He tilted her chin up so she was looking into his eyes.

"Is your name really Jody?"

"Y...yes. Jody Vanessa Ingram." She hated that her voice came out a breathy whisper.

He smiled. "Well, Jody Vanessa. I think it's time you called me Adam. Don't you?"

His deep voice and cool blue eyes seemed to cast a spell on her. She couldn't think with him this close, could barely even breathe.

"McKenzie... I mean, Adam. What's the plan here? Why did you—"

He tugged the rope, pulling them even closer together. "This is where that trust part comes into play."

He grabbed her around the waist.

She read the truth in his eyes and suddenly realized what he was going to do. The rope. The fact that he'd tied the two of them together. "No. No, no, no. Please. I can't do this. I'm too scared. I can't."

Sympathy filled his gaze. He brushed a featherlight caress down the side of her face. "Then I'll just have to do it for both of us."

Adam yanked her forward. She screamed as they tumbled over the cliff.

TREACHEROUS MOUNTAIN TRAIL

LENA DIAZ

&

USA TODAY Bestselling Author

DEBBIE HERBERT

Previously published as *Smoky Mountains Ranger*
and *Appalachian Abduction*

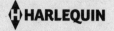

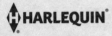 HARLEQUIN®

PLEASE RECYCLE · THIS PRODUCT IS RECYCLABLE

ISBN-13: 978-1-335-42482-2

Recycling programs for this product may not exist in your area.

Treacherous Mountain Trail

Copyright © 2021 by Harlequin Books S.A.

Smoky Mountains Ranger
First published in 2019. This edition published in 2021.
Copyright © 2019 by Lena Diaz

Appalachian Abduction
First published in 2018. This edition published in 2021.
Copyright © 2018 by Debbie Herbert

This edition published by arrangement with Harlequin Books S.A.

For questions and comments about the quality of this book, please contact us at CustomerService@Harlequin.com.

Harlequin Enterprises ULC
22 Adelaide St. West, 41st Floor
Toronto, Ontario M5H 4E3, Canada
www.Harlequin.com

Printed in U.S.A.

CONTENTS

Lena Diaz was born in Kentucky and has also lived in California, Louisiana and Florida, where she now resides with her husband and two children. Before becoming a romantic suspense author, she was a computer programmer. A Romance Writers of America Golden Heart® Award finalist, she has also won the prestigious Daphne du Maurier Award for Excellence in Mystery/Suspense. To get the latest news about Lena, please visit her website, lenadiaz.com.

Books by Lena Diaz

Harlequin Intrigue

The Justice Seekers

Cowboy Under Fire
Agent Under Siege
Killer Conspiracy
Deadly Double-Cross

The Mighty McKenzies

Smoky Mountains Ranger
Smokies Special Agent
Conflicting Evidence
Undercover Rebel

Tennessee SWAT

Mountain Witness
Secret Stalker
Stranded with the Detective
SWAT Standoff

Visit the Author Profile page
at Harlequin.com for more titles.

SMOKY MOUNTAINS RANGER

Lena Diaz

This book is dedicated to my dear friends
and fellow authors Jan Jackson and Connie Mann.
Your constant cheerleading and friendship are
priceless. Jan, thank you for helping me through
my plot tangles on this one. I hope you approve
of the final product.

Chapter 1

Adam ducked behind a massive, uprooted tree, the tangle of dead roots and blackened branches his only cover on this wildfire-blighted section of the Great Smoky Mountains. Had the man holding the pistol seen him? He ticked off the seconds as he slid his left hand to the Glock 22 holstered at his waist. When half a minute passed without sounds of pursuit, he inched over to peer up the trail and moved his hand to the radio strapped to his belt. After switching to the emergency channel, he pressed the button on his shoulder mic.

"This is Ranger McKenzie on the Sugarland Mountain Trail." He kept his voice low, just above a whisper. "There's a yahoo with a gun up here, about a quarter mile northwest of the intersection with the Appalachian Trail. Requesting backup. Over."

Nothing but silence met his request. He tilted the

radio to see the small screen. After verifying the frequency and noting the battery was fully charged, he pressed the mic again.

"Ranger McKenzie requesting backup. Over." Again he waited. Again, the radio was silent. Cell phone coverage in the Great Smoky Mountains National Park was hit-or-miss. It didn't matter if someone was coming up from the Tennessee side, like Adam, or hiking in from the North Carolina border. Cell phones up here were unreliable. Period. Which was why he and the rest of the staff carried powerful two-way radios that worked everywhere in the park.

With one exception.

The Sugarland Mountain Trail, where the devastating Chimney Tops wildfire had destroyed a communication tower.

Budget cuts meant the rebuilding was slow and had to be prioritized. Rehabilitating habitats, the visitors' center and the more popular, heavily used trails near the park's entrance were high on that list. Putting up a new tower was close to the bottom. So, naturally, the first and only time that Adam had ever encountered someone with a gun in the park, it happened in the middle of the only dead zone.

There would be no backup.

If the guy was just a good old boy out for target practice, the situation wouldn't even warrant a call back to base. Adam could handle it on his own and be on his way. But the stakes were higher today—much higher—because of two things.

One, the faded blue ink tattoos on the gunman's bulging biceps that marked him as an ex-con, which likely meant he couldn't legally possess a firearm and wouldn't welcome a federal officer catching him with one.

Two, the alarmingly pale, obviously terrified young woman on the business end of Tattoo Guy's pistol.

Even from twenty yards away, peering through branches, Adam could tell the gunman had a tenuous grasp on an explosive temper. He gestured wildly with his free hand, his face bright red as he said something in response to whatever the petite redhead had just said.

Her hands were empty and down at her sides. Unless she'd shoved a pistol in the back waistband of her denim shorts, she didn't appear to have a weapon to defend herself. The formfitting white blouse she wore didn't have any pockets. Even if she'd hidden a small gun, like a derringer, in her bra, there was no way she could get it out faster than the gunman could pull the trigger.

Did they know each other? Was this a case of domestic violence? Since the two were arguing, it seemed likely that they *did* know each other. So what had brought them to the brink of violence? And what had brought them to *this* particular trail?

Neither of them was wearing a backpack. Unless they had supplies at a base camp somewhere, that ruled them out as NOBOs on the AT who'd gone seriously off course and gotten lost. Not that he'd expect any northbound through-hikers on the Appalachian Trail in the middle of summer anyway. Most NOBOs started out on the two-thousand-plus-mile hike around March or April so they could reach Mount Katahdin in Maine before blizzards made the AT impassable. But even if they were day hikers, they had no business being on the Sugarland Trail. It was closed, for good reason. The wildfire damage made this area exceedingly dangerous. Now it was dangerous for an entirely different reason.

An idiot with a pistol.

So much for the peaceful workday he'd expected when he'd started his trail inspection earlier this morning.

He switched the worthless radio off, not wanting to risk a sudden burst of static alerting the gunman to his presence. The element of surprise was on his side and he aimed to keep it that way as long as possible, or at least until he came up with a plan.

He belatedly wished he'd dusted off his Kevlar and put it on this morning. But even though he was the law enforcement variety of ranger, as opposed to an informational officer, the kind of dangers he ran into up here didn't typically warrant wearing a bullet-resistant vest. The heat and extra weight tended to outweigh the risks of not having a vest on since the possibility of getting into a gunfight while patrolling half a million acres of mostly uninhabited mountains and forests was close to zero.

Until today.

Still, it wasn't the bullets that concerned him the most. It was the steep drop-off behind the woman. One wrong step and she'd go flying off the mountain. The edge was loose and crumbling in many places, particularly in this section of the trail. The couple—if that's what they were—couldn't have picked a worse spot for their argument.

Sharp boulders and the charred remains of dozens of trees littered the ravine fifty feet below. Branches

stuck up like sharp spikes ready to impale anything—
or any*one*—unlucky enough to fall on them.

Twenty feet farther north or south on this section of
the Sugarland path would provide a much better chance
of survival if the worst happened. The slope wasn't as
steep and was carpeted with thick wild grasses. Fledg-
ling scrub brush dotting the mountainside might help
break someone's fall if they lost their footing. They'd
still be banged up, might twist an ankle or even crack a
bone. But that was preferable to plunging into a rocky
ravine with no chance of survival.

The gunman and the woman were still arguing.
But Adam couldn't figure out what they were saying.
Sometimes sounds carried for miles out here. Other
times a person could barely hear someone a few yards
away. It all depended on the wind and the configura-
tion of mountains, rocks and trees nearby.

At the man's back, a vertical wall of sheer rock went
straight up to a higher peak. In front of him was the
woman and the sharp drop-off. Sneaking up on him
just wasn't going to happen. Either by luck or by design, he'd chosen a spot that was impossible to approach without being seen.

As Adam watched, the man gestured with his pistol
for the woman to head south, away from Adam. When
she didn't move, he stepped forward. She backed up,
moving perilously closer to the edge. Adam drew a
sharp breath. If he didn't do something fast, this was
going to end in tragedy. He'd have to approach openly,
giving up his element of surprise, and hope that cooler
heads prevailed.

He unsnapped the safety flap on his holster—just
in case—and straightened. Keeping his gaze trained

on the ground, he boldly stepped onto the path in plain sight and whistled a tune—AC/DC's "Highway to Hell." It seemed appropriate at the moment.

Continuing to look down and pretending not to notice the couple, his hope was to get as close to them as possible and appear nonthreatening—just a ranger in the mountains, doing his job. Most people didn't realize the difference between informational officers and federal law enforcement rangers anyway. They'd assume the pistol holstered on his belt was for protection against bears or other dangerous wildlife. Usually, it was.

In his peripheral vision, he saw the man shove his pistol into his pants pocket. Adam kept moving forward, head down, increasing the volume of his whistling and tapping his thigh to the beat.

"You gonna run into us or what?" the man's voice snapped.

Adam jerked his head up as if in surprise, stopping a few feet away from the couple. "Sorry, folks. Must have been daydreaming. Pretty morning for it, don't you think?" He smiled and waved toward the mountains around them. "Even with the blight from the wildfires, it's still beautiful up here."

The man watched him with open suspicion as if sizing him up and trying to decide whether Adam really hadn't seen the gun. The woman stared at him, her green eyes big and round behind matching green-framed glasses. But instead of seeming relieved to have help, she appeared to be even more terrified than before.

Adam struggled to maintain his smile. "I'm Ranger Adam McKenzie. You folks lost? Got to admit I'm a bit surprised to see you on this particular trail. Know why?"

Tattoo Guy seemed to come to some kind of decision and offered his own smile that didn't quite reach his dark eyes. "Afraid I don't. Why?"

"Because the trail is closed, for your safety. It's because of the fires last season. You heard about those? Burned over seventeen thousand acres, ten thousand of them right here in the park. Killed fourteen people, too." He didn't have to fake his wince. The fire had been horrible, tragic. Innocent civilians—including children—had perished in the flames. Families had been destroyed. The community was still struggling to recover as best they could. But nothing could replace the precious lives that were lost.

The man glanced at the woman, his eyes narrowed as if in warning. "Can't say that I've heard about that. I'm not from around here."

"What about you, miss?" Adam grinned again. "Sorry. Where are my manners? I didn't catch your name. I'm Adam McKenzie. And you are?" He held out his hand to shake hers, purposely leaving enough space between them so that she'd have to move away from the edge to take his hand.

She looked at the other man as if for permission, then leaned toward Adam, her hand out. As soon as she grasped his hand, he pumped it up and down in a vigorous shake, pulling her even farther away from the edge.

"Your name, ma'am?"

"I, um… Jody. My name's Jody Ingram." She shook his hand, eyes wide with fear.

"Pleased to meet you." Adam let her go and held his hand out toward the gunman. "And you are?"

The man's nearly black eyes dropped to Adam's out-stretched hand while he clearly debated his response. A handshake required that he use his right hand, his dominant hand, the one that had held the pistol earlier. He'd be giving up precious seconds of reaction time if he decided that Adam was a threat and he needed to draw his gun. Which of course was exactly why Adam wanted to shake his hand.

Adam was left-handed.

And his pistol was holstered just a few inches from where his left hand currently hung down by his side.

Come on, come on. Shake the clueless cop's hand.

An awkward silence stretched out between them as no one moved. Adam pretended not to notice. He kept his hand out, waiting, a goofy grin on his face. From the corner of his eye, Adam saw the woman watching them closely, her gaze sweeping back and forth.

Finally, the man mumbled something beneath his breath that sounded suspiciously like "stupid hillbilly" before gripping Adam's hand.

Adam yanked hard, jerking the man off balance. The man stumbled as Adam grabbed the butt of his gun in the holster. But Tattoo Guy was lightning fast. Even as Adam began to draw his pistol, the other guy was already drawing his and swinging it toward him.

Chapter 2

"Drop your weapon. *Now.*" Adam had both hands wrapped around the butt of his Glock. The bore of his gun was aimed directly at the other man's head.

Tattoo Guy stood statue still, his weapon aimed slightly to Adam's left, frozen in midmotion. But one quick twist and a squeeze of the trigger would blast a hole through Adam's gut. The only question was whether Adam could blow the man's brains out before that happened. Not exactly a competition he wanted to wage, especially with a woman a few feet away who was dangerously close to the kill zone.

The seconds ticked by. They stood frozen. The only sounds were the woman's short gasping breaths as she watched the standoff, apparently too terrified to back away to a safer location—preferably behind a thick, solid tree.

Adam didn't dare say a word to her. He didn't even blink as he kept his gaze glued to his opponent and his finger on the frame of his gun, just millimeters from the trigger. He narrowed his eyes, letting the stranger know that he wasn't kidding, wasn't bluffing and wasn't the head-in-the-clouds idiot he'd pretended to be moments earlier.

Tattoo Guy must have read the truth and determination in Adam's eyes, in his stance. He tossed his gun to the ground.

Adam kept his finger right above the trigger, ready to fire at the slightest provocation. Everything about the man screamed danger, and he wasn't taking any chances. "Turn around."

The man hesitated, his gaze darting past Adam.

The urge to check over his shoulder to see what Tattoo Guy was looking at was almost impossible to resist. Did the man have a partner in crime creeping up on Adam? Or was he trying to trick him, distract him? His shoulder blades itched, expecting a bullet to slam into them any second. But he didn't turn around. He focused on the known threat in front of him and waited.

The man finally did as Adam had ordered and turned to face the wall of rock.

Adam kicked the pistol out of reach. "Down on the ground. Put your hands behind your back."

Again Tattoo Guy hesitated. Adam pulled a pair of handcuffs from one of the leather cases attached to his utility belt. He desperately wanted to check on the woman, make sure she was safe, that no one was sneaking up behind *her*. But he didn't dare. Not until he had this guy secured.

When the man finally put his hands behind his back,

Adam holstered his pistol in one smooth motion and dropped down on top of him, jamming his knee against the man's spine to hold him down. The man cursed and tried to buck him off. But Adam used every bit of his six-foot-three-inch bulk to keep the stranger pinned.

He slapped the cuffs on the man's wrists, then sat back, drawing deep breaths as adrenaline pumped through him. A bead of sweat ran down the side of his face in spite of the mild, springlike temps this high up in the mountains. From the moment he'd seen the gunman to the moment he'd cuffed him had probably only been five minutes. But it had felt like an eternity.

He stood and pulled his prisoner up with him. After patting the man down to make sure he wasn't hiding more weapons, he grabbed the man's pistol and popped out the magazine. After ejecting the chambered round and verifying that the weapon was now empty, he pocketed the gun and the magazine. Then he slid the man's wallet out of his back jeans pocket, jumping back when the man jerked around, glowering at him.

"Give that back." The man's tone communicated a deadly, unmistakable threat.

"After I check your ID."

A smug look crossed the man's face, a look Adam understood when he opened the wallet. Tucked inside was a hefty amount of cash: twenties, tens, a few ones—a thousand dollars, easy. A heck of a lot of money for someone wandering through the mountains. But that was it. No driver's license, no credit cards, nothing that could shed any light on his identity.

He forced the man to face the rock wall again and returned the wallet with its cache of money to the man's pocket. "What's your name?"

Silence met his question.

"What were you doing up here on a closed trail with a pistol? Why were you pointing it at Miss Ingram?"

Tattoo Guy turned his head to the side, watching Adam over his shoulder. Still, he said nothing. He just studied Adam intently, his eyes dark and cold, like a serpent.

Adam glanced toward the woman, then stiffened. During the altercation between him and the gunman, instead of moving down the trail or ducking for cover behind a tree, she'd backed up close to the edge again.

"Miss Ingram." He kept his voice low and soothing so he wouldn't startle her. "Jody, right?"

She swallowed, then nodded.

"Jody, I'd feel a whole lot better if you'd step away from that sharp drop-off."

She glanced over her shoulder. A visible shudder ran through her as she hurried forward and to the side. She'd been mere inches from falling off the cliff and was exceedingly lucky the unstable edge hadn't given way.

"How about you move over there?" He directed her closer to the wall of rock, a little farther up the path and out of reach of his prisoner if the man decided to launch himself at either of them.

She did as he'd directed. But instead of looking relieved that she no longer had a pistol pointing at her, she seemed even more anxious than before. Her face was chalk white, making her green eyes and matching glasses stand out in stark contrast. Even her lips had lost their color, and her whole body was shaking.

Why?

"Everything's okay now," he reassured her. "You're safe. What's this guy's name?"

She exchanged an uneasy glance with the hand-cuffed man, then shook her head. "I...I don't know. We, ah, ran into each other on the trail."

Adam glanced back and forth between them, beginning to wonder whether he should put her in hand-cuffs, too. They were hiding something. What was going on here?

"You're strangers? You've never met before?"

She swallowed. "We've never met. I'd just rounded the curve and he was...there. I...ah...startled him, which is why he drew his gun." She gave a nervous laugh. "I guess he thought I was a bear." Again, she gave a nervous laugh that was anything but convincing.

A smile creased Tattoo Guy's lips as he watched the exchange over his shoulder.

"You don't know each other's names?" Adam asked, giving her another chance to answer him truthfully.

"No."

He shook his head, not even trying to hide his dis-belief. "You have a habit of getting into heated argu-ments with strangers?"

Her face flushed guiltily. "He drew a gun on me. I wasn't happy about that. Things did get a bit...heated... with him demanding to know why I'd snuck up on him. Which, of course, I hadn't. But looking back, I can see how it appeared that way to him." She wouldn't meet his gaze. Subterfuge obviously didn't come naturally to her. So why was she covering for this guy? Or was she covering for both of them?

He tried again, working hard to inject patience into

his tone. "You were arguing with each other over him putting the gun down?"

She cleared her throat. "Yes, pretty much." Another nervous laugh.

Her story had more holes in it than a white-tailed fawn had spots. Instead of rescuing her from a domestic dispute between a couple, had he interrupted a disagreement between a couple of criminals? Were they out here doing something illegal and they'd turned on each other? Or maybe whatever they'd planned was still to come, something far worse than trespassing on a closed trail or carrying a gun into a national park. Adam backed up the path several feet so he could keep Jody—if that was her real name—in his line of sight at a safer distance, just in case she and Tattoo Guy decided to join forces against him.

"Let me guess," he said. "You don't have ID on you, either?"

She cleared her throat again. "Actually, no. I don't. I left my purse in my car, at the trailhead. All I have with me are my keys and my phone."

"Empty your pockets."

Her brow furrowed, and she finally looked at him. "Excuse me?"

"Would you prefer that I pat you down like I did your friend?"

Twin spots of color darkened her cheeks, making her freckles stand out in stark contrast to her pale complexion. Her eyes flashed with anger. "I assure you, he's *not* my friend."

That statement, at least, appeared to be true. But he could tell she immediately regretted her outburst by the way her teeth tugged at her full lower lip.

His prisoner's eyes narrowed at her, as if in warning. Something was definitely rotten in the state of Denmark, or in this case, the Smoky Mountains. And Adam was determined to get to the bottom of it.

"Your pockets, ma'am?"

Without a word, she pulled her phone out of one pocket, a set of keys out of the other. Clutching them both in one hand, she turned out the lining of her pockets to show they were empty. "That's it. There's nothing else."

"Back pockets, too."

Her mouth tightened but she turned around and turned those pockets inside out.

"All right," Adam conceded. "You can turn around." To perform a complete search, he should pat down her bra. But his years of reading people told him that wasn't necessary. She wasn't carrying.

"Where do you live?"

Again, another look at the handcuffed man as she shoved her keys and phone back into her pockets. "Not far from here. I've got an apartment in town."

"Gatlinburg?"

Again, she hesitated. "Yes."

"Why were you two up here today?"

She chewed her bottom lip.

Tattoo Guy simply stared at him, eyes narrowed with the promise of retribution over Adam's interference in whatever was going on.

"Maybe my question wasn't clear," Adam said. "Why were you both on a closed trail?"

"Closed?" The man sounded shocked. "Really? Miss Ingram, did you see any signs saying the trail was closed?" Laughter was heavy in his voice as he watched her.

"N…no." Her voice was barely above a whisper. "I didn't. I guess I was…enjoying nature too much and wasn't paying attention."

Disgusted with both of them, Adam flipped the radio on again. "Ranger McKenzie to base. Come in. Over." He tried two more times, then gave up.

"I don't know what you two are hiding. But at a minimum you're guilty of criminal trespass. This trail is closed for a reason. The recent wildfires have burned away brush that used to hold the topsoil in place. What the high winds and fire didn't destroy, recent rains did. Entire sections of the trail have been washed away. Trees have been toppled, their roots ripping up most of what was left. The trail is more a memory than a reality anymore. The part we're standing on is one of the best sections left. But it's the exception rather than the rule. You already know that, of course. Because you had to climb over and around some of the damage on your way up. No way you missed it."

He waited for their response and wasn't surprised when neither of them said anything.

"It's also against the law for civilians to carry guns into the park. Care to explain why you had a loaded pistol up here, sir?"

"Protection, of course. I've heard there are all kinds of dangers in these mountains." He kept his gaze fastened on Jody.

As if she felt his eyes on her, she shivered.

What the heck was going on? Had Tattoo Guy just given the woman a veiled threat? Was *he* one of the dangers he'd just mentioned? Even though Adam had zero doubt that Jody Ingram was covering something, his instincts were telling him that she was a victim here. But since neither of them would talk, he had no choice but to bring both of them in.

"Am I under arrest, *Ranger*?" The man drew out Adam's title into several extra syllables, then chuckled. He wasn't the first to make fun of the ranger title. But Adam wasn't inclined to care. He just wanted this guy off the mountain before he hurt someone.

"For now, you're just being detained, for everyone's safety. We'll sort it all out at headquarters. Those are prison tats on your arms, aren't they? I'm sure your fingerprints are on file. Won't take but a minute to find out who you are once I get you back to base. And if you're a felon with a gun, well, we'll just have to deal with that issue, won't we?"

If looks could kill, Adam would be six feet under right now.

He'd dealt with all types over the years, the worst of the worst back when he'd first started out in law enforcement as a beat cop in some of the rougher parts of Memphis. But because of Adam's own intimidating size, he could count on one hand the number of men who made him uncomfortable. This man was one of them. There was something sinister, jaded, so…empty about him. As if long ago he'd poured out his soul and filled the emptiness with pure evil.

He motioned for him to start down the trail, in the direction toward the Appalachian Trail intersection and Clingmans Dome—a famous lookout point high in the Smoky Mountains. "Take it slow and easy."

His prisoner calmly pushed away from the rock wall. As he started walking down the path, he whistled the same tune that Adam had whistled earlier, "Highway to Hell."

Jody watched him go, fear and trepidation playing a game of tug-of-war across her face. Adam wanted to reassure her. But she'd done nothing but lie to him. Trusting her would be a mistake. Instead, he gestured for her to fall in beside him and they started down the steep incline about ten feet behind his prisoner.

"He can't hear you now." Adam kept his voice low as they carefully stepped around boulders and climbed over downed trees. "What was really going on back there?"

She accepted his hand to help her over a pile of rocks and busted branches. There were pieces of splintered wood and rocks everywhere, making it slow going. The prisoner up ahead navigated the same obstacles with surprising ease for a man with his hands behind him. There was now twelve feet of space between them. Adam frowned and motioned for Jody to speed up.

"Well?" he prodded, watching Tattoo Guy's back.

"I already told you. I didn't see the closed-trail signs and I was walking through the park enjoying the scenery. I rounded a curve and scared that man. He drew his gun. I'm sure he would have put it away, but then you came up and things got…complicated."

"That's how you're going to play this?"

She stared straight ahead.

Frustration curled inside him. "You don't have to be afraid of him. I can protect you, help you find a way out of whatever trouble you're in. Just tell me the truth."

She made a choked sound, then cleared her throat. "I am telling you the truth."

He let out a deep sigh. This was going to be a very long day.

Up ahead, the rock wall made a sharp curve to the left.

"Hold it," Adam called out to Tattoo Guy. "The trail gets much steeper and more treacherous there. I'll have to help you."

The man took off running.

Adam grabbed his pistol out of the holster. "Stay here!" He sprinted after his prisoner.

Chapter 3

Stay here? Was he worried that she'd run after the bad guy? It took courage to chase a man who'd pointed a pistol at you and made threats. She wasn't courageous. If she was, she would have fought harder after the auditor absolved her adoptive father of any wrongdoing in regards to her trust. She would have taken back what she believed he'd stolen from her. But she hadn't. She wouldn't. Because she was a coward. Being courageous and fighting back had never done her any good. It had only made things worse. So somewhere along the line, just giving in had become a habit.

Still, not at least checking on the ranger seemed wrong. So she kept moving forward, toward where he'd disappeared, even though she had no idea what she'd do if he needed help. She certainly hadn't done anything to help her best friend, the friend who was the only reason she'd survived her awful foster, later turned adoptive, family.

Where are you, Tracy? That man had to be lying. You have to be hiding somewhere, safe, not some thug's prisoner.

The curve where the ranger and his prisoner had disappeared loomed up ahead. What was the officer's name? Adam something. McKenzie, maybe? Yes, that was it. Cool name for a hot guy. Of course, she hadn't been thinking about his good looks during that frightening standoff. She'd stared up into those deep blue eyes and all she could think was that her friend Tracy was about to die, because of Jody's own stupidity. Her only chance to save her friend had been to lie, or so she'd thought. But she hadn't lied convincingly. She'd been too dang scared to pull it off.

Hysterical laughter bubbled up in her chest. Pull what off? What had she thought she could do? Convince a police officer that someone pointing a gun at someone else was no more significant than changing lanes on a highway without signaling? That Adam McKenzie would give them a warning and let them go on their merry way?

Once again, she'd had a choice to make. Once again, she'd made the wrong one. What she should have done was be honest, tell the ranger exactly what was going on. The time for going it alone had evaporated the second a man with scary tattoos had pulled a gun on her. What was she supposed to do now? If she told McKenzie the truth, would that sign Tracy's death warrant? Probably. Maybe. All she knew for sure was that Tracy needed help. But when help had arrived, in the form of a handsome, dark-haired ranger, she'd squandered the opportunity. And put him in danger, too.

Why hadn't he come back yet?

She stopped and peered down the trail, or what was left of it. McKenzie hadn't exaggerated its hazardous condition. She'd leaped over rock slides and logs a dozen times as she'd run from the man with the gun. He'd caught her, of course. Had she really thought she'd get away? Just like one of those too-stupid-to-live women in a horror movie, she'd run up the stairs instead of out of the house. Or, in this case, up the trail instead of back to her car.

Idiot. Stupid, cowardly idiot.

Her hands fisted at her sides. To be fair, she couldn't have reached her car. He was standing in the way, and there really had been nowhere else to go. Self-recriminations weren't helping. She was in deep, deep trouble and had no clue how to fix it, or even whether it *could* be fixed. But she at least needed to try. Standing here, waiting, wasn't accomplishing anything. It certainly wasn't finding her missing friend or saving an officer who might be in trouble.

She took a hesitant step toward the curve, then another. Her hand itched for the security of her pistol. But, of course, the one time she actually needed her gun it was locked in the safe in her apartment. That decision, at least, she couldn't feel bad about. There was no way she could have predicted what would happen when she drove up here in response to Tracy's text. That she might be in danger had never entered her mind.

When she reached the curve, she squatted down by the wall of rock and peered around the edge. Her stomach sank, as if she'd plummeted down a steep rollercoaster drop. McKenzie no longer had his gun. Instead, he stood about twenty feet away from her, hands in the air. And directly in front of him was another man pointing a pistol directly at McKenzie's chest.

The man McKenzie had handcuffed was still cuffed. But he was leaning against a tree another ten feet beyond the ranger and the other gunman. His face bore an angry, impatient expression as he watched the standoff.

McKenzie shifted slightly, revealing some bloody cuts on the right side of his face. She drew a sharp breath. All three men jerked their heads toward her. She pressed a hand to her throat, belatedly realizing she must have made a sound.

"Nice of you to join us, Jody," the handcuffed man called out, his earlier cocky grin back in place. "Stay right where you are. Remember what I told you." He half turned, looking over his shoulder at the other gunman as he flexed his hands. "Owen, just get the dang keys already and get these things off me. Officer Mayberry can wait."

Jody swallowed, his earlier threats running through her mind. Somehow he'd gotten it into his head that she had something he wanted. And he was using Tracy as leverage. It stood to reason that she could do the opposite, couldn't she? Leverage whatever he thought she had in return for Tracy's safety? If she helped McKenzie, wouldn't the bad guy have to keep Tracy alive until he got what he wanted?

She curled her nails against her palms. Why was she even debating with herself? It wasn't like she could just run away. No matter what, she couldn't ignore the fact that Adam McKenzie was right here, unarmed and outnumbered, with a gun pointed at him. He needed help. She had to do something. But what could she do?

The man named Owen had keys in his left hand now, keys that he must have taken from McKenzie. His gaze stayed on the ranger as he trained the pistol on him and backed toward the tree.

McKenzie's gaze locked on Jody. He glanced to the right, toward the curve of rock wall and subtly jerked his head. Clearly, he wanted her to run up the path, to escape while she could.

She shook her head, even though she really, *really* wanted to give in to her cowardice and do exactly that—retreat, run, hide. But she'd just had this particular argument with herself. And lost.

His jaw clenched. He obviously wasn't happy with her response. He jerked his head again.

Ignoring his unspoken command, she studied the other two men. The one with the gun was fumbling with the set of keys. Their attention was temporarily diverted. McKenzie must have realized the same thing. He edged toward her. One foot. Two feet. When he was about ten feet away, he took off running toward her.

A shout sounded behind him. He grabbed Jody's arm and yanked her around the corner as more shouts and curses sounded.

"The cuffs, the cuffs! Hurry!" The handcuffed guy was apparently ordering Owen to remove the cuffs before they took off in pursuit.

"Go, go, go!" McKenzie's fingers tightened around her upper arm, pulling her up the trail. When a downed tree blocked their way, he lifted her up as if she weighed nothing and leaped over the tree. He set her on her feet and they took off again.

The *clomp-clomp* of boots pounding up the path sounded behind them. She looked over her shoulder. The first gunman didn't have his hands cuffed anymore. The short delay of removing them had given her and McKenzie a head start. But their lead was dwindling.

"Come on." McKenzie pulled her around rocks, over branches, at an impossibly fast pace.

"I'm trying," she gasped, struggling to match his long strides. She already knew she couldn't outrun the man behind them going uphill. She'd tried once and failed. Keeping up with the tall, long-legged McKenzie was impossible.

"Stop or we'll shoot!" the man named Owen yelled at them.

She started to look over her shoulder again. But McKenzie tugged her forward.

"Don't look back. It'll only slow you down." He yanked her around another curve in the trail.

A shot rang out. Jody instinctively ducked. But McKenzie was already pulling her under some thick branches from another downed tree. He came out the other side, hopped over more branches, then lifted her over.

A bullet whined past them. She let out a startled gasp and pressed a hand to her galloping heart. Good grief, that was close. McKenzie didn't react at all. Was the man used to getting shot at? He pulled her behind a huge boulder that was clustered with several others and pushed her down. He scanned the area around them, up the trail, out toward the open vista of mountains that alternated between blackened bald spots and new spring greenery poking up through the ashes.

The twin peaks of the Chimney Tops, two of the higher mountains in the park, stood out in stark relief from the destruction around them. She'd never even been in the park before, other than sitting in a car looking out the window as her adoptive father wheeled and dealed for yet another parcel of land. The only reason she recognized that particular landmark was because a new client had shown her pictures of them a few weeks ago and was considering hiring her to take new ones for a tourist brochure. What she didn't understand was why McKenzie was looking at the Chimney Tops. It wasn't like they had a helicopter and could magically fly to them and escape.

His gaze flicked back to her. "I need to know whether I can trust you."

The cuts on his face had guilt flooding through her. "I could have run when you told me to. But I didn't leave you behind. Isn't that proof enough?"

He seemed to consider that, then shrugged. "For now, *you're* going to have to trust *me*."

She gave a nervous laugh. "Well, I certainly don't trust the guys shooting at us. Where are they?" She tried to peek around the largest boulder. He stopped her with a hand on her shoulder.

"Don't. They've hunkered down behind the last tree we jumped over, about forty feet back. I imagine they're waiting to see if I'm going to pull a weapon from my backpack, since they made me toss my pistol into the ravine and took Tattoo Guy's pistol away from me."

Hope unfurled in her chest. "Do you? Have a backup gun?"

He shook his head. "I've got a hunting knife. But

you know the saying about bringing a knife to a gun-fight."

"I'm really good with a knife. I could throw it at them. All I'd need is some kind of diversion to get one of them to stand up and give me a clear target."

As soon as she said it, she realized she'd made a mistake. He was looking at her with open suspicion again.

"In college," she rushed to explain, "I hired a guy who ran a gun range to teach me to defend myself. He taught me to shoot. But he also taught me how to throw a knife."

"Ever thrown a knife at a real, live person?"

"No, of course not, but—"

Bam! Bam!

They both ducked at the shockingly loud sound of pistol fire.

She drew a shaky breath. "Well?" She held out her hand for the knife.

"I'm not giving up my only weapon just yet."

She dropped her hand. "You have a better suggestion?"

He looked toward the Chimney Tops again. "I'm considering a few possibilities."

"Is one of them to crouch down and use these boulders to block them from seeing us retreat up the path, back the way you came? We might be able to get pretty far up the trail before they realize we're gone."

"That's a good suggestion, except for one problem." He shrugged out of his backpack and unzipped the top. "The trail straightens out after that next curve, with no cover of any kind for about three hundred yards. It's also unstable. There's a lot of debris but nothing sizable enough to hide us from view. The odds of us making it that far before those guys work up the courage to storm our little hideout are too low to make it worth the risk." He pulled out a length of white nylon rope and the knife he'd mentioned earlier.

She was about to argue with him, but the rope made her pause. "What's the rope for?"

"So we don't die."

It took several seconds for her to realize he wasn't going to expand on his cryptic answer. Instead, he shoved the knife into a leather holder and tucked it into his backpack. After slipping the pack onto his shoulders, he connected some extra straps on the pack that he hadn't bothered to fasten earlier. One went over his chest. Two more attached the pack to his belt loops with metal clips. She thought they might be called carabiners, like she'd used when Tracy had badgered her into going on a zip-lining trip in Pigeon Forge to celebrate Jody's new, second job at Campbell Investigations.

"What are you doing?" she tried again.

He picked up the length of rope that he'd cut. His fingers fairly flew as he tied knots and created loops.

She watched him with growing frustration. The gunmen could be creeping up on them this very minute. So why was he tying knots? She hated being kept in the dark. Her life was on the line just as much as his.

And Tracy's.

He pulled on one of the loops as if testing it, then let out a few more inches, making it larger.

"Are you going to tie them up or try to lasso them or what?" she snapped, unable to hide her frustration any longer.

For the first time since he'd appeared on the trail with a goofy, dumb-as-a-rock grin, he gave her a genuine smile. It lit up his eyes and made him look years younger than the thirty-one or -two that she'd assumed him to be. Maybe he was only in his late twenties?

"Lasso them? Can't say that's ever been part of my law enforcement training. Might be a good skill to learn, though."

He continued to work the rope through the metal clips. "Hypothetical. We figure out a way to get Owen or Tattoo Guy to stand up and give us a clear target. You do a Wonder Woman move and take him out. That leaves the second thug with two pistols, and potentially other weapons we don't even know about. We're left without even a knife to defend ourselves. What would we do then?"

"Maybe I do another Wonder Woman move and lasso the second guy."

His lips twitched as if he was trying not to laugh. He looped the rope through one of the backpack's metal clips.

She curled her fingers against her thighs. It was either that or shake him. She closed her eyes for a moment and drew deep, calming breaths. Their lives were on the line and this man was pushing all her buttons. What she needed to do was calm down and think. There had to be something they could do instead of just waiting here playing with a rope. She opened her eyes again, then frowned. "What *are* you doing?"

He swept the ground between them clear of debris, scattering several broken pieces of branches and twigs, then motioned for her to move toward him. Exasperated, but curious enough to see if he actually had some kind of plan, she scooted toward him on her knees. He closed the distance and slid the rope through one of the belt loops on her shorts.

"McKenzie. What are—"

"Give me a minute."

She blew out an irritated breath and held her hands out of the way as he threaded the rope through all the loops on her shorts. When he was done, he tied the end of the rope to another metal loop on his backpack, effectively anchoring them to each other, with just a few feet in between.

"McKenzie?"

He tilted her chin up so she was looking into his eyes. "Is your name really Jody?"

She swallowed, her whole body flushing with heat when she realized just how close her breasts were to his chest, her lips to his. "Y...yes. Jody Vanessa Ingram." She hated that her voice came out a breathy whisper.

"Pretty name."

"Vanessa was my biological mom's name." Why had she said that? It didn't matter one bit under the circumstances.

He smiled. "Well, Jody Vanessa. We're about to explore one of those possibilities I mentioned earlier. And I think it's time you called me Adam. Don't you?"

His deep voice and cool blue eyes seemed to cast a spell on her. She couldn't think with him this close, could barely even breathe.

"Come on out from behind that rock and we won't kill you," Owen shouted. "All we want to do is talk."

She blinked. The spell was broken. Thank goodness. "McKenzie... I mean, Adam. What's the plan here? Why did you—"

He tugged the rope, pulling them even closer together. "This is where that trust part comes into play."

She licked her suddenly dry lips. "I'm not sure what you—"

He grabbed one of the short, broken pieces of branch that he'd swept out of the way earlier and tossed it over the top of the boulder.

Boom! The stick exploded into sawdust.

Jody ducked down, even though she was already behind the boulder.

Adam winced but didn't duck. "They're better shots than I'd hoped. This is going to be close."

"Close? What are you—"

He grabbed her around the waist.

She read the truth in his eyes and suddenly realized what he was going to do. The rope. The fact that he'd tied the two of them together. Him staring out at the Chimney Tops and telling her she needed to trust him. Her stomach lurched, and she pushed against his chest, to no avail. He didn't budge and the rope wouldn't have let her move very far anyway. "No. No, no, no. *Please.* I can't do this. I'm too scared. I *can't.*"

Sympathy filled his gaze. He brushed a featherlight caress down the side of her face. "Then I'll just have to do it for both of us." He grabbed two more sticks and threw them high into the air. Shots rang out. He yanked her forward, clasping her tightly against his chest as he raced in a crouch behind the boulders toward where the trail disappeared over the edge of the mountain.

"No!" she cried, desperately pushing against him. "Please!"

The gunmen shouted.

Adam yanked her forward. She screamed as they tumbled over the cliff.

Chapter 4

They hit the ground hard, a tangle of arms and legs flopping end over end. Jody's head snapped against Adam's chest. Blood filled her mouth. She was too busy trying to grab a tree, a root, anything to stop their out-of-control roll down the steep mountainside to even cry out in pain.

"Hold on," his voice rumbled next to her ear as his arms squeezed her against his chest.

She caught a glimpse of another steep drop, then sucked in a startled breath and closed her eyes. Shots rang out from somewhere above them as they plummeted into open space again.

We're going to die.

Strong arms clasped her so tightly she thought her body would break in two. Then she hit something hard—or he did, because she was on top of him. Their entwined bodies bounced several more times and slid a heart-stopping few more yards. Then, just as suddenly as their wild flight had begun, it was over. His chest rose and fell beneath hers, his ragged breaths fanning against the top of her head. But other than that, and her own gasping breaths, the world was blessedly still.

We didn't die.

Yet.

Her eyes flew open. Miraculously, her glasses had somehow survived the tumble down the mountain and were still on. Which gave her a startlingly clear view of a pair of brilliant blue eyes staring directly into hers from just inches away. It was only then that she realized just how intimately she was pressed against him. Her breasts were crushed to his chest, her cleavage straining the top of her lacy bra, her blouse having surrendered several buttons. Her right thigh was sandwiched between both of his legs, pressing against a very warm spot that left little to the imagination about just how well-proportioned he was to his taller-than-average height. Her cheeks flaming, she tried to scramble off him.

"Hold it, wait." His harsh whisper had her going still as his hands tightened on her arms. He tilted his head back and looked up the mountain they'd just tumbled down, apparently searching for the gunmen.

Her gaze followed his. She didn't see anyone. But what she did see had her shaking again. How they'd managed to fall so far through such rough terrain without being killed was a mystery. As she noticed the deep skid and slide marks down the grassy and rocky terrain, and the broken tree branches that marked their path, she realized that maybe it wasn't such a mystery after all. Her benefactor had rolled and tugged and pulled her to him the entire ride down. That was the only thing that explained how they hadn't crashed into boulders and trees and been killed. He'd done that. He'd protected both of them.

Or he'd protected *her*, at least.

Her eyes filled with tears as she realized just what his noble actions had cost him. Blood was drying on his face from his earlier cuts, likely from an altercation or ambush by the second gunman, the one named Owen. More blood streaked his arms and neck. A long gash marred his left biceps, blood trickling from a wound that was smeared with dirt. A black shadow was already darkening on his forehead where he'd obviously smacked it against something. And her? Other than a bitten tongue, dirty and torn clothes, and a few stinging minor cuts on her arms and legs, she was unharmed.

"You're hurt," she said. "I'm so sorry. Do you have a first-aid kit in your backpack? I can dress your wounds."

His gaze shot to hers. "Are you okay? You're crying."

The concern in his voice as he reached a hand toward her had shame and guilt flaring up inside. She jerked back to scramble off him but slammed down against his chest because of the rope that still connected them.

"Sorry, sorry. Dang it." She wiped the tears away and tried to tug the rope free.

"Here, let me." His deep voice was soft again, gentle, as he pressed the carabiners on each side of his pack. A few quick tugs on the knots and they seemed to magically unravel. Another yank and the slick nylon rope pulled free from her belt loops.

She pressed against the ground on either side of his chest and pushed herself up off him, then sat back on her heels and yanked the ends of her blouse back together to cover her bra.

"Are you okay?" he asked again, sitting up.

She nodded. "Thanks to you, I'm fine. But you're not." She waved toward the dozens of cuts on his arms, his face. "You took the brunt of the fall to protect me. Why would you do that?"

He frowned as if in confusion. "Why wouldn't I? It's my job."

She shook her head, unable to fathom such selfless thinking. "First-aid kit?"

"Later." He pushed to his knees and looked up again. "I don't see our two friends."

She followed his gaze to the cliff, which seemed impossibly far away. She still couldn't believe they'd rolled down the mountain and hadn't gotten killed, or shot, or both. But thankfully the gunmen weren't standing there, aiming a pistol at them.

"Why aren't they still up there, trying to shoot us?" she asked. "Maybe they didn't think we'd survive the drop?" She shivered and wrapped her hands around her waist. "Maybe they're worried someone heard the shots, so they took off?"

He shook his head. "Unless there are more trespassers ignoring the trail-closed signs, there's no one else to hear the gunshots. And I don't see our friends just moseying to their car and heading back where they came from after all the trouble they went to. They're after something. And they don't have it yet." His eyes stared deep into hers, once again darkening with suspicion. "How much motivation do they have, Jody? Enough to figure out a way down that mountain to come after us?"

A cold chill shot through her. She looked up again. But the only thing above them was a bright blue sky and a hawk gliding over the mountaintops.

"Jody? Who were those men? Why are they after you?" He climbed to his feet and helped her stand.

She stepped back so she could meet his gaze without getting a crick in her neck. "You're bleeding. I really think we should get the first aid kit." She took another step back.

He grabbed her waist and yanked her to the side. "Haven't you ever been in the mountains before? Never back up without looking first."

She glanced over her shoulder and sucked in a breath. The blood seemed to drain from her body, leaving her cold and shaking. Once again, she'd been close to the edge of another drop-off and had nearly plunged over the side.

Swallowing hard, she pressed a shaking hand to her throat. "Thank you. You've saved me more times than I can count and we've known each other for less than an hour."

"We need to go." He put a hand to the small of her back and urged her toward the charred woods to their right.

"Go where? It looks like we're heading toward another cliff." She tried to stop, but his hand was firm, pushing her forward.

"We'll make our own path. We have to. Out here

we're too much in the open." He held back a branch on a new sapling that had sprouted from the destruction.

They rounded a curve in the mountain, the going steep, treacherous, with loose rocks underfoot. A few yards farther and they were surrounded by trees, half of them scorched but miraculously still standing. Some of them supported canopies of new growth in spite of their blackened trunks. The underbrush had resurged here. Many of the bushes were taller than both of them.

Far below, water gurgled and rushed over boulders. She caught glimpses of it through breaks in the trees. Rocks in the middle of the stream created eddies and little rapids. The artist in her craved a few moments to stand there and gape at the beauty below, to frame it in her mind's eye like she'd frame a camera shot. But the reality of their situation, and the imposing ranger beside her, had her hurrying as fast as she could manage through the rough terrain.

He took the outside, near the steep drop, using the rise of the mountain as a barrier against her falling over the edge. His gaze was never still. He constantly scanned the woods around them, looking up at the mountain that rose above their heads. His constant vigilance should have made her feel secure. Instead, it only reminded her of the danger they were in.

She finally grabbed one of the saplings they were passing and used it as an anchor in the sea of fear that threatened to pull her under. "Wait."

He stopped beside her, brows raised in question.

"Your arms—some of the cuts are still bleeding. And they need to be cleaned so they don't get infected. Do you have medical supplies in your pack?"

"You're stalling, Jody. We need to get moving."

She waved a hand toward the trees surrounding them. "Unless those gunmen take a swan dive over a cliff or have billy goat ancestors, I don't see how they could follow us. It's too steep and rocky."

"They don't have to get too close. They just need one clear shot. Up on the trail, we were jumping over downed trees and weaving around curves. Plus, their adrenaline was probably pumping pretty good. Otherwise they wouldn't have missed. I don't want to hang around in one spot and give them a perfect target."

Her hand tightened around the sapling. "You're not helping."

He frowned again. "Helping with what?"

She huffed out an impatient breath. "I'm scared, okay? Right now I'm more afraid of plunging head-first over a cliff again than some gunmen who may or may not be following us."

His expression softened. "I wish I didn't have to force you to keep going. But I don't see those guys giving up that easily."

She swallowed. "Why do you say that?"

"Because they thought nothing of trying to shoot a federal officer. Your average thug thinks twice in a situation like that. They don't want to risk bringing the wrath of the feds down on them. But our guys not only shot at us multiple times, they risked their own lives running up a dangerous trail to do it. My guess is they might lie low for a little while to see whether backup arrives. But not for long. Then they'll be looking for a way to hike down here and find us."

He motioned toward the radio hooked to his belt. "I've turned this thing on half a dozen times since our flight down the mountain. There's no signal, not even a burst of static. One of the radio towers was destroyed in the wildfires. What we have to do is get within range of another tower so we can radio for help. Until then, we keep going." He arched a brow. "Unless you can tell me why those men might decide to hightail it out of here without finishing us off. Just what are they after? Who are they?"

She hesitated.

His jaw tightened. "Jody—"

"I don't know their names, other than the one calling the other Owen in front of both of us."

"You're splitting hairs. Not knowing their full names and not knowing what they want are two very different things. You were arguing with the first man when I approached. He later warned you to remember what he'd told you. What were you arguing about? What did he want you to remember?"

Without waiting for her reply, he pried her hand from the tree and tugged her through the woods.

Her foot skidded on some loose rocks. She let out a yelp, but he grabbed her around the waist and steadied her before she could fall.

"I've got you," he said. "Try not to worry. My boots hold the trail a lot better than your sneakers. I'm not going to let anything happen to you, okay?"

His voice was gentle again. But there was an underlying thread of steel. He wanted answers. And he deserved them. Even if it meant she might go to jail, or at the least, have all her career aspirations ruined. All those years of college, the sacrifices she'd made, the two jobs she was holding down were for nothing. In one stupid week, she'd destroyed it all.

She jerked to a halt, pressing a hand to her throat. "I

can't believe how selfish I'm being, thinking about my future career and prison when Tracy's missing." She moved her hand to her stomach. "That's just the kind of thing my adoptive father would do." She squeezed her eyes shut. "I think I'm going to be sick."

"Your career? Prison? Wait, who's Tracy?"

Chapter 5

Jody groaned and whirled around, gagging as she dropped to her knees and emptied the contents of her stomach.

Suddenly a strong arm was around her waist and a gentle hand swept her hair back from her face, holding it loosely behind her as Adam spoke soothing words in her ear. She was too sick and miserable to protest his help. The spasms wouldn't seem to stop and she started dry heaving.

"Deep breaths," he said. "Slow, deep breaths. You'll be okay. Slow and easy."

Somehow the sound of his voice calmed her. She dragged in a deep breath, then another. The knots in her stomach eased, and she could finally breathe normally without feeling like her stomach was trying to kill her.

Her world suddenly tilted as he scooped her up into

his arms. Before she could even ask him what he was doing, he'd set her down several feet away beneath the branches of a thick stand of trees. The realization that he was giving them cover in case the bad guys were around had her stomach clenching with dread. She pressed a hand to her belly.

"This should help." A bottle of water and a wet cloth appeared as if by magic as he handed them to her from the backpack he'd been carrying.

She rinsed her mouth out and spit. After a long drink, she washed her face with the cloth.

"Better?" He was on his knees in front of her, his brow furrowed with concern.

"Better. Thank you." She swept her hair back from her shoulders. Heat flushed her skin at the realization of what had just happened. She groaned and covered her face. "I can't believe you witnessed that. And that you helped me. I'm so embarrassed."

He tugged her hands down. "Jody, what made you so upset? Who's Tracy? Is she in trouble?"

She nodded miserably. "I think so. She texted me. That's why I was on the trail. Well, partly, anyway. I mean, I was in the parking lot. But she wasn't there, so I checked the bathrooms, and when I came out, that guy was there…and he started toward me. I saw his gun sticking out of his pocket, so I ran. I just ran. Then he was there, on the trail, with the gun—"

"Take a breath." He took one of her hands in his. "Back up. Who is Tracy?"

A ragged breath shuddered out of her. "My sister." She waved her hand. "Not a real sister. She's my friend. My very best friend. I don't have any biological siblings, just adoptive sisters and brothers. Not that I'm knocking adoptive families in general. I think they can be wonderful, for other people. But it hasn't turned out so well for me. We don't exactly visit each other or exchange Christmas cards." She drew a deep breath. "Tracy is not part of my adoptive family. She's my friend, my best friend, more of a sister to me than my adoptive sisters ever were. And her family is more of a family to me than my adoptive one." She closed her eyes and fisted her hands against the tops of her thighs.

"Tattoo Guy, he did something to her? To Tracy?"

She nodded and looked at him. "He abducted her. At least, that's what he told me. I didn't know, or I swear I would have called the police. I would never do anything to risk her life." She pressed her hand to her throat. "I think I may have just killed her. By running, with you. I shouldn't have done that." She squeezed her eyes shut again.

"Jody, I need you to be strong. For your friend, okay? I know it's hard. But you have to hold it together so we can figure out what to do. All right?"

She nodded and opened her eyes. "Okay. I'm sorry."

"Nothing to apologize for. I'm going to ask you some questions and I need you to give me the answers. Short and to the point. And we need to keep moving while we talk." He pulled her to her feet. "Can you do that?"

"I'll try. Yes. I'm sorry." She grimaced. "I know. Quit saying that."

He smiled and pulled her with him through the trees. "What's Tracy's full name?"

"Larson. Her name is Tracy Larson."

"Is she your age?"

"Yes. Twenty-four. We went to school together, from

grade school through high school. She didn't go to college. I went to TSU, Tennessee State University, I… Sorry. Short and to the point. I forgot. Sorry."

"It's okay. I went to TSU, too. When's the last time you saw her?"

She patted her pocket to check the time of Tracy's last text messages on her phone. But her pocket was empty. They all were. "My phone and keys are gone." She shook her head. "I know. Doesn't matter. I think the last I heard from her was at work yesterday. She's full-time. I'm part-time. I left at my usual two o'clock."

He steered her around a downed tree. "Friday at 2:00 p.m.? You're sure?"

"Pretty sure. I'm not counting the fake text this morning. The guy with the gun must have sent that. He tricked me."

"We'll get to that in a second. Are you sure you didn't talk to Tracy on the phone after 2:00 p.m.?"

"Talk?"

His mouth quirked up in a smile. "Forgive me. I'm a doddering thirty-year-old who actually uses phones for spoken conversations. Let me rephrase. Did you text each other? Share anything on social media?"

She surprised herself by laughing, which seemed obscene given the situation. She quickly sobered. "Sorry. But the idea of you being described as doddering is ridiculous. Trust me, most women my age would count themselves lucky to be with a guy as smokin' hot as you."

Her face flushed with heat as soon as the words left her mouth. She absolutely refused to look at him. "Text, yes, we texted a few times. Nothing seemed out of the norm. Then, this morning, I got a new text from her saying she needed to meet me, that it was urgent. She said she'd be waiting in the parking lot at the Sugarland Mountain trailhead. I went to the visitor center, and her car wasn't there. I texted her to ask where she was, and she said in the parking lot on the other end of the trail, not the visitor center. So I headed there. Only, when I got there, her car wasn't there, either."

Tears burned the backs of her eyes, but she refused to give in to the urge to cry again. She swallowed against her tight throat and continued. "There were a couple of cars besides mine on the other side of the lot. One of them was a minivan with a family and kids. I didn't see anyone in the other car, a black Charger. Not then. The family went to use the public facilities by the beginning of the trail. Tracy texted back that she'd be there in a few minutes and to wait. I ducked into the restroom, chatted with some of the people from the minivan. They left before me. When I came out, they were just pulling out of the parking lot. That's when he got out of the car."

"Who? The guy with the tattoos?"

"Yes. I started toward my car, then stopped. He was walking really fast, straight toward me. But there wasn't anyone else around. And the men's restrooms were on the other side of the lot. There was no reason for him to be hurrying toward me. I don't know how to explain it. But he gave me the creeps, and he was between me and my car. I didn't want to let him get too close. So I walked toward the trail. I looked over my shoulder, and that's when I saw the gun." She swallowed. "He had a pistol sticking out of his pants pocket. I ran. I hopped over the cattle gate blocking the trail and took off. And he took off after me."

"Did he fire the gun?"

She frowned. "No. No, he never did. Not until you and I were running up the trail later."

He nodded as if that made sense to him. "Go on. You ran. Then what happened?"

"I used to run track in high school. I was pretty fast. But I'm not used to running up mountains or having to hop over downed trees. I couldn't sprint and pull away like I would in a flat footrace. He caught up to me right where you saw us. And he…he pointed his gun at me. And he…" She drew a ragged breath.

"You're doing great, Jody. Slow, deep breaths. What did he do next? What did he say to you?"

As much as she wanted to be strong for her friend, she was having a hard time holding back her terror. What was happening to Tracy right now? What had that man done to her? Was she even alive or had he lied to her?

"Jody. What did the man do when he caught you on the trail?" He steered her around a particularly rocky section and past some thorny shrubs.

She murmured her thanks and straightened. She could do this. She had to. For Tracy's sake. "He told me I had something of his and he wanted it. He said if I didn't give it to him, he would…he would kill Tracy." In spite of her efforts to stay calm, tears tracked down her cheeks. "He had her phone, showed it to me. That's how I knew he was telling the truth. He must have texted me to meet him there, pretending he was her. No way could he have gotten her phone without taking it from her. That thing is practically attached at her hip."

He pulled her to a halt and grasped her shoulders. "What do you have that he wants?"

"I don't have anything. I swear. He insisted I have pictures, maybe a video, or knew where they were. He said my boss had seen something he shouldn't have and that there was a gap in the time stamps on the pictures."

"Your boss?"

"Sam Campbell. He's a private investigator. Tracy and I work for him." She looked away, panic swelling inside her again. She'd been so stupid. So very, very stupid.

"You know what he's after, don't you?" The thread of steel was back in his voice.

She glanced up at him and wiped at the tears on her cheeks. "Not specifically, no. I assume that Sam performed surveillance on him, that he's one of Sam's clients. But all of Sam's pictures and videos are locked up at the office. I told him that. He shook his head, said that he'd searched there already. That's when we heard you whistling. He told me to keep my mouth shut, that Tracy would die if I told you anything."

His eyes widened. "You lied to me up on the trail to get me to leave you two alone, knowing he had a gun? If I'd bought your story, you would have been all alone with him. He could have killed you."

"I know. Looking back, it was stupid. But I didn't know what else to do. Tracy—" Her voice broke.

"You thought he would kill her if you didn't do what he told you. You risked your life for her. Whatever happens, you can't blame yourself. You did what you could."

She shook her head. "No. I was stupid, too scared to think straight. You don't make deals with criminals. What I should have done was shove him or something when you came up and yelled a warning." Her hand shook as she raked her hair back from her face. "You could have been killed."

He frowned. "Is that why you came looking for me after I chased Tattoo Guy down the trail? You were trying to save me?"

She snorted. "Fat lot of good it did. I just slowed you down. And now you're all scratched up and out here with me, without a weapon, with a couple of thugs possibly coming after us. I'm such an idiot."

His warm, strong hand gently urged her chin up so she had to look at him.

She pushed his hand away. "Go ahead. Yell at me. My stupidity has probably gotten my friend killed and nearly got you killed. Every decision I made was wrong. You'd have thought I would have learned better at college."

"What do you mean?"

"I studied criminal justice, graduated with honors. Not that it means I have any sense. Might as well tear up that piece of paper."

He frowned. "Aren't you being a bit hard on yourself? You drove up here because a friend said she needed you. A man chased you with a gun, threatened to kill your friend if you didn't do what he said. And as soon as you had a chance to escape, instead, you went *toward* trouble, to help a law enforcement officer you thought was in need. From where I stand, that's pretty darn amazing."

She blinked. "What?"

"You have the education, but not the training or the experience. And you're a civilian, unarmed. You did the best you could. I can't find fault with any of your decisions."

"Th...thank you?"

He smiled. "Come on. There are a lot of gaps in your story, like why someone with a criminal justice degree is working part-time as a private investigator." He tugged her hand, then stopped and looked over his shoulder at her when she pulled back. "Jody?"

"I'm not a private investigator," she confessed. "And when I tell you the rest, you aren't going to think I did the best I could or made good decisions. I didn't."

He turned to face her. "Go on."

"Tracy pretty much runs the office. I guess you'd call her an administrative assistant. I help Sam with his cases. But I'm not a licensed investigator, just a recent criminal justice grad trying to get some experience to help me get the job I really want—as a criminal investigator with the prosecutor's office. But those jobs are few and far between, so I'm working two jobs to make ends meet and trying to get a step up on the competition when the job I want opens up."

She waved her hand again. "Anyway, my point is that I'm his gofer, his researcher. Sometimes I interview clients and things like that. Sam does all the heavy lifting, and I take care of the grunt work."

He studied her intently, as if weighing her every word. "So far I'm not hearing any bad decisions or things for you to be worried about."

She tightened her hands into fists by her sides. "There's more. I screwed up. I mean, really, really screwed up." She let out a shaky breath and met his gaze again. "Sam disappeared a week ago. And before you ask, no, it's not unusual. He's had a tough time since his wife died of ovarian cancer about a year ago. He hits the bottle too hard. He usually shows up a few days later and will be fine for a while." She clenched her fists so hard the nails dug into her palms. "We always cover for him when he's on a binge. Do you understand what I'm telling you? He could lose his license if clients complain that he's a drunk and messes up cases. And besides that, if he messes up the cases, the income stops rolling in. And, well, Tracy and I both rely on that income. We live paycheck to paycheck. No paycheck means no food, no rent."

He stared at her intently. "You did more than run errands, didn't you?"

She nodded. "We may have…pretended to be Sam to some of the clients, through correspondence in the mail…to close out cases, resolve issues."

"You operated as PIs without a license. You're worried that you may have committed fraud. Even worse, mail fraud. That's a felony."

She winced and looked away.

The silence stretched out between them.

"Jody. There's more, isn't there?"

She nodded slowly.

His sigh could have knocked over a tree. "Go on. Might as well tell me the rest."

She swallowed, then forced herself to meet his gaze. Surprisingly, it wasn't the cold, judgmental look she'd expected. Instead, he looked at her with something far worse.

Pity.

She stiffened her spine and confessed the rest of her sins.

"Sam is dead. Tracy and I killed him."

Chapter 6

Adam dropped his chin to his chest and shook his head. If for even one second he thought Jody was telling the truth, he'd have pulled out his second set of handcuffs and Mirandized her. But in spite of her low opinion of herself, she struck him as painfully honest. In the span of a few hours, she'd confessed more to him than most people confessed to their priests. This young woman didn't know how to lie convincingly, as proven by the fiasco up on the trail. And she'd apologized at least a dozen times in the past few minutes, and meant it. She was riddled with guilt over things she shouldn't even feel guilty about. No way had she murdered someone.

"Okay," he said. "Tell me how you two did the dirty deed. Poison? Butcher knife? Machete?"

"Are you seriously making fun of me?"

He raised his head and gave her a baleful glance. "Are you seriously going to try to convince me you murdered someone?"

"Well, not directly, we didn't. But we might as well have. When Sam disappeared, we should have gone to the police, filled out a missing-persons report and—"

"Which the police would have set aside. They would have told you to give it a few more days because there was no evidence of foul play and your boss has a history of going off on drinking binges."

She crossed her arms, her mouth drawn into a tight line.

"Am I wrong? You said he disappeared all the time."

"That's not fair to Sam. He's a great man, more of a father to me than my adoptive father ever was. He doesn't disappear *all* the time. Just sometimes. And it's not like I think we should have reported it the first morning he didn't show up. There was no reason to think anything was wrong. But he's never been gone a whole week before. We should have done something on day five instead of…of…committing fraud. And then maybe Sam would be okay."

Everything about her posture and her tone told him she truly felt responsible. And he hadn't missed the hurt look in her eyes the last time she'd met his gaze. Which was several minutes ago. Now she was staring off into the woods, her pretty face mottled, her jaw tight. She was obviously upset, both because she took the weight of the world on her shoulders and because he'd made light of her claims. She'd really be angry if she knew how hard he was struggling not to laugh, or at least not to smile.

He cocked his head, studying her profile. She'd been

through a traumatic experience. Her boss was missing—even though Adam was inclined to think the man would show up alive and well with a wicked hangover. Adam had met Sam Campbell a few times over the years and was well-acquainted with his reputation around town for going on occasional drinking binges—even before his wife's death. Not that Jody apparently knew that. His employees were trying to hide a secret that wasn't even a secret.

But Jody's best friend was *really* missing. And Tracy Larson was *not* likely to show up alive and well. Jody had been chased, threatened, shot at, pulled off a cliff—all in all the kind of morning that would crush most civilians. But here she stood, her back ramrod straight, her mouth compressed into a mutinous line as she glared her hurt feelings at the mountains around them.

And his teasing, his refusal to take her seriously had only added to her burden.

His shoulders slumped. He'd handled this all wrong. He started to apologize but stopped. What was he supposed to say? *Sorry I didn't believe that you could kill someone in cold blood*? She seemed so young in so many ways. At twenty-four, she was only six years younger than him. His last girlfriend had been younger, twenty-three. But Brandy had been just as bruised by the world and jaded as he was. The years between them hadn't mattered. This girl didn't seem world-weary or jaded and he didn't get the impression that she realized just how horrible or cruel people could sometimes be.

She crossed her arms, the movement pushing up her small breasts in the delicate, lacy bra that her torn blouse did little to conceal. His body's reaction to that innocent display surprised him. He could feel himself tightening, heat pulsing through his veins. And he had to admit, now that he *really* looked at her for the first time since this had all started, there was nothing girlish about her figure.

She was all woman, from her luscious red hair that bounced around her shoulders to the full, pink lips that gave her mouth a pouty, sultry look to her narrow waist that begged for a man's hands to span its narrow curves. Her legs weren't long and lean like Brandy's had been. But on Jody, her short, toned, silky-looking legs were the perfect complement to the rest of her. Even those green glasses on her perky nose were cute. All in all, she was one sexy package. And now that he'd finally noticed, he was cursing himself for the lust that shot through him. Jody needed a protector, not some guy drooling after her.

He forced his gaze back to her face and cleared his throat.

She arched a brow and looked at him in question, the hurt and anger still broadcast in her expression like a neon sign flashing at him. If she ever played poker, she'd lose every round. The art of bluffing was beyond her. Which was, all in all, refreshing. Most people he knew were great liars and couldn't be trusted. He had a feeling he could trust Jody in any situation, and she wouldn't let him down.

Maybe it was time he told her that. And confessed his own half-truths he'd tossed out earlier.

"You didn't sign your boss's name on anything you mailed, did you?"

She frowned. "No, why?"

"Then it's unlikely you committed fraud. All you

did was manage the office, continue to send your boss's mail for him, tie up loose ends—stuff administrative assistants do for their bosses every day of the week all over the world. Unless you actually went up to someone and claimed to be a private investigator, you can let that guilt go. You didn't do anything wrong."

"But—"

"But nothing." He squeezed her hand. "I'm sorry I didn't treat your concerns more seriously earlier. You've been through a lot, and you're worried about your boss and your friend. I should have been a better listener and commiserated more."

She cleared her throat. "Well, maybe. But I was being a bit over-the-top when I said we'd killed Sam. It's just that I'm really worried about him. I wish I'd done something more when he didn't show up. Now, with Tracy missing, and that creepy man with the gun thinking Sam had more pictures of him somewhere, I can't help worrying everything's connected and both Tracy and Sam are either in real trouble or—"

"Leave the 'or' to me, okay? That's my job, to worry about stuff like that." He tugged her forward and they started through the woods again. "Let's focus on getting you to safety and then I'll work with the local police to start an investigation and search for your friend. If I were a betting man, I'd bet you that Sam is alive and well, passed out on his couch at home. And your friend is alive, too."

Her hand tightened in his. "You really think so?"

"I do," he lied, seeing no point in making her even more miserable. "And as long as Tattoo Guy thinks you have something he needs, he won't hurt Tracy. He needs her as leverage. His threats up on the trail were a complete bluff."

She stopped, and he did, too, facing her.

"Why do you think it was a bluff?"

"Because he didn't shoot you. In the parking lot, you said he chased you up the trail, then confronted you. If he'd wanted to kill you, he could have. Instead, he threatened you, threatened your friend's life, to get you to talk. To tell him where the pictures are that he thinks are floating around somewhere. That's your bargaining chip. As long as he thinks you have something he needs, he'll keep Tracy safe as leverage."

"Then…those were just warning shots? He wouldn't really shoot us?"

Adam laughed harshly. "Oh no. He'll kill me the first chance he gets. No doubt. And his type, he'll hurt you in a heartbeat. Might even try to shoot you in the leg or bust your kneecap to get you to talk. Or worse." He forced a smile he was far from feeling when he saw the worry in her eyes. "Which is why we don't want to risk him catching up to us if he wasn't smart enough to head back to his car and hightail it out of here."

A deep rumble sounded in the distance.

They both looked up at the sky. Instead of the brilliant blue it had been earlier, it was rapidly turning dark and ominous with heavy rainclouds blowing in to cover the sun.

"A storm's rolling in. And we aren't anywhere near the next cell tower yet to radio for someone to get us out of here before the lightning show starts."

"That's crazy. There was no hint of an oncoming storm a few minutes ago."

"Oh, I'm sure there were hints. We were just more

focused on watching out for thugs than keeping an eye on the weather." He studied the terrain around them, then pointed off to the right. "There, see how the mountain forms a natural depression over there? Away from trees or rocks that will conduct electricity? That's the safest place around here to hunker down when the lightning starts. Won't keep us dry in the rain, but it's safer than being under trees or becoming human lightning rods out here in the open like we are now. Let's go."

He motioned for her to join him and led her down a steeper descent than they'd been taking before. He hadn't wanted to risk her twisting an ankle or getting scraped up on the rocks if she lost her footing, so he'd been leading her around the mountain, taking a more gradual slope down toward the valley below. But storms up here could be deadly. There was no time to waste.

Sure enough, her sneakers weren't up to the task of navigating the rocky path. She wobbled and skittered across some loose stones, her arms flailing as she tried to maintain her balance. He grabbed her waist, steadying her.

"Next time you hike in the mountains, wear some decent shoes," he teased.

She smiled up at him. And it did crazy things to his breathing.

He swallowed and urged her forward again. The breeze that had kicked up helped cool his body and bring clarity to his thoughts. They really did need to find shelter, fast, or they could get struck by lightning, or even drown in a flash flood if they were crossing one of the dry creek beds when the rains started.

Boom!

Jody looked up at the sky. Adam tackled her, wrapping his arms protectively around her as they both fell to the ground. He heard her gasp of pain when they landed, the breath leaving her in a whoosh as her chin smacked his chest. The back of his head snapped against a rock, practically making his teeth rattle.

She shoved against him. "What was that for? The thunder—"

"It wasn't thunder. Move, move, move!" He rolled and grabbed her around the waist, yanking her up with him in a crouch.

Boom! Boom!

A chunk of rock exploded inches from Adam's head.

Jody let out a startled yelp and looked over her shoulder. "Was that—"

"Gunfire!" He shoved her in front of him, shielding her body with his. "Run, Jody. Run!"

Chapter 7

C*hh-chh.*

The ominous sound didn't have to be explained. Jody had heard it dozens of times in action movies. It was the sound of a shotgun being pumped.

Adam was already pulling her to the ground before she could react.

Boom! Chh-chh. Boom!

Leaves and sawdust rained down on them from the tree above. Jody let out a squeak of fear before she could stop herself. She started to push off the ground to run again, but Adam pressed her back down.

He held his fingers to his mouth, signaling her to be quiet, then pointed to his right and motioned for her to precede him.

She nodded to let him know she understood, even though she wanted to yell at him for always making himself a human target to protect her. It wasn't right, regardless of what his job title might be. But arguing would only make him more of a target as the men pursuing them homed in on the sounds.

Her bare knees screamed in protest as she half crawled, half duckwalked through the woods, behind clumps of bushes and trees, toward another group of boulders. She tried to avoid dried leaves, twigs, anything that could crunch or snap and give away their location. But everything in this half-burned section of the mountains seemed to make noise when she touched it. All she could do was hope the sound didn't carry to the men chasing them. Their only chance was to give them the slip, find a hiding place and hunker down.

A hand tapped her shoulder. She looked back at Adam. He held up one finger, pointed off to their left and then held his hands out together as if he were holding a shotgun. Her stomach sank, but she nodded in understanding. He held up a finger again and pointed a little farther to the left, almost behind them. This time he held his other hand out, pointer finger extended, thumb raised, in an imitation of a handgun. He must have seen Owen and Tattoo Guy, both closing in on them. One of them had a pistol. How had the other one gotten a shotgun? Had they hidden one in the woods, just in case the threat about Tracy failed? In case Jody managed to escape and they had to give chase?

She nodded, again letting him know she understood. Then she held her hands out in a gesture of helplessness and mouthed, "What do we do now?"

He pointed to the right and once again held both his hands out as if he were holding a shotgun, or maybe a rifle. She bit her lip to keep from crying out in frustration. At least now she knew where Tattoo Guy and Owen had gotten a shotgun. A third man was after them. He must have been a reinforcement, and he'd brought more weapons.

Please don't let there be a fourth thug out here with yet another gun.

He pointed to her, then himself, then motioned behind him. She frowned. That couldn't be right. He wanted them to go back the way they'd already come? She shook her head and pointed straight in front of them, a direct line that would keep the two guys to their left and the other to the right.

His brows drew down, and he shook his head. "Trust me," he mouthed silently. "Come on."

She didn't protest when he grasped her shoulders and turned her around. All she could do was put her faith in him and, as he'd told her, trust him. He was the professional, and she presumed he knew his way around this mountain. She sure didn't.

Her instincts screamed at her to jump up and run. It would be much faster. The ground was almost level in this section of the mountain. They'd descended to a valley or a plateau, perfect for stretching out her legs and putting on a burst of speed and stamina that would take her far away from this place in no time. Years of running, both in school and out, would finally come in handy—if Adam would give her the chance. As long as she didn't have to run an obstacle course—leaping over rocks and trees that had slowed her down on the trail above them—she was confident she could outrun these thugs.

But she couldn't outrun a bullet.

Feeling all kinds of wrong about it, she did as Adam

directed. Half crawling, half walking in a deep crouch, turning left or right each time he thumped her on one of her shoulders from behind to let her know which direction to go.

It seemed like an eternity had passed by the time he tugged her hair in what she assumed was his way of telling her to stop. The man was treating her like a horse with his tapping and hair pulling. She wanted to scream in frustration. Instead, she looked over her shoulder and arched a brow to ask him what to do next. But he wasn't looking at her. He was staring off into the woods, eyes narrowed, every muscle tense and alert. He reminded her of a panther: stealthy, alert, searching for prey. Except that in this case, she and Adam were the prey. They were the ones being hunted.

His eyes widened, and he suddenly grabbed her waist, hauling her backward with him. She scrabbled with her feet, pushing back to help him. Once they were behind a downed tree, he shoved her onto the ground and covered her with his body.

Good grief, he was heavy. About six feet, three inches of pure muscle squashed her into the dirt, the musty smell of pine needles and wet moss seeping into her lungs. Drawing a deep breath was impossible, so she breathed shallowly, one after the other, struggling to get enough oxygen.

The sharp crack of a snapping twig sounded close by. She froze. Adam pressed her even harder into the ground, and it dawned on her that he had dark clothes on and she had a white blouse. In the gloom of this part of the forest, her white shirt would stand out like a beacon. He was doing everything he could to keep her hidden and make sure her shirt didn't alert their pursuers.

Another crack sounded, but it was farther away. The men searching for them must not have seen them and were moving off in another direction.

Her lungs screamed for air. Dark spots began to fill her vision. She could feel her energy seeping away. Her limbs went limp like noodles. A strange buzzing sounded in her ears. The weight lifted and everything turned on its axis.

"Jody."

She gasped, drawing a deep lungful of air, then another and another. The dark veil fell away. She blinked and looked up into Adam's beautiful eyes just inches from hers. His brow was lined with worry, his mouth tight as he gently shook her.

"Jody," he whispered harshly. "Are you okay?" He shook her again, his gaze searching hers.

She shoved his hands away. "I'm fine," she whispered. "Couldn't breathe."

He winced. "Sorry," he mouthed silently and held his fingers to his lips, letting her know they weren't alone, that the gunmen were still hunting them.

She pushed against his chest so she could get to her knees and follow wherever he led. Instead, he scooped her up into his arms and ran. He was bent over at the waist, keeping as low as possible so the bushes and trees could conceal them.

She clutched his shirt, holding on for dear life, the trees and bushes rushing past, making her dizzy. She squeezed her eyes shut and focused on making herself as small as possible, pulling in her arms and legs. It was a wild ride, with her bobbing up and down in his arms, feeling like she was going to fall any second. But he didn't let her fall. He protected her, as he'd done since the first moment he'd met her.

Where were the men who were after them? For him to be running like this, they must be close. But no one was shooting at them, so they must not have seen them. Not yet, anyway. She felt his chest rise and fall against hers. Carrying her and running in such an unnatural, bent-over position was taking its toll. His strides were slowing, his breaths coming faster and faster as he struggled to keep up his blistering pace.

"Put. Me. Down." Each word bounced out of her in unison with his strides.

Instead of stopping, he pulled her tighter against him, his mouth pressed next to her ear. "Too close," he rasped.

"I can run faster than you think. Put me down. *Please.*"

He stumbled and cursed, then stumbled again. He dropped to the ground, spilling her out of his arms onto a carpet of thick leaves and wild grasses. She scrambled to her knees and turned to check on him and ask which way they should run.

Then she froze.

She clasped her hand over her mouth to keep from crying out in dismay, mindful of the footfalls in the distance, pounding against the forest floor. Coming closer.

She scrambled to Adam, careful to stay low behind the grasses and bushes. Tears stung the backs of her eyes as she met his pain-racked gaze. From midchest down, his body was wedged in some kind of hole, a sinkhole or maybe a wild animal's den. He'd braced his arms beside him and was struggling to pull himself free. But every time he moved, his face went pale. He was obviously in terrible pain.

Footfalls sounded harder against the ground, louder, coming closer.

Someone shouted. Another man answered, though Jody couldn't quite make out the words.

"Hide," Adam ordered, his voice low, gritty. Talking was obviously a struggle.

"I'm not leaving you in this hole," she whispered.

"Go." He pushed her hands away when she reached out to help him. He motioned toward the nearest stand of trees. "Hurry, before they see you."

Another shout sounded.

She reached for him again, but he shoved her hand away.

"Jody, get out of here. Head into those trees. There's nothing you can do to help me." He pressed his hands against the ground and strained, his arms shaking from the effort. His body barely moved. He was good and stuck.

She turned in a circle, desperate to find something that might help. There, a thick, broken piece of a branch a few feet away. She lunged for it, grabbed it and yanked it over to Adam. What now? There wasn't any room around his chest to shove the stick into the hole and try to pry him out.

"Over there," a shout sounded. "I think I saw something."

Adam grabbed her arm and yanked her close. "Leave me. Run into the woods. Save yourself, Jody. Hurry!"

"They'll kill you. I can't just hide while they find you and shoot you."

"There's no other choice. I'm stuck. Better that you survive than both of us die. *Go.*"

She whirled around again on her knees, looking for something else, anything, to give him a chance. There were boulders close by, but they wouldn't hide him for long. He was a sitting duck out here. Wait. Boulders. The branch she'd dragged over was too short, but if she got a longer one...

"Hold on," she whispered.

"Jody—"

She scrambled away from him, her heart pounding in rhythm with the footfalls she could hear. Taking a risk, she lifted up just enough to see over the closest bush, then ducked back down. All three men were in sight, about twenty feet apart from each other, maybe fifty yards away. They were searching behind every bush, every tree. They'd be here in a couple of minutes, maybe less. She turned around and around, then she saw it. Another branch, this one thicker, longer, like a bat or a thick cane. It would work. It had to.

She scrambled to it, then dragged it back to Adam and shoved both ends of the branch between some boulders. The main part of the branch was about a foot above him. He gave her a furious look, then grabbed the branch. It held. He strained against it, twisting and pulling. The ground around his chest moved. It was working.

"Did you hear something, Owen? Where did that come from?"

Adam froze and looked at Jody. "Go," he ordered again.

She hesitated.

He strained, pushing and pulling on the branch, twisting his body. He rose an inch, two, then fell back, his face a mirror of pain. The men were almost upon them. They would shoot him, kill him. Maybe they'd shoot her, too, wing her as he'd warned, take her prisoner so they could interrogate her for whatever they thought she had.

She glanced toward the trees where Adam had told her to run, to hide. The boulders and bushes might block her from sight long enough for her to reach cover. But that wouldn't save the honorable man caught in the hole, a man who'd risked his life repeatedly for her.

He was waving at her, his face a mask of fury as he tried to get her to run into the woods. She ignored him. She looked past the woods to the left. The trees were sparser there. But the ground was nearly level. A fast track, as her old high school coach would have said. And it wasn't close to Adam like the trees where he wanted her to hide.

She looked back at Adam, who looked like he wanted to murder her himself.

Please, please let this work. Let him live.

She bent over and ran in a crouch about thirty feet away from him. Then she stood.

"Over there!" Tattoo Guy yelled. "She's over there!"

Jody took off, arms and legs pumping as she sprinted across the open field.

Chapter 8

Jody whirled around, swinging the knobby length of branch like a baseball bat when one of the men got too close.

The other two laughed as they continued to toy with her, slowly tightening their circle around her in the small clearing.

"What do you want from me?" she demanded.

The pockmarked one named Owen grinned and lunged toward her.

She swung the branch in a wide arc.

He jumped back, laughing and grinning the whole time. "She's feistier than her friend."

Her stomach dropped. "Where is she? Where's Tracy?" She tightened her grip on the branch, twisting and turning, trying to keep tabs on all three of them.

"She's alive," Tattoo Guy told her. "But she won't

be for long if you don't tell me where your boss keeps all his pictures and videos."

She gritted her teeth. "Why don't you ask Sam?"

His mouth quirked in a cruel smile. "Already did. He wasn't any more forthcoming than your little friend. I was hoping you'd be more cooperative."

"I told you. I don't know where any more pictures or videos are. Sam locks them all up in the office every day. Are you a client of his? Maybe you got things mixed up. Maybe you thought Sam had more information but he didn't—"

"Where's the cop, Jody girl?"

She clutched the branch harder. "He...he didn't make it. When we went over the cliff. I...had to leave his body there."

"Now, now, Jody." He stopped in front of her, just out of reach of her tree branch while the others kept circling. "And here I thought we were beginning to understand each other. But then you lie to me." He shook his head. "I don't like liars." He made a quick motion with his left hand.

Jody spun around in that direction, swinging her branch as hard and fast as she could. *Crack!* It slammed into the side of Owen's head. His eyes rolled up and he dropped to the ground, blood dribbling from the corner of his mouth.

She stared down at him in horror. Had she killed him? No, his chest moved. It moved again. He was breathing.

"Go on, Thad. Teach her a lesson."

She jerked her head up. Tattoo Guy was standing off to the side, still out of reach. The other man, Thad, was circling her again. But he wasn't smiling. And he was holding a knife.

She tightened her grip on the branch. Her heart was beating so hard her pulse thudded in her ears. Had she really endured this whole horrible day only to die here, two hundred yards from where she'd left Adam? She hadn't managed to give him much distance to get away. Would he be able to escape before they backtracked and found him?

Thad darted toward her, knife extended.

She swung the branch.

He leaped back just in time, laughing again. He was enjoying this.

He feinted left, then jabbed toward her right.

She jumped to the side, bringing the branch around just in time to slap the knife back. That was close, too close. Her breaths came in short, choppy pants. They circled each other like two boxers. She tried to watch out for Tattoo Guy, keeping him in her peripheral vision. But Thad kept circling and she had to keep turning or risk him stabbing her from behind.

"We're wasting time, Thad. Just stick her already."

Jody's stomach clenched.

Thad's face scrunched up with concentration as he moved in for the kill. He raised the knife over his head, moved closer, closer.

She clutched the branch, knowing she might only get one chance.

Thad let out a guttural yell, a battle cry that made Jody's blood run cold. He lunged forward, knife raised. She screamed her fear, frustration and rage as she swung the branch with every ounce of strength she had.

"No!" Thad yelled, a split second before a dark shape barreled into him, slamming him to the ground.

Jody's swing met empty air. Her momentum sent her crashing to the ground, and the branch flew from her hand.

Vicious curses sounded from a few feet off to her left. Behind her came more swearing and thumps. She shoved herself up to her knees and looked around. Tattoo Guy was the one to her left, his face contorted in rage as he drew his gun. She jerked around to look behind her. Thad was on the ground, wrestling with the man who'd tackled him—Adam! And just a few feet away, the knife blade winked in the light, the prize Thad was struggling to grab.

Bam!

She ducked down and whirled around to see Tattoo Guy, gun out, pointing it at the two men locked in combat. He must have tried to shoot Adam. His jaw was clenched and the pistol kept moving in his two-handed grip as he waited for an opening between the fighting men on the ground.

Jody spun around and dived for the knife. Out of the corner of her eye, she saw Tattoo Guy turning toward her. She grabbed the hilt and threw the knife in one quick motion, twisting around and falling back onto the dirt.

A shout full of rage and pain filled the clearing. Tattoo Guy's pistol dropped to the ground. The knife's blade was buried in his left shoulder, blood quickly seeping around it and darkening his shirt. His eyes shined with malevolence and a promise of retribution as he stared at Jody. A shudder racked his body, and he dropped to his knees. His left arm hung useless at his side, but his right hand was already reaching for the pistol.

Scrambling away, Jody looked around for the only weapon she had, the branch.

Strong arms grabbed her from behind and yanked her backward. She struggled against them as she was picked up.

Tattoo Guy brought up his gun, shouting curses as he raised it.

She fell, something dark filling her vision as she slammed into the ground again.

Bam! Bam! Bam!

She recoiled against the sound of gunshots, but all she could see was the solid bulk of a downed tree directly in front of her face. She started to turn, but strong arms shoved her down—just like they'd done so many times before. Adam!

"Stay down," he whispered harshly.

More gunshots sounded. Wood splintered above her and rained down on her head.

Adam rose to his knees, beside her now, lifting a gun he must have taken from Thad and pointing it at the clearing. His return fire was deafening. Jody covered her ears, squeezing herself into a tight ball as more shots rang out.

A scuffling noise and more cursing sounded from a new direction. She could feel Adam's body against hers, pivoting to the right. He fired once, twice.

Bam! Another shot rang out from the left again.

Adam whirled around, cursing as he ducked behind the tree.

Footsteps pounded against the ground, the sound of men running away. The sounds faded, leaving only

Adam's harsh breathing and her own shallow gasps to break the silence.

He looked down at her, gun still clenched in his hand. "They're gone. For now. Are you okay?"

She blinked up at him, noting the fresh blood on the side of his face, his hands, the white line of his lips, clenched in obvious pain. She uncurled and sat up, her gaze sweeping over him. His clothes were filthy and torn, matted with dirt and sweat. Then she saw it, finally, the reason he was in such terrible pain.

"Oh no." Her words clogged her suddenly tight throat as she stared in horror at the thick length of splintered wood that pierced his left calf, protruding through bloody holes torn in the front and back of his pant leg.

"Are you okay?" he repeated, his voice a gritty mixture of concern and raw pain.

"What? Yes, yes, I'm fine. But you, Adam, I can't even imagine how much that hurts." She reached for his left leg, but he jerked back.

"Leave it. We have to get moving. They'll lick their wounds, but they'll be back. It's not about whatever information you have anymore. It's about revenge. They'll kill both of us when they get the chance. We have to get out of here."

"But your leg. You can't possibly walk on that. You have to let me help you. I'll fashion a splint—"

"I made it this far. I can make it a little farther. We have to get to a defensible position. Hurry." He shoved the pistol into his front pocket then braced himself against the downed tree, pushing himself up.

Jody scrambled to her feet and stood beside him, reaching out to help him. Then she saw the body lying in the middle of the clearing. It wasn't Tattoo Guy or Owen. It was Thad. Sightless eyes stared up at the dark sky with its threatening storm that was still holding off, a single small dot of red in the center of his forehead. The ground beneath his head was saturated in blood.

She pressed a hand to her throat.

Adam's jaw worked, his hands clenched into fists at his sides. "That's the handiwork of our nemesis, Tattoo Guy. My guess is he didn't want to leave anyone behind who might give us information about him."

Her gaze flew to his. "He killed his own man?"

He nodded. "Which means he won't hesitate to kill us, especially since you managed to hit him with that knife. He doesn't strike me as the forgive-and-forget type. As soon as he binds his wound and is able to come after us again, he will. And it wouldn't surprise me if he brings reinforcements. We have to get out of here, fall back to somewhere more secure, keep moving until we get in range of a cell tower and can radio for help."

He wobbled on his feet, then braced himself against the tree.

She bit her lip to keep from crying out in sympathy. He was being unbelievably strong, had managed to somehow crawl out of that hole where she'd left him. And even with his leg so horribly damaged, he'd come to her rescue. Somehow she had to find the inner strength to match his, so she could get him somewhere safe and finally look in his backpack for a first-aid kit. Her mouth twisted bitterly. He needed far more than a kit. He needed an emergency room with a trauma unit.

"Let's go. That way." He pointed off toward the left.

"Deeper into the mountains? Are you sure? Shouldn't we head back toward town—"

He shook his head. "Our only real chance is to get in range of a cell tower so I can radio for a rescue team. Back the way we came is by the broken tower, the one destroyed in the wildfires. If we head west, we should be in range of a working tower within a few minutes."

"A few minutes?"

"Give or take."

Relief made her legs go weak. Soon they would have other rangers with guns to protect them, and medical help for Adam. And then they could bring in the FBI or whoever they needed in order to find her friend Tracy. And Sam, if he was still alive. Then they could put Tattoo Guy and Owen in prison where they belonged.

Maybe, just maybe, they'd make it out of here after all.

Adam turned and limped forward.

"Wait." She motioned for him to stay where he was and hurried around the downed tree.

"Jody, what are you—"

"This." She held up the thick piece of branch she'd used like a bat to defend herself after the thugs had caught up to her and surrounded her. "It's thick and heavy and just about long enough to work as a cane." She rushed over to him and held it out.

The lines of pain bracketing his mouth eased, and he offered her a small smile. "That should do the job. Thanks. The one I used to pull myself out of the hole broke in half or it would have been a perfect walking stick." He tested it out, pressing the length of branch against the ground as he took a step forward. He grimaced but quickly smoothed his features. "Works great. Let's go."

Together they hobbled and walked west, keeping near the tree line to give them cover in case the bad guys came looking for them. By staying out of the woods, the going was easier, with fewer obstacles for Adam to navigate around.

"Shouldn't we stop and pull that wood out of your leg?"

He shook his head. "It's controlling the bleeding. It's better to leave it in, even though it hurts like the devil."

She nodded, unconvinced. But since her most recent medical training was CPR in the fifth grade, it wasn't like she had any true wisdom to offer.

"At least the storm is holding off. That's good," she said.

He looked up and nodded. "Looks like it's moving east. We should be okay."

At first, he managed a steady clip. But as they began a gradual climb into the foothills of the next mountain, his pace began to lag. He was leaning heavier and heavier on the makeshift cane. If the broken piece of wood piercing his leg was truly stanching the bleeding, she couldn't imagine how bad it would be if the wood was out. A dark, wet spot was slowly spreading down his pant leg.

She glanced at the ground behind him. Bright spots of blood marked their trail. She worried her bottom lip, not sure whether it mattered at this point. They weren't going fast enough to outrun anyone. Once the bad guys decided to come back to look for them, they'd find them pretty quickly, with or without a blood trail to follow.

"What is it?" Adam asked, his voice husky from the pain.

"Nothing."

He stopped, using the cane for support as he drew a ragged breath. "It's not nothing. What's wrong?"

"It's just that, well, we're leaving a pretty obvious trail. I doubt it matters, but—"

He glanced back, then swore. "My backpack. There should be an extra shirt inside. We can wrap it—"

"I'm on it." She moved behind him and quickly located the shirt, then zipped the pack. A moment later, she stepped back to take a look. The shirt had been wrapped tight around his leg, just under where the stick protruded. It was soaking up the blood and had the added advantage of stabilizing the stick. There'd been some white-lipped moments as he'd endured her ministrations. "That should do the trick," she said. "Hopefully it will help ease the pain a bit when you walk, too."

He took a step forward then another. No blood was left on the ground behind him. But his white-knuckled grip on the makeshift cane told her the pain, if anything, was worse.

They had to get him help. Soon.

"Do you think we're in range of a tower yet?" She moved to his side, wedging her shoulder beneath his to help him hobble forward. It was a testament to his agony that he didn't refuse her help like he'd done earlier.

"Let's give it a few more minutes before we try," he said. "I can picture the park map in my head. I think once we get right about to that tree over there—" he waved toward a group of trees about a football field's length away "—that should do it."

As they hobbled toward their goal, she said, "I never thanked you for saving me in the clearing. I don't know how you managed it. But I was a goner until you got there. Thank you."

"Don't thank me. I'm just doing—"

"Your job, yes, I know. But I guarantee most people wouldn't go to the lengths you've gone to in order to help a stranger. So maybe instead of arguing with me when I thank you, you can just say 'you're welcome.'"

His mouth twitched but didn't quite manage to form a smile. "You're welcome."

She squeezed his side in response, and they continued forward.

An eternity seemed to pass before they reached the trees he'd pointed to. She helped him turn around and sit on some rocks.

He let out a shaky breath and gave her a reassuring smile. "It's going to be okay, Jody. We're going to make it."

"No offense," she said, "but once your fellow rangers finally get here and get us off these mountains, I'm never planning on coming back again. I've had my fill of the Great Smoky Mountains National Park."

He chuckled and unsnapped his radio from his utility belt. Then he lifted it and froze.

Jody swung around, looking behind them. But she didn't see anyone. Or hear anyone. As far as she could tell, they were alone. "What's wrong?" She turned back around to see him staring off into space, a defeated expression on his face. "Adam?"

Without a word, he held up the radio. A bullet hole had been blasted right through the screen.

Chapter 9

Jody stared at the bullet hole. "Maybe...maybe the radio will work anyway."

He turned some dials. "It's busted. Useless."

"But—"

"Forget it." He snapped the radio back onto his belt and looked past her, his gaze scanning the horizon. "I figure Tattoo Guy will get that shoulder stitched up and some painkillers on board before he and reinforcements come after us. As fast as he got that third guy out here—"

"Thad."

He nodded. "Thad. As fast he got him out here, he's probably got more resources close by. It won't take long." He pulled Thad's pistol out of his holster and popped out the magazine. Then he popped it back in and shoved the gun into the holster. "Six shots left in the magazine and one in the chamber. It's a .40 caliber, like my Glock was. So the extra magazines in my backpack will work. We won't be completely defenseless. We'll need to find a defensible position and settle in, make a plan."

"A plan sounds good. What's our first move?"

He shrugged the backpack off his shoulders and let it drop to the ground. "That first aid kit you've been nagging me about?"

"I don't nag."

He winked, which was amazing considering that he had a piece of wood sticking through his leg.

"The kit is in the bottom of the pack. Can you get it for me?"

"Of course." She dropped to her knees, grimacing when the cuts and scrapes on her skin started stinging all over again. She rummaged through the pack, noting he had some water and energy bars, which would come in handy when they weren't busy running for their lives. She grabbed one of the bottles and handed it to him. "Drink that."

"Not yet." He set the unopened bottle on top of the rock.

She pulled the medical kit out and handed it to him. "You need to hydrate to help your body fight its injuries and replenish the blood you've lost. Why won't you drink now?"

"Because there's something else we need to do first."

He clicked the top of the plastic box open, rummaged inside, then pulled out a spool of black thread and a long, wicked-looking needle.

"If we're going to face off with our enemies," he said, "I can't afford to lose any more blood. And I need to be mobile. I'm going to pull the stick out of my leg. And you're going to stitch me up."

Adam would have sworn Jody's face turned green when he asked her to sew him up. Now it was completely washed out, almost translucent. Her right hand went to her stomach.

"St...stitch you up?"

"It's a lot to expect," he said. "And I hate asking it of you. But once I pull out the wood, I'll be bleeding from the front and back of my leg. It's going to take both of us to stanch the bleeding and sew the wounds closed."

She shook her head, stepping back from him. "I threw up earlier just because I was upset. Sticking a needle in someone's flesh is a whole other level. I can't do it."

"You can. You're much stronger than you think you are. How many people do you know who could have taken off like you did, leading the bad guys away from me? You saved my life, Jody. You know it. And then you faced down three men with guns and knives and lived to tell the tale. You're a hero and a fighter. You *can* do this."

Her shoulders straightened as his words sank in. Some of the color came back to her cheeks. Then she glanced down at the needle and thread and went pale again. "Please tell me you have anesthesia to numb the pain."

He slowly shook his head. "No. I don't."

"Alcohol?"

"The drinking kind or the rubbing kind?" he teased.

"Either! You have to have something for the pain, and germs."

"Afraid I'm all out of whiskey. But I do have an antiseptic spray. And rolls of gauze."

She raised a shaky hand to her throat. "It will hurt like crazy."

"It already hurts like crazy. Nothing you do could make it worse." He leaned forward and took her hand in his. "I need your help. We're sitting ducks out here. Not enough cover. I'd keep going, look for somewhere better to do this if I could. But in case you hadn't noticed, that shirt you wrapped around my leg is soaked through already. We're leaving a blood trail again. And I'm getting woozy. We have to stop the bleeding, now, or I won't be any use to you at all. I won't be able to defend you. I'll be passed out."

"I'm so sorry," she whispered.

He frowned, thinking she was still refusing to work on his leg. But then she took the thread and needle from him and dropped to her knees. She was probably apologizing because she didn't want to hurt him. He didn't think he'd ever met anyone more sensitive and kindhearted than her.

She set the first-aid kit beside her and located the antiseptic spray. He stretched his leg out in front of him to give her better access. She used his knife to slit his pants and roll the ends up to his knee, out of the way.

Once Jody Ingram set her mind on something, she fully committed to it. She was like a drill sergeant, giving him orders, setting out what she needed.

Getting his boot off to give her more room to stitch the wound was agony. But it was over quickly.

Another of his shirts, the only other one he had in the pack, was sacrificed for the cause. She wrapped it around his calf just below the entry and exit points of the piece of wood, ready to apply pressure as soon as the wood came out.

The confidence she'd displayed as she prepared his leg seemed to evaporate when she looked up at him with shiny eyes. "I'm going to do this," she assured him. "But I'm probably going to cry the whole time and I might even throw up. You'll just have to deal with it, all right?"

He was surprised that she could make him laugh when he was in so much pain. "All right."

She nodded. "Go ahead, then. I'm ready. Pull it out." She squeezed her eyes shut and braced his calf.

In spite of the pain—and the even more pain that was yet to come—he couldn't help but smile at her and admire her. He'd meant what he said. She really was courageous, heroic and strong. She was also sensitive and kind, a rare combination these days.

He crossed his ankles, using his good leg as a brace to keep his other leg still. Then he grasped the two-inch-thick length of tree branch that had impaled him when he'd slid into the pit. His calf already throbbed just from grasping the wood. This was going to hurt like the dickens. And he had to be quiet, no matter how much it hurt, so he wouldn't upset Jody any more than she already was. And so he didn't broadcast their location to the thugs in case they were already back in the mountains looking for them.

He mentally counted. One. Two. Three. He locked his good leg down hard on the bad one, and pulled. The pain was instantaneous, blinding in its intensity, molten lava searing every nerve ending. There was a sickening sucking sound as he tugged and pulled the stick forward and up. It slid through his leg, scraping against bone, rough bumps on the wood tearing his flesh anew much like an arrow might have done. It finally came free with a popping sound.

Jody gasped and clamped her hands down hard against his leg to stop the fresh rush of blood.

Agony ripped through him. He had to clench his jaw not to yell. His lungs heaved. Sweat poured off him. He gasped for air, quick pants as he tried to breathe through the pain.

"It's bleeding too much. I can't stop it."

Her words came to him through a long black tunnel. He struggled against it, desperately tried to clear his vision.

"Adam? Adam!"

He surrendered to the darkness.

Jody's hand shook so hard that she almost couldn't sew the last stitch. Only the fact that it was the very last one kept her going. Because she knew it would soon be over. Her stomach clenched as she pierced Adam's skin and pulled the last of his ragged flesh together. She shuddered as she used the knife to cut the thread.

He was still unconscious. But his chest rose and fell in steady, deep breaths. And she'd checked his pulse about ten times out of fear. It too was strong and steady. Maybe the universe was being kind to him by knocking him out so he wouldn't experience the pain of being stitched up. She'd barely managed to keep him from knocking his head when he'd fallen back.

But she hadn't been able to keep him from sliding off the boulder.

Now he was lying on his side on the ground, which had ended up being easier for her to stitch the wounds. But without him awake to help her put pressure on them while she stitched them up, he'd lost far more blood than he could probably afford. And she'd had to work fast to try to limit the bleeding. There'd been absolutely no finesse in her needlework. He was going to have horrible scars.

She bent over his leg, inspecting her work, and winced. Hopefully men didn't care about such things. Or maybe a plastic surgeon could fix it later. She glanced around. If there *was* a later. He was right about them being out in the open here. It was called a bald, if she remembered right from the brochures she'd seen. A part of the mountains where there was a huge gap in the trees, where nothing but grass grew. It could have been caused by disease, but judging by the charring on the few trees that were close by, more likely it was a part of the woods that had burned all the way to the ground, leaving nothing in its wake.

And nothing but a few rocks and trees to hide behind.

She grabbed a bottle of water and a bandana from the backpack and gently wiped away the blood on his leg. Thankfully, the stitches had done their job. The bleeding had stopped. Her next worry was infection. She'd sprayed the disinfectant on it throughout the process. And she sprayed it liberally one more time before carefully rolling gauze around his calf.

Once that was done, she pulled a clean sock up over the wound to help protect it. After another quick check to make sure he was still breathing, she worked his boot back on. She almost gave up, but knowing it would probably hurt like crazy if he was awake for the procedure, she persevered until the boot was in place.

She put everything into one of the baggies in his backpack, remembering the "take nothing, leave nothing" mantra the commercials were always touting to tourists. Then she sat beside him and wondered what to do next. Shouldn't he have woken up by now? She pressed the back of her hand to his forehead. It seemed normal, as far as she could tell. No sign of fever. Not yet, anyway. So why wasn't he waking up?

She shook his shoulders. "Adam, it's Jody. Adam, can you hear me?" She shook him again, then sat back and looked around. There were a few trees close by, and the group of boulders he was lying beside. But it wasn't enough to make her feel safe by any means. And she hated for him to be so vulnerable. Maybe she could pull him behind the boulders at least? It would block anyone's view from the woods back where they'd emerged when running from Tattoo Guy. It was worth a try.

A few minutes later, she gave up. A five-foot featherweight like her just wasn't going to be able to drag tall, dark and gorgeous anywhere. It was hopeless. She thought about trying to roll him, but she was worried she'd hurt his leg. There was only one other thing she could think to do—guard him. She pulled the pistol out of his pocket. It was a Ruger, not a brand she'd ever owned or shot before. But it was similar to the Glock she had in the safe at her apartment. It was small enough to fit comfortably in her hand.

After unloading it, she dry fired it a few times. Not the best thing for the gun. But she wanted to be familiar with the trigger pull, see how hard she had to squeeze to make it shoot. It was a little trickier than her own gun, but not overly difficult.

She loaded it again and dug the two extra magazines of ammo from the bottom of the backpack and put them in her pocket. Then she scooted her back against the boulder beside Adam's unconscious form.

Clutching the pistol with both hands, she rested it in her lap, sitting cross-legged on the ground. Then she stared toward the woods, and waited.

Chapter 10

Blinding, sharp pain shot through Adam's body. He jerked upright, clawing for the pistol holstered on his belt. It wasn't there. He shoved his hands in his pockets, desperately searching for his weapon.

"Whoa, whoa, Adam, stop. You're okay. Everything's okay."

His hands clutched nothing but emptiness in his pockets. He blinked in confusion at the beautiful woman kneeling in front of him. Thick red hair formed a messy, wavy halo around her heart-shaped face, falling to just below her shoulders. Her blouse was partly undone, revealing a lacy bra and the delicious upper curves of her breasts. His mouth watered as his gaze traveled to her full, pink lips, which were curved in a smile as she leaned close.

"Sorry for thumping your leg. You'd slept so long.

I was getting worried and thought that might be the only way to wake you up. Looks like it worked." She smiled sheepishly, then her smile faded. "Adam? It's me. Jody. Don't you recognize me?"

He watched her lips move like a blind man seeking the light.

She put her hand on his shoulder and leaned in closer. "Adam?"

It was all the invitation he needed. He wrapped one arm around her waist, sank the other deep into her fall of gorgeous red hair and pulled her mouth to his. Her lips parted on a gasp, and he groaned, tasting their honeyed sweetness and delving deeper inside.

She was so hot and sweet and soft. He tasted and treasured her mouth, ran his hand down her back, down the sexy curve of her bottom, wanting her with a desperation that didn't make sense. Nothing made sense. He didn't know how he'd gotten here or why this woman—Jody—was in his bed. But he wasn't going to complain or waste the opportunity.

She moaned deep in her throat and clutched his shoulders. Then, finally, she was kissing him back. For such a tiny thing, she was full of passion and exploded like a firecracker in his arms. Her breasts crushed against his chest, and she threaded her hands through his hair, her tongue dueling with his.

He shuddered and caressed her through her shorts. She jerked against him. For a moment he thought she might push him away. But then she was kissing him again. His body hardened painfully. He couldn't take this much longer. He had to have her. Now. He slid his hands back to her blouse and fumbled with the buttons.

She was too close. His big hands couldn't maneuver between them and he was afraid he'd rip the fabric.

He broke the kiss and drew a ragged breath as he gently pushed her back so he could finish taking off her shirt. Deep green eyes stared back at him in wonder over green-framed glasses perched crookedly on her nose. A delightful smattering of freckles marched across her flushed cheeks as her gaze dropped to his lips. He undid one button, then another, then he stopped.

A pistol lay discarded on the ground between them, cradled between her thighs. He frowned. That wasn't his pistol. He looked at his utility belt and saw the radio, its cracked screen glinting in the fading light. Fading light? He leaned back and looked around. Little puffs of white mist dotted the mountains all around them, looking like signals from some Indian campfire of old. The Smoky Mountains. They were outside, in the middle of the Smokies. And the sun was going down?

He made a more careful inspection of their surroundings, noting they were out in the open, in a bald near the foothills. His legs were stretched out in front of him. His lap was full of gorgeous redhead. And his left leg was shooting hot jolts of lava up his calf. He winced and bent to the side to see why it hurt. White gauze was wrapped around it just above where his boot ended. The whole lower part of his pants was gone, the hem ragged and ripped, like someone had torn it, or sawed it with a serrated knife.

"Adam?" Her husky voice made his body jerk in response, blood heating his veins, scorching him from the inside out. Good grief, this woman was sexy. He drew a deep breath and turned back toward her.

And blinked.

Recognition slammed into him. Everything clicked together. The hazy fog of lust cleared instantly, and his mouth dropped open in shock. "Jody?"

Her perfectly shaped brows arched in confusion. "Adam? Why are you…" Her eyes widened, a look of horror crossing her face. "You didn't know it was me?"

He stared at her, his face flushing with guilty heat. "I…I knew there was a beautiful woman—"

She scrambled off his lap, smooth toned arms and glorious legs flailing awkwardly in her rush to get away from him. One of her legs slammed into his left calf. Fire ripped through his body. He sucked in a breath and jerked back, clenching his jaw to keep from shouting.

"Oh no, your leg. I'm so sorry. So, so sorry."

She reached for him, but he shook his head and held a hand up to stop her. "Don't." His voice was a harsh croak, the pain so intense he couldn't say anything else. He drew several deep breaths, holding as still as possible, waiting, hoping the pain would ease its grip.

"I'm sorry," she whispered miserably, her eyes looking suspiciously bright, like she was holding back tears.

On a scale of one to ten, his pain was about fifty-two. He rode it out, his fingers clawing at the dirt, panting like a wounded animal. Darkness wavered at the edges of his vision. But he couldn't give in. He realized he must have passed out before, when he'd pulled out the piece of wood embedded in his leg. Thankfully, their pursuers hadn't come back yet or they'd be dead. Or maybe not. As the pain began to ease to about a thirty, he noted Jody had grabbed the gun, expertly holding it with her finger on the frame, not the trigger, pointing it away from him.

"You've…" He cleared his gritty throat and tried again. "You've fired guns before. You know how… how to handle them."

He tried to focus on her rather than the pain. Had he noticed how beautiful her hair was before? It was fire red and hung in thick waves past her shoulders.

She looked down at the pistol in her hand and frowned. "Well, yes. Of course I know how to handle guns. Once I left home and went to college, I was determined to never be a victim again, so I…" Her eyes widened, as if she'd just realized what she'd let slip. "I mean, that I would never *become* a victim, so I learned about guns and—"

"Jody? Who hurt you?"

She looked away. "I never said anyone hurt me."

"You mentioned your family before, that you weren't close. Did one of them—"

"I'm really sorry about your leg," she blurted out, obviously desperate to change the subject. "Is it feeling any better? I didn't mean to bump it. I'm so sorry."

"Stop." The fire in his left leg was bearable now, a paltry eleven or twelve. He let out a shuddering breath. "Stop apologizing all the time. All the bad in the world isn't your fault or your responsibility. Okay?"

She nodded but didn't look like she believed him. "I didn't mean to hit your leg just then. Earlier I did— just a tiny nudge, though. I was worried about you and wanted to wake you…" Her voice trailed off, and her gaze fell to his lips. Her pink tongue darted out to moisten her mouth.

His entire body clenched. He forced himself to look

away from the tempting little siren. And just how had that happened anyway? How had she gone from being the young, barely-out-of-college girl to a sexy, mature woman who could tempt a saint? He must have a fever. That was it. It was the only explanation. Jody was far too pure and innocent and sweet for a jaded man like him.

"Make me laugh."

She blinked. "What?"

"Make me laugh. Say something funny." When she continued to look blankly at him, he said, "The pain, to take my mind off the pain. Tell me something funny." What he really needed to do was take his mind off how sexy she was. He clenched his hands into fists to keep from reaching for her.

Her brow furrowed in concentration, as if he'd asked her to calculate some complex scientific equation instead of trying to come up with a lame joke. Didn't she ever laugh? Or really smile and have fun? He found himself craving her smile and laughter even more than he craved her body.

And that was saying something.

"Peter, Patricia, Patience, Patrick and Paul," she blurted out.

He waited for the punch line. "Picked a peck of pickled peppers?"

She frowned. "No. The names. Peter, Patricia, Patience, Patrick and Paul. Those are the names of my adoptive father and my adoptive sisters and brothers."

"Wait, seriously?"

She nodded, looking even more serious than she had a few moments earlier.

"What's your adoptive mother's name? Penelope?"

She shook her head. "Her name is Amelia."

Adam threw his head back and laughed. He laughed so hard he got a stitch in his side. Then Jody had to ruin it by smiling, a genuine, real smile that reached her gorgeous green eyes and made her so beautiful he ached. Again. Oh, how he wanted her, needed her. He sobered and stared at her, his breath hitching when he noticed the tantalizing display she obviously wasn't aware that she was offering. "Jody. Your blouse is, ah, gaping a bit."

She didn't even look down at her shirt. "So?"

His mouth was watering, just from that one glimpse of heaven he'd had, before he'd forced himself to look up, at her face. She obviously hadn't understood what he was trying to tell her. "I can see…ah…your…your bra is…showing."

"In case you didn't notice, I was letting you unbutton my blouse earlier. I'm well aware of the state of my clothes. You may have temporarily lost your mind, forgetting who I was. But I didn't. And I'm not ashamed of that. You're a gorgeous guy. And I like you, a lot. Okay, a whole lot. I wouldn't mind picking up where we left off."

His mouth fell open. He snapped it closed.

"What?" She sounded angry this time, on top of being frustrated. "Does that shock you?"

He cleared his throat. "Well, yes, actually, it does. A little. You're so, so…"

Her eyes narrowed. "I'm so what?"

"Young," he blurted out.

Her expression changed to one of confusion. "I'm twenty-four. Yes, I'm young. But I'm not *that* young. I'm a full-grown woman, Adam. Not some child.

Where on earth did you get this hang-up about women who are younger than you?"

He scrubbed the stubble on his face, wondering just how this conversation had turned so bizarre. "You're right." He dropped his hands to his sides. "When we met, I got it in my head that you were much younger than you are, and I didn't for a second imagine ever, well, being attracted to you."

She stiffened.

"Oh, come on," he said. "Don't get insulted now. There can't be any doubt about the state of my attraction for you at this point." He waved at his overly tight pants and his still-painful erection. "I think we crossed that barrier about the time you stuck your tongue down my throat."

She made a choking sound, her eyes wide. She coughed, then covered her mouth with her hands. He had the crazy suspicion that she was laughing at him and didn't want him to know. Likely she was trying to spare his feelings. Because that would be typical for someone who felt guilty over everything from global warming to La Niña and everything else she had no control over.

"I want you, okay?" he gritted out. "And the age thing isn't the problem anymore. The problem, if there is one, is that you're too nice."

Her hand fell to her lap. "I'm too nice? What's that supposed to mean?"

"It means you're too pure, too sweet, too…nice. You deserve someone way better than me. I'd destroy everything good about you. I'd destroy you. You don't want me."

"I don't?" She sounded suspiciously like she wanted

to laugh again. "Because you'll ruin me? That's a bit old-fashioned of you. Besides, I'm not a virgin, Adam."

Something dark passed in her eyes, but it was gone too quickly for him to be sure what he'd seen. Pain? Anger? Resentment? At who? Him, or someone in her past?

"Jody, I'm sorry if I offended you, or hurt you. I didn't—"

"Stop apologizing." She parroted his earlier words back at him. "It's not like I was asking for a long-term commitment." She pulled the edges of her blouse together. "We were just two adults who were about to have fun." She looked wistfully at his lap. "A *lot* of fun. But the moment has passed. And I think that ship has definitely sailed."

His hands curled against his thighs. It was either that or grab her and prove that the ship had definitely *not* sailed. This ridiculous conversation had only done one thing to his appetite for her—whet it.

She pushed herself up and wiped dirt off her legs before straightening. "I need a moment of privacy. When I come back, we'll work on a plan to get out of here and back to civilization."

What should have been a dramatic exit when she whirled around to leave was ruined when she tripped on a tree root. Her arms cartwheeled and she managed to regain her balance without falling. Her spine snapped ramrod straight and her face was flaming red when she once again turned her back on him and marched off to the nearest stand of trees.

Adam groaned and dropped his head to his chest. Everything about this day, from the moment he'd stepped on the Sugarland Mountain Trail, was a disaster. And every attempt he made to fix it only seemed to make things worse.

He shook his head. He wouldn't let anything happen to the complicated, intriguing, sexy redhead who'd just declared that she was no longer interested in him. It was just as well. Because he needed to focus, to figure out a plan. They needed to alert someone about Tracy, get them searching for her. Which meant he needed to be fully mobile and find that defensible position he'd mentioned earlier.

Even if they didn't find a way out of the mountains to get help, he knew his team would come looking for him soon, if they weren't already. The sun had slipped low on the horizon, and night was falling. His shift had ended hours ago and he'd never called in to report status updates.

His truck was still parked in the employee lot behind the visitor's center. It wasn't like he worked in an office building. He worked in the wilderness. No one would just assume that if he didn't show up he'd gone bar-hopping with a friend to drink away his Saturday night. They had each other's backs and took it seriously when a member of the team didn't report in. But there were thousands of acres of mountain range out here. Without a last known location, they could have several teams of search and rescue out here and never find him.

It had happened before.

Two different people on separate occasions had disappeared in the Smoky Mountains National Park over the past couple of years. They were never found. Not alive, anyway. What Adam had to do was figure out a way to improve their odds, to help the searchers find them. Or reach the searchers themselves.

Which meant he had to stand up.

He also needed a few moments of privacy, like Jody. His bladder was near to bursting. Which meant he *really* needed to stand up. And walk. Neither option appealed to him with his leg throbbing painfully in rhythm with his heartbeat. He had no desire to experience the agony he'd felt when he'd pulled the stick free from his leg, or when Jody had accidentally kicked his leg while scrambling off his lap. But there was no getting around it. He was destined for a bit of torture no matter what. Might as well get it over with. Of course, deciding that he needed to get up and figuring out how to do it were two entirely different problems.

His burning, aching leg wouldn't support him enough to rise to standing. Even rolling over on all fours failed. The leg was pretty much useless. He was beginning to wonder about the wisdom of having pulled out the stick. It had seemed like the only way to stop the bleeding. But his muscles were like jelly now, unable to bear up under any kind of strain.

After yet another try, he got halfway up before his leg collapsed beneath him and he fell face-first into the dirt. He cursed viciously and rolled to his side, panting like a dog as he fought through yet another episode of stabbing pain that set his insides on fire.

When the pain finally subsided to a dull roar rather than a blistering inferno, he stared toward the trees they'd come from several hours ago. The sun had set. The moon was bright, the sky clear, or he wouldn't have been able to see anything this far away from any man-made light sources. Still, the woods were little more than a dark void.

Had Tattoo Guy given up on coming after them?

Figuring they'd die of exposure out here? Or was he biding his time, waiting to see where Jody was before shooting at Adam?

Jody. He looked to his right where she'd disappeared earlier. How long had she been gone? More than five minutes, which was all it should have taken her if she had to empty her bladder. Had it been ten minutes? Fifteen?

He hated himself for having spent so much energy and time on his repeated attempts to stand. He had no true concept of the passage of time. And no clue whether she was in trouble, or admiring the stars, or walking off her anger at him and how badly he'd bungled things between them. Regardless, she should have been back by now. He *had* to get up and go check on her. There was no other option.

He looked around, searching for something to use as leverage. The makeshift walking stick might have helped. But the tall grasses and rocks dotting the landscape were hiding it well and good. Wait, rocks. They'd stopped by some boulders to work on his leg. He'd been sitting on one before he'd passed out. He jerked around and let out a string of curses when he realized the boulder had been behind him this whole time. Bracing his arms on either side of him, he scooted back until he was against the rock. Then he rolled over, breathing through the worst of the pain before bracing his hands on the boulder.

With his good leg beneath him and his hands pushing against the rock, he finally made it to his feet. Correction, foot. His bad leg crumpled as soon as he put weight on it. He had to balance on one foot to keep from falling. Leaning against the boulder to remain upright, he looked toward the small group of trees again for Jody. No sign of her. Where was she? At least she had his gun for protection.

Or did she?

He looked around, then groaned. The gun was lying on the ground by the boulder. She hadn't taken it. He swiped it and checked the loading, then slid it into his pocket. Where was his walking stick? He didn't see it anywhere. He snagged his backpack, too, and clipped the strap across his chest to keep it in place so it wouldn't fall with him hopping around like a kangaroo.

On a hunch, he continued his kangaroo impression around the boulder to the back side. *Yes.* The walking stick was lying there, probably having fallen when he'd sat down. He grabbed it and tested it out.

At first his leg wobbled so much he could barely take a step. But he did take a step, so he was encouraged by that. He took another then another. After about ten feet, the leg began to go numb. Probably not a good sign. But it made walking more bearable. And faster. He hurried as quickly as he could across the open space from the boulder to the trees. Then he stopped. Beyond the trees was more empty space.

And no sign of Jody.

"Jody," he called out, his voice just above a whisper. A cool mountain breeze ruffled his hair, bringing with it the scent of rain. The storm that had threatened earlier seemed to be brewing again instead of moving off to the east as he'd expected. "Jody," he called out, louder this time. The only answer he heard was the distant rumble of thunder. A flash of lightning followed, off to the left.

He took another step past the trees and looked around in a full circle for something, anything, that might tell him where she'd wandered off to. Thunder rumbled again, followed by another flash of light. But this time the light didn't turn off. It kept coming. Toward him, low to the ground. That wasn't lightning. And the sound he'd heard wasn't thunder.

It was an ATV, its engine making a dull roar now, the headlights bouncing crazily as it rushed toward him.

He dived for the cover of trees, pulling himself behind them just as the headlights swept past where he'd been standing moments ago.

The ATV wasn't an ATV after all. It was a dune buggy. Tattoo Guy was driving. Owen and another man were in the back seat, Owen with a rifle in his hand, pointed up at the sky. And in the front, her eyes wide with terror, her hands tied to the roll bar above her, was Jody.

Chapter 11

Jody bit her lip to keep from shouting a warning to Adam as the buggy bounced across the bald and headed toward the group of rocks and boulders where she'd seen him last. She could only hope that he'd heard the engine, seen the headlights and been able to hobble to another hiding place in time. If he was just crouching down behind the boulder, the men would see him in about, three, two, one...he wasn't there. Her breath stuttered out in relief.

The backpack was gone, too. And the gun.

The buggy continued on its way, circling the area as the men looked for Adam. He was injured. He was also experienced and trained. He would know what to do, wouldn't he? He'd mentioned earlier getting to a more defensible position. Had he done that now? She hoped so. Because there was no doubt what the men with her would do if they found him.

They'd kill him.

"He ain't here, Damien," Owen called out.

Tattoo Guy—now she knew his name was Damien—aimed a sour look at Owen in the rearview mirror. "Unless he sprouted wings, he's here. You saw that stick through his leg in the clearing. He won't be running any marathons any time soon. He's hiding. We just have to find him."

He slammed his foot on the brake, wincing when the action obviously jostled his hurt shoulder. His left arm was in a sling. Adam had been right. He'd had resources close by and got medical treatment, then returned with reinforcements—including the man whom Owen had called Ned, sitting quietly in the back seat studying the terrain, and four more men in a second buggy that was searching the other side of the bald.

The buggy slid to a stop, its headlights illuminating the boulder where she and Adam had been earlier—before she'd gone into the woods to relieve her bladder. It was a mixed blessing that she'd chosen not to stop at the first stand of trees. Because when Tattoo Guy, Damien, had found her, she'd been far away from Adam. And that was the only reason he was still alive.

She'd wanted more privacy, which seemed silly given how intimate they'd already been. Still, it had been good luck that she'd continued on. And that after she'd answered nature's call, she'd seen a beautiful stream sparkling in the moonlight in the distance. She'd been unable to quell the artistic excitement inside her that wanted to see nature's beauty. As soon as she'd stepped up to the stream, Damien had grabbed her.

The radio sitting on the console crackled to life. He picked it up and spoke to his other team, comparing notes about where they'd searched.

Jody rubbed her tongue against the inside of her sore cheek, trying to ease the ache where he'd punched her when she'd refused to tell him where "the cop" was. She imagined the only reason he hadn't beaten her more was that he figured Adam was close by and they'd find him quickly. Since that hadn't happened, would he hit her again?

He slammed the radio back into the console. "Where's the cop?" He called her a foul name and raised his fist in warning. "Where is he?"

She backed against the door. "I don't know. I told you, we split up after the clearing. We were trying to find a cabin, or a road, and I got lost. I couldn't figure out how to get back to where we'd agreed to rendezvous."

"She's probably telling the truth," Owen offered from the back seat. "You know how redheads are."

Damien frowned and glanced back at him. "Don't you mean blondes?"

"Oh, yeah. Those, too. See?"

Damien closed his eyes and shook his head, then looked at Jody again. "Where was the rendezvous point?"

Keep it simple, stupid. The KISS principle one of her criminal justice professors had badgered them with every time they came up with some convoluted answer to a question came to her rescue now. There was evidence by that boulder—blood on the ground, footprints—that would corroborate her story without giving up Adam's current location, wherever that happened to be.

"There!" She poured excitement into her voice. "That boulder, see? I remember it now. I'm sure there have to be some footprints or something showing you we were there." She bit her lip. "At least, I think that's the right boulder."

He stared at her a long moment, apparently not nearly as willing as his pal Owen to believe she was a "dumb redhead."

"Check it out," Damien ordered, waving toward the boulder.

Owen popped his door open.

"Not you," Damien said. "Ned. See what you can find."

With a barely perceptible nod, the second man hopped over the door frame and landed nimbly on the ground. He produced a pen-size flashlight from one of his pockets and shined it around the base of the boulder. As Jody watched, he crouched down and feathered his fingers over some depressions in the grass.

He shined the light all around, his intense gaze seeming to take everything in, as if he could picture what had happened there. Then he aimed his flashlight farther out, toward the trees where she'd run earlier. He stood and motioned toward the trees.

"She's telling the truth. There were two people here, one slight, one heavier, larger. The bigger one—"

"The cop," Damien spit, as if it was an obscenity.

"He lost a lot of blood." He trained the light on the grass again, back to the boulder. "He must have climbed up here, used some kind of stick to push himself to his feet." The light bounced and moved across the rocks, the grass, then toward the stand of trees where she'd gone. "She went that way. He followed."

She sucked in a breath. He'd found Adam's trail? Adam had followed her?

"Back in the buggy," Damien ordered.

Ned hopped over the side and the buggy took off, straight for the trees where she'd run. And, apparently, unbeknownst to her until now, where Adam had gone, too. That must be where he was hiding. And she'd led them straight to him.

She pressed a hand to her throat. What had she done?

Chapter 12

Like a rubbernecker on the highway, unable to look away from the scene of an accident in spite of being horrified, Jody stared at the beam of Ned's flashlight as it got smaller and smaller in the distance. Her relief that Adam had not been hiding behind any of the trees in this part of the bald had been short-lived. Like a bloodhound, Ned had easily picked up his trail again, leading straight toward the water.

While she sat in the front passenger seat of the buggy, her hands going numb tied to the roll bar above her, Owen continued to whine in the back seat.

"Why can't I help search for him? I'm just as good a tracker as he is."

"Oh, really?" Damien clutched the steering wheel with his good hand and stared at Owen in the mirror.

"When's the last time you tracked anything, or anyone?"

"I tracked that Tracy girl down just fine. It may have been in town instead of mountains. But I tracked her good."

Jody stiffened and looked at Damien. He was staring at her now, probably waiting for her reaction. A slow, cruel smile curved his lips.

"That you did, little brother. Guess I forgot about that. Still, it wasn't like she got very far before we'd realized she took off. And it wasn't at night, so it was a lot easier to recapture her."

Recapture? Had Tracy escaped, only to be caught again? "Where is she?" Jody demanded. "What have you done to her?"

"You really want to know?"

She nodded.

"Then tell me where your boss keeps the rest of his surveillance equipment. Where are the other pictures and videos? Audio recordings?"

"I told you, I don't know of anywhere else he would keep anything. As far as I know, he always keeps it at the office. I don't even think he took his work home with him. It…it was a habit from when his wife was still alive. She made him promise to leave work at the office, literally and figuratively. So both of them could relax and not think about their cases when the workday was over."

"Ah, now. Isn't that sweet?" He leaned toward her, forcing her to press herself against the door to the limits of her bound hands above her. "Tell you a secret, honey. He didn't keep his promise to that dear old lady of his. We found plenty of work files and pictures at his house." His smile faded. "Just not the right ones."

"You…you went to his house?"

He grinned again and relaxed against the seat. "Don't worry. It's not like Sammy boy cares anymore." His laughter made her stomach clench with dread.

Please be bluffing. Please don't have hurt Sam.

Owen chuckled in the back seat, as if the two of them shared a private joke.

"Where's Sam?" she asked, her throat tight. "Please tell me you didn't hurt him."

"Well, now. I would, but then, I wouldn't want to lie."

Bile rose in her throat as Owen and Damien both laughed. Damien hadn't mentioned using Sam as leverage, only Tracy. And from what he'd just said, he wasn't even trying to pretend that Sam was okay. Or was he just saying that, making her think Sam was… that he *wasn't* okay, to make her scared of what he might do to her if she didn't talk? She had to cling to the hope that the dear old man who'd been like a father to her was still alive. She wouldn't be able to function otherwise.

She swallowed and drew a steadying breath. Tracy was still alive. Wasn't she? He was still using her friend as a bargaining chip. She *had* to be alive.

She stared through the windshield toward the water, moonlight sparkling off the little eddies and ripples caused by boulders just beneath the surface as the current rushed over them. Adam was out there somewhere, hopefully okay and hiding. Had he seen Ned? Did he know about both dune buggies loaded with thugs with guns? There was no way he could fight off all of Damien's men with only one pistol.

Don't worry about me, Adam. There's nothing you can do to save me. Don't be a hero. Don't get yourself killed.

The portable two-way radio sitting in the console crackled, startling her.

"It's Ned. Pick up."

Damien grabbed the radio and clicked the button on the side. "Damien here. Go ahead."

"His trail leads directly to the water and stops. Either he fell in or he went in on purpose." Ned's voice, deadly calm and matter-of-fact, sounded through the speaker.

Damien swore. "I want that cop. If he drowned, I want his body as proof. He's seen my face, my jailhouse ink. He knows I'm an ex-con. If he makes it back to civilization, he'll eventually figure out who I am. Once he does, if he pulls the wrong thread, connects the right dots, you can kiss your cut bye-bye. You got me?"

"Understood."

They were talking about killing Adam as if they were making a grocery list. Who *were* these people?

"What's your theory?" Damien asked through the radio.

"If he didn't fall in, he could be walking in the shallow part to keep from leaving a blood trail. With a wound like his, and judging by the blood he lost back at that boulder, I don't see him doing much more than that. The stream is too wide, the current too fast, for an injured man to cross to the other side. But I don't know this guy, how strong or motivated he might be. We'll need to check the far side, just to be sure."

"Owen can do that."

"Bro, I don't want to swim across a freezing-cold stream. Make someone else—"

"Shut up, Owen. Get out of the buggy."

Owen cursed a blue streak, but he popped the door open and got out. His boots crunched on some rocks just outside the car as he started down the rise toward the water.

"What else do you need?" Damien asked through the mic.

"If I'm going hunting, I'll need my pack, plenty of ammo for my nine millimeter and the rifle."

"Owen." Damien motioned to the other man, who stopped to look at him. "Get back here."

When Owen trudged to the driver's side, Damien gestured with his thumb to the back seat. "Get Ned's backpack for him. And your rifle and ammo. Get some nine-millimeter magazines, too."

"My rifle? He's got a pistol. Why's he want my rifle?"

Damien narrowed his eyes. "Who bought that rifle for you? Like I buy everything else?"

Owen threw his hands up in the air. "Fine. Whatever. I'll get it."

When Owen was jogging down the hillside again, this time with a backpack and rifle, Damien turned in his seat to face Jody. "Don't worry. They'll find him."

He chuckled, as if amused by her distress. But any sign of humor quickly faded as he stared at her. "You've wasted my time all day and caused me way more trouble than you're worth." He motioned toward the sling that immobilized his left arm. "I haven't forgotten that I owe you for this. But I'm willing to forgive this one time, if you give me what I want. Normally I'm a patient guy." He chuckled again, which clearly meant he *wasn't*. "But that little PI firm of yours has been a thorn in my side for three days. And I didn't have time to spare to begin with. Where are the rest of the pictures? You want that friend of yours to live, then tell me what I need to know."

She raised her chin, trying to act brave even though inside she wanted to curl up into a fetal position. "Which friend? Sam, Tracy or Adam?" She swallowed, every muscle tensed as she waited for his answer.

His brows arched up. "Well, now. That's a question, isn't it? I think we both know that Sam's a lost cause at this point." He winked and grinned when she pressed her lips together to keep from crying out.

Sam. Oh no, Sam.

"I admit, I might have been a little hasty with your boss." He let out a laborious sigh. "Regrets can be a terrible thing. Interrogating him first would have saved me a lot of trouble, for sure. As for that cop of yours, well, once again, lost cause. He's not getting out of here alive. That's not negotiable. I've got big plans, and him mouthing off to other law enforcement pigs could ruin everything. I'm not letting that happen. Guess that leaves you with just one friend to be worried about. Your fellow office worker, that Amazon warrior woman with legs that go all the way up. Tall women aren't normally my taste. But she's got some curves, nice melons. I could enjoy some of that. What's her name? Tracy? Yeah, that's it. Tracy Larson. You worried about her?" He leaned forward, his eyes blazing with menace. "Because you should be."

Her stomach clenched, and she pressed back against the door. "Where is she?"

"In safekeeping, for now. But only if you start talking. My infamous patience is about gone. Where are the recordings?"

She flexed her bound hands, which were tingling in the night chill with them tied above her head. "They have to be in Sam's office. That's where he keeps everything."

"Yeah, well, not this time. I've tossed that place high and low, went through every SD card and flash drive I could find. You and that Tracy girl are the only two other people who worked there. So it's up to you to spill the beans."

"What...what makes you so sure there are more recordings?"

He rolled his eyes. "You think I'm dumb? Your boss had date and time stamps on all of his pictures. And there's a gap in them, on a very specific day. He was watching us for a whole week based on the other time stamps. And there's one day smack-dab in the middle that's missing. Tell me where the rest of the stuff is and I'm gone, like I was never here. You'll never see me again. Promise."

She could feel the blood draining from her face. He might have thought his little speech would convince her that Tracy was still alive, that if she gave him what he wanted, she could still save her friend. But after hearing his callous talk about Sam and Adam, and fitting the pieces together, she realized she'd been kidding herself all this time.

Damien's tactics were to kill first, ask questions later. After killing Sam, he'd realized he'd made a mistake. So he'd taken Tracy. He'd no doubt *interrogated* her, and when Tracy had nothing to share, he'd likely killed her. That was the only reason Jody could come up with for why *she* was still sitting here, alive, relatively unhurt. She was Damien's last chance to get the information he needed. He had to make sure it was secured, maybe destroyed, so no one else would find it. And once he did that, he'd kill her to keep her from talking.

"Good," he said. "You're obviously thinking hard about what I've said. Just hurry it up. Your friend's life, and yours, depends on it. If you take too long, I'll order her killed and cut the truth out of your flesh. You feel me, girl?" He didn't wait for her reply. He turned away and stared toward the water.

Tears burned the backs of Jody's eyes as she followed his gaze. She hated that she cried so easily. But in this case, maybe it had helped her. Damien had to have seen the tears she was trying so hard to hold back and figured she was on the verge of breaking and telling him what he needed to know.

He was right, of course.

She wasn't a strong person, never had been. If she had any clue where other recordings or pictures were, she'd probably have spewed that information back on the Sugarland Mountain Trail. And he would have killed her right then.

She blinked hard, forcing the tears back. If she'd died up on that trail, Adam would have found a dead body instead of ever seeing Damien. He'd be sitting in an office somewhere investigating her death, or maybe others would take on that chore while he went off to do whatever it was law enforcement rangers did. The important thing was that he'd be safe, having never become a target of Damien's wrath.

She clenched her fingers together, trying to keep the blood flowing as she looked through the windshield in the same direction where Damien was looking—down at the water. The second dune buggy was parked by the river now. Flashlight beams pointed down at the ground as the four men from that buggy, plus Ned and Owen, searched for Adam. Six men searching for one, all so they could ensure his silence, that he'd never tell anyone about Damien. Any doubts she'd had about Tracy maybe still being alive died a quick death.

The man beside her didn't value life. And he didn't like being inconvenienced. He'd shot and killed one of his own men to keep him from talking, or maybe to save himself the trouble of dragging him to safety. He was being greatly inconvenienced by Jody right now. No way would he do that if he had another option.

Her best friend in the whole world was dead. And Adam McKenzie—an honorable, kind man willing to risk everything to save a stranger—was going to be dead, too, if she didn't do something to help him. Assuming he wasn't dead already, lying on the bald somewhere, his wound torn open and bleeding out. But what could she do? How could she help him?

She wasn't lying about the pictures. She really didn't know where Sam might have hidden them if he'd stumbled onto something bad and wanted to hide it from her and Tracy for some reason. So where did that leave her?

For the moment, it left her with leverage. As long as this bloodthirsty idiot beside her thought she could give him what he wanted, he'd keep her alive. She could make something up, bluff, buy some time. He'd kill her anyway. Not much she could do about that. But if she could buy Adam some time, maybe, just maybe, with his law enforcement experience and knowledge of these mountains, maybe that would be enough to let him get away and get some help…and survive.

If the legacy of her twenty-four short years on this planet was that she managed to save Adam McKenzie's life, well, that wouldn't be too bad. She could take comfort in that—if she could make it happen.

She watched the lights in the distance. They were still searching, which meant they hadn't caught Adam yet. If he'd passed out from blood loss, they would have found his body by now, wouldn't they? So he was still alive. There was still time to save him.

While she watched the flashlights bobbing through the trees that lined the stream, she came up with a plan. Not a very good one, but better than nothing.

"Damien?"

He frowned and looked at her, obviously not pleased with her using his name. "What?"

"I'll… I'm willing to show you where the other pictures are. But I have conditions."

He grabbed her chin and squeezed it in a painful grip. "How about this condition? You tell me what I need to know. Period. And then maybe I don't kill you."

She jerked her head, but he only tightened his fingers, the nails biting into her skin.

"Kill me and those pictures will be found and made public. I guarantee it. I'm the one in charge of storing all our case files. And part of that responsibility is making sure the files are sent back to Sam if something happens to me. It's…it's in my will, the location of those files. It'll all come out. Whoever handles Sam's estate will get the files. Then they'll be made public."

"You're lying. You're a kid, probably fresh out of college. You don't even have a will."

"Oh, really? I'm a criminal justice major and I work for a private investigator. You think my professors, and Sam, didn't drill into me the importance of ensuring that I have a will, and that any important documents are preserved and turned over to the executor of that will upon my death?"

She wasn't lying about that. Her professors and Sam *had* drilled that information into her. But the glaring flaw in her story was that the papers, and pictures, that she'd mentioned in her will were of course her own, not Sam's. Her storage unit was full of her cameras and SD cards and file cabinets loaded with pictures that she'd taken as part of her other job, as a professional photographer. She had mentioned the unit in her will and left a copy of her key with the lawyer who'd drawn it up. That was part of securing *her* assets. Not Sam's.

But Damien didn't know that.

If she could get him to believe her now, and take her to her storage unit, he could spend days going through all her SD cards looking for the specific pictures he believed to be there. That would buy her a little time, hopefully enough to escape. If not, maybe she'd at least be able to get a note under a door to another storage unit, or somehow leave it for someone else to find, a note that would let them know about Adam so they could send him help.

"Load up your guys into the buggies and take me back to town. If you do that, if you leave Adam alone,

I'll take you to where the pictures are stored. And you'll let Tracy go. She's safe and sound, like you said, right?"

She bit her bottom lip, trying to look hopeful, even though she was convinced that her friend was already dead.

He straightened in his seat. "Sure, sure. She's safe and sound. I'll take you back to town, get the pictures and both of you will go free."

"And Ranger McKenzie? What about him?"

His jaw tightened. "He's a threat to me, him being a cop and all." His gaze darted back and forth as he appeared to consider her deal. "Okay, my plans will be taken care of in the next few days. I can pull my guys back, have them watch the trails to make sure your cop doesn't find his way back, for two days. After that, it won't matter. We'll be gone. Of course, I'll have to accommodate you as a guest for those two days as well. You understand. But after that, I'll let you go—if you take me to the pictures."

"And Tracy? You'll let her go, too?"

"Oh, right, right. Her too. Do we have a deal?"

Her heart shattered at how casual he was about Tracy. He'd already forgotten about her. It was so hard to keep up her pretense without giving in to grief, to pretend she was buying the snake oil this viper was selling. "Cut my hands free and we'll shake on it."

He snickered. "No can do. You'll try to get away."

"It's not like we can drive back into Gatlinburg with my hands tied to the roll bar. I'm not going to try to escape. I'm not betting Adam's or Tracy's lives on that."

"I'll cross that bridge when we get there. Your hands stay tied."

She shrugged, as if it didn't matter. Her hands really

were going numb. But mainly she'd wanted them free to give her more options. Like maybe she could grab his gun. But he was too careful for that.

"We have a deal?" she asked.

"We do."

She nodded toward the stream. "Your men?"

"Oh, of course." He was all smiles and acting like her friend now that he thought he was going to get what he wanted.

He radioed the change in plans. "Got that, boys?"

"Got it, boss," Owen answered.

Damien frowned. "Why do you have the radio instead of Ned?"

A pause, then, "Ned was worried the chatter would warn the cop. He didn't want the radio. He gave it to me so he could track him."

As Damien took the opportunity to tell Owen what an idiot he thought he was, Jody tried to focus on the coming challenge, how to draw the time out once they got to the storage unit. Was there something she could use inside to try to get word to someone to come help Adam? Not that she believed that Damien would truly follow through, that he'd pull all of his men off the search permanently. He'd said "your cut" earlier, which implied there was money riding on whatever Sam had seen. He wasn't going to risk Adam making it out of here and ruining that. But at least getting them all out of these mountains for the time being, until Damien could get more men out here searching, would give Adam a head start.

The lawn mower–type roar of the second buggy started up in the distance. All she could see were the beams from flashlights bouncing around as, she assumed, the men got into the buggy. Then the flashlights flicked off. She could tell there were men in the buggy. But she had no way of counting them from this far away.

"Looks like they're ready," Damien announced. "They'll follow us out of the mountains, like I promised." He started up the engine. It sputtered then caught, adding its dull, throaty roar to the sound of the other buggy that was idling down by the water and hadn't yet moved.

"I need to see them," she insisted. "I need to see six men in that buggy. Then *they* can take the lead. We'll follow them out. I have to make sure they're all there, that none of them are looking for Adam."

His eyes narrowed. "You thinking I ain't holding up my end of our deal? You calling me a liar?"

"Trust but verify."

He surprised her by laughing. "You're a lot more like me than you probably think you are. Wheeling and dealing, probably lying but playing the innocent." He laughed again. "You think I don't see that hamster wheel spinning around in your head a hundred miles an hour? You think you're clever, getting me to call off the search and let you and your friend go. If I thought there was a good chance of your boyfriend making it out of here in the next twenty-four hours, I wouldn't go along with whatever game you're playing. Just make sure you haven't outsmarted yourself. 'Cause if you don't take me to those pictures, I'm not drawing this out any longer. I'll slit your throat and take my chances. And I'll come back here personally and kill that cop."

He floored the gas and the buggy took off, bumping over the rocky field.

Jody squinted toward the other buggy, trying to make out the different silhouettes. The one in the driver's seat was most likely Owen, because he was leaning back against the headrest as if bored, probably whining to everyone else about being cold or something. The others seemed to have their backs to them, looking out at the water.

She tensed. Had they seen something? If Adam was hiding and had made some kind of noise, would they draw their weapons and shoot him, in spite of the fragile deal she had with Damien?

The buggy pulled to a stop perpendicular to the other one, headlights illuminating the group of men.

Jody sucked in a shocked breath.

"What the—" Damien stood up in his seat to get a better view.

There weren't six men in the buggy. There were only five. Ned was missing. But the rest of them were bound and gagged, including Owen. Their own clothes had been used to tie them up. All of them were shirtless. Shoestrings tied their hands together.

Damien let out a guttural roar of rage and slammed the gas, whipping the steering wheel hard left. The buggy spun in the dirt, then took off in the direction of the Sugarland Trail, leaving a wide-eyed and gagged Owen behind along with the other men. A tree loomed up ahead. Damien turned the wheel to avoid it. The headlights suddenly revealed a man standing in their path, about fifty yards ahead, aiming a rifle directly at them.

It was Adam. He was alive!

Damien floored the gas, heading right for him.

Chapter 13

The dune buggy barreled down on Adam. He didn't move out of the way. He carefully aimed his rifle at the driver's side of the windshield, painfully aware that Jody was just a few feet away from the driver. He squeezed the trigger.

Bam!

He heard the crack of the windshield and guttural cursing from behind the blinding headlights. Had he hit Damien? Had he hit Jody? That possibility had his stomach clenching with dread. But he'd had to take the shot. If he let Damien take her out of these mountains, she was as good as dead. He'd had to risk it.

The buggy was still barreling down on him. He aimed for the driver's side headlight, then lowered the rifle bore to just beneath it, going for the tire.

Bam! Whoosh!

The left front tire blew. The buggy hop-skipped sideways. The headlights arced away from him, and he got his first clear look at Jody. Her eyes were wide with fright, but she seemed okay. Relief flooded through him, but not for long. The buggy bounced like crazy, sliding toward him. Damien was wrestling for control with his one good arm, even as he shrugged off the sling on his bad arm. Moonlight glinted off the pistol clutched awkwardly in his left hand, pointing at Adam.

Adam leveled the rifle again.

"No!" Jody yelled. She yanked herself up in the air toward the roll bar and slammed her legs into Damien's shoulders. The pistol went flying.

Adam jerked his rifle up so he wouldn't hit her.

The buggy made a sickening lurch, then careened toward him.

Adam dived out of the way, rolling across the ground, the buggy coming to a bouncing stop about ten yards away, miraculously still upright.

His left leg was on fire, but he fought through the pain, limping as fast as he could to reach the buggy. He rounded the driver's seat, aiming his rifle inside. The seat was empty. Damien was gone.

"Where is he, Jody?"

She motioned with her chin. "He jumped out, ran toward the water."

Adam yanked his knife out of his boot and leaned across the opening. He sliced the rope on the roll bar, freeing her. "Can you drive?"

"The tire—"

"Don't make any sudden turns or stops and we should be able to ride on the rim for a bit on this soft ground. We have to get out of here, now, before Damien finds the cache of guns I took away from his men, or the one who took off looking for me returns. He would have heard the gunshots and could be back any second."

She was shaking her hands, working her fingers. "I'll try. My hands feel like a thousand needles are stabbing them." She stepped over the middle console and plopped down behind the wheel. "What about you? How will you get into the—"

He rolled over the side of the buggy and fell into the back seat. "Go! Head that way." He motioned toward where they'd come from earlier in the day, back toward the Sugarland Trail.

"Your leg. Are you okay? How did you—"
Boom!
The crack of another rifle sounded from the direction of the water.

"Go, go, go!" Adam yelled even as he returned fire.
The buggy took off, tilting dangerously to the right.

"Back off the gas, ease into it!" Adam fired several more rounds, laying cover fire as Jody brought the buggy under control, then took off more slowly.

The buggy straightened out, the ride so bumpy and lopsided that Adam fell back. He scrambled across the seat on his knees, cursing when his makeshift splint caught on a seat belt and pulled his hurt leg. Fire shot up to his thigh, but he couldn't give in to the pain now. He gritted his teeth and brought up his rifle, exchanging shot after shot with the thugs by the other buggy until it fell out of sight behind a rise.

He collapsed, clutching his useless leg.

Jody looked at him in the mirror. "Should I pull over?"

"No! Keep going. I slashed all four tires in the other vehicle and tossed the keys in the water. That should give us a good chance. But it's still a dune buggy. They can ride it with flat tires on this ground just like we're doing. All it takes is one guy who knows how to hot-wire it and they'll be after us in no time."

"Then…what can we do? This buggy can't get back up the mountain where we came down. I don't remember a road."

"There's a road—several. Access roads we rangers use, more like wide footpaths than roads, but they'll do the job. I assume Damien and his men came down one of them to get to us as fast they did. We'll have to keep ahead of them. That's our best chance right now."

A dull roar sounded in the distance. The other buggy, back over the rise they'd just come down.

Jody's tortured gaze met his again in the mirror. "Is there a plan B?"

This was his plan B. Plan A had pretty much ended when he'd had to shoot out the buggy tire to get Damien to stop. He'd hoped to use that buggy for his and Jody's escape. Without a flat tire, they could be going twice as fast as they were now, and escape would have been easy.

He forced a smile even though his leg was throbbing so hard he could barely think straight. And it was bleeding again. And he was pretty sure he was close to passing out. Again. "I'll think of something."

A bright spotlight popped on ahead of them.

Jody slammed the brakes.

Adam grabbed the roll bar and swung himself into the seat beside her, dropping onto his knees and aiming his rifle straight ahead over the top of the windshield.

Lena Diaz 135

They came to a shuddering stop, turned sideways, with Adam's side the one facing the lights.

"Drop your weapon!" a voice called out over a loudspeaker.

Adam hesitated.

The spotlight swept off to the side, still lighting up the buggy but not in his eyes anymore. He got his first clear glimpse at what they were facing. A group of at least fifteen men and women formed a semicircle about a hundred feet away. They were all aiming rifles at them.

"Drop it!" the voice ordered again.

Adam pitched his rifle out and held his hands up in the air.

Jody stared at him in shock. "What are you doing?"

He was about to tell her when the loudspeaker buzzed again. "Step out of the vehicle, hands up."

"Go ahead," he told her. "These are—"

Chh-chh. Four men materialized from out of the darkness on either side of them. One had just pumped his shotgun.

"Put the guns away," Adam told them, sounding furious as he leaned over Jody as if to shield her. "I'm Ranger Adam McKenzie."

"Lower your weapons!" Another man jogged into view, shaking his head as he reached the buggy. "What have you gotten yourself into this time, Adam?"

Jody's eyes were wide, her face pale as she looked back and forth between them, her hands in the air.

Adam rolled his eyes at him, but he couldn't help but grin as he gently pressed Jody's arms down. "Jody Ingram, meet National Park Service Investigative Officer, Special Agent Duncan McKenzie. My brother."

Chapter 14

Adam looked over his brother's head, past the foot of the hospital bed to where Jody was curled into a completely uncomfortable-looking chair by the window, passed out from exhaustion.

"Earth to Adam," Duncan said. "She's fine. The doctor checked her out last night, and other than some bumps and bruises, she's okay. You can quit checking on her every thirty seconds."

Adam shoved his brother's arm off the bed railing. "And you can stop exaggerating. I've only checked on her a few times since you came in."

"Yeah. Whatever." He didn't look convinced as he waved a hand toward Adam's left leg, heavily bandaged and propped up on some pillows. "I'm surprised they didn't cut that thing off while I was dealing with your mountain buddies all morning." He winced with sympathy. "It looked awful yesterday. Had to hurt like a son of a gun. What's the prognosis?"

He started to glance at Jody again but caught himself.

Duncan grinned, as if he could read his mind. Maybe he could. The two of them were the closest in age of all of his brothers. They were only ten months apart—Irish twins, as the saying went. Most strangers had difficulty telling them apart. Every time he had to tell someone in front of his mom that, no, they weren't twins, they were ten months apart, she'd blush bright red. His dad would grin with pride, as if his virility had been confirmed. He didn't mind at all being the stereotype behind the slang Irish twins saying that some found offensive. He just pointed to his other two sons and smiled. Or, most of the time to his other *one* son, since the fourth son was rarely ever home, doing everything he could to keep his title as the reigning black sheep of the family.

"The doctor threw all kinds of medical jargon at me. The best I can tell, I pretty much ripped the main muscles apart when I pulled that piece of wood out. Creating a makeshift splint out of tree branches and my shirt and chasing down the bad guys destroyed the rest. If I'm lucky and the antibiotics work like they're supposed to, I might get full use of the leg with a year or so of physical therapy."

Duncan winced again. "And if you're not lucky?"

Adam's hands tightened on the blanket covering him. "They lop it off." He shrugged. "Jody's alive. I'm alive. That's a miracle considering what we were up against. If I end up losing a leg out of it, I consider myself lucky."

"You have a warped view of good luck," Jody's soft, feminine voice called out from her window seat. "And there was no luck involved. You almost killed yourself saving both of us. If the National Park Service hands out medals, you deserve a drawer full of them."

She uncurled her legs and headed toward the bed. She held her hand across Adam to the other side, offering it to his brother. "Thank you for rescuing us, Duncan. But knowing your brother, he'd have found a way to finish the job and bring us both home, even without your help. He's pretty amazing."

Duncan shook her hand. "I'm sure you're right, Miss Ingram. Adam would have found a way. He's a pretty resourceful guy and I'm proud to have him as a fellow officer, and a brother."

Adam rolled his eyes.

Duncan dropped down into his chair as Jody took the one on the other side of the bed. He picked up an electronic tablet from the bedside table and tapped the screen, bringing it to life. "I'm actually on duty, in spite of the obscenely late hour of seven on a Sunday evening—well past my normal dinnertime. I need to take Adam's statement now that he's finally out of surgery and no longer under the influence of anesthesia. My team's heading up the investigation in conjunction with the local police."

"So sorry to have inconvenienced you by having a long surgery," Adam said, rolling his eyes.

Duncan grinned.

"Have they found Tracy? Or Sam?" Jody asked.

"Not yet, ma'am. But I promise you we have every available resource searching for them. We've also got a team looking for that Damien fellow and his right-hand guy, Ned. The rest of them we captured and put into lockup, waiting to be processed. We know their names because of their fingerprints. They're all in the system. We just have to figure out last names for Damien and Ned and make the connections, figure out how and why they ended up together. We're on this. Don't you worry."

She nodded her thanks and rubbed her hands up and down her arms, as if chilled.

Adam started to pull his blanket off to give to her.

She put her hand on his, stopping him. "Don't you dare. I'll go ask the nurse for an extra one. Be right back."

As soon as the door to the hospital room closed, Adam rolled his head on his pillow to look at his brother. "Waiting to be processed? No one has interrogated the thugs you captured?"

"Every single one lawyered up. We didn't get squat from any of them."

"Any idea what their connection is to each other?"

"Career criminals, and not the garden-variety street thugs, either. They all have long records with everything from grand theft auto to breaking and entering. One of them was charged with murder but beat the rap. No question he did it—the prosecutor made some stupid mistakes and he got off on a technicality. But finding links between them has proven difficult. If anything, the lack of links is what's so glaring and concerning. They've all done some time, either in jail or prison, but never at the same places, not at the same time, at least. Two of them aren't even from Tennessee. And the states they're from aren't the same, either. So, again, no links, other than them being lowlifes who will do anything for a buck."

Adam drew the obvious conclusions. "Damien's the leader, so he probably hired all the guys working for him. Instead of bringing on guys he did time with or knew in some way, he purposely went out of his way to hire strangers. He didn't want to risk anything coming back to point to him."

Duncan nodded. "That's my take, too. Which makes me think that either Damien has some kind of connection to whatever is behind the abductions, or someone who hired him does. And that someone is going to great lengths to distance themselves from whatever happens. Even if everything hits the fan, they want to come out lily-white."

"You think someone hired Damien? That he's not the one behind this?" Adam asked.

"Did he strike you as smart enough to mastermind all of this?"

"Hard to say. Didn't you find his fingerprints on the buggy he drove? He has to be in the system. Those were prison tattoos on his arms."

Duncan's mouth flattened. "Unfortunately, the steering wheel and the rest of the interior of the buggies isn't conducive to giving us viable sets of prints. They're textured, don't provide anything useful in the fingerprint department."

"What about the outside of the buggies, the painted surfaces? Can't you get prints off those?"

"Oh, we've got plenty of prints from the outside. So far, every one matches up to the guys we've already got locked up. Not one of them leads to this Damien guy. Also, the buggies were stolen. So tracing registration is a dead end."

"Figures." Adam blew out a breath in frustration. "The lack of prints doesn't make sense. He wasn't wearing gloves. And I didn't see him wipe down anything. He sure didn't have time to later, when he took off running."

"If he took precautions to only touch the textured plastic door handle on the outside, he wouldn't have left prints. A guy who went to the care he did in order to hire guys who weren't connected to him in any way could have been careful enough to think about fingerprints before touching anything."

Adam stretched his leg, wincing when a sharp pain radiated up his calf. "You have to have a theory about all of this. A group of thugs kidnaps all three employees of a PI firm and threatens one of them if she doesn't show them where some supposed pictures are. Makes sense it's all related to one of Campbell's cases, don't you think?"

Duncan nodded. "The possibility has crossed my mind. This Damien fellow was worried about surveillance photos. The client who hired Sam would have wanted the photos taken. And there wouldn't be any reason for Sam to hide the photos from the guy paying his bills."

"So whoever was in the photos found out that the client hired a private investigator and wants any pictures he took. The question is how did the person in the photos find out. You think Sam got sloppy? That someone saw him taking pictures?"

"Seems like the simplest scenario, and it matches what Miss Ingram said on the chopper on the way to the hospital. Whoever is being followed by Sam sees him and hires Damien to kill Sam and hire a group of guys to toss Campbell's home and office. Only they're still searching the office when Tracy Larson goes to work, and she catches them in the act."

Adam nodded, following the scenario. "There's a struggle, maybe they kill her—either accidentally or on purpose—and then they realize the pictures they're looking for are nowhere to be found. Now they're getting desperate. Was there anything in Campbell's office to let them know that Jody worked there, too? And that she was the only remaining employee?"

"Absolutely. Campbell was meticulous. His payroll records were right in his filing cabinet. Damien knew there were three of them. Without Sam or Tracy around to interrogate, Miss Ingram was the last link to making sure those pictures never find their way into anyone's hands. That's why they went after her." He shrugged. "Makes sense as a hypothetical. But I have to keep an open mind and follow the evidence. We may be on a completely wrong track. If Miss Ingram can remember more details about what Damien and the others may have said in front of her when you weren't with her, that could give us the clues we need to make all the puzzle pieces fit," Duncan said.

"I assume you're talking to all of Campbell's clients?"

"Of course. We sent the files from the office to our team of investigators. They're following up with everyone who hired him in the past month. If we don't get any leads out of that, we'll go back further. Don't worry. We'll figure it out."

"What about finding Sam Campbell and Tracy Larson?" When his brother hesitated, Adam narrowed his eyes. "You found them, didn't you? That's what you really came in here to tell me. But since Jody was here you couldn't."

"I came in here to check on my brother and take a more detailed statement now that you're coherent and off drugs. But, yes, you're right. We found something. Or, rather, some*one*. A body. The autopsy isn't finished yet. They'll need DNA results or dental records to confirm the identity."

"Male or female?"

"Male."

"Sam Campbell."

Duncan nodded. "Most likely but it hasn't been confirmed. Physical description and approximate age matches the body, and there aren't any other open missing-persons cases that could fit. He was dumped in a ditch not far from his office, beside a rural road. Critters and decomp took their toll. Thus the need to wait for dental records or DNA results before making it official."

"Understood. What about her friend Tracy Larson?"

"Based on the quick statement you gave me while the search-and-rescue team hauled you two out in the chopper, I can't imagine that she's still alive. But without a body, we're still treating it as a search and rescue, not a recovery. Not yet."

"No leads?"

"None. Her car was parked at the office, so it seems likely that's where she was taken. No witnesses so far, though. We've canvassed her apartment complex, too, in case this was planned in advance and someone suspicious was hanging out watching her place in the week before she disappeared. Gatlinburg PD is doing a knock and talk, going door to door to follow up with anyone who wasn't home when they did their initial canvass. But the last reported sighting of Miss Larson so far is Friday afternoon, when Miss Ingram left the office."

"I prefer Jody to Miss Ingram."

They both looked toward the door. Jody was just inside, her face pale, her freckles standing out in stark relief.

"How long have you been listening?" Adam asked.

Two bright spots of color darkened her cheeks as she clutched a beige blanket in her arms. "I wasn't purposely trying to eavesdrop. I was about to step inside when I heard you mention Tracy. I didn't want to interrupt, or make you stop, because everyone has been so tight-lipped. It's frustrating. No one seems to want to tell me anything."

She stepped to the plastic chair on Adam's right and sat down, bringing the blanket up to her chin.

Adam exchanged a relieved looked with his brother. If Jody had only started listening at the mention of Tracy, then she hadn't heard that a body had been found and might be Sam. He wanted to keep it that way until the coroner confirmed the identity. "Duncan, can you—"

"Yeah, yeah." He set the tablet on the table and stood. "I'll give you both a few minutes. But then I really need that statement."

"Make it ten."

Duncan nodded. "Ten it is. I'll bring back some coffee. Miss Ingram—"

"Jody."

He smiled broadly, pouring on the charm. "Jody.

Lovely name for a fine, Irish-looking lass. Your red hair and green eyes are a perfect foil to black Irish here, with those blue eyes and black hair."

"You have the same blue eyes and black hair," Adam growled. "And stop with the fake accent. You've never even been to Ireland."

Duncan's grin widened as he continued to stare at Jody. "How do you take your coffee, sweet colleen?"

Adam wanted to strangle him.

Jody smiled. "Cream and sugar, please."

"My pleasure." He headed out of the room.

"Is he always that cheeky?" she asked.

Adam blinked. "Cheeky? Are you going to start talking in a British accent now?"

"I bloody well might," she teased, her inflections a perfect imitation of an English lady's, even if the language she used wasn't.

"Don't fall for his *cheekiness*," he said. "He's married to his job."

"And you aren't?"

He shook his head. "Haven't been on the job long enough to be married to it yet. I transferred from Memphis a few months ago." He held his right hand out, unable to resist the need to touch her, to remind himself there was still some good left in this world. There were many dark times, like now, when he wasn't so sure.

There was no hesitation on her part. She slid her hand through the large opening in the railing. She entwined her fingers with his and rested their joined hands on the mattress.

He squeezed reassuringly and searched her face. She was dressed in clothes a policewoman had brought from her apartment, another white blouse—that unfortunately had all its buttons—and a pair of faded jeans that hugged the curves of her hips and offered a tempting view of her backside whenever she walked across the room. He had availed himself of that view far too often since waking up from recovery to find her in his room this afternoon.

He cleared his throat, forcing himself to focus on the case, not his ridiculous fascination with the beautiful woman just a few feet away. "I'm sorry you heard that, about Tracy. No one has given up hope. They're still searching for her."

She nodded, looking sad but resigned. "You don't think she's alive any more than I do. Even from the beginning, as soon as you heard about her and knew that Damien had confronted me on the trail. You put the pieces together pretty fast, figured out that Damien would have killed me to eliminate witnesses if Tracy was still alive and could tell him what he needed."

He wanted to lie. But she deserved better than that, and she was too smart to fall for it anyway. "You're right. I figured he was eliminating witnesses to whatever he was trying to hide right from the get-go. He didn't strike me as the ruminating type. Act first, regret later. That seems to be his motto." He squeezed her fingers again. "But miracles do happen. Maybe instead of…well, maybe Tracy escaped after all. Damien may have gone after you because you were his last lead and he was desperate to make sure the pictures don't fall into someone else's hands. Your friend may be hiding somewhere this very minute, not sure where to go or what to do. I guarantee she's got the very best possible men and women out trying to find her, both in the mountains and in town. No one's giving up."

She nodded her thanks and pulled her hand free to tug the blanket up higher around her where it had started to fall. The loss of her touch sent a sharp pang of longing through him. He had to force himself not to reach for her again. She was too good for him. There was no chance of a future between them, in spite of the attraction that seemed to simmer every time she was in the same room—a mutual attraction, judging by the hungry looks she'd been casting his way all afternoon as he'd endured exams and bandage changes and listened to long lectures from his doctor on what to do and what not to do.

He frowned and waved at her clothing. "Your hospital gown is gone. I'm assuming they discharged you after keeping you for observation last night. Where do you plan on going when you leave?"

"One of the police officers brought me a key to my apartment that she got from the manager. I guess I'll go there—home. And before you say it, I'm sure I'll be okay. My Glock is locked up there. If Damien or Ned or any other thugs he wants to send after me show up, they won't find a defenseless woman waiting for them. And I've got a phone again if I needed to call for help. A victim's advocate that one of your people called gave me some cash and a pay-as-you-go cell phone from the hospital gift shop to replace mine."

"None of that sounds especially comforting. What about transportation?"

"I can call a cab. You don't have to worry about me. I'll be okay."

"You need protection. Have you asked the police—"

She laughed, without humor. "They're great and all. But they have a limited budget and can't afford to assign officers to watch over witnesses who may or may not be in danger. Especially when half the Park Service is out searching for the guys I'm allegedly in danger from. Apparently, the odds of them being able to get to me are extremely low."

"Is that a direct quote from some jerk police officer?"

"Pretty much. But to be fair, Gatlinburg PD and the Park Service have been great. It was only one jerk. And it's not anyone's fault that they have a limited budget. If I need protection, I've been told to hire my own."

He stared at his bum leg, hating himself for that one unguarded moment when he hadn't been careful enough and had stepped into a hole. "Will you? Hire someone?"

"I have a limited budget, too."

"When Duncan gets back, I'll tell him to withdraw some money from my account. I can hire someone to guard you for a few days."

She was already shaking her head before he finished. "No. Thank you very much, Adam. But you don't owe me anything. There's no reason for you to spend your money on me."

"I could make it a loan. With a really long payback time frame. Like forever."

She smiled. "You're amazing, you know that? But, like I said. I'll be fine. Now that I know to be careful, I'll be on my guard. And I'll keep my gun beside me tonight, ready to grab. Plus my phone. My apartment's just five minutes from the police station. Seriously, there's nothing to worry about. But thanks, just the same, for being concerned."

"I know you aren't close with your adoptive family.

But surely they'd let you stay with them for a while. Wouldn't they?"

She stiffened, but before she could answer, the door clicked open and Duncan stepped inside. As soon as Adam saw the look on his brother's face, he reached for Jody's hand. She clutched it like a lifeline, her face pale as she waited for Duncan to speak.

"I'm so sorry, Jody. They found your friend Tracy Larson. She's dead."

Chapter 15

Jody dried her face with a washcloth and stared at her reflection above the sink in Adam's hospital bathroom.

They found your friend Tracy Larson. She's dead.

Even though she'd been expecting those words, her heart didn't want to accept the truth.

She could see Tracy in her mind's eye, hear her voice, feel her arms around her whenever she'd needed a hug. Which was a whole lot more often than her strong, beautiful friend had ever needed. Tracy was a rock, always had been. Jody had been her weak, needy friend. During the most difficult years of Jody's life, Tracy and her family had been her comfort, her solace, her refuge from the storm. Jody would never have survived if it weren't for their love and support.

She swiped at her tears and straightened her shoulders. Hiding in this bathroom wasn't helping anyone. It was time to pull herself together and tell Adam and his brother everything she could remember about Damien and his thugs. Hopefully some of the details that were coming back to her now that she had finally gotten some sleep would provide the clues necessary to bring justice to her friend, and to Sam, if he too was dead, as Damien had taunted.

She opened the door and stepped out. Two very similar pairs of deep blue eyes looked at her with concern. She forced a smile and stepped around Duncan to take her seat beside Adam's bed.

"I want to help you catch Damien," she told Duncan. "I know that my earlier statement wasn't all that useful. I was exhausted and wasn't thinking straight. But I'm remembering more details now. Like that Damien and Owen are brothers."

Adam and Duncan exchanged a surprised look. "Brothers?" they echoed each other.

"I think so. In the buggy, Damien called Owen his little brother. He only said it once. It could have been a nickname. But if it wasn't, that could help you figure out more about Damien. Right?"

"Absolutely." Duncan pulled out his cell phone and started texting someone. A few moments later, he gave Jody a big smile. "Bingo. My guy brought up Owen Flint's bio. We knew he had a brother, Raymond D. Flint. But hadn't made the connection yet. The D stands for Damien." He held up his phone and turned it around. "Mugshot look familiar?"

"That's him," they both said.

"That's Damien," Jody confirmed. "He's the one who sent those men to kill Adam."

"And *you*," Adam said, frowning.

"Do you remember any other details you didn't mention before?" Duncan asked.

"Three days," she said. "It was part of that same conversation in the buggy. Damien said Sam's PI business had been causing him problems for three days. He had plans, big plans, and Owen wouldn't get his cut if Adam made it out of the mountains and connected the dots."

Adam and Duncan exchanged another look.

"Big plans?" Duncan asked.

"Connected the dots?" Adam asked.

She nodded. "They didn't talk about his plans or what he meant, other than that Adam was a cop and knew he was an ex-con—"

"Because of the tattoos," Adam said.

"I think so, yes. He was worried you'd figure out who he was before he could do whatever it is that he's planning."

"Are you looking at all of Sam Campbell's active cases?" Adam asked his brother.

"His office was crammed with hundreds of case files. We're using his planner to reconstruct a timeline for last week to start, so we can determine which cases he was actively working. So far we're up to twenty."

"He was meticulous with that planner," Jody said. "If he worked a case last week, it's definitely written down."

"Good to know. On the chopper when we were flying you and Adam to the hospital, you said that Damien insisted there were some pictures missing from Sam's office. Any idea why he thought any were missing? And where Sam might have put them?"

"I don't know where Sam would have put them other

than the office. But as for thinking some were missing, I imagine Damien was referring to time stamps. I'm not sure if he meant actual dates and times printed on the photos, like I put on most of the pictures that I take for brochures before processing them through an editing program. He might have been referring to the metadata on SD cards that tell you when each picture was taken."

"Photography?" Adam asked. "Is that the second job you mentioned in the mountains? You work for a studio?"

"I work for myself, as far as the pictures are concerned. Sam couldn't afford to hire me full-time. So I run my own photography business on the side. Actually, calling it a business is probably stretching it. I get my clients through word of mouth. I don't have an office or anything like that."

"What do you do, exactly?" Adam asked.

"Work with hotels and cabin rental companies mainly, taking pictures and creating ads and brochures they can use to target tourists." She glanced back and forth between them. "If you're thinking some of Sam's photos could be mixed with mine, I assure you, the chances of that happening are zero."

"How can you be that positive?" Duncan asked.

"Because my photography work is run out of my apartment and a storage unit outside town. And Sam would never allow someone to bring work home. He likes to keep everything under lock and key at the office."

"Assuming you're right—"

"I am." She arched a brow at Duncan.

He smiled. "Okay. Then does Sam have a habit of

losing pictures at the office? Maybe putting them in the wrong files?"

She shook her head. "Not in the six months that I've been working there. He's extremely detail oriented, and careful. He'd keep all of the pictures for one case together. It doesn't make sense that any could have been misplaced."

Adam rubbed his left leg as if to try to ease the ache. "It makes sense if Sam purposely put the pictures somewhere else for safekeeping. Maybe he realized he had something important and was checking on some details before going to the police."

Duncan picked his computer tablet up from the table beside the bed. "Looks like it's going to be a long night for us investigators. We should have a preliminary timeline put together by morning. If you don't mind reviewing it, to make sure it looks right, I can bring it to you tomorrow. Does that work for you, Jody?"

"Of course. They've already discharged me from the hospital. I'll take a cab to my apartment in a little while. The address is—"

"No way are you going home," Adam interrupted. "It's not safe."

"I agree," Duncan said. "Damien and his men are likely looking for you. It's too dangerous. You should go to a hotel until we have him locked up."

She laughed. "Seriously? Did you miss the part where I work two jobs to make ends meet? I live paycheck to paycheck. If I have to pay for a hotel, I don't eat for a week."

"Not a problem," Adam said. "The doctor is discharging me later today. You can stay at my place."

Chapter 16

Adam had expected Jody's apartment to be small. He hadn't expected it to be the size of one of those tiny houses that were all the rage on TV these days. Jody's apartment wasn't even a one-bedroom. It was an efficiency. She didn't have a bed. She had a day bed. If she'd had a couch, there wouldn't have been room for it. She had a lawn chair pulled up to a cardboard box, which apparently acted as her desk.

"Well," he said. "This is…cozy."

"I think you mean minuscule. Now you can see why I keep my cameras and equipment in a storage unit. My goal is to eventually get a full-time job as an investigator with the prosecutor's office. But until that miraculous day happens, I'm stuck in an efficiency."

She opened a door on the far wall, revealing a tiny closet. "I'll pack a bag and grab my Glock from the gun safe. Then we can take that fancy limo you rented and go to your place. Where do you live?"

He was about to answer when he realized she was pulling articles of clothing out of open boxes neatly lined up beneath her hanging clothes and shoving them into what amounted to a large book bag. She didn't even have a chest of drawers or a suitcase.

Thinking about his own home, he suddenly felt self-conscious. He worked hard because he wanted to, not because he had to. He'd never had to struggle financially.

He cleared his throat.

Jody glanced up. "Almost done." She stood and took all of three steps to reach the sink in the bathroom beside the closet. "You never answered me. Where do you live?" She grabbed a few items out of a drawer and snagged her toothbrush from a cup by the sink. "Well?"

"It's, ah, a bit larger than this place."

"I hope your house is huge. We'd be like sardines if we both had to stay here together."

Some of the tension went out of his shoulders. "Then it wouldn't bother you if I had a really big house with a few acres of land?"

"Tell me you have a million dollars in the bank and I'm yours forever."

"I have a million dollars in the bank. I guess we're getting married now."

She laughed and brushed past him to grab her bag. He reached to take it from her, and she rolled her eyes, moving it out of his reach. "You're on crutches. I can carry my own bag. Come on, Mr. Millionaire. I hope you have some New York strip or filet mignon in your freezer and a giant grill to cook them on."

He followed her to the front door, struggling to keep up since he wasn't used to crutches. When she reached to open the door, he said, "Hold it."

She glanced up at him expectantly.

"I do have steaks in the freezer."

She smiled. "Great."

"And a grill."

"Sounds perfect."

"And an outdoor kitchen."

"Okay."

"And a heated pool."

Her smile began to dim. "Any other deep confessions you want to make?"

"I really do have a million dollars in the bank. And then some."

She blinked, all signs of amusement gone. "That wasn't a joke?"

He slowly shook his head. "That wasn't a joke. Do you hate me now?"

She shoved her hair back from her face. "Look, I'm not prejudiced against rich people. Well, not *all* rich people. Just Amelia, Peter, Patricia, Patience, Patrick and Paul. I never mentioned that my estranged adoptive family is wealthy, did I?"

"No. You didn't. Your family has money but they don't share it with you?"

Shadows seemed to darken her eyes, just like they'd done up in the mountains when she'd mentioned her adoptive father.

"Jody?"

"It's…complicated. I don't want to talk about it."

"All right. Then, we're good? You don't mind going to my place?"

"We're good. Just as long as you don't live in Rutherford Estates. It's a ritzy development in the mountains outside of town where my real estate mogul adoptive father lives, along with my adoptive mom." She shivered dramatically. "It's like Mordor and the evil eye looking my way. That's why I'm over here in The Shire, making do with my little hobbit house." She grinned.

"Rutherford Estates?" He forced a laugh. "What would be the odds of your family and me living in the same area?"

"Exactly! Right? I shouldn't have even brought it up. Let's go."

Jody stomped past Adam into the foyer of his mansion—the one in Rutherford Estates—and didn't even spare him a glance. She was so angry she could spit. Seeing the expensive travertine floors spread out before her for miles made it even more tempting. She'd grown up in a place like this. And she had no desire to go back, or be within a few streets of where her family lived. He knew that and had brought her here anyway.

She clutched her bag and marched to the massive staircase just past the equally massive living area on the left side of the room, keeping her back turned to him. "I assume the bedrooms are upstairs. Which one is mine?"

Click. Click. The crutches sounded behind her as he approached. Part of her wanted to ignore him and run up the stairs, knowing he couldn't follow easily. The other part—the part she really hated right now—wanted to turn around and help him, ease him into one of the surprisingly cozy-looking leather chairs that sprinkled the room and get him a beer. Assuming he even had beer. More likely he drank wine, something French with a hoity-toity label.

The clicks stopped.

"Jody?" As always with her, his deep voice was gentle and kind.

"I'm sorry," he said. "I should have told you where I lived when you asked me instead of tricking you into coming here. But there's an electrified fence around this property, motion sensors, alarms. This is the safest place I could think of to take you."

When she didn't reply, he said, "If you really want to, we can go. I'll call the limo driver back."

She clutched the banister. "Why are you always so nice to me?"

"You want me to be mean?"

She sighed and turned around. "Of course not."

"Okay." He looked thoroughly confused. "I'll book us a room in a nice hotel downtown. I can hire a security guy to watch the door—"

"Stop. Just stop. I'll stay here. And like you said, it's safe. I'll just have to do my best to forget that we're within walking distance of my evil adoptive dad." She forced a laugh and dropped her gaze to his chest.

His fingers gently tilted her chin up. His deep blue eyes searched hers. "I'm a good listener if you want to talk."

"I don't."

"If you change your mind—"

"I won't. Where's my room?"

His mouth tightened with disappointment. "There are four guest rooms upstairs, each with its own bathroom. Pick whichever one you like. My room is down here if you need me."

"Adam, I…"

"Yes?"

She shook her head. "Thank you. I mean it. You've done so much for me. I really appreciate it."

He nodded but didn't say anything.

She started up the stairs, then stopped and looked over her shoulder.

He hadn't moved. He was balancing on his crutches, watching her with an unreadable expression.

"You're not a real estate entrepreneur, are you?" she asked.

His brows raised. "If you're wondering where my money comes from, my great-great-grandfather was a business whiz and started a dozen companies. My parents gave ownership of some of those companies to my siblings and me as we each turned twenty-one."

Her face flushed with embarrassment. "I wasn't trying to find out how you got your money. I just… I'm glad you're not in real estate. That's all."

"Because of your adoptive father being in real estate?"

She swallowed, then nodded.

"But you don't want to talk about him?"

"I really don't. But…if I did…you would be the one I'd want to talk to." She gave him a watery smile, already struggling to hold back the tears that were threatening. "Good night, Adam."

"Good night, Jody."

She hurried up the rest of the stairs and went into the first bedroom she found. After shutting the door, she slid down to the thick, plush carpet and drew her knees up to her chin. She wasn't going to get a wink of sleep knowing that the man she'd hated and feared all her life was just a short walk away. She couldn't tell Adam what Peter Ingram had done to her. She couldn't bear the revulsion that would cross his face. Or worse. She couldn't bear it if he turned out to be just like the rest of her adoptive family. She couldn't bear it if he didn't believe her.

She dropped her chin onto her knees and did what she'd done all her life when times got hard. She wept.

Chapter 17

Jody hesitated at the top of the landing. She hadn't expected any lights to be on downstairs at two in the morning. She didn't want to intrude if Adam was still up, maybe watching a late movie or something.

Everything was quiet. And there were only a *few* lights on. Maybe he'd left them on for her, since she was in an unfamiliar house. He was like that. Nice. Kind. Considerate. Exactly the kind of man she'd always dreamed of, and exactly the kind of man she could never have because she was so dang screwed up.

She sighed and headed downstairs with no particular destination in mind. But she was going stir-crazy in her room, unable to sleep with so much rattling around in her brain. And her heart. Grief was a constant ache in her chest.

Figuring Adam wouldn't mind, she wandered

through the sprawling house. It was refreshing to see that not everyone with money decorated their homes like a museum, the way her adoptive father decorated his.

The paintings here weren't modern atrocities of splattered paint with no form or function, calling itself art. Adam's paintings were comfortable, accessible, warm. His love of the outdoors was obvious in his choice of landscapes, most of them featuring mountains, lakes and ethereal forests that seemed so real she could swear she smelled the pine trees.

For such a big house, it didn't feel intimidating. She wasn't afraid that if she touched something it might break. She could easily see children running across the area rugs and bounding up the stairs, giggling and laughing and loving life—as all kids should.

She forced away the dark memories of her own childhood that tried to press in on her and continued her exploration. To the right of the foyer was a short hallway that she assumed led to Adam's bedroom. She paused, longing to go to him. Not because she *wanted* him, although she couldn't imagine ever *not* wanting him. Tonight she *needed* him, needed someone to care about her, to hug her and hold her and tell her that she mattered. That would be selfish, though, waking him up just to give her a hug, no matter how deeply she craved his arms around her. So she forced herself to move past the hallway to the kitchen.

Of all the rooms in the house that she'd seen so far, this one was the most typical of what she'd expect in a place like this. He hadn't stamped his personality in here, his warmth. It was functional and beautiful, with cherry cabinets and black granite countertops.

But there was nothing homey. It was too sterile, too impersonal, to be a reflection of him. Which made her doubt he used it much. Maybe he cooked out a lot in the outdoor kitchen that he'd mentioned earlier, or brought a lot of takeout food home.

Thinking of takeout had her tummy rumbling. She hadn't been hungry at the hospital and had only picked at the food on her plate. She had to search for the refrigerator and finally realized it was disguised with cabinet fronts to blend in with everything else.

Mission accomplished. It definitely blended.

Shaking her head, she opened the doors, then laughed. She pressed her hand to her mouth, belatedly hoping she hadn't been too loud. Then she rummaged through the containers of Chinese takeout, barbecue and leftover pizza. Most of the food still looked edible, and she was about to grab a slice of pepperoni pizza when she saw a plastic-wrapped plate sitting on the next shelf down. There was a note taped to the top.

Jody, just in case you wake up hungry, I cooked you a steak and grilled a potato. Wasn't sure how you like it, so I left the steak medium. —Adam

His thoughtfulness did funny things to her heart and of course had her eyes moist with tears. After all the tears she'd shed tonight, she hadn't expected that. She furiously wiped her eyes and then took out the plate. After warming it in the microwave and preparing the potato, she grabbed a beer—relieved to see he wasn't a wine drinker—and headed toward the dining room. Pausing at the entrance, she eyed the massive, lonely-looking table and changed directions, heading into the living room to the left of the stairs instead.

Now this room was exactly to her taste. Decorated in rich browns and golds, the furniture was plush leather with reclining seats. And a giant TV mounted over the fireplace. She set her beer in the cup holder on the big, cushy recliner that directly faced the TV, then settled down to eat her meal.

The first bite of steak melted in her mouth. She didn't think she'd ever had anything so good. Then again, she hadn't eaten a real meal in a few days, so that could have had something to do with it. She'd eaten half the potato and steak before she finally got full enough to slow down and leisurely enjoy the rest.

As she chewed, she glanced behind her to judge the distance between the living room and Adam's bedroom. She didn't think he'd hear her this far away, so she swiped the remote from the end table and clicked on the television. Just to make sure she didn't disturb him, she kept the volume low. Then she settled back to catch up on what had been happening in the world since she'd received that fateful text from Tracy's phone.

Since it was so late—or early, depending on how she wanted to look at it—local news wasn't an option. So she clicked on one of the twenty-four-hour national news channels. As usual, it was a kaleidoscope of unrest in the world, terrorist plots and political pundits offering so-called expert opinions based on hearsay and no firsthand knowledge. She was about to turn off the TV when one of the news anchors mentioned Gatlinburg.

Curious, she turned up the volume a couple of notches and leaned forward. Their little town was a tourist mecca. But other than the wildfires last season, nothing much happened around here to catch the attention of the national news shows.

Until now.

A picture of one of the local city councilmen, Eddie Hicks, flashed up on the screen. The anchor reminded the audience that Hicks had been killed in a car crash earlier in the week, the same day that Sam had gone missing.

Sam. Tracy. She missed them both so much.

The anchor gave details about the memorial service being held later today. Jody wasn't sure why that made the national news, until another picture flashed up on the screen—Tennessee state senator Ron Sinclair. He was well-known in Gatlinburg and heavily lauded for bringing several economy-boosting projects to town because of his work on an infrastructure subcommittee. Apparently, he was friends with the councilman and would be in town for the memorial. The mayor and other dignitaries would also be in attendance.

The anchor droned on about other events around the world as Jody finished her meal. Then she clicked off the TV and headed into the kitchen to clean up. After loading her plate and utensils in the dishwasher and making sure the kitchen was as pristine as she'd found it, she started toward the stairs again to go up to her room.

Then she noticed the pool through the back wall of French doors.

The water was a gorgeous cornflower blue, lit by lights from underneath. Since the homes around here were separated by several acres, none of them were close enough to have a view of the backyard. It was completely private and looked so peaceful and serene that it drew her forward like a magnet.

She started to open one of the doors, then stopped. There was an electronic keypad on the wall to the right. The security alarm. She hadn't even thought to ask Adam for the code. She pressed her face to the glass in frustration, then froze.

There was a man outside.

She stepped back, ready to run to Adam's room, then hesitated. The man's back was to her and he wasn't skulking around as if he was looking for a way into the house. He was sitting in one of the deck chairs facing the pool. As she watched, he turned his head to look down and picked up a bottle of beer she hadn't noticed before.

Adam.

She let out a shaky breath, relieved that Damien or one of his men hadn't found her. Then she frowned, noticing more details as her eyes adjusted to the dim light through the glass panes in the door. A holstered pistol sat on a small glass table beside his chair next to a legal pad. Dozens of balled-up pieces of paper lay discarded on the ground all around him. His phone was facedown on the concrete as if it had fallen from the table and he hadn't noticed.

What was going on? Why was he out there? Was his leg hurting so much that he couldn't sleep? That thought had her turning the knob and rushing outside.

"Adam, are you okay?" She hurried toward his chair. "Is your leg hurting too much to—" She stopped and blinked down at him. He didn't have a shirt on. He didn't have much of anything on. Actually, all he had on was his underwear—sexy boxer briefs that hugged all his…attributes…like a second skin.

Her mouth went dry as she stared at him, her gaze caressing every inch from his toes to his rippling abs to his lightly furred chest and, finally, up to eyes that reflected a deep blue in the light from the pool. But he wasn't looking at her. He was staring out at the darkness beyond the pool, his jaw clenched with agitation.

"Adam?"

He tipped the bottle of beer up to his lips and took a deep swig, emptying the bottle. Then he tossed it over his head into the pool. It landed with a splash and bobbed up and down before filling with water and slowly sinking beneath the surface.

Jody didn't have to look down into the pool to know the bottle he'd just emptied wasn't his first. And apparently it wasn't going to be his last, judging by the flush on his cheeks and the six-pack carton on the other side of his chair with one more bottle in it.

She put her hands on her hips. "You're drunk."

His eyes slowly rose to hers. "Not drunk enough." He picked up the other bottle and stared at it a moment, then squeezed his eyes shut as if in pain before throwing it unopened into the pool.

Jody lowered herself to her knees beside his chair. "Is it your leg?" She reached for his phone on the ground. "I can call the doctor, get him to phone in a stronger pain prescr—"

"I know about your adoptive father, Peter Ingram."

She went still, the phone clutched in her hand. "Excuse me?" she whispered.

His jaw clenched so tight the skin along his jawbone turned white. "The way you reacted when you mentioned him earlier, calling him your evil adoptive dad, how angry you were that I'd tricked you into coming here…" He scrubbed his face, covering his eyes with his hands before dropping them to his lap. "I know it was your story to tell. But I couldn't let it go. I had to know why you were so afraid of him." His tortured gaze finally rose to hers. "I'm so, so sorry."

"You had no right." Her voice came out a harsh croak. "You had no right."

"I know. Believe me, I know. I'm so sorry—"

"Stop saying that!" She jumped to her feet, finally finding her voice. "What are you sorry for anyway? Abusing your authority and opening a closed file you shouldn't have been able to open? That's what you had to have done. I was a juvenile. They sealed the record. No way could you have gotten that information without breaking a law or some kind of law enforcement code or something. Or are you sorry that you violated my privacy, violated *me* by prying into secrets that were mine to tell or not to tell?"

"Both. I shouldn't have pried, you're right. I abused your trust, my position as a federal officer. I never should have done it."

"No. You shouldn't have. I'm leaving, going back to my apartment. Don't bother driving me. You're too drunk to drive anyway. I'll call a cab." She turned and ran for the house.

"Jody, wait."

His chair creaked. She heard the click of his crutches as she threw open the door.

"Jody!"

She rushed inside.

A loud crack followed by the sound of shattering glass had her whirling around.

Adam lay on his back on the patio, his face twisted in agony as he clutched his hurt leg. His crutches had skittered out from beneath him and lay several feet away, right next to the shattered glass table that had been sitting beside his chair.

She ran back outside.

"No!" His voice was a hoarse whisper. "The glass. You'll get cut."

She stepped around the larger shards as she knelt beside him. "What can I do? How can I help? Are you cut?"

"Stop, Jody. You're barefoot."

"So are you. Can't you just accept help when you need it?" She grabbed his crutches, but when she tried to help him up, there was no way she could lift him. It took all her strength and a lot of cajoling and threatening to get him to even try to help her. Half-drunk Adam was ornery as all get-out and had an incredibly colorful vocabulary.

Finally she got him inside. Once they'd reached the living room, she was so exhausted she didn't even try to steer him down the hallway. Instead she jerked his crutches away and let him fall onto one of the mammoth couches.

He grunted when he landed, bounced a couple of times, then promptly passed out.

Jody's mouth dropped open in shock. Then she snapped it closed in anger. "Adam?" She grabbed his shoulder and shook him. "Adam?"

He started snoring.

She fisted her hands at her sides and kicked one of

his crutches. It skittered across the room before spinning around and sliding halfway under a recliner. How dare he? How dare he invade her privacy, look into the most intimate details of her life without her permission, then not even stay awake long enough for her to yell at him? He should be begging her forgiveness and groveling at her feet.

She closed her eyes. Dang it. He *had* groveled. He *had* begged her forgiveness. And he'd nearly killed himself trying to chase after her because she'd refused to listen to him. She sagged down onto the couch beside him.

"Oh, Adam. What am I going to do with you?"

His soft snore was apparently the only answer she was going to get any time soon.

Obviously leaving him when he was passed out wasn't a good idea. Especially with his injured leg. Plus, she really didn't want to head out the front door with Damien possibly lurking around somewhere. All in all, she was pretty much a prisoner here for the time being. But come morning, when Adam was groaning with a headache over a cup of hot coffee, she'd make him take her back home. She had a gun. If Damien tried to come into her apartment, she'd gladly pull the trigger.

Adam's jaw tightened in his sleep, and his legs shifted restlessly. He reached toward his hurt leg, groaning, obviously in pain.

"You don't deserve my help, you know that, Adam?"

He winced and mumbled something incoherent but didn't wake up.

She shook her head and set about doing everything she could to ease his pain. Which basically amounted to straightening his leg, elevating it on a pillow and applying a cold compress that she'd found in his cavernous refrigerator. But it seemed to help, because he settled down and was no longer twitching in pain.

She sighed and raked a hand through her hair. A slight breeze had her realizing she'd left one of the French doors open. Outside the little pieces of crumpled-up paper still lay by Adam's chair. The broken table glass twinkled in the moonlight like a thousand little diamonds scattered across the concrete.

"A thousand little diamonds I get to sweep up," she grumbled.

Once again she trudged into the kitchen, locating the broom and dustpan in the pantry, exactly where it made sense they would be. Of course they were hanging on hooks, and what little food he had was lined up in neat rows on the shelves.

"I wonder if he folds his underwear, too." Her bin of underwear in her closet was a chaotic jumble. It would probably give him a heart attack. She grabbed a trash bag, conveniently on a shelf next to the broom, and headed outside.

The little table had obviously been made of safety glass, probably the only reason she hadn't cut her feet when she ran outside. But even though the little pieces weren't wicked sharp, there were a lot of them. It took a good ten minutes before she was satisfied that she'd gotten up all the glass. She dumped the last of it into the garbage bag, then set about picking up the pieces of crumpled paper by Adam's chair.

Back inside, she set the legal pad and his phone on the counter and was about to stuff the garbage bag into the can under the sink when she noticed the writing on the pad. She grew still, then very slowly pulled the pad toward her and read the rest of it. By the time she'd read it all, tears were blurring her vision.

She hated that she was such a crier.

She wiped at her eyes, then slid to the floor and pulled the trash bag toward her. She picked out every piece of balled-up paper, unfolded them and smoothed them out so she could read them. Anyone else would probably be horrified at what he'd written. They might even call the police, thinking that he was dangerous. But Jody understood his anger, his fury and his desire for revenge better than anyone. And if she hadn't only known the man for a few days, she'd think she was half in love with him.

Because he was the only person, ever, who'd truly believed her.

The fact that she hadn't personally told him the details about the abuse she'd suffered at the hands of the man who'd adopted her didn't matter. Adam had read the police reports. He'd read the testimony in juvenile court. He'd read what the judge had decided, most likely after being given a substantial bribe by Jody's adoptive father. And still, Adam had believed her. That was what these pieces of paper told her. And to her they were a precious gift, something to treasure.

She carefully set each wrinkled piece of paper on the counter in a neat stack on top of the legal pad and threw the trash away. Then she headed into the family room. She set the pages on the end table, grabbed a blanket off the back of one of the chairs, sat down beside Adam. She gently lifted his head and slipped closer, cradling his head on her lap. Then she covered both of them with the blanket and closed her eyes.

Chapter 18

The smell of bacon had Adam bolting upright, then falling back with a groan. Pressing a hand to his throbbing head, he blinked up at the familiar coffered ceiling above him. Why was he on the couch? With a pillow beneath his head? And a blanket covering him? The last thing he remembered was sitting by the pool, nursing a beer to dull the pain in his leg, dreaming up all the different ways he could torture and kill Jody's adoptive father for what he'd done to her.

Jody. She'd been there, too. Hadn't she? There was an argument. Blinding pain as he'd fallen against… something. A loud crash. What in the world had happened?

He blinked his bleary eyes and forced himself to sit up. Then he looked over the end of the couch toward the kitchen, where the delicious—and nauseating, given his current state—smells were coming from.

Was she cooking breakfast? He could just catch a glimpse of her as she moved around inside the kitchen. Was she…humming?

She stuck her head around the corner. "About time you woke up. Breakfast will be ready in about ten minutes. Duncan will be here at nine to give us an update on the case. You should hurry up and get ready."

He blinked, certain he'd heard her wrong. "My brother? He called you?"

"Well, actually he called you." She picked up his phone off the island and held it up. "Hope you don't mind that I answered on your behalf." She motioned toward him. "There's a glass of water and some aspirin beside you, and something to settle your stomach if you need it." She looked over her shoulder. "The clock above your oven says you've used up one of your ten minutes. Chop, chop. I don't want your breakfast to get cold while you're dillydallying in the shower."

She disappeared into the kitchen.

Adam had a million questions for her, the most important being why she was so cheerful when he was pretty sure he'd been a moron and a jerk last night. But his roiling stomach, aching head and throbbing leg were taking center stage in his world at the moment. And they wouldn't be ignored.

He gratefully downed several aspirin, chasing them with a huge swig of Pepto and half a bottle of water.

"Six minutes," Jody called out from the kitchen, sounding disgustingly cheerful.

Was this the calm before the storm? Was she planning on poisoning him in return for whatever he'd done last night? He had a feeling he deserved it.

He grabbed the crutches she'd thoughtfully left on the floor beside the couch and hobbled his way into his bedroom. He tried to get ready quickly according to her timetable, but his attempts to shower without getting the bandage around his leg wet were a complete fiasco and he fell twice, finally giving up and just taking a normal shower—to hell with his stitches.

A few minutes later, feeling far more human than he should have thanks to the aspirin and Pepto, he made his way to the kitchen island.

The kitchen was empty.

"You're late."

He turned at the sound of her voice behind him. She was wearing curve-hugging blue jeans and an emerald-green button-up shirt that perfectly matched her eyes and her adorable glasses. Her gorgeous, thick red hair tumbled over her shoulders to hang halfway down her back. Just a touch of makeup made her eyes pop even more than usual. His mouth went dry just looking at her.

"You're beautiful," he breathed.

Her frown evaporated. "You're forgiven. Come on. Your plate's in the dining room."

He stood in confusion, but she seemed determined for him to eat and had gone to a lot of trouble, so he dutifully sat down. She'd made scrambled eggs, biscuits, bacon and hash browns. They were all expertly prepared. She was definitely talented in the kitchen. But in spite of how good everything tasted, he didn't want any of it. He wanted to talk instead, to beg her forgiveness for what little he remembered of his behavior last night, to rebuild the bridges he'd torn down. But she seemed so…happy…content to sit across from him. There were no recriminations on her tongue, no accusations, no tears.

That part bothered him the most.

He was used to her tears. He expected them. This smiling Jody without a seeming care in the world was an enigma. And he didn't know what to make of it.

When he'd finally eaten enough to feel that he wouldn't insult her if he stopped, he set his fork down. "You're a wonderful cook. You shouldn't have gone to all that trouble. But I appreciate it. Thank you."

She beamed at him. "You're very welcome." She took a sip of her orange juice.

"Jody?"

She looked at him over the rim of her glass, brows raised in question.

"Why are you doing this? Why did you cook me breakfast? And why are you being so sweet when I don't deserve any of this?"

She set the glass down and wiped her mouth with the napkin. "Wait here."

He started to ask her what she was talking about. But she hurried out of the room.

He clenched his fists on the table in frustration. He'd wanted to talk it out, see if they could move beyond last night. But she was putting up a front, not letting him in. Where had she gone? Was she upstairs, crying, after trying to be nice in spite of her hurt feelings? All alone? That thought had him pushing back his chair.

"No, please." She'd come back into the room. "Don't leave. We need to talk."

Now this he'd expected. He scooted his chair back

under the table. "I know. I was a jerk last night. I abused my authority and—"

"Looked into my sealed juvenile records. Yes, I know." She pulled a stack of wrinkled pages from behind her back and set them on the table.

Adam's stomach clenched. He was glad his appetite hadn't been what it normally was or he'd probably have thrown up right then and there.

"Do you know what these are?" She smoothed her hand over the top page.

He slowly nodded. "The ramblings of an idiot who drank far more than he should have. Jody, I had no right to—"

"No. You didn't. You shouldn't have gone behind my back and used your authority to find out details that were mine to share. Or not to share. I admit, when I realized what you'd done, I was furious, and hurt, and felt betrayed. I was ready to storm out of here."

"Why didn't you? Don't get me wrong. I'm glad you didn't. I'd have been worried about you and would have had to tear this town apart to find you. But why did you tuck me in on the couch and leave pills for my hangover and go to all that trouble to cook me breakfast? I should have been the one waiting on you, not the other way around. Why did you do all of that for me?"

She tapped the stack of pages on the table. "This. This is why I'm still here, why I'm not mad at you anymore." She held up the first page and squinted at it. "You have really bad penmanship, by the way."

"I was drunk."

"True, which means your inhibitions were lowered and you poured your emotions out onto these pages. Your true emotions, not subterfuge."

"Jody, I didn't mean for you to see—"

"'Castration,'" she read from the first page.

He choked and started coughing.

She looked at him over the top of her glasses and continued reading what he'd scribbled while under the influence of alcohol and an all-consuming rage.

"'Castration would be a good way to kill Jody's father. Bastards like that shouldn't be allowed to procreate.'"

She set the page to the side. "I agree. They shouldn't." She picked up the next page. "'Gunshot wound. Nothing quick or easy. I'd shoot him in the gut and tie him out in the sun to slowly and painfully bleed to death.'"

He cleared his throat again. "I'm actually not as bloodthirsty as I sound. I was just…fantasizing. I wouldn't *actually* do that to someone."

She picked up the next page. "'Caning. Maybe it's time that caning was brought to this country. I'd give cane poles to everyone who'd ever been abused by someone who'd sworn to love them and let them each have a turn at him until the lecherous light faded from his serpent's eyes.'"

"A bit melodramatic," he said, trying to smile as if he thought the whole thing was amusing. But he was pretty sure he failed spectacularly.

"This is a pretty good one." Her voice was tight. She cleared her throat and picked up the next paper, her hands slowly smoothing it out. "'I'd get one of my old buddies from the vice squad to plant seized child pornography pictures on his computer. Once in prison, the other inmates would enact their own form of punishment.'"

"I wouldn't really plant evidence."

"I'm sure you wouldn't," she agreed. She pulled another piece of paper from the very bottom of the stack. "This one is my personal favorite." The paper shook in her hands as she read. "'I'd tie him to a chair and, with his family watching—the vipers who turned their backs on Jody—I'd let her confront him about everything he did to her. I wouldn't let him go until he admitted what he'd done and begged for her forgiveness. And once her family realized they'd been wrong all this time, they'd beg her for forgiveness, too, and she could laugh in their faces. I'd take Jody away from those horrible, awful people and do everything I could to make her forget every bad thing that ever happened to her.'" Her chin wobbled as she read the last part of it. "I would *love* her."

Tears spilled over and ran down her cheeks.

He scooted his chair back, ready to go to her, but he hesitated. Was she angry or hurt or…what? He wasn't sure and didn't know what to do. How was he going to fix this?

"Thank you," she whispered brokenly.

"I'm sorry—what? You're…thanking me? Why?"

"You believed me. When no one else did. You have no idea what that did to me when I read those pages." She waved her hand in the air. "Oh, I know you would never actually do all of those things to Peter. But the fact that you believed in me enough to be that angry on my behalf goes a long way toward healing the holes in my heart." She stood and circled the table to stand in front of him. Then, to his shock, she straddled him in his chair.

He jerked against her, swearing, a bead of sweat

popping out on his forehead as he grabbed her arms to lift her off him. "I don't think you're thinking straight. You should—"

She shoved his arms away and cupped his face in her hands. "I'm thinking with more clarity than I have in ages. And you were thinking more clearly when you wrote those pages than you realize. Your heart shined through in the concern you showed for me. And in that last sentence you wrote. I agree with you, Adam. Love really is the cure. Will you love me?"

"Sweetheart." He cleared his throat. "I mean… Jody—"

"I like *sweetheart* better." She pressed a soft kiss against his right cheek.

He shuddered and drew a ragged breath. "*Jody,* we've been through a traumatic few days together. Sometimes that makes people have, ah, feelings that might not prove to be real later on."

She kissed his other cheek, then shifted her bottom in a delightfully sinful way against his lap.

He grabbed the arms of the chair to keep from doing something he knew he would regret, like grabbing her. "Have *you* been drinking this morning?"

"Nope," she breathed against his neck. "I'm stone-cold sober. Love me, Adam."

He grasped her arms and pulled her against him, then swore when he realized what he was doing. He gently pushed her back against the table. "Be careful. My control is hanging by a thread here. I'm trying to do the honorable thing."

She let out a deep sigh and scooted farther back on his thighs but didn't get up. "I don't know why you think making love to me isn't honorable. It would be two consenting adults who care about each other and want to show their feelings in the most wonderful way possible."

He started to protest her warped view of honorable, but she shook her head and held a finger to his lips.

"Knowing you, I imagine that you're worried I'm vulnerable. But I've never felt so empowered in my life. By believing in me, you've helped me feel less hopeless, more in control, than I have in years. Thank you for that."

He cleared his throat. "Um. You're welcome?"

She smiled, then took his hands in hers. "My parents, my biological parents, were killed in a car wreck when I was a toddler. I barely remember them. Mostly I just know their names—Lance and Vanessa Radcliffe—and that they loved me enough to make sure that I was taken care of when they died. Or at least, that's what they thought—that I'd be well taken care of because of everything they put into place, like designating their best friends, the Ingrams, as my guardians."

"Jody, you don't have to tell me any of this."

"I know. And that's why I want to, because I don't have to. And because…because I've never told anyone the whole story. Not even the judge who oversaw the hearing against Peter Ingram. Not even the prosecutor who pressed the case. Not even Tracy. She knew bits and pieces, but no one knows it all. Except me."

She shoved her hair back from her face and drew a deep breath. "After my parents were killed, the Ingrams took me in, eventually adopted me. Everyone thought they were being good Samaritans, honoring their friends. But they never really wanted me. They wanted the Radcliffe family home here in Rutherford Estates that came with me, and my trust fund. The house has its own trust fund just for its upkeep and taxes, to ensure that I'd never have to worry about having a home."

Adam frowned. "But you live in an apartment. Shouldn't the house be yours now that you're a legal adult?"

She shrugged. "You would think so. The Ingrams showed me the deed and a copy of my parents' will giving them ownership in exchange for taking care of me. I guess my biological parents thought the trust fund they set up for me would be enough once I was out on my own, that I could buy my own house at that point."

"It wasn't enough?"

Her mouth tightened. "It should have been. But the Ingrams made large withdrawals against the fund while I was growing up, supposedly for my care. There was barely enough to get me through college when I came into ownership of the fund and they lost control of it." She held her hand up. "And before you ask, yes, I petitioned the court for an accounting of their stewardship, hoping I could force them to pay back some of the money. But after an accountant reviewed the records, a judge ruled that they hadn't done anything illegal. I could have appealed, but I decided to let it drop at that point."

Adam didn't like what he was hearing. It sounded fishy to him. Maybe he could look into it sometime, if she wanted him to. But it wasn't the financial misdeeds of the Ingrams—if indeed they had done anything illegal—that worried him right now. It was the way Jody had turned pale as she prepared to tell him the details about her childhood.

He didn't want to know any more than what he'd read in the court transcripts.

The house she'd grown up in was just a few blocks away. He knew because he'd looked it up when he'd looked into her background. He already cared deeply about her. How was he supposed to sit here and not run over there and kill the man who'd hurt her? He was afraid of what he might do if she told him in her own words what her adoptive father had done to her.

He was about to remind her again that she didn't need to tell him any of the details. But she was staring at him, her green eyes searching his with a mixture of trust, and hope, and fear. And he knew he couldn't tell her no. She wanted this, needed this, needed to share with him what had happened to her. And he was in awe that it was him she trusted to share it with. So even though it almost killed him, he endeavored to listen and be there for her, and to not go kill Peter Ingram once she was finished.

He drew her against his chest.

She clung to him for several minutes, then relaxed. "The first time he came into my room at night, when everyone else in the house was asleep, I was nine."

Dear God. He closed his eyes and spent the next twenty minutes in agony listening to the harrowing details of her abuse. He remembered, in the mountains, thinking about how young she was, and that she was naive, inexperienced and sheltered in the horrors that existed in the world around her. What a fool he'd been. She was none of those things. She'd suffered horrendous abuse and learned about the ugliness that existed in this world far sooner than she ever should have. He felt like such an idiot for judging her, making assumptions. And now, as he sat here, listening to what had happened to her, all he wanted to do was grab his gun and storm out of the house. He wanted to kill the man who'd hurt her. If Jody wasn't nestled in his arms right now, so trusting and needing him in this moment, he very well might have. He stayed, for her, but it tore him up inside.

The abuse she'd suffered was horrific, far worse than anything listed in the court records. He didn't know how she'd managed to survive and become the well-adjusted, caring, kind person that she was today. She'd been abused by her adoptive father. And then abused again, betrayed, victimized by every member of her supposed family when they took their father's side against her after she finally told a counselor at school what was going on.

And if that wasn't enough, the social worker in the case and the court-appointed psychiatrist took the father's side as well. They claimed that Jody was lying, acting out, wanting attention. And when the proceedings were over, they found the father innocent and forced Jody to attend psychiatric sessions for years— to work on her issues with being needy and attention seeking and being a pathological liar.

And they sent her back to live with her abuser and his family.

As far as Adam was concerned, all of them—her adoptive father, his family, the judge, the psychiatrist, the social worker—should have gone to prison, lost their jobs and anything else that could be legally done to punish them for failing to protect the innocent little girl entrusted to their care.

"After that," she continued, whispering against his chest, "I was treated like a servant, like Cinderella, doing all the chores, eating alone, being pulled out of my school and sent off to the bad kids' school. It was as if I didn't exist to them anymore. I was invisible and I didn't matter. The only good thing was that Peter never touched me again. I think he was worried that his wife was suspicious, that maybe she believed me but wouldn't go against him. The only reason I think that is because the day after the judge made his ruling, a steel bolt showed up on my door. I could bar it from the inside and there wasn't any way to unlock it from the hallway. No one ever said who put it there. No one even mentioned it. But I think it was my adoptive mom. Whoever did it, that bolt was the only thing that kept me sane, gave me hope that one day maybe things would get better."

She sat back and brushed at the tears on her cheeks. "I think I would have died of loneliness and despair if it hadn't been for Tracy and her family. I began spending more and more time with them, until I rarely ever went home. My family didn't care, of course, as long as the trust fund checks kept coming in every month. The moment I turned eighteen, I was out of there. And I've never been back."

She let out a shuddering breath. "Tracy and her family loved me and supported me, but even they were skeptical. It was the one wound in my heart where they were concerned. My family, and the experts, had painted such a terrible picture of me that even Tracy believed I was damaged, maybe traumatized from los-

ing my biological parents at such a young age and that
I was an attention seeker."

"How could you have stayed friends with her after
that?"

She shrugged. "That's life. It's how it's always been.
No one truly believed everything that I said happened.
Until you. Why, Adam? Why did you believe me when
no one else did?"

"Because I know you, know what's in your heart.
We've been through more together in a few days than
most people survive in a lifetime. I've seen the good
in you, the kindness, the honesty. Why would I doubt
you?" He opened his arms, and she fell against him.

It didn't surprise him when she began weeping. If
anything, it was reassuring. Crying was her way of
coping. She'd just relived her horrible ordeal by saying
it out loud to him. The copious tears meant that she'd
be okay. Or as okay as she could be with everything
she'd been through.

When she started hiccupping, she pulled back. "I'm
so sorry. I cry at the drop of a hat. It must be incredibly annoying."

"Not at all. It's part of who you are. It shows you're
sensitive and have a wonderful, full heart in spite of
everything that's happened to you. It would break my
heart if you ever stop having that capacity to care and
feel so deeply that you *don't* cry. Don't ever apologize
for feeling and being honest about your emotions."

She lay back against him, her arms around his waist.
He rested his chin on the top of her head and gently
stroked her back. They sat that way for a long time,
until the air around them seemed to subtly change. Her
fingers curled against his shirt. Her breathing turned

ragged. She slowly slid her hands up his chest and entwined her arms around his neck.

"Adam."

Just one whispered word, said with such a mixture of longing and desire, was all it took to send a jolt of raw lust straight through his body.

Then she pressed her open mouth against his neck and lightly touched her tongue to his overheated skin.

He almost came right out of his chair.

His hands tightened around her, trying to stop her wandering mouth. "Jody," he rasped. "Don't."

She kissed him again.

"Jody, no. Stop. You're vulnerable, emotional. You'll regret this later if you—"

She moved to his ear, her tongue doing wicked things that had him hardening in an instant.

He shuddered, his arms tightening around her, drawing her close. *No!* What was he doing? This was wrong. He couldn't act on the chemistry that flared between them every time they were close. Not now, not like this.

"Jody, you're not thinking clearly. You're not—"

She pressed her mouth against his neck and sucked.

He jerked back.

She pulled back and stared up at him and ran her fingers through the hair at the nape of his neck. "I want you Adam. I need you."

"You'll hate me later. When you're thinking more clearly, you'll realize that—"

"Do you want me?"

He swallowed, hard. "You know I do."

"Then love me." She didn't wait for his response. She pulled him down to her and kissed his mouth.

He should have been stronger. Should have set her away from him. But he wanted her so badly he ached. There was something about this beautiful, smart, incredibly sweet woman in his arms that turned his knees to jelly. By the time her tongue darted inside his mouth and stroked his, he was already waving the white flag of surrender. He couldn't have stopped now if a whole army was at his door, trying to break it down. For some reason she needed him. And he needed her just as desperately.

He broke the kiss and gasped for air. Then leaned in and tortured her the same way she'd tortured him earlier. He pressed his mouth against her neck and sucked.

She gasped and almost overturned the chair.

He laughed and pulled back, his mouth hovering inches from hers. "What time did you say Duncan would be here?"

She swallowed, with obvious difficulty. "N...nine o'clock... I think."

He looked past her to the digital readout over the oven. "That's not nearly enough time."

"We'll make it work!" She jumped off his lap, grabbing the table to keep from falling when she tripped over her own feet. She picked up his crutches. "Hurry." She shoved them into his hands and took off down the hall, her bare feet slapping against the tile.

Adam was laughing so hard he could barely keep the crutches under his arms as he followed her to the bedroom at his aggravatingly much slower pace.

Chapter 19

Jody stood naked in the middle of Adam's bedroom, her clothes discarded in a pile at her feet. The *click, click* of his crutches echoed through the house beyond the bedroom door as he slowly made his way toward her. And even though she'd had the occasional tryst in college and had always wanted them this way—fast, furious, two sweaty bodies seeking quick solace before she shoved the man of the hour out the door—suddenly everything about this seemed wrong.

Because this was Adam.

He wasn't like the men who'd drifted in and out of her life. Men who, according to her college counselors when she'd sought therapy on her own, were Jody's way of taking control of her body, in response to the abuse she'd suffered as a child when she'd been completely helpless to stop it. But Adam was different, special. Shouldn't that make…this…different? She looked down at her clothes, her naked body, and suddenly felt shy, nervous.

Click. Click.

She lunged for the chair by the bed and grabbed the blanket off the back.

The door opened behind her.

She spun around, clutching the blanket against her breasts, quickly shaking it out to cover more of her naked skin.

Adam stopped in the doorway, leaning heavily on his crutches, his face pale, eyes wide as they swept her from head to toe. "What's wrong? Second thoughts?"

"What?" She looked down at the blanket, clutched like a lifeline in her hands. "Oh. No, no, of course not. It's just that…" She looked up at him again, took a step toward him. "Are you okay? You look like you're in pain."

"And you look scared. Jody, it's all right. We don't have to do this. I'll just go back—"

"No!" She hurried to him, stopping a few feet away. "It's just…nerves. It's been a while, since college." She took off her glasses and tossed them onto her pile of clothes. "I'm not scared. I could never be afraid of you, Adam. I want you, very much. Don't you want me?" She dropped the blanket.

His gaze dipped. His throat worked. "You have no idea how badly I want you." His voice was thick with desire.

Feeling more confident now, she smiled and slipped into the role she'd always taken with these encounters. She put her hand on his arm and led him toward the bed. Then she shoved the covers back and lay down.

She lifted her heavy fall of hair and fanned it out on the pillow, then held her arms up for him to join her.

Some of the heat seemed to leave his eyes as he stared down at her.

She suddenly felt self-conscious again. "Adam? What's wrong? Don't you like the way I look?" Men always did. They loved her thick red hair, her narrow waist, her curvy hips. Her breasts weren't as large as she would have preferred. But they were firm and well shaped. No one had ever had any complaints. "Adam?"

He swallowed again, his knuckles whitening where he was holding on to the crutches. "I think you're the most beautiful creature I've ever seen. And I want you, more than you could possibly imagine. But I want you to want me, too, really want me."

She frowned. "I do. I'm here, aren't I? I'm ready. Let's do it."

He winced. "You make it sound like a chore."

Her face flushed with heat, and she curled her fingers into the sheets. "Well if it is, I'm good at it. No one's ever said otherwise." She grabbed for the covers, pulling them up to her neck. "I don't understand you. We're both adults. We want each other. We should be rolling in the sheets right now, halfway done."

"Halfway *done*? Oh, sweetheart. It would take a lifetime for me to love you the way I want to, the way you deserve to be loved. I assure you we wouldn't be *halfway done* by now."

She frowned in confusion. "Are we going to have sex or not?"

The mattress dipped as he sat beside her. "No. We are not going to *have sex*."

She crossed her arms and stared up at the ceiling.

"We're going to make love. If you want to."

She turned her head on the pillow to look at him. "What's the difference?"

He smiled sadly. "Everything." He reached for her hand.

Aggravated, frustrated, she resisted, keeping her fingers curled into her palm.

He didn't try to uncurl her fingers. Instead, he leaned down and pressed an achingly soft kiss against the back of her wrist. Her skin heated beneath his touch. He moved his mouth along her thumb, kissing, caressing.

Raw pleasure zinged straight to her core.

She drew a ragged breath, fascinated as she watched his long lashes form crescents against his cheeks when he closed his eyes and bent over her arm. The incredibly erotic treatment continued. He worshipped her skin with his mouth, his tongue blazing a trail of lava everywhere he touched. She uncurled her fingers, curious what else he might do. He pulled one of them into his mouth…and sucked.

She jerked against the mattress, her other hand curling into the sheets. Heat unfurled in her belly. Every muscle tightened. Her pulse leaped, her breaths ragged.

And he was only kissing her hand.

He raised his head, breaking contact with her skin. She almost whimpered at the loss of his heat.

"Do you want me to stop?" he whispered.

"Hell no," she gasped.

His mouth curved into a hungry smile that *did* have her whimpering this time. She shifted her legs restlessly against each other and held her arms out to him. But he didn't climb on top of her. Instead, he lowered his mouth to her elbow.

The man seemed to know where every nerve ending in her body was located. He massaged, caressed and kissed her into a frenzy. When he moved to her inner thigh, she came off the mattress, bucking against him.

Still, he refused to hurry, to take what he wanted from her, to slake his body in hers as others had done. The realization shot through her. With others, she'd had sex. This, this was what making love was about. Giving, not taking. Cherishing, gifting her with his body instead of making demands. She'd never experienced anything so incredible, so sweet, so beautiful.

"Jody? Sweetheart? Are you okay?" His breath fanned out across her thigh as he looked up at her.

She realized she was crying. Again. She swiped at the tears. "I'm more than okay. I'm in awe."

"Good tears, then?"

She drew a ragged breath. "Good tears. Um, you're not going to stop yet, are you?"

He grinned and slowly shook his head. "We're a long way from done." Then he lowered his head and flicked her core with his tongue.

"Adam!"

Where before he'd been gentle, slow, tender, now he was a demanding lover, ruthless in wringing every ounce of pleasure from her that he could. She thrashed against the bed, her hands threaded in his hair as her climax exploded through her. Still he kissed her, stroked her, drawing it out until colors burst behind her eyelids and her toes curled against the bed.

She heard the familiar sound of a foil packet being ripped open, felt the bed dip and knew he was protecting her. Then, finally, he moved up her body, fitting himself to her. She was limp, spent, but the feel of him hard and thick against her sent a jolt of heat straight through her. She dragged his lips to hers and lifted her legs, wrapping them around his waist, inviting him in.

This time, he didn't hesitate. He claimed her mouth and her body at the same time, thrusting into her. His hands moved between them, doing wicked things, building the pressure again, spiraling her up to even greater heights. He filled her so completely, so perfectly, his body fitting to hers like they were made for each other. She'd never felt such pleasure, such completeness, such joy before. As if this was meant to be. Destiny. Fate.

She felt him tighten inside her, knew he was close. But her ever-considerate lover placed her needs above his own once again, holding back, caressing, kissing, molding her body with his hands until she was again at those lofty heights, on the brink. Then he thrust into her again, sending them both tumbling over the edge. She cried out in wonder, clasping him to her as they both shattered into pieces and then slowly drifted back down to earth. Together.

Chapter 20

Duncan set his coffee down on the dining room table and glanced back and forth between Jody and Adam. "Am I missing something? Both of you are yawning like there's no tomorrow. You're either sleepy or you're worn-out. What have you been doing?"

Jody choked.

Adam coughed, then cleared his throat. Jody was so red with embarrassment that he wanted to grin. But he didn't dare. She'd probably murder him if he did.

"You have new information about the investigation?" he asked his brother.

When Jody wasn't looking, Duncan grinned and winked at Adam, letting him know he knew full well what they'd been doing.

Adam narrowed his eyes in warning. What he'd shared with Jody had been life changing. No way was he going to let his brother's juvenile teasing cheapen it in any way, for either of them.

He gave Jody an apologetic smile. It had been like a bucket of cold water having to hurry and wash and dress before his brother got there. Both of them had wanted to lie in bed all day, exploring the newfound closeness between them. But life wouldn't let them. Cold reality had intruded all too soon. He hadn't even gotten a chance to talk to her about what had happened between them, and whether her heart was as tangled up in the experience as his.

They'd only met a few days ago. But he already couldn't imagine his life without her in it somehow. Did she feel the same way? He desperately wanted to know. Instead, he was stuck here at his dining room table with his brother sitting across from him.

"Why are you frowning at me?" Duncan teased. "Did you wake up on the wrong side of the bed or something?"

"Or something," Adam gritted out, belatedly wishing he'd called his brother and told him not to come over at all. But that would have been selfish. Jody's safety rested on Duncan solving the case. Everything else, no matter how pleasurable, needed to come second.

"Just tell us what updates you have."

Duncan set his briefcase on the dining room table and popped it open. "Saying I have updates is stretching it. For as many threads as we have on this thing, they're unraveling far too slowly and not really leading anywhere."

He took out several folders and plopped them onto the table, then snapped his briefcase closed and set it on the floor. "These are the five cases Sam seemed to be focused on the most in the week before he was killed." He winced. "Sorry, Jody. I should have led with that, with a lot more finesse. The coroner confirmed a body we found was Sam. I'm very sorry for your loss."

She blinked and shook her head as if to clear it. She appeared to be having as much trouble as Adam focusing on the case. "It's okay. I mean, it's not okay. But I'd pretty much accepted that he had to be, that he was gone. To hear you confirm it isn't a shock at this point. It's just sad, and so unfair." She waved toward the folders. "Please, continue."

Adam wanted to pull her onto his lap and hold her, comfort her. But he didn't know how she'd feel about that in front of his brother. Damn it. They needed to talk, privately.

"Like I said, these are the five cases we determined that he was actively working. All of them have stacks of photographs in them."

Adam let out a deep breath and resolved to pay attention, no matter how difficult. He pulled one of the folders toward him and flipped through the small stack of pictures. "I'm not noticing any gaps in time stamps in this one."

Jody pulled another one of the folders toward her and opened it.

"There aren't any gaps in *any* of them," Duncan said.

She frowned. "No gaps?"

"None. We looked in all of the other case folders, too. Like you said, your boss was very detail oriented. Each case has an index listing the pictures that should be there. Everything matches up. We've hit a dead end."

Adam shook his head. "No. You haven't. You've learned something important."

Duncan arched a brow in question, and Jody looked at him, both waiting.

"You've learned that whatever Damien is after isn't related to any cases that Sam was officially working on."

Duncan stared at him intently. Then he sat back in his chair. "You should be an investigator, Adam. That makes complete sense. We've been looking at this all wrong. Sam must have been investigating something else, on his own. Not for a client. That would explain the gap. If he was working something on the side, he'd have no reason to keep the information at his office with his regular cases. He'd put it somewhere else. I would think it would be at his home, so he could keep it separate from regular work. But we searched there, found nothing." He shook his head. "We're still at an impasse. I'm not sure where to go with this. But I'll update the guy working on it. Maybe he can find a thread I haven't thought of."

"Guy? Not guys, plural?" Adam rested his forearms on the table. "What's going on? I thought you had a whole team working on this."

"Yeah, well, I did. We want justice for Mr. Campbell and Miss Larson. And we want to get Damien and Ned and anyone else who may be involved off the streets and locked up where they belong. But, well, resources being what they are, the guys higher up than me make executive decisions based on budget and higher priorities."

Adam swore. "What's a higher priority than making sure Jody isn't murdered? I thought the press had wind of this case and was putting pressure on you to solve it?"

Jody put her hand on his. "Please. Don't fight over me. I'll be okay."

He laced their fingers together. Even with her life on the line, she focused on others, on him. After what she'd suffered in her life, it was a miracle that she wasn't bitter and angry all the time. Instead she was selfless and sweet. He squeezed her hand in his.

"You *will* be okay," he said. "Because I'm not going to let anything happen to you. But you shouldn't have to live in fear wondering when Damien might try to strike. We need to end this. And that means the government needs to put its resources back on the case." He shot his brother an accusing look. "What are you working on if not this?"

"Something that's being kept hush-hush right now. I'm not at liberty to discuss it."

Adam leaned forward. "I'd expect that from Ian, not from you. Spill. Tell me what's going on."

"Who's Ian?" Jody asked.

Duncan gave her an apologetic smile. "Sorry. Ian is our youngest brother. He's always been a bit, well, rebellious. Doesn't exactly get along with the rest of us on the rare occasions that we even see him."

"Us? Just how big is your family?" she asked.

Duncan turned an accusing look at Adam. "Were you in too much of a hurry to even go through the niceties first?"

Jody's brows drew together in obvious confusion. But Adam wasn't confused in the least. His brother was berating him for making love to Jody without the two of them really getting to know each other first. And he had every right to shame him. Jody deserved better, and he hadn't bothered to share anything substantive about himself with her even though she'd shared the most intimate details of her life with him.

"I'm sorry I didn't tell you more about myself or my family," Adam said. "Really short version for now, I have three brothers—Duncan, Colin and Ian. My dad, William, is a retired federal judge. Margaret, my mom, is a retired prosecutor and—"

"Wait, Judge William McKenzie? I should have made the connection earlier. You're a part of the infamous Mighty McKenzies, aren't you? Your family's a legend at the courthouse. Every member is in law-enforcement in one way or the other, right?"

He winced. "We're not fans of that label. But yes, that's us. Except for Ian. But that's not important right now. The point, that we need to get back to, is that Duncan should be working this case with a full team of investigators. And he's not leaving until he tells us what so-called higher priority trumps protecting you by finding the guys who are trying to hurt you."

This time it was Duncan's turn to look uncomfortable. "I wouldn't put it that way exactly." He held up his hand to stop Adam. "But I'll remind you that I don't set the priorities. I didn't want to tell you what I was working on because I knew it would only upset you even more."

"Duncan—"

"But I'll tell you anyway. Eddie Hicks, a local city councilman, was murdered last week. Turns out he was assisting Senator Sinclair with some local research for an infrastructure bill that was passed by Congress a few days ago after pending in subcommittee for well over a year."

"Infrastructure?" Adam asked. "I vaguely remember seeing something about that on the news. Wasn't the government looking into buying up all the land associated with it?"

Duncan nodded. "A highway and bridge bill. This local councilman has been assisting Sinclair with surveys and research on the tracts of land involved, title searches and things like that. Getting appraisals and, as you said, buying up the land in preparation for the passage of the bill." He idly straightened the folders sitting on the table. "Sinclair and Hicks were apparently good friends."

Adam clenched a fist on the table. "So the senator is using his power to push the National Park Service and everyone else to steer their resources toward finding out who killed his friend instead of protecting Jody. Our taxpayer dollars at work. Nepotism is alive and well."

Duncan shoved back from the table and stood. "Like I said, I knew you'd be upset. I argued against this. In the end there was nothing I could do. I was fortunate just to get them to agree to leave one investigator assigned to the case." He set a business card on the table. "Here's his contact information, Jody, if you think of anything else that might help. I'll check back in with him as often as I can to ensure he keeps at it. And as soon as the councilman's case is resolved, I'll push to get more resources reassigned to your case." He spread his hands out beside him. "I'm really sorry. It's out of my control." He turned and headed toward the front door.

Adam followed, clicking after him on his crutches. In the opening, he let out an exasperated breath. "I'm sorry I'm taking my anger out on you, Duncan. I know none of this is your fault."

His brother gave him a sympathetic look. "You care about her."

"Well, of course I care about her." He kept his voice low, even though he doubted that Jody could hear him back in the dining room. "She's a good person. She doesn't deserve any of what's happening to her. I want Damien and whoever put him up to this found before she gets hurt."

"I know. I'm doing everything I can to help, officially and unofficially. In the meantime, just keep watching over her. And don't hesitate to call me if you need me. No matter what."

"I will. Did you mean to leave those folders?"

"They're copies. I don't think you'll find anything useful in them. But it couldn't hurt to have another pair of eyes on the case. I told the lone remaining investigator to email you if he found anything else significant."

"Thanks. I know that's against the rules. I appreciate it."

Duncan bumped him on the shoulder, his version of a hug, then headed outside.

Adam shut the door and leaned back against it. He was furious with the government for letting politics decide their priorities. But he also knew his brother well, and he knew that Duncan would have already done everything possible to change their minds. Since Duncan hadn't been successful, Adam needed to pick up where the government had left off. He was effectively on leave until his leg healed anyway. Might as well use that time to do what the government should have been doing—solving the case.

He headed to the table, his crutches making a tapping sound on the tile that drove him to distraction. When he stopped beside Jody's chair, she looked up at him in question. He wanted to kiss her so badly right now. But he knew where that would end. And his desire to make her safe outweighed everything else at the moment.

"Pretend you're Sam Campbell."

She blinked. "What? Why?"

"You knew him pretty well, right? Think like him. Tell me about his daily routine."

"I already told Duncan, during the chopper flight to the hospital—"

"I was a bit out of it during that flight. Tell me what you told him."

"Okay. I'll try."

He pulled out the chair beside her and listened to her tell him about her boss. He could see the love and admiration she felt for him. And it broke his heart that she'd suffered two devastating losses of people close to her in a handful of days. But what mattered the most was making sure that she didn't become victim number three.

"Okay," he said, when she finished talking about Sam. "What I'm hearing is he had a regimented schedule and documented everything. Other than when his grief for his wife overcame him, he never veered from that routine. So if he was working a secret case in the week before he died, he would have documented it just like everything else, right?"

"Right. Makes sense."

"But he didn't keep the documents at the office."

"Agreed. But I still don't know where he would have put them."

He tapped the table as he thought some more. "Did he seem afraid before he disappeared?"

"No. Not at all."

"Did he do anything different, out of the ordinary? Anything at all that you noticed?"

She started to shake her head, then stopped. "Well, it seems silly, really. I'm sure it's not related."

"Let me be the judge of that."

"A few days before he disappeared, he was extra nice to me. Not that he wasn't always nice. But he did more things with me than usual. I was his assistant, so usually he worked a case and I was his gofer, running errands for him. But that last week, just a few times, it was like he was *my* assistant instead. I remember it was the anniversary of his wife's death that week, and I attributed it to him being lonely."

"Be specific, Jody. What did he do?"

She thought about it a moment. "He talked to me, in the car, about my family, both my birth parents and my adoptive ones. It was awkward because I never tell anyone about them, or what happened. So it was a short conversation. I certainly didn't tell him about the abuse. He had lunch with me two or three times, asking more questions, like he was just trying to get to know me better. Oh, and one night, after work, he knew I was going to my storage unit and he said he'd like to see what I do when I'm not working for him. He seemed so lonely, so I let him come along."

"Did he give Tracy any extra attention that week?"

She shook her head. "I don't think so. Not that I recall."

"What kinds of questions did he ask you about your family?"

"The usual—whether I had brothers and sisters, where I grew up. I told him I was adopted, that my biological parents were killed in a crash. I remember he asked my birth parents' names, but after that he dropped the questions. I think he could tell I was uncomfortable and he changed the subject."

Adam shoved back from his chair. "Where's that storage unit of yours located?"

"In the middle of nowhere—not far from here, actually. We passed it on the way to your house last night. It's in the last flat section in the valley right before you climb into these foothills. Why?"

He held out his hand toward her. "We're going to take a little trip. If I'm right, we'll find the evidence that Damien was looking for hidden in your storage unit."

She took his hand and slowly stood. "You think Sam was working on a secret investigation and that he put something in my storage unit to hide it? Why would he do that?"

"I don't know. But it's the only place that makes sense, given your accounting of what he did that last week."

"Wait." She tugged her hand from his. "I'm getting my gun. It's in my room."

He tapped the holster on his hip. "I've got mine. It's my job to protect you."

"And it's my job to protect you."

She turned away before he could argue and headed up the stairs.

Chapter 21

Jody rubbed her hands up and down her arms. On the other side of the small table in the middle of her storage unit, Adam sat flipping through the folder they'd found.

"I can't believe Sam snuck that in here, or that he hid it in a pile of my photographs. Why would he do that?"

Adam didn't answer. She wasn't even sure that he'd heard her. He seemed engrossed in whatever he was reading.

"Adam?"

"Hmm?"

She sighed and glanced over her shoulder at the opening. The rolling door was down. Adam was so worried about keeping her safe that he'd insisted on keeping them locked inside while they searched the place. She never usually shut the door when she was here. It was too much like a cave. Or a prison.

Or her room back home, when she'd watched a similar slit beneath her door and prayed she wouldn't hear footsteps in the hallway.

She swallowed and turned back toward Adam. He was frowning down at a piece of paper.

"More title searches and real estate transactions?" she asked.

"Pretty much. And bills of sale. I'm no expert on that infrastructure bill Duncan mentioned earlier in relation to that city councilman and Senator Sinclair. But I remember a few local news reports about the government buying up land for right of way." He lifted his gaze to hers. "A lot of these tracts of land mentioned in these bills of sale are ones from the news reports. The buyer is the government. The seller on most of these is a company named Preferred Parcel Purchasing Corporation. That's a lot of P's. Remind you of anyone connected to you?"

Her pulse leaped in her throat. "Peter, Patricia, Patience, Patrick, Paul. You think my adoptive father set up a shell company? And that he's involved in some kind of crooked real estate deals that Sam discovered?"

"We've already established that Peter Ingram is a lowlife. Connecting the dots to shady business deals isn't much of a stretch. Another company listed on some of these transactions is Amelia Enterprises. Isn't your adoptive mother's name Amelia?"

She nodded, her entire body flushing hot and cold. She'd always thought of her adoptive father as evil. But could he be evil enough to have had someone kill Sam and Tracy? Was he trying to have her killed, too? Because of land deals? And money?

"I don't understand," she said. "He's wealthy.

There's no reason for him to do anything illegal to get more money."

"Maybe Peter isn't as well-off as you think. Bad investments, a struggling economy, poor decisions—they can quickly ruin someone financially. If he's had heavy losses, he might be desperate enough to make deals with some pretty bad people—like Damien Flint." He held one of the documents up and pointed to a bold signature scrawled across the bottom. "The witness on *all* of these documents is Judge Martin Jackson. Ever heard of him?"

Something about the name sent butterflies loose in her stomach. "I'm not sure. It sounds familiar. But it's not an uncommon name."

"Maybe." He didn't sound convinced. "I know I've seen it somewhere recently." He flipped the folder closed. "It will come to me. In the meantime, I think we should head back to my house. I'll tell Duncan what we've found and have him send someone for this folder. He'll want to search the rest of the storage unit." His jaw tightened. "When he has resources. Is that okay with you?"

"Of course. If it helps with the case, by all means. Did you find anything in the folder to explain why someone would want to hurt Sam? Or Tracy?"

"Or you?"

She swallowed. "Or me."

"I haven't found a connection yet. But I will. Or Duncan will. Don't worry, Jody. I'll take care of you."

"I'll take care of you, too, Adam."

He smiled, the first smile she'd seen in a long while.

"We'll take care of each other, then," he said.

A few moments later they were heading down the

two-lane road back toward town. Barbed-wire fences ran along both sides of the road with cows grazing in the green fields behind them. How ironic that such beauty and serenity could exist just a few feet from their car when her world seemed to be turning upside down.

Adam tensed beside her.

"What is it?" she asked.

"I remember where I saw that signature before, the name Judge Martin Jackson. That's the same judge who ruled on the case involving your adoptive father."

Her hands curled against the seat beside her. "You mean...the abuse case? My abuse case?"

He nodded. "I told you that my dad's a retired federal judge. From what I heard growing up, judges specialize and tend to stay in their specialties. It doesn't make sense to me that a family court judge is signing a bunch of real estate transaction documents. Even if he did switch specialties, the coincidence is sending up all kinds of red flags."

"What coincidence? The real estate transactions have nothing to do with me."

"They have everything to do with you. Your boss was looking into them and hid the evidence in your storage unit. Those have to be the documents Damien was talking about. He said pictures, and maybe there are some pictures, too. But maybe he meant documents, or whoever hired him didn't know if someone had physical printouts or just photographs." He waved his hand. "Doesn't matter. What does matter is that the same judge who signed them played a huge role in your life early on, signing other legal papers associated with you. Sam asked you about your birth parents.

And your adoptive parents. Then he hid those papers where you'd eventually find them. Why would he do that if all of this isn't connected?"

He stared through the windshield at the winding road in front of them. His hands tightened on the steering wheel. "Didn't you tell me that Peter was a real estate developer? That he was always amassing property in the mountains?"

A cold chill seemed to run up her spine. "You think…you think he's somehow connected to all of this? Because the papers are about real estate?" She gave a humorless laugh. "That's quite a leap."

They drove in silence for a moment, then Adam slammed a hand against the steering wheel. "The timeline. That's it."

"What?"

"The timeline. Three days. You said Damien told you that Sam's PI firm had been a problem for three days. That was on Saturday. What happened three days before Saturday? What happened on Wednesday of last week?"

The truth slammed into her. She started to shake. "The councilman was murdered."

"Exactly. And he was helping a senator with the infrastructure bill. The government has to buy out everyone who owns land that they need for right of way. Which means researching titles and deeds and finding out who the owners are. That's what the councilman was helping with, because the land involved was here in Gatlinburg."

"Where my adoptive father owns a lot of real estate."

"Do *you*?"

She frowned. "What?"

"You told me your biological parents wanted to make sure you were taken care of. And yet their house passed to your adoptive family instead of to you. That seems unusual, to say the least. Isn't it also surprising that they didn't give you a generous enough trust fund to see you through life, not just college, but they left a huge fund for the Ingrams to take care of a house?"

She rubbed her arms again. "The thought has definitely crossed my mind before, yes."

"A judge ruled against you when you had the trust fund audited. Was that Judge Jackson, too?"

"No. I don't remember the judge's name, but it was a woman. It wasn't Martin Jackson."

"Then the audit may have been legit. Which again brings to question why your parents wouldn't provide better for you. The answer could be that they left you other investments, like real estate. They may have left you a fortune in land thinking it always appreciates in value and you'd be set for life, that you could sell some of it whenever you needed more money."

"But I didn't get *any* assets in the will other than the trust fund."

He tapped the folder on the seat between them. "You sure about that? Wills can be faked. Sam was tracing the titles on all of the land in this folder, either for a secret client that we haven't found yet or because he heard something himself that made him suspicious and decided to follow up. Either way, it leads back to you. Because he left the information in your storage unit, for you to find. Maybe the land in that folder was actually owned at one time by the Radcliffes—your biological parents. Which means the land should have passed to you but never did. Sam got sloppy, took one picture too many, and Damien or maybe Peter saw him. They went through his things, realized he'd figured out what they were doing—making a killing, probably millions of dollars—selling your land to the government as part of that infrastructure bill. They have to destroy any hint of impropriety about those land deals or they'll lose everything and wind up in prison."

She pressed a hand against her throat. "If you're right, my adoptive father wants me—"

"Dead. So he can enjoy the millions of dollars that were supposed to be yours." He tapped the folder again. "This is what he wants. Once he has it and any pictures that Sam hid, there's no reason to keep you alive any longer. You're a liability, a time bomb waiting to blow up his financial empire if you ever decide to contest the will and dig into your parents' financial history. As soon as we get this information to Duncan, we'll both grab a suitcase and head out of town to lie low somewhere until this is resolved. No arguments. I want you safe and as far away from Peter Ingram as possible."

"No arguments from me."

A black Dodge Charger came into view on the next hill up ahead, coming toward them.

Jody blinked and leaned forward in her seat. "Adam, that car. It looks just like the one that was parked near the Sugarland Mountain trailhead. The one Damien was driving."

Adam stared hard at the car coming their way. The Charger sped past them with a familiar profile sitting in the driver's seat.

"Adam—"

"I know. It was Damien. Grab my phone. Call Duncan." He kept driving down the road, heading toward his house. When he glanced in the rearview mirror, he swore.

Jody whirled around in her seat. The Charger had hit the brakes. Damien was making a three-point turn in the middle of the road. The car took off, heading straight for them.

"My phone, Jody. Forget Duncan. Call 911."

She grabbed his cell phone out of his pants pocket, her breaths coming in ragged gasps. "What's your pass code?"

He told her, and she punched in the numbers.

Adam grabbed his pistol out of the holster and slammed the accelerator. His car was a sleek sedan with leather seats and all the creature comforts his money could buy. But it didn't have the horsepower the Charger had. Damien was rapidly gaining on them.

"We're four miles from my house. We aren't going to make it." He reached up and slammed back the inside cover of the moon roof.

"What are you doing?" Jody punched Send on the call.

"You're going to hold the wheel while I shoot the bastard. Did you call 911?"

"I did but nothing's happening!" She yanked the phone back to look at the screen. "The call didn't go through!" Her hands shook as she redialed.

Tat-tat-tat-tat-tat-tat-tat!

Bam! Bam!

The car bumped and swerved, skidding toward the drainage ditch on the side of the road.

Adam fought the wheel. "The tires! Hold on!"

"Nine-one-one, what's your emergency?" A tinny voice came through the phone.

She clung to the armrest as the car headed toward the ditch and a group of trees on the edge of the road. "This is Jody Ingram and Special Agent Adam McKenzie," she said so fast the words ran together. "Damien Flint's shooting at us on the road to Rutherford—"

"Brace yourself!" Adam yelled.

She screamed. The car slid off the road, hopped the ditch and slammed into a tree. Everything went black.

Chapter 22

"You idiot! Bringing them here was the last thing you should have done. What if someone saw you?"

"No one saw me. I brought you the folder! After all the trouble I've gone through, including getting stabbed, you should be thanking me instead of yelling at me. My guys are hiding the car. No harm done."

A string of violent curses followed.

The words drifted through Jody's mind like a canoe slogging through mud. Someone was shouting at someone else. Both of the voices seemed to be coming through a long tunnel. They were achingly familiar. Not in a good way. She groaned and pressed a hand to her throbbing head.

"Jody?" Another voice, whispering next to her ear. Deep, soothing, full of concern.

"Adam?"

"Thank God." He pulled her close. "Where do you hurt?"

She blinked and opened her eyes. Then promptly closed them, her stomach lurching. "The room is spinning."

"You lost consciousness. You probably have a concussion. What about your arms? Your legs? I didn't see any cuts or obvious breaks. Does anything other than your head hurt?"

"Everything hurts."

"I know, sweetheart. I'm so sorry. Can you try to open your eyes again?"

More shouting. Something about deeds and pictures and...infrastructure? That voice. She knew that voice. It was...oh no!

Her eyes popped open. The room was still moving, but not as badly as before. She was sitting on the floor, her back against a wall. Adam knelt in front of her, the side of his head smeared with blood yet again.

He smiled. "There you are. Better now? The room isn't spinning?"

She reached out a shaky hand. "Your head. You're always getting hurt."

He ducked away. "I'm fine. Now that you're back in the land of the living, let's work on getting out of here. Do you know where we are?"

She looked past him and winced. "My room. My old room. When I was a little girl."

"One of Damien's men carried you up here. After Damien shot out our tires, we crashed. You hit your head on the side window." He framed her face in his hands and pressed a whisper-soft kiss against her lips. "You scared me to death. I thought I might lose you."

She clung to his hands. "What happened? Why are we here? Is that my...is Peter downstairs?"

He nodded again. "Damien had a submachine gun. I lost my pistol in the crash and couldn't do anything to stop him."

She reached down to her side.

"Your gun is gone, too," he told her. "We don't have any weapons. But that doesn't mean we're defenseless. As long as they're arguing, we know where they are. Can you stand?" He didn't wait for her reply. He grabbed her around the waist and lifted her to her feet.

She'd squeezed her eyes shut because the room was spinning again. But when she realized she was clutching his shoulders to steady herself, and that she was bending over at the waist to do it, she forced her eyes open again. Adam was still kneeling on the floor.

"Good job," he said. "I've tied some bedsheets together and anchored them to the four-poster bed. You need to climb out that window and run. Looks like there are some trees ten yards out. That should give you good cover." He tugged her hand to get her moving.

She pulled her hand out of his grasp. "Where are your crutches? Did those monsters take them away from you? I'm not leaving you here."

He frowned. "Jody, we don't have time to argue. We don't know whether that 911 call did any good. You didn't have time to give them an address. We have to assume that help isn't coming."

"I told them Rutherford Estates. And we crashed. They'll see our car, look for us. They have our names. Why are you shaking your head?"

"You said Rutherford. And you gave them our

names. They'll look me up and realize I live in Rutherford Estates, so they'll go to my house. Not here."

"But the car. Surely they'll see the crash, know something is wrong. When they don't find us at your house, won't they search the whole subdivision, go door to door? Canvassing. That's what it's called, right?"

"From what I could tell from the yelling downstairs, it sounds like Damien and his guys cleaned up the accident scene. I don't know that the police will have cause to go door to door searching for us." He frowned and glanced past her toward the door, which she noted no longer had the dead bolt on it that someone had installed for her years ago.

"I don't hear them anymore," he said. "You need to hurry. I'll do what I can to stall them. But you have to get out of here." He pushed her toward the window again.

She shoved his hand away. "You can't even stand. I'm not leaving you."

He grabbed one of the posts on the bed's footboard and shoved to his feet. "There. I'm standing. I'm not helpless. Now go."

"You're as white as a sheet."

"It hurts, all right? But I'm fine. Please, Jody. Just go."

Fresh blood marked the denim of his jeans. He wasn't even close to fine, and they both knew it. She took a quick look around. Everything in the room was eerily similar to the way it had looked when she was little, probably because the house was so large there was no reason to redecorate this particular room. Dust covers were draped over the bed, the chair in the corner, the desk. If all of her things were still here, there were crutches she'd used when her adoptive father had slammed her into a wall and broken her leg. They'd be too short. But maybe Adam could still use them like canes to help him walk, like he'd done with the tree branch in the mountains. She ran to the closet.

"Jody, what are you doing? Get out of here."

"I'm not leaving you. So quit telling me to go." She flipped the light on and rushed inside. Her stomach dropped when she saw nothing that looked familiar. The large closet was obviously being used for storage now. There were boxes stacked in neat rows all across the back. Labels declared them as "crafts." Probably for Amelia. She'd always loved making things and took up new craft hobbies all the time. Or at least she used to. There might be something in these boxes Jody could use.

She started tearing them open. In the third one, she found nylon rope used for macramé, along with a pair of scissors. In another box she found picture frames and a shadow box. She yanked out the shadow box and broke it apart. The pieces of wood were thick and long, perfect for making a splint. She'd have Adam fixed up in no time. Then both of them could climb out of the window together.

Holding the rope and wood in one hand, scissors in the other, she hurried back into the bedroom. Her mouth dropped open in horror, and she stumbled to a halt. Adam was still standing with one hand holding the bedpost. But he had a wicked-looking long gun pointed at him, and Damien was holding it.

"Well, well, well. The last little PI finally makes an appearance." He nodded toward his left arm, still in a sling. "Maybe I'll get a chance for payback after all.

Drop the scissors and that other junk." He jerked his head toward the open bedroom door. "Daddy's waiting."

She cast a miserable glance toward Adam and dropped her splint supplies to the floor. He was right. She should have gone out the window. Now there would be no help for him, or her. "I'm so sorry, Adam."

He gave her an encouraging smile without a hint of anger. "Go on. We'll be okay."

Damien laughed. "Sure, yeah, you'll be okay." He chuckled and jerked his head again. "After you."

Jody straightened her spine and headed into the hallway.

"Now you, *cop.* Go."

A loud thump sounded behind her, followed by a pained grunt.

Damien cursed.

Jody spun around.

Adam was on his hands and knees. He must have fallen. Damien pulled his leg back as if to kick him.

Jody ran forward. "Don't touch him!"

Damien turned the gun on her. "Back. Off." He aimed his gun at her abdomen.

"I'm okay. Jody, get out of here. Go." Adam hauled himself upright, using the bed for support again. "I'm okay."

She rushed to him in spite of his protests and the gun following her every move. She shoved her shoulder under his left arm, acting as his crutch.

He gave her an admonishing look, once again not happy that she'd put herself in more danger to help him. But he didn't argue as he limped with her out of the room under the watchful gaze of Damien and his gun.

Going downstairs was much easier because he used the banister and hopped down each step. But once they were on the ground floor without a banister to hold, he had to lean on her in order to limp into the family room.

"Stop right there," Damien ordered.

They stopped in the middle of the room. Ned and another armed man they'd never seen before lounged against the left side of the massive fireplace. A third gunman stood on the right side of the fireplace. Damien crossed the room and joined him. And directly in the middle, ten feet away from her and Adam, stood the man who'd made her childhood worse than any nightmare.

His dark brown hair was stylishly short with just a hint of gray at the temples. The charcoal-colored suit he wore was tailored perfectly to compliment his broad shoulders and trim waist. Gold cuff links winked in the light of the chandelier suspended from the twenty-foot ceiling above them. To anyone else, he'd look like a handsome businessman, perfectly groomed and ready for an important meeting. To Jody, he looked like a monster.

She started to shake.

Adam's arm tightened around her shoulders.

A loud crash sounded off to their left. Everyone turned toward the sound, except the monster. He let out a deep sigh and simply turned his head to look at the woman who'd just emerged from the kitchen and had dropped a tray of drinks onto the travertine floor, shattering the glasses. She stared at Jody, her eyes big and round, her mouth dropping open.

"Amelia," the monster said. "Our daughter has finally come home to visit."

Her mother didn't move, didn't say anything. She just stared at Jody in obvious horror.

Footsteps sounded.

Jody looked toward her adoptive father. His polished shoes clicked against the floor as he strode toward her.

Adam tensed.

Peter stopped three feet away and sighed heavily again. "Jody, Jody, Jody. Always the troublemaker. Maybe I should take you upstairs and turn you over my knee, eh? Teach you another lesson?"

"You'll never touch a hair on her head again, you lecherous pervert," Adam snapped.

Peter's eyes narrowed.

A muffled sob sounded from Amelia. She whirled around and ran into the kitchen.

Peter rolled his eyes and shook his head. Ignoring Adam, he stared at Jody, a nauseatingly hungry look in his eyes. "If I only had more time." He clucked his tongue. "But I have a funeral to attend. A dear friend died tragically in a car crash last week." He chuckled again. "Seems to happen a lot to my friends. Car crashes." He winked.

Jody's stomach lurched at the implication. Her parents, her real ones, had died in a car crash. Had Peter had something to do with that too?

"Fortunately for me—" his voice was lowered in a conspiratorial tone "—my dear friend had finished the task I gave him before his...demise."

"Forging land leases?" Adam accused. "Helping you arrange accidents for the true owners? Convincing Senator Sinclair to push an infrastructure bill so you could sell all the land you stole to the government and make a fortune?"

Peter slowly turned his head like a snake and speared Adam with his dark-eyed gaze. "To be fair, I bought some of that land legitimately."

"You didn't buy *Jody's* land legitimately. You stole her inheritance. Including this house."

"Well, well, well. Someone's been busy, haven't they? Faking that damn will cost me a pretty penny. I spent years covering that up. And all it took was one very stupid drunk councilman in a bar to complain to the wrong PI about the problems he was having performing title searches to bring it all crashing down around my ears. I gave him explicit instructions to exclude the Radcliffe properties from those searches. But he wasn't the detail-oriented man he should have been. And Sam Campbell started sticking his nose where it didn't belong. Who knew he'd recognize the Radcliffe name? My bad luck that you were working for him. Doesn't matter now, though."

"I'll bet you killed the councilman. And you killed Sam," Jody accused. "And Tracy. And my real parents. For what? Land? Money?" She waved her hand to encompass the mansion. "By all accounts you were quite wealthy even before my parents' deaths. And now you have this. Don't you have enough already?"

He smiled. "You poor, silly girl. You can never have enough when it comes to money."

She surged forward, wanting to slam her fists into his smiling face. But Adam tightened his arm around her shoulders, anchoring her against him. He turned his body slightly as if to protect her from her adoptive father. It caused her arm around his waist to bump against something beneath his shirt, something in his back pocket.

She glanced up at him. He was staring intently at her. *The scissors.*

That's what was in his pocket. He must have fallen on purpose in her bedroom so he could grab them. And he was letting her know he would use them when the time was right. But how could the time ever be right with four gunmen twenty feet away? And who knew if Peter was armed? She cleared her throat and looked back at the monster.

"You have the land and the folder," she said. "I don't have any proof that you stole anything from me. It would just be my word against yours. You can let us go."

He clucked his tongue again. "Right. And your boyfriend here would just ignore everything that's happened? He's a cop. Cops don't ignore and let things go. At least, not the honest ones who refuse to take bribes. And word on the street is that he's one of the good guys. Which means, of course, you both have to die."

"Bribes?" Adam said, obviously stalling for time. "Just like you bribed Judge Jackson when Jody went to court? And bribed him again to file those bogus land claims?"

Peter speared him with a look full of hate. "You know way too much, cop."

"What about the pictures?" Damien stepped forward. "I chased them through those stupid mountains to find out where that PI hid the pictures. There weren't any pictures in the folder."

Peter rolled his eyes, a pained expression on his face. "There were never any pictures, *you moron*. I made that up because you didn't need to know exactly what I was looking for. You were just supposed to find out where

Campbell might hide any information he collected." He pointed at a folder lying on a decorative table against the wall. The folder that had been in Jody's storage unit. "Everything I need is in there. Now all you have to do is kill these two and I'll be on my way."

"No." The voice, barely above a whisper, came from the kitchen doorway.

Everyone turned to see Amelia once again standing there. This time she was holding a pistol. And it was pointed at her husband.

"Ho, ho," Damien exclaimed, laughing. "Trouble in paradise, boss?"

"Shut up." Peter stared at his wife. "What do you think you're doing, Amelia?"

"What I should have done when Jody was a little girl. Stopping you." Her lower lip wobbled and the gun shook in her hand. "I'm so sorry, Jody. I swear I never even suspected that he might be hurting you until that counselor from your school talked to me."

"Shut *up*, woman." Peter strode toward Amelia. "She lied. I never did *anything* to her."

Amelia wrapped both hands around the gun and brought it up higher, pointing directly at Peter's head. This time, her hands weren't shaking. "Not one step closer. I'll shoot you. I will."

He stopped, his eyes narrowing. "Now why would you do that?"

"Because you hurt little girls!" she cried out. She looked toward Jody. "I swear, I never knew. I asked Patricia and Patience when your counselor brought those charges against Peter. But they said you were lying, that their daddy would never do that. He would never do those horrible, awful things." Tears spilled over and slid down her cheeks. The gun started shaking again. "They were little girls, too. I believed them. I never knew they were scared of him, that they lied. For him. Until Patricia had her baby last month. And she and her husband wouldn't let Peter near the baby." A sob burst between her clenched teeth. "Oh, God. Your own daughters. How could you, Peter?"

His face turned a bright red. He looked at Damien. "Shoot her."

Damien's men raised their guns.

Adam took a limping step forward, his hand going behind his back. Jody grabbed his arm, but he shook it off.

"Adam," she whispered, "please don't. They'll kill you."

He took another wobbling step and pulled the scissors out of his waistband.

"Hold it," Damien said, raising his hand and motioning toward his men. "Lower your weapons."

Adam stopped, the scissors clutched in his right hand. But no one seemed to notice. They were all looking back and forth between Amelia, Peter and Damien.

Adam took another step, and another, moving closer to Peter, the scissors down by his side, half concealed by his hand.

Jody wanted to grab him, stop him. Instead, she moved with him, trying to keep from having a big gap between them to make it less obvious that he'd moved closer to Peter.

Damien faced his boss. "You some kind of perv, man? You like to hurt little girls?"

Peter looked down his nose at Damien. "You're a

murderer and a thug. Don't tell me you're suddenly developing a conscience."

Sirens sounded in the distance.

Damien and his men exchanged worried glances.

"Don't be idiots," Peter said. "They're going somewhere else. Not here."

"Yeah, well. We ain't taking that chance," Damien replied. "Not for some sicko who hurts kids." He motioned to his men and they headed for the door.

Peter stepped toward them. "One million dollars. I'll give one million dollars to the man who shoots my wife."

Jody gasped.

Amelia's eyes widened.

All four men turned around.

"A million?" one of them asked, aiming his gun at Amelia.

"No." This time it was Adam who stepped forward.

The man turned his gun toward Adam.

Jody stepped forward. "No!"

Adam shoved her behind him. "You really want to go to jail for a pedophile?"

The man's gaze darted to Peter, who was now glaring at Adam.

"Even if you don't care what he's done," Adam continued, his voice calm, matter-of-fact, "do you think you can trust him to follow through with the money?"

"Two million!" Peter yelled.

The man swung his pistol back toward Amelia.

She stood frozen, tears tracking down her chin. She didn't seem to know what to do and was obviously too scared to pull the trigger on her gun to defend herself.

"Wait!" Adam yelled.

The man looked at him but kept his gun trained on Amelia.

"He's asking you to kill his wife," Adam said. "You really think he'll honor his word to you, someone he barely knows? Everything he does is about money and protecting himself. And you think he'll give you a million dollars, two million dollars? More likely he'll hire someone else to take you out for a few thousand. He kills everyone who gets in his way or threatens what he wants. Listen to the sirens. The police are almost here."

The sirens were much louder now. But were they coming here? Or to Adam's house a few blocks away?

Adam took another step forward. "When the police get here and find Amelia dead, what do you think Peter will tell them? That you killed her. A home invasion. He'll blame everything that happens here on you. The forensics will back him up. You go to prison. He goes on to enjoy his millions."

The gunmen shared concerned looks. One of them headed out the door. Ned followed, leaving Damien and the other gunman.

"Those cops aren't coming here," Damien said, looking like he was considering cashing in on Peter's offer.

"Of course they aren't," Peter said. "No one has any reason to suspect me of anything. You and your men made sure of it."

"Jody called 911," Adam rushed to say. "Right before the crash. They're definitely coming here. Sounds to me like they're three or four minutes out. You'd better hurry and decide whether you want to go to prison or get out of here."

"Check her phone," Damien ordered the other gunman. "Hurry."

"I don't have it," Jody started to say, thinking she'd lost Adam's phone in the crash. But the gunman pulled the phone out of his own pocket.

"Pass code," Damien said. "What's the code to unlock it?"

She gave him the code that Adam had given her in the car. The gunman keyed it in and swiped the screen a few times. His face went pale. "She ain't lying. She called 911."

"Screw it," Damien said. "Let's get out of here. Wait in the Charger. I'll be right there."

His partner threw the phone down and ran out the door.

"Did he really hurt you as a little girl?" Damien asked, looking straight at Jody.

Her face flushed with heat. "Yes."

"Sick bastard." Damien pointed his gun at Peter.

Peter threw his hands up. "My lawyer is working to get your brother out of jail. You kill me and what do you think he'll do?"

"Come on, man!" A yell came from outside.

Damien's hand flexed on the gun. "You'd better not renege on our deal or I'll come after you, you sicko." He tossed his gun toward Peter and ran.

Peter caught the gun and swung it toward Amelia.

"No!" Adam threw the scissors like a javelin toward Peter.

Boom! Boom!

Peter fell to the floor, the scissors embedded deep in his neck. He gagged and clasped his hands around the wound, blood pouring through the gaps between his fingers. His knees drew up, blood darkening his pants where Amelia's bullet had found its mark.

He'd never hurt another little girl again.

Jody whirled around toward Amelia. "Oh no! Mom!"

Amelia blinked in confusion and looked down. Red bloomed on her breast above her heart and quickly spread, saturating her shirt. Peter's bullet had found its mark, too.

Jody ran to her, catching her just as Amelia's knees buckled beneath her. She couldn't hold her up and fell with her to the floor.

"Mom, Mom. Oh no, please. Mom." She pressed her hands against the wound, desperately trying to stop the bleeding.

Adam dropped to the floor beside her, his phone in his hand. "We need an ambulance." He rattled off the address that he'd found on the internet just last night while looking into Jody's past. "Send the police, too," he said. "I hear them in the subdivision. They're probably at my home from a previous 911 call, but we're here. We're the ones who called them."

"Jody?" Amelia blinked up at her. "Are you there?"

Tears flooded Jody's eyes. "Yes. I'm here."

Adam yanked off his shirt and pushed Jody's hands away. "I've got it." He pressed his shirt hard against the wound.

Amelia gasped, her lips turning white.

"Sorry, Mrs. Ingram. I have to press hard to stop the bleeding."

Jody grabbed Amelia's hand and held it tightly in her own as she gently wiped the hair out of Amelia's face. "Hold on. Help is on the way."

232 Smoky Mountains Ranger

Amelia blinked, and her vision seemed to clear, her hand tightening on Jody's. "Sweet, sweet girl. I'm so sorry. I swear, I never knew. I didn't."

"It's okay," Jody whispered, her tears dropping onto their joined hands. "It's okay."

"No. It's not." Amelia coughed, and bright red blood bubbled out of her mouth.

"Don't try to talk." Jody gently wiped the blood away. "Save your strength."

"I put the lock on your door." Amelia clung to Jody's hand and searched her gaze. "I didn't think you were telling the truth. But I put the lock on your door to be sure, as a test. He never...he never said anything, never took it off. So I thought... I thought that proved me right. That he wasn't the man you said he was." She coughed again and started choking.

"Jody, back up."

She scooted back and Adam rolled Amelia onto her side. She stopped coughing. He moved forward, his knees propping her up while he applied pressure to her wound again.

Jody bent down, maintaining eye contact. Amelia was frighteningly pale, her eyes turning glassy.

"Jody?"

"I'm here." Her voice broke as she clasped Amelia's hands. "I won't leave you. I'm here."

"I loved you, Jody. I should have been stronger, smarter. I should have fought for you."

"You did. He never hurt me again after you put that lock on my door," Jody said, her heart breaking. "I love you, too. You were the only mother I ever knew. It's okay. Everything is going to be okay."

"Forgive me?" Amelia pleaded. "Please forgive me."

"I forgive you."

A smile curved her mother's red-stained lips. Then her hand went slack in Jody's.

"Mama?" She shook Amelia's hand. "Mama?"

"Miss, let us help her," a voice said behind her.

"Mama?"

Adam was suddenly there, pulling her back. "Let her go, Jody. You have to let her go."

"No! Mama?"

Adam lifted her in his arms, then limped to one of the couches and collapsed onto the cushions, holding her tightly against him.

"Shh," he whispered against the top of her head. "Shh."

He stroked her back and rocked her as the paramedics worked on Amelia. Jody drew a ragged breath and closed her eyes, clinging to him and doing something she hadn't done since she was a little girl and a judge sent her back to live with the monster.

She prayed.

Chapter 23

Three months later, Jody stood at the entrance to the Sugarland Mountain Trail, a jacket around her to ward off the chilly autumn temps up high in the mountains. A backpack of supplies was strapped on her shoulders. Sensible boots protected her feet, gave her sure footing.

There was no cattle gate across the entrance this time, no warning signs declaring that the trail was closed, no man with a gun chasing her. She was all alone and ready to begin another journey, another chapter of her life.

She pulled her cell phone out of her pants pocket. No bars, no service. But it showed the time. She'd been checking it every few minutes. When she realized the wait was over, a mixture of dread and excitement sent a shot of adrenaline through her. This was it. No turning back now. She started up the path.

Her steps were measured, careful. She kept glancing at her phone, checking the time, checking her surroundings to get her bearings. She didn't want to be late. Or early. She wanted everything to be perfect.

A few minutes later, she reached the curve in the path, the one where Adam had disappeared all those months ago as he chased Damien. The one where she and Adam had run back the other way with two gunmen after them.

Her pulse sped up, her body shaking. She pushed back the fear, knowing it was silly now. Damien and his men weren't chasing her this time. The police had rounded up everyone involved in Peter Ingram's schemes, and they were all either already convicted and in prison or in jail waiting for their trials. She was safe. No reason to be afraid.

Well, at least not about bad guys, anyway.

She forced her feet forward and rounded the curve, then hurried to her destination. When she reached the spot where Adam had forced her to take that huge leap of faith, she stopped. And looked out at the mountains and the Chimney Tops beyond. And waited.

"Jody?"

His voice sent a jolt of yearning straight through her. She drew a deep breath and turned.

Adam stood ten feet away, having just come around the corner from the other direction. He was wearing his ranger's uniform again, his gun holstered at his side, his new radio clipped to his belt.

"How's the leg?" She waved toward his left leg, which had a metal brace around it from ankle to knee.

He took a step toward her, then stopped again, his gaze wary. "It's fine. Thanks."

She swallowed, hating that she'd been the reason for that wariness. "This is your first day back on the job, isn't it?"

He frowned. "How did you know?"

She took a step toward him. "I asked your brother. Duncan."

His jaw tightened. "He told you I was walking this trail, didn't he?"

She nodded.

"Why? Why are you here?"

She took another step forward. "You're not going to make this easy, are you?"

He looked away, out toward the Chimney Tops. "I don't know what you want from me, Jody. I tried visiting, calling, texting, emailing, until I felt like a stalker and had to stop." He looked back at her. "It's been three months since your...since Peter Ingram died. You haven't contacted me once."

She moved closer. "I know. I'm sorry. I'm so sorry."

"You say that all the time. It doesn't mean anything anymore."

She sighed and raked her hair back. "You're right. I'm trying to stop apologizing so much. I've been going to therapy again, trying to move on, letting go of all the guilt I've been carrying around." She let out a harsh laugh. "At least I've finally figured out why I've always felt so guilty."

"Your sisters. You blame yourself for leaving when you turned eighteen. You've worried that you didn't fight for them, too. You left them behind, and it's always bothered you."

She blinked. "How do you know that?"

He gave her a sad smile. "Because I know *you*, Jody Vanessa Radcliffe."

She blinked again. "How did you know I changed my last name?"

He tapped the badge clipped to his belt. "Cop." He dropped his hand to his side. "Or I might have heard it from Duncan. He told me he'd offered you an investigator job with the National Park Service. You had to put your legal name on the paperwork."

She smiled. "You've been keeping tabs on me."

"Not since the first month. Like I said, I felt like a stalker, so I quit. Duncan, on the other hand, won't stop talking about you. He's torturing me." He clamped his lips together and looked away.

"Torturing you?" She took another step. "Hearing about me is torture?"

His fingers curled into his palms, but he didn't say anything.

"It's been torture for me, too," she admitted. "Being away from you."

His gaze shot to hers. Still, he said nothing.

"My mom's fine, in case you're wondering. You saved her life that day. You kept your cool, thought to grab the phone and call for help when I was completely losing it. The doctors said if you hadn't gotten the EMTs there so fast, if you hadn't kept pressure on the wound, she'd be dead. Thank you, Adam. Thank you for saving her."

He shook his head. "I did my job. And we were lucky you'd called 911 and the police and EMTs were already at my house."

"Maybe. Maybe not. You have a talent for saving

people." She took another step forward. "You saved me. So many times. In so many ways."

He stared at her, some of the hostility and frustration easing from his expression. The wariness was back. But along with it was something else. Hope.

"I needed the time, the distance," she said. "From you, from my overwhelming feelings for you. Because I didn't believe it could be real. We'd known each other for, what, a few days? Less than a week? Under traumatic circumstances. I didn't trust my feelings. I had to process them. And I had to process my 'unhealthy attitude' toward sex." She used air quotes. "Apparently my adoptive father did a number on my psyche and I never understood what a normal physical relationship was supposed to be like. Until you."

"You're giving me too much credit."

She shrugged. "Not in my opinion. But I'm working through my relationship hang-ups. And my relationships with my adoptive family. I had to deal with my mother in the hospital, her recovery, getting to know my sisters and brothers, unraveling the legal tangle that Peter Ingram left for all of us." She shook her head. "It was a mess. I was a mess. That's why I've been going to a therapist."

He started to step forward, then stopped. "Are you okay?" He cleared his throat. "I mean, your adoptive family, the legal stuff."

"My adoptive…my *family* is…well, awkward might be the best way to put it. My sisters weren't abused in spite of Amelia's fears, by the way. Thank God for that. But they suspected what their father had done to me. That's why Patricia wouldn't let him be alone with her new daughter. She didn't trust him. Still, they grew up with him as their dad, loving him as best they could with all that poison running just beneath the surface. I think they blame me for what's happened to the family now. I can understand that. But I don't apologize to anyone for it. Like I said, I'm moving on. From the guilt, from my past." She stepped closer. "I'm moving toward my future now."

He looked down at her feet and smiled. "You're wearing boots."

"And a shiny new backpack with supplies. I learned my lesson from the best. Always be prepared for the worst." She took another step. "But hope for the best."

He stared at her intently, longingly, and took a step toward her. "I saw that your family house is for sale."

She nodded. "The courts awarded me all of the money, the house, even the land that Peter tried to swindle from me. The infrastructure deal is still going through. I didn't try to stop it. But all the money from the land sales went to me."

"You're rich now."

"In some people's eyes, maybe. I gave a huge chunk of it to my mother and siblings. Including the house. But no one wants to live there because of everything that happened. It was their decision to sell."

"You gave a multimillion-dollar mansion plus more money on top of that to your family? After they turned their backs on you? And didn't protect you?" His tone wasn't accusing, just curious and concerned. As always, it was her he was worried about. Which reassured her that this little trip into the mountains had been the right thing to do. She hadn't built him up in her mind as larger-than-life after all. He really was the wonderful, caring, protective man that she remembered from that dark time in her life that seemed so long ago now.

"I don't blame my adoptive family," she explained. "Not anymore. In their own way, they were all just as much victims as I was. If I kept all that money, it would make me feel like the villain of their lives. There's been too much hurt, too much hate in my life already. I didn't want that. I did it for me, more than for them. I also gave some to Tracy's family. They were there for me, always. So, for once, I was there for them. I'm here for you, now, Adam. If you still want me, that is."

"If I still want you?" He gave her an incredulous look. "Is that a joke?"

"I hope not."

He quickly closed the remaining distance between them. He pulled her into his arms and looked down at her, a fierce, hungry expression on his face. "I'll never stop wanting you. I want to kiss you. If you don't want that, you'd better tell me right now."

She wrapped her arms around his neck. "It's about time."

He groaned and claimed her mouth with his. It wasn't sweet or gentle like he'd been the first time he'd kissed her, when he'd shown her how a man who really cared about a woman treated her. This kiss was out of control, full of longing, yearning, and wild with desire. He was consuming her, and she was bursting into flames in his arms.

His tongue tangled with hers, and his hands roamed over her body, stroking, teasing, tempting. When he finally broke the kiss, they were both panting.

She stared up into his gorgeous blue eyes, gazing down at her with such yearning it nearly broke her heart. "I'm so sorry that I took so long to—"

"No apologizing." His voice was ragged, strained. He kissed her forehead and dragged her against him, his arms holding her tight. "I thought it was all in my head, that I was the only one who felt this way."

She pulled back so she could look up into his eyes, needing to hear the words. "Felt what way?"

He frowned, looking uncertain again. "I love you, Jody. Don't you know that?"

She burst into tears.

He lifted her in his arms. He carried her to one of the leftover stumps that still needed to be cleared from the trail and sat down with her in his lap. He rocked her and stroked her back. "Good tears?"

She hugged him tight. "Good tears. I'm trying not to cry so much. But it's going to take some work to change."

He set her back from him and cupped her face in his hands. "Don't change for me, Jody. Don't ever change. I love you just the way you are. Tears and all."

She hiccupped, and they both laughed.

"I love you, too, Adam. I think I loved you from the moment you threw me off that stupid cliff and sacrificed your own body to protect mine."

"I didn't throw you. I pulled you with me."

She rolled her eyes. "Just don't ever do it again. You scared me to death."

He kissed her, gently, softly, a fluttering caress like soft butterfly wings brushing against her heart. Then he smiled down at her with such reverence and love in his deep blue eyes that her tears started up again.

"I love you, Jody. I may not know everything about you. But I know what matters—your caring heart, your courageous, selfless soul, your kind and giving spirit. And I want to spend the rest of my life getting to know all of the fascinating details that go along with that. I want to build a future with you. If you'll have me."

She straightened in his arms. "What are you saying, Adam?"

His hands shook as he gently feathered her hair back from her face. "I'm saying that I want to marry you. But I know we've only really known each other a short time. I don't count the three months we've been apart. So I'll start out slow. We can date for a while. I'll introduce you to my family—my other brothers, Ian, too, if I can even locate him and convince him to come home for a visit. My mom, my dad. They have a cabin in the mountains where we grew up, where I got my love for the outdoors. I want to take you to Memphis, too. That's where I started my career, as a beat cop, before the ranger position opened up and I could come back here, to my hometown. I want to share everything with you. And then, when you're ready, once you feel you know me well enough, if you still think you love me, maybe then we can work on forever."

She shook her head in wonder. "You're an amazing man, Adam McKenzie. And far more patient than me." She shoved her hand into her jacket pocket and pulled out a small velvet box and held it out to him. "Open it."

He frowned. "What are you doing?"

"What do you think I'm doing? I'm asking you to marry me. There's a gold band in that box. I know it's not the customary thing for a guy to wear an engagement ring. But you're blazing hot and I want every woman who looks at you to know you're taken."

"No."

She grew still in his arms. "No? You don't want to marry me? But... I thought—"

He pressed a finger to her lips. "Hold that thought."

He reached behind him and unsnapped one of the small leather holders clipped to his belt. Then he held his hand out toward her. A large diamond sparkled in the sunlight, surrounded by a smaller cluster of diamonds on a white-gold band.

Tears flowed again, and she didn't even bother to wipe them away. There was no point. She seemed to have an endless supply. Her chin wobbled as she held out her left hand.

He slid the ring onto her finger, then handed her the gold band she'd gotten him. She put it on his finger and stared up at him in wonder.

"When? When did you get that ring?" she asked.

"Right after the whole debacle at your old house. Every time one of those thugs pointed a gun your way, I felt like I was dying inside. I knew I was in love with you and there was no point in fighting it. I've carried that ring with me ever since, all the while hoping and praying you'd come back to me. If, or when, you were ever ready."

He lifted her off his lap and set her on the stump, then got down on his one good knee.

"Jody Vanessa Radcliffe, will you make me the happiest man alive and agree to be my wife?"

"Only if you'll agree to make me the happiest woman in the world by being my husband."

He grinned. "I'll do my best."

"You always do, Adam. You always do."

He took her in his arms, and into his heart, and once again, he saved her.

* * * * *

APPALACHIAN ABDUCTION

Debbie Herbert

This book is dedicated to all my author friends
who help me, especially: Gwen Knight, Lexi George,
Ash Fitzsimmons, Michelle Edwards, Tammy Lynn,
Fran Holland and Audrey Jordan!

And, as always, to my husband, Tim,
my dad, J.W. Gainey, and my sons, Byron and Jacob.

Chapter 1

Only one road climbed Blood Mountain to the exclusive Falling Rock community and its luxury mansions. But Charlotte had no interest in accessing the gated community through the pretty lane lined with oaks and vistas of manicured lawns and gardens.

No, the backside view of the swanky neighborhood was where she'd find clues to the ugly mystery of Jenny's whereabouts. And to get to this precious vantage point in the hollow, she'd hiked a good two miles down from neighboring Lavender Mountain. She raised her binoculars and focused on the nearest cabin's massive wooden deck.

Nobody milling about there.

She slanted them to the cabin's impressive wall of windows, hoping to catch a glimpse of Jenny—or any other young teenage girl, for that matter. The bastards.

Still nothing.

But she wasn't discouraged. If nothing else, her career as an undercover cop had taught her patience. She waited and, after a few minutes, scanned the row of houses yet again before dropping the binoculars and taking a swig from her water bottle.

Faint voices rumbled through the air, low, deep and indecipherable. Quickly she raised the binoculars to search for the source. But the field glasses weren't necessary. Near the base of the cabin, only one hundred yards away, stood two men armed with shotguns and wearing walkie-talkies belted at their waists. Where had they come from?

Suddenly the muscular guy on the left raised an arm and pointed a pair of binoculars at *her*.

Oh, no.

She'd been spotted, despite the fact that she was dressed in camouflage and had tucked her red hair into an olive ski cap. The man on the right raised a shotgun to his shoulder and scanned the area. Charlotte dropped to the ground on her stomach, praying she was out of sight. Three deep breaths, and she raised her binoculars again. The men had disappeared.

Strangely, she wasn't comforted by that realization. They could be creeping their way downhill to find her. Time to get the heck out of Dodge. Charlotte tucked the binoculars and water bottle into her backpack and withdrew her pistol. Not the standard-issue one provided by the Atlanta Police Department—they'd forced her to turn that in—but the personal one she always kept stashed in her nightstand. If they found her, she'd be ready for them. The cool, hard wood snuggled in her right hand provided a surge of comfort, just as it always had on those nights when she'd been home alone and whispers of danger made her imagine some ex-con had discovered where she lived.

Charlotte eased the backpack onto her shoulders. Cocking her head to the side, she paused, listening for anything out of the ordinary.

Wind moaned through the trees, and dead leaves gusted in noisy spirals. Then she heard it: a methodical crunching of the forest underbrush that thickly carpeted the ground. At least one of the men was headed her way.

Damn it.

She jumped to her feet and ran, heart savagely skittering. Its pounding beat pulsed in her ears, loud as the echo of dynamite. A slug whistled high above her, and bark exploded from near the top of a pine sapling eight feet ahead.

Did they mean to kill her or merely frighten her off? Because if their aim was the latter, it was working. Charlotte kept running, this time darting behind trees every ten yards or so. No sense providing them with an easy target. The path seemed to stretch on forever, though, and a stitch in her side finally screamed in protest at the brisk pace. Charlotte stumbled behind a wide oak and sucked oxygen into her burning lungs.

Another shot rent the air, but she couldn't tell where the bullet landed. Hopefully not anywhere nearby. She pushed off and ran once more. Wind blasted her ears and cheeks, stinging her eyes as she sped down the trail, mentally calculating her best escape. If only she knew how close they were.

There were three options. One, return to the nearby abandoned cabin and hope they didn't see her sneak inside. Two, if there was enough time, hightail it to her truck hidden in a copse of trees and take off. The problem with the first two was that her cover might be compromised if she were spotted. The third option was riskier, but it would leave her free to continue her planned surveillance.

Another shot torpedoed by like an angry hornet, grazing the side of a nearby oak. This shot was much closer. Again, she ran. Gnarled roots gripped her right foot and she fell flat. A pained cry slipped past her lips. She stared down at her twisted knee and the ripped denim on the outside of her right thigh where brambles and rocks had cut deep. Blood oozed and created a widening stain on her pants. Her right temple throbbed and she knew a knot would form on her scalp. Charlotte swallowed hard, pushing back the sudden stab of dizziness that narrowed her vision. No allowing the blessed relief of unconsciousness to take hold. The things men like them could do…she'd seen way too many victims and knew a thousand ways evil people could inflict pain upon another.

Focus. You can't let them catch you.

Option three it was, then. Quickly she ripped off her jacket and pressed it against her wound. Couldn't let blood drip to the ground and become a trail that would lead the men to her. Not to mention the danger of passing out from blood loss.

She hissed at the wave of pain that slammed into her knee. It was as if someone had tripped a live wire inside her that burned through her veins and traveled up and down her body. Even her mouth had a metallic, coppery taste. Charlotte spit a mouthful of blood, clamped her teeth shut and crouched low. Plenty of time later to moan and groan. Right now she had to find cover.

It hurt like hell, but she managed a stumbling trot, forsaking the main path and stumbling through shrubs and bands of trees. Winter was a hell of a time to seek shelter in the Appalachian forest. The plants were practically stripped bare, their only foliage a few withered, stubborn leaves that had not yet broken loose. But there were patches of evergreen shrubs and small pine trees still to be found. She'd checked on that in her earlier recon of the area.

"Where'd he go?" one of the men shouted from afar.

The answering voice was much closer. "Lost sight of him."

She dove behind a clump of rhododendrons and curled into a tight ball. If they hadn't seen her, she had a chance. Her breath sawed in and out—to her ears, loud enough to doom any hope of going unnoticed. She crossed her left hand over her thigh and pressed down on the wound to staunch the bleeding. Those damn briars ripped flesh like tiny surgical knives. The pistol was in her right hand, loaded, with the safety off. If they came too close and found her hidey-hole, she might be able to fire at them first.

They tromped through the area and continued the search. Subtlety wasn't their strength.

"You go that way," one of them shouted, pointing in the opposite direction, "and I'll head this way."

A tide of relief whooshed through her body. One would be easier than two if it came to a showdown.

Footsteps approached, and she rounded into herself even tighter, not daring to breathe.

Please don't stop. Keep walking, she prayed as the

nearest man stomped not twenty yards away. He wore black leather boots and dark denims—that much she could see—but she didn't dare lift her face and examine him further.

He stumbled on a rock and tumbled forward several steps, managing to catch his balance at the last minute. "Damn it," he snarled, then yelled, "Anyone out there?"

Right. Like she was going to raise her hand and pop up like a jack-in-the-box to answer him.

"If you can hear me, you were trespassing. Stay away from Falling Rock, got it? Hey, Ricky, let's get back to the house," he called to his fellow tracker, then walked back toward the main trail.

Another voice, deeper and more gravelly, spoke. "Probably just a hunter, anyway."

"I didn't see no shotgun on him, but he was wearing camouflage. Scrawny little fella."

"Might not have been hunting animals. Could be one of them 'sengers."

What the heck was a 'senger? Whatever they were, she was grateful they provided another plausible explanation for a person roaming the woods in camouflage attire.

Her breathing slowed at the sound of receding footsteps. Today had almost been disastrous, and she wasn't in the clear yet.

If those men were smart, they'd linger a bit, hoping that their prey would be cocky enough, or stupid enough, to reemerge on the trail, mistakenly believing the danger had passed. But six years on the force had honed her methods and instincts. *Never believe your opponent isn't as smart, or smarter, than yourself*, she'd been warned.

And so she waited. As shock and adrenaline faded, the pain in her knee and temple increased. As soon as she got to the cabin, she'd clean the wound and patch it up with the first aid kit she'd brought along. She also had Ace bandages to wrap her knee. It had to be a superficial injury, since she'd been able to put weight on her leg and run. The air chilled her skin, although not enough to counteract the burn of ripped flesh. Were the men still lying in wait? She wasn't sure how much longer she could stay. Every moment the wound went unattended increased the likelihood of infection, and she desperately wanted to take something for the building headache.

Gingerly Charlotte rose and tested putting weight on her right leg. A bolt of pain traveled up from her knee, and she bit her lip to keep from crying out. Hurt or not, she had to leave. Those men might return with a larger force. And even if her damn cell phone worked out here in the boonies, who could she call? Right now, she was a pariah to her coworkers, and if she called the local authorities, they'd pepper her with questions.

She gripped her pistol more tightly and set off toward the main trail. Once she got there, she'd walk along the outskirts until she was sure the men were truly gone.

The trail looked as forlorn and barren as when she'd first hiked it that morning. Charlotte ran a hand through her hair and then stopped cold. At some point, her hat had been blown away by the wind. Good thing the men were gone. Now she needed to push through the pain and walk. She could do that. There was no choice.

It appeared she'd survived this encounter. Some-

times the best option was to hide and live to fight another day. Justice delayed beat justice denied. Besides,
it wasn't as if she harbored a death wish, though death
would be preferable to what these men were capable
of doing.

They might have succeeded in running her off for
the day, but she wasn't giving up. She couldn't give
up. Not today, not ever. She was the last, best hope for
Jenny and the other lost girls.

The near-deserted roads suited James just fine. Oc-
tober, while beautiful in the Appalachians, had drawn
crowds of tourists flocking to view the scenic foliage.
But November's gray skies and biting wind meant that
Lavender Mountain was back to its usual calmness—
and he could sure use some peace and quiet. Returning
from Afghanistan hadn't exactly led to the grand family homecoming he'd once envisioned. Instead, murder had wiped out half his family before he'd even set
foot in Elmore County. That tragedy, combined with
what the doctors deemed a mild case of PTSD, had left
him edgy and filled with uncertainty about the future.

With no conscious plan, James meandered the deputy sheriff's cruiser up the mountain road, and he startled at the sudden sight of his father's old cabin. How
often had he done this very thing on routine patrols?
Ended up driving right here, precisely at the place he'd
rather *not* be?

He shook his head in disgust and hit the accelerator. Memory Lane had zip appeal.

Twenty yards down the road, a flash of beige slashed
through his peripheral vision. What was that? He did
a U-turn and craned his neck, searching the brown-

and-gray woods. *There*, he spotted it again. Curious, he pulled onto his father's old property and exited the cruiser, shrugging into his jacket. He strode along the tree line until he solved the riddle: someone had parked their truck toward the back of the property behind a couple of large trees. He retrieved his cell phone and hurried over on the off chance that someone might be injured or stranded.

It was locked, but he peered in the tinted windows. No clues there. The interior was practically empty and spotlessly clean. He headed to the back of the truck and took a photo of the license plate. He'd call in the numbers shortly.

No damn reason it should be here. No *good* reason, anyway. Frowning, he went to the cabin and pulled out his keys. Better make sure some squatter hadn't decided to take up free residence.

He inserted the key in the lock, but it wouldn't turn. James withdrew it and checked—yes, this was the correct key. Someone had changed the locks. He felt a prickle of unease mixed with anger, and the twin emotions churned in his gut. Anger won.

"Open up," he bellowed, rapping his knuckles on the old wooden door. "Sheriff's department."

Silence.

He stepped back on the porch and noticed for the first time that every window was taped up with plain brown wrapping paper. This was *his* place, damn it. He'd chosen not to live in the cabin he'd inherited, but that didn't mean just anyone could help themselves to it and move in. James rapped on the door again, louder. "Open up now, or I'll break down the door."

Still no answer.

With a quick burst of energy, he kicked the door. Splinters flew, and the frame rattled. He kicked again, and it burst open. James shuffled to the side and removed his sidearm, then proceeded cautiously inside with his gun raised. The room was abnormally dark from the taped windows, and only the light from the open doorway illuminated the den. At least his sister had gotten rid of most of the furniture. In this room, only an old couch remained. No place to hide.

James flicked the light switch, grateful he'd kept the power on. The Realtor had insisted on it so she could show the place to potential buyers. *That* was a laugh—the place had sat empty for months. Seemed fixer-upper cabins in remote Appalachia weren't a hot commodity. Hardly a shocker.

He made his way to the kitchen, gun still drawn. Like the truck and the den, it was pristine, and mostly empty. No signs of forced entry or habitation. Three more rooms to check. He padded down the short hallway, gun at the ready. The guest bedroom and bathroom doors stood open, but the main bedroom door was shut.

Gotcha, he almost whispered aloud. He spared a cursory glance in the guest room that housed only a bed. Nothing was underneath the tucked comforter, so he eased toward the closed door. Spots of spilled liquid, still wet, stained the pine flooring leading from the bedroom into the bathroom. He flipped on the bathroom switch, careful to keep his gun aimed at the closed bedroom door.

Smeared blood and dirt formed a drag pattern on the floor and basin and continued their path to the side of the tub. A wet towel lay beside the tub, as well as strips of gauze and a bottle of rubbing alcohol. Some-one had been hurt—and recently.

A grating metal sound came from behind the closed bedroom door, and James barreled into the room. A mattress lay on the floor, and food provisions and clothes were neatly stacked in plastic containers along the side wall. But it was the open window that drew his immediate focus. Oh, *hell* no, they weren't slipping away. He was going to get answers. James rushed to the window and stuck his head out.

Red hair whipped in the breeze. A petite woman wearing a camouflage shirt and black panties—no pants, no shoes—ran through the yard. Blood oozed from ripped flesh on her right leg, and she limped as she headed toward the truck.

Okay, that was far from the thug or drugged-out squatter he'd expected. "Halt," he ordered.

She didn't even bother looking back at him as she continued a gimpy run to the tree line.

"For Christ's sake," he muttered, tucking his side-arm back into its holster and rushing through the cabin. He exited the busted front door and stormed down the porch steps to the side yard. "Stop right now," he called out.

Again she ignored his command. Stubborn, foolish woman. He couldn't let her get in that truck. But as he ran toward her, she spun around, raising a pistol in both hands and aiming it straight at his heart.

James threw up his hands and cautiously walked forward before pointing at his badge. "Lady, you don't want to shoot an officer of the law." He nodded at her leg. "Looks like you need medical attention."

"You're a cop? Let me take a look at that badge."

She approached and examined the badge on his uniform. The harsh glint in her eyes softened, and she lowered the gun. "Sorry. I didn't stop to see who broke in when I ran."

"I identified myself as from the *Sheriff's department*," he said grimly. She might be pretty as all get-out and pretend compliance, but people weren't always what they seemed. This job and his tour of duty had taught him those lessons well. "Now gently lay down the gun and step away from it," he ordered.

She kept her eyes on him as she bent her knees and placed her weapon on the ground. "No problem, Officer. I always—"

Her right leg gave out from underneath, and she swooned forward—which put her hands right by her gun, he couldn't help noticing. Quickly he crossed the distance between them and kicked it several yards away.

"Suspicious much?" she drawled.

"I'll call for an ambulance or drive you to the hospital in my vehicle. Do you have a preference?"

"Neither. I'm fine. It's not as bad as it looks."

"There's blood on the right side of your scalp. Not to mention your mangled leg. Might need stitches, at the very least. Antibiotics, too."

"I said no." She struggled to stand and then limped past him. "Just let me get dressed."

"Not until you explain how you got hurt and what you were doing in my cabin."

That got through to the woman, and she whirled around. "*Your* cabin?" She bit her lip and mumbled, "Of all the damn luck."

"You can explain on the way to the hospital."

"I don't need a doctor."

She hobbled to the door, and he scrambled to retrieve the fallen weapon before following her, trying to deduce this stranger's game. "You hiding from an abusive husband?" he guessed.

"No," she said flatly, grabbing onto the porch rail and wincing as she climbed the steps.

"There are shelters that can help, you know. In fact, there's one less than thirty miles—"

"I don't need a shelter. I can protect myself."

Like hell she could. "Fine. You want to clam up? Let's go down to the station. I'll run your license plate and clear up this mystery."

She sighed, resignation rounding her shoulders. "If you don't mind, I'd like to get my clothes on."

Woman was probably freezing her butt off. "Of course. Look, whatever kind of trouble you're in, we can help."

She blinked and nodded her head. "Thank you, Officer. I'm sorry about intruding and…and pulling that gun on you."

About time she saw sense. "Fine. I'll wait here." He took in her pale face, and his eyes traveled down to her right leg. "Can you manage by yourself?" he asked gruffly.

"Of course. Any chance I can have my gun back now? After you unload it, of course."

What kind of fool did she think he was? "No, you may not."

She cast her eyes down in a demure manner. "Be back in a minute."

He watched as she made her faltering way down the hall, her back ramrod straight. What kind of man could hurt a woman that way? It looked as though she'd taken a hard tumble. Her ex was obviously dangerous. He'd see that whoever the man was, he'd get his due punishment.

James paced the empty den, thinking of his dad and sister Darla, both murdered at the hands of another family member. How sad that the ones we most loved were often our worst enemies and betrayers of our trust.

He shook his head and strode to the windows, stripping off the papers the woman had taped up to avoid detection. It shouldn't matter, but he hated the thought of the cabin being shrouded in darkness night and day. Bad enough he'd abandoned it to die a slow death from neglect.

What was taking her so long? Had she passed out from loss of blood?

A flash of red in the barren landscape caught his eye.

Damn it to hell. She was running away again, this time fully clothed and with a backpack strapped to her shoulders.

Should have known the minute he'd seen those teal eyes and titian-colored hair that this woman spelled trouble.

Chapter 2

Charlotte suppressed a wince as she collapsed into the seat across from his desk at the Lavender Mountain Sheriff's Office. She glanced at his nameplate. Officer James Tedder. The name had a familiar ring.

"Driver's license, please," he said matter-of-factly, firing up the computer on his battered wooden desk. He examined her gun and wrote down the serial number before opening his desk drawer and locking it away.

"License. Right." She made a show of rummaging through her backpack. "Shoot," she mumbled. "It's not here. Must have left it at the cabin. Sorry."

He quirked a brow. "How convenient. Tell me your name."

The officer was bound to get her real name from the truck's license plate numbers. No use lying. "Charlotte Helms."

262 *Appalachian Abduction*

He picked up his cell phone, and she saw a photo of the rental tag as he typed. But there was no need to panic just because he had her name. He'd run a standard background check and see she had no priors. No reason for him to look further and check out her employment record. A little fast talking on her part to avoid trespassing charges, and her cover would remain uncompromised.

"The truck's a rental," she volunteered. "Thought it would be easier to keep my ex-boyfriend off the trail that way." She trembled her lips and let her eyes fill with tears. This wouldn't be her first performance for getting out of a jam. And acting was so much easier when she actually felt like crying from pain. "You were right. I'm running from someone."

"How did you wind up in my cabin?"

Bad spot of luck there. It'd looked perfect when she'd scouted the area earlier—practically deserted but sturdy, and the location so close to Falling Rock. She'd figured it would be less conspicuous to camp there than to rent a room at a local motel. The tourist season was long over and she didn't want to attract attention.

"It...seemed safe," she hedged. "I was afraid if I stayed at a motel he'd track me down. I don't have much cash on me, only credit cards." She added a hitch to her voice. "I left in a bit of a hurry."

He paused a heartbeat, drumming his fingers on the desk. "How did he hurt you?"

His face and voice were neutral and she couldn't tell if he was buying her story or not. Charlotte thought fast.

"It wasn't my ex-boyfriend. I'd gone for a walk," she lied. "Got a little stir crazy holed up in the cabin. I must have ended up on someone's property because a shot came out of nowhere. Might have been an irate land owner. Or…maybe it was a hunter mistaking me for a deer? I didn't stick around to find out. In my hurry, I stumbled and took a hard fall."

"Exactly where were you when this incident occurred?"

"About a mile or two south of the cabin? I can't say. I was focused on getting the hell out of there."

A *ding* sounded on the computer and he turned to the screen. "Truck was rented from Atlanta," he read. "Two days ago. The contract states you've rented it for two weeks."

"That's right." Charlotte swiped at her eyes and sniffed. "I apologize for staying at your cabin. I'll be glad to pay for a new door and any other damages incurred."

He leaned back in his chair and steepled his fingers. "A crime's been committed here."

"Please don't arrest me for trespassing. I've never been in trouble with the law." Then she remembered. "And, um, sorry for that other incident, too."

"You drew a gun on me," he stated flatly, a muscle flexing in his jaw.

"I thought you were my ex."

"Again, I identified myself before entering the cabin. Fleeing an officer is a crime."

"But I didn't *see* you," she argued. "I couldn't be sure who you really were."

"And then there's the matter of someone taking potshots at you. I'm going to need more details on that."

She waved a hand in the air dismissively. "Why? I'm fine. I won't be pressing charges even if you find the one who fired. I just want to move on. I decided during that long walk today that I want to stay with my parents in South Carolina for a bit. Get my life together and put distance between me and my ex."

"Move on all you like, but I still have the problem of a rogue shooter in the woods. We're going back there and you're going to show me where you were when this happened."

"But…my leg."

"You claim the injury's not serious enough for medical attention."

Her temper rose. "But I can't walk a mile and go scouting around the wilderness."

"I have a four-wheeler. You won't have to walk."

"I see." She cleared her throat and pressed a hand to her head injury. "Could we do this tomorrow?"

His blank expression never wavered. "You have a permit to carry a weapon?"

Charlotte blinked at the sudden change of topic. The damn gun. Once he ran the serial numbers he'd have her employment history. And then her cover was blown.

"Of course I have a permit."

If only she could be sure he was a clean cop. It would be amazing to have assistance in saving Jenny. And he acted sincere with his direct manner. His face was rugged while at the same time maintaining a certain boyish charm. She couldn't deny that she found him appealing and his forthright air inexplicably tugged at her to confide everything. But this was a small town, one that Jenny Ashbury's kidnappers had chosen for a reason. And that reason might very well be that local law enforcement had been paid to turn a blind eye on the abductor's comings and goings.

She couldn't take that chance with Jenny's life.

A middle-aged lady with dark hair and bifocals stuck her head in the door. "Harlan needs to speak with you ASAP."

Officer Tedder frowned. "Can't it wait?"

"Nope."

Charlotte's paranoia radar activated. Harlan Sampson was the county sheriff. Was there any way he knew who she was and why she was here? Was that why he wanted to speak with Officer Tedder?

"Be right back," he said.

Alone, Charlotte leaned over the desk and peeked at the computer screen. Her not-so-flattering driver's license photo was on display. Feeling restless, she stood and strolled to the open window, wincing at the burst of pain.

Downtown Lavender Mountain was picturesque with its gift shops and cafés. From here she could see the local coffee shop and a gourmet cheese store. Despite the off season, a few people were out and about.

Leave. Just leave. Now.

Charlotte bit her lip, debating the wisdom of her inner voice. It's not like Officer Tedder had arrested her, right? And he didn't issue an order to stay when he left. If she could keep out of sight for a couple of hours and then hitch a ride back to her truck, maybe he'd give up on questioning her.

Yeah…but then what? Stay the next town over? It wouldn't be as convenient, but she could rent a different vehicle, find an inconspicuous place to park it near Falling Rock, and then continue on as before. All it took was one photograph of any of the lost girls by a window, one slip-up by the kidnappers transporting their captives, or one girl to escape their cabin and make a run for it. Then she'd have the needed proof to obtain a search warrant and rescue Jenny.

It was worth the risk. Hell, she'd already damaged her career by coming to Lavender Mountain anyway. So what if a local cop got angry with her and eventually charged her with trespassing? That was the least of her worries.

With a longing glance at the locked drawer housing her gun, Charlotte scooped up her backpack. She'd get another weapon. If nothing else, she was resourceful and a risk-taker. With that, and a whole lot of luck, she'd bring down that human trafficking ring.

Something about her story didn't jibe. James hurried back to his office. More than anyone, he realized these mountains were as dangerous a place as any city. He need look no further than his own family for confirmation of that sad fact. But hunters shooting at a woman didn't sound right. Hunters around these parts knew you shot by sight, not sound. Was it an irate property owner? It was possible they'd fired a warning shot or two in the air. People 'round these parts didn't take kindly to trespassers on their land.

And what was she so afraid of? If Charlotte Helms could afford to rent a truck, she could afford a motel. No reason an ex from Atlanta would ever think to look in this area.

Time for answers.

Squaring his shoulders, he stepped back into his office. His empty office. No, surely she didn't run again. She wouldn't, would she?

"Sammy," he bellowed, scurrying down the hall.

"What's up?" Samuel Armstrong asked, not looking up from his computer.

"Did you see a woman leave the building a minute ago? A redhead limping on her right leg?"

"Nah," he drawled with a wry grin. "Saw y'all come in, though. You manage to lose her?"

"Maybe." James hurried over to Zelda's cubicle. "Did you see that woman in my office leave?"

Zelda laid down her pencil and crossword puzzle book. "No, my back's been to the door. Want me to check the ladies' room?"

"Please."

She rose from her chair with a sigh. He followed Harlan's secretary to the lobby restroom. But he guessed Zelda's answer before she emerged half a minute later.

"She's gone."

Aggravating woman. "Thanks," he mumbled, hurrying back to his office for his jacket. He pulled it on as he rushed out of the lobby. He'd spoken with Harlan about five minutes, tops. Charlotte couldn't have gone far with an injured leg and no vehicle. He glanced up and down the road, but no flash of red was in sight. James crossed the street and entered the coffee shop. This was as good a place to start as any.

Myrtle waved as he entered. "What'll it be, Jim Bob? Your regular with two sugars and one cream?"

His campaign to have people address him as James instead of his boyhood nickname was not a success.

"No, I'm looking for a woman. A petite redhead. Seen her?"

"You have very particular tastes," Myrtle said with a wink. "Didn't know you were partial to redheads and leather."

He was *so* not in the mood for jokes. "Sheriff's business. Has she been here or not?"

"Touchy today, huh? Nope, haven't seen your mysterious lady."

"Call me if you do."

He exited the shop and tried half a dozen others. No one had seen Charlotte. He stood in the middle of town square, hands on hips. Every minute that went by increased the likelihood that she'd succeeded in giving him the slip. *Think.* Where would he go if he were in her shoes? Probably slink around the alleys and slip into a shop's back door if someone approached. He hustled behind the coffee shop and scanned the alley lined with garbage bins. Down at the far end, he spotted Charlotte rounding a corner, red hair flaming like a beacon.

I've got you now, he thought with grim satisfaction. He hurried to the end of the backstreet in time to see her slip into the Dixie Diner.

Now he'd get answers.

Inside the diner, the aroma of fried chicken, biscuits and gravy made his mouth water. Chasing Charlotte was hard work and it was past lunchtime. He scanned the tables filled with families.

No Charlotte.

He proceeded to the back exit and stuck his head out to check the alleyway.

Still no Charlotte.

Only one place left unchecked. He rapped on the ladies' room door once and then entered.

Lucille Bozeman, an elderly member of the local Red Hat Society, shrieked and clutched her pearls. "James Robert Tedder," she said breathlessly, "what on earth do you think you are doing?"

At least she'd used his full name instead of Jim Bob. Normally, he found her and the other members of the Red Hats a hoot—amusing older ladies with their red hats, purple attire and carefree spirit. But not today. Heat traveled up the nape of his neck. "Sorry, Mrs. Bozeman. I'm looking for a woman."

"You've come to the right place, but this is hardly appropriate behavior. I'll speak to Harlan Sampson about this. How dare you…"

But he tuned her out and bent over. No feet were visible under the stalls, but one door was closed. He knocked on it.

"Come on out, ma'am."

A long sigh, and then a dry voice answered. "You going to order me to put my hands up or you'll shoot?"

"I don't think that'll be necessary," he answered in kind. "Unless you try to flee from an officer of the law again."

Charlotte emerged with a wry smile and leaned against the wall, arms folded. "Sorry. You never arrested me so I'd assumed I was free to leave earlier."

Despite her flippant attitude, James noted that her face had paled and her eyes were slightly glazed. "Right. So that's why you ran and tried to give me the slip." He nodded at the bump on her head. "You might be concussed. Change your mind about going to the hospital to have that looked at?"

"Not at all. I'm fine."

"Are you in some kind of trouble, young lady?" Lucille walked over, the brim of her outlandish purple hat brushing against his shoulders. Her gaze swept Charlotte from head to toe. "You appear a mite peaked."

Charlotte's smile was tight. "Just a few superficial wounds."

"Jim Bob, you should take her to see Miss Glory. She's a sight better helping folks than any doctor."

Actually, that wasn't a bad idea—and the healer's shop was only two doors down.

He addressed Charlotte. "What do you say? No forms to fill out or insurance cards to process."

"All I need is over-the-counter pain medication. If you could point me in the direction of the local pharmacy?" She pushed past them both and made for the bathroom door.

James took her arm. "You're coming with me. Stop being so stubborn. It's obvious you're hurt. Miss Glory can fix you right up."

He caught a glimpse of Lucille gaping at them in the bathroom mirror. News of this bathroom encounter would be all over town in an hour.

"Thanks for the suggestion, Mrs. Bozeman." He leaned into Charlotte, whispering in her ear, "If you don't want your business common knowledge, let's continue this outside."

He stayed near her as they walked through the diner. Charlotte briefly glanced at every face in the crowd, as if taking their measure. She opened the door and stumbled, pitching forward a half step. The full weight of her body leaned against him. She smelled like some kind of flower—a rose, perhaps. It was as though a touch of spring had breathed life into a dreary November day.

Charlotte stiffened and drew back. A prickly rose, this one—beautiful but full of thorns. James clenched his jaw. Didn't matter how she looked or smelled or felt. This woman was a whole host of complications he didn't need or want. He'd get her medical attention, find out why she came to Lavender Mountain and then escort her to her truck and wish her well.

"If you're on the run as you claim, the last thing you want is an infection to set in that injury. Miss Glory really can help you."

"If I agree, will you give me a ride to my truck afterward and let me go?"

"You're in no position to negotiate. You trespassed on my property and pointed a gun at me, as well. I believe I'm holding the trump card."

"Okay, okay," she muttered.

She hobbled beside him until they reached the store. Miss Glory's shop, The Root Worker, was dark. Glory claimed the light deteriorated the herbs strung along the rafters. The placed smelled like chamomile and always reminded him of the time he and his sisters, Darla and Lilah, had all come down with the flu at the same time. Their mother had infused the small cabin with a medicinal tonic provided by Miss Glory.

"What brings you here today, Jim Bob?" Glory asked, grinding herbs with a mortar and pestle. She swiped at the gray fringe of hair on her forehead. Her deeply lined face focused on Charlotte. "And who's your friend?"

James quickly made introductions. "She's here because of a lump on her head, a twisted knee and cut skin on her right thigh. She refuses to see a doctor, so I thought I'd bring her to you."

Glory didn't even blink an eye. No telling how many strange stories she'd heard over the years.

"I've already cleaned it out and bandaged it," Charlotte said. "Don't see the need for anything else."

"How bad do your injuries hurt?" Glory asked gently.

"I wouldn't turn down some aspirin."

"Hope you're not so stubborn that you ignore any signs of a concussion or infection. You start runnin' a fever or see red streaks flame out from the flesh, you get to a doctor quick, ya hear?"

Surprisingly, Charlotte nodded her head slightly. "I will."

"You seein' double or got the collywobbles in yer tummy?"

"None of that."

Every moment he spent in her company, his doubts about her story grew. He remembered her steady aim and fierce eyes as she aimed a gun dead center on his chest. This wasn't a woman who ran away from danger. She'd confront it head-on.

"Tell you what I'm gonna do, darlin'. I'm sending you home with a gallon of my sassafras tea. You drink a big ole glass of it at least three times a day. That sassafras is my special tonic that'll clear up any nasty germs brewing in yer body."

Miss Glory went behind the counter and rummaged a few moments, returning with a couple of items.

"A little poultice to draw out infection," she said, pressing it into Charlotte's palm. "And a few capsules filled with feverfew, devil's claw and a couple other goodies. Much better than an ole aspirin."

Charlotte shook her head. "I don't—"

"Now don't you fight me on this, child. I see the pain in them eyes of yers. You'll need a sharp mind to be of any use to anyone and you can't have that without rest. Take it before you go to bed at night."

"Thank you," Charlotte murmured, stuffing the poultice and pain packet in her backpack.

"Jim Bob, grab a gallon jug of sassafras tea on yer way out. It's in the cooler by the door." Glory rested an arthritic-weathered hand on Charlotte's shoulder. "I see danger surrounding you, child. They's people wish you would go away from here and never come back."

James was used to Miss Glory's eerie predictions. He wasn't sure he believed in all that hocus-pocus, but people around here claimed she had the sight. Couldn't hurt to pick her brain. "What do you know?" he asked sharply.

"Me?" She threw up her hands and cackled. "I'm just an old woman who's been around too many years to remember, and can sense people's energy."

He was reading too much into the old lady's ramblings. Wouldn't have even bothered coming to her shop, but Lilah swore that Miss Glory was the only one who helped her get through a difficult pregnancy and then again helped with her colicky baby.

Charlotte backed away to the door, suspicion hardening her classical features. "Who am I in danger from?" she asked sharply.

"That's not for me to say. But I suspect you know the answer to your own question."

Charlotte nodded and continued edging to the door.

He wasn't going to let her run again. James plopped down a couple twenties on the counter. "Will that cover everything?"

Miss Glory nodded and leaned in, her breath a whisper against his ear. "Watch after her. She needs help whether she likes it or not."

James shook his head. "I'm no one's protector," he grumbled. He had his own demons to fight. His tour of duty overseas had left him unwilling to get involved in others' problems, beyond what was required as an officer. Lilah often fussed that he'd become too withdrawn. But whatever—all he wanted was to perform his duties and be left alone.

Charlotte gasped suddenly and flung herself against the side wall, away from the shop door. A couple of mason jars filled with herbs crashed to the floor. The scent of something earthy, like loam in a newly plowed field, wafted upward.

"What is it?" Instinctively, his right hand went to his sidearm and he surveyed the scene outside. On Main Street, a sleek black sedan accelerated and turned out of sight from the town square.

"Are they gone?" Charlotte asked past stiff lips.

"Whoever was in that vehicle? Yes. What's this all about?"

Charlotte lifted her chin and carefully picked her way through the strewn herbs and glass shards. "Sorry, Miss Glory. I'll pay, of course. Where's your broom? I'll sweep up the mess."

Glory shooed her off, then bent over and whispered something in Charlotte's ear before addressing them both. "I'll take care of this. You go on, now, and do what you have to do."

Charlotte rummaged through the backpack and dug out a wad of bills. She lifted a hand at the sight of Glory's open mouth. "Take it. I insist. And thanks for your help."

James grabbed a jug of tea and followed Charlotte outside. He took her arm. "What really brings you to Lavender Mountain?"

Chapter 3

"Anyone ever tell you that you're stubborn as hell?" Charlotte grumbled. She climbed into James's truck, slowly swinging her injured leg into the cab, and then eased back onto the leather seat with a sigh. She wouldn't admit it for a month's salary, but running from his office had been a mistake. Her first instinct, born from years of busting street gangs and drug rings, was to flee until she'd formed a plan and was ready to strike.

James got in beside her and slammed his door shut. "Start talking."

"You're taking me back to my truck, right? I'll be out of your hair soon enough."

"That wasn't the deal. What's your game?"

She opened her mouth, and he started the engine. "Don't lie," he said. "You're not running from some ex."

She had no choice. Once he ran the gun paperwork, he'd know. "I'm an undercover cop. Atlanta PD Special Crimes Unit."

He shot her an assessing glance, then pulled the truck away from the station and into town. "What are you doing ninety miles from the big city? Anything going on around here, we should be part of the investigation. Atlanta's urban area may sprawl for miles, but this is still our jurisdiction."

He might have her cornered, but she didn't have to tell him the whole truth. "I don't suppose you'd accept the proposition that the less you know, the better?"

James snorted.

"Right. Okay, I'm investigating a missing girl and have reason to believe she's being held in the Falling Rock community."

His brow furrowed. "Why? Give me details."

"How can I be sure you're trustworthy? Well, not necessarily *you*," she amended. "But what about your boss and coworkers? Any of them could compromise—"

"I trust the sheriff explicitly," he ground out. "Harlan Sampson is as honest as they come, and I'm not saying that because he's my brother-in-law. I've known him all my life. We've been friends since third grade."

"That's fine for you, but it doesn't assure me. Far as my research shows, the previous sheriff is doing time for twenty years of covering up moonshine and murders."

"And Harlan has been working for over a year now to clean up the force," James said with a scowl.

"Are you sure he's finished? Most criminals don't work in a vacuum."

"Two officers were fired. That's out of an office with a dozen employees. I have complete faith in the ones remaining."

"But you've only worked with them six months." She'd done a cursory background search on every officer.

He shot her a glance, eyes widened in surprise. "You've done your homework," he noted, driving away from the downtown area and starting the drive up a winding mountain road.

"I know you've done a couple tours in Afghanistan. Army Special Forces."

"You seem to have me at a disadvantage," he said coolly. "I know nothing about you. Yet."

"No doubt you'll check the gun paperwork and confirm my story. I'd do the same in your position."

"So why did you break into my cabin? Couldn't you survey the Falling Rock area more directly?"

Typical cop. A rookie one, no less. "That's the difference between working undercover versus running routine patrols and answering callouts. Direct isn't best in my line of work. I picked your cabin because it's within walking distance of where I can get a behind-the-scenes view of most of the Falling Rock houses."

"What do you expect to find? Are you hoping by some miracle that the missing girl is going to step outside? I don't foresee that happening."

Charlotte squirmed. Put that way, it did sound like a lame plan. But then, he didn't know all the particulars. He didn't know that she was investigating a ring, and as such, she hoped to observe vehicles pulling into backyards to hide the drivers' comings and goings. Even license plate numbers would provide worthwhile leads to pursue. So let him think she was foolish. The less she revealed, the less interference and lower possibility of word getting back to the traffickers that she was closing in on their operation.

"Don't make this hard," James warned. "Either voluntarily give us the information so we can help find this missing girl, or drag your feet until we force the information out of your supervisors. Your choice."

Damn it. If he contacted Atlanta, she'd be ordered—again—to stop searching. And that was the best-case scenario. Worst case, it was entirely possible she'd lose her job. But she'd weighed the risks from the start, and the decision had been easy. Jenny was her best friend's daughter. If she didn't try her best, how could she live with that knowledge? How would she be able to face her best friend for the rest of her days? She couldn't.

"If I tell you more, can we keep it between us?"

"No way. I can't keep this secret from Harlan and the others. Like you said, I'm pretty new here. Everyone else will have more experience. Don't you want the full resources the sheriff's office can provide?"

Hell, yeah. No question. Charlotte gazed out the passenger window, where shadows already lengthened with a hint of the coming twilight. To his credit, James didn't press her as she weighed the pros and cons of telling him everything. But it wasn't much of a choice, really. She had a bum leg now, and she'd been seen by the bodyguards who were obviously protecting the traffickers.

"I do need your help," she admitted. "But if you go to the sheriff, he'll contact my boss for verification of my story, and then all hell will break loose."

James's eyes narrowed. "If you're on the up-and-up, what's the problem?"

"I've been suspended." There, she'd said it. Six years of exemplary service, and now she was in the hot seat. James would think she was a total screwup.

He pulled into the cabin's driveway, shut off the engine and faced her, arms folded. "Why?"

She jerked her head from his piercing gaze and stared down at her folded hands. "Because I won't give up on this case. That's why. The official charge against me is insubordination."

"Go on," he urged at the beat of silence between them.

Charlotte lifted her head. Officer Tedder had been more than patient. He could have arrested her for trespassing, or even decided she was too much trouble and not searched for her after she'd fled. But he'd found her and coaxed her into getting help for her injury. A good man, she decided. Perhaps even a trustworthy one. She'd been burned before, but mostly, her gut and intuition had served her well in a dangerous profession.

"Can we talk somewhere other than here? Sitting in the open in your truck is an invitation for trouble." Her stomach churned as she remembered the black sedan with tinted windows that had cruised through town.

He countered with a question of his own. "Is this where you run from me again?"

"No running. You can follow me in my truck while I get a motel room, or we can go in your cabin to talk."

James drummed his fingers on the steering wheel. "My cabin. I'll park my truck behind yours. No casual observer passing by would notice it. Probably safer than you spending the night at the local motel with your vehicle in plain view, anyway."

"Agreed."

He drove across the yard and parked behind her rental truck. Charlotte opened her door and eased onto the ground, putting most of her weight on her left leg. If it came down to another chase by land, she was doomed.

They walked across the yard, but try as she might, a low hiss of pain escaped her lips as she started up the porch steps. James placed a hand on her right forearm, and she leaned into his strength, hobbling across the wooden porch.

Damn if it wasn't heaven to feel his strong muscles taut and solid against her. For the first time since arriving at Lavender Mountain, Charlotte felt safe and protected. Not an emotional luxury she often indulged in with her line of work.

James frowned at the broken door frame as he ushered her inside. "Stay here while I check the cabin," he murmured, setting down the jug of sassafras tea from Miss Glory.

She nodded, grateful. Ordinarily that kind of take-command attitude by male coworkers annoyed her, but he was the only one around with a gun and two good legs. And he was her best hope for rescuing Jenny.

"All's clear," James announced, returning to the den and placing the gun in his holster. "And I closed the back bedroom window you opened earlier this morning. You remember, the one you crawled out to run from me."

Charlotte nodded, making no apologies, and limped

to the couch. Instead of collapsing into an exhausted heap, she settled in primly, back straight and feet crossed at the ankles.

What a striking woman. In the dark shadows, her hair glowed like sun fire and her eyes gleamed with intelligence, determination and...sorry to say, still a trace of wariness. Not that he blamed her for the mistrust. She'd most likely seen the worst of human nature, just as he had in Afghanistan.

He picked up the jug of tea and strode to the kitchen, where he located a glass in the near-empty cabinets. Miss Glory's tonic was purported to do wonders, and he hoped it lived up to its hype. He added ice to the glass and poured the pale, caramel-colored drink. Charlotte was being damn foolish about treating her injuries, but he couldn't force her to accept medical attention. A wry smile twitched the edges of his mouth. He imagined Charlotte Helms could be mighty stubborn when it came to changing her mind.

That was okay—he could be as damn stubborn as Charlotte, and he meant to draw out everything from her about this case. The greatest lesson he'd learned in the military was to work with others as a team. It enhanced the chance of success for any mission. He preferred a quiet, solitary life these days, but when it came to his new job, he was all about teamwork.

James returned to the den. "Drink up," he ordered, handing Charlotte the glass. "I'll be back in a minute."

"Where are you going?"

"To get my tool kit."

And his tablet, because he wasn't letting this woman out of sight again. While she slept tonight, he'd double-check her story. Insomnia came in handy every now and then.

James scanned the yard and then strode to his truck, retrieving the toolbox, the tablet, a box of crackers and a cooler packed with water bottles. Another thing the military had taught him was to be prepared. The water and crackers would satisfy their basic needs for the evening, but he longingly recalled the smell of fried chicken and mashed potatoes at the Dixie Diner. Tomorrow he'd go back and eat his fill at the lunch buffet.

Inside, Charlotte sipped tea and raised a brow. "Quite an armful. You must have been a Boy Scout."

"Lucky for you. What did Miss Glory whisper to you back at the shop?"

She blinked at the sudden question. "I couldn't understand what she muttered. Her Southern accent's pretty strong."

Again, he suspected she wasn't truthful, but in this instance, it didn't matter. Not in the grand scheme of things. He let it go. "What do you think of Miss Glory's tea?"

"Has a licorice taste. I like it. Either that, or I'm really thirsty. You believe in this stuff?"

"People who refuse standard medical treatment can hardly complain."

A surprised chuckle escaped her lips, and her eyes sparkled. "Touché."

James nearly dropped the supplies in his hand. He'd known she was attractive—that was plain to any fool—but when she smiled? Stunning.

Charlotte's eyes widened and their teal hue deepened. The space between them grew electric, humming with energy. He swallowed hard and turned away, setting down the supplies and then gripping his hammer like a lifeline. Sexual attraction was the last thing he needed in this sticky situation.

"I don't have replacement hardware, but I can nail up this door and make do for tonight. That is, if you still want to stay here?"

"You'll let me stay?" Her voice was husky, and she cleared her throat. "Thank you."

"For now. Unless your safety becomes compromised. First thing in the morning, we'll—"

"*We?* I don't need you to stay with me."

"You think I'd leave you alone out here?" He might be reluctant to get involved with people, but he always did the right thing. Or tried to. "As I was saying, at dawn, we'll get my four-wheeler, and you can show me where you were shot at."

She slowly nodded. "Like I said, I don't need your protection, but it's your cabin, after all. As far as returning to that place, it's a needle-in-a-haystack possibility, but if we can find those shell casings, it could be important down the road."

He set to work, quickly repairing the door. Satisfied, he returned to the kitchen with the cooler and put the water bottles in the fridge. The only thing edible in the refrigerator was a jar of peanut butter, and so James set the crackers and peanut butter on the table with two paper plates and a roll of paper towels.

"Dinner's served," he announced. "Basic protein and carbs."

Charlotte took a seat. "I'm used to it. If we want to get really fancy, there are some granola bars and apples and such in my—I mean *your*—bedroom."

She started to rise, but he motioned her to stop. "I'll get them."

It wasn't fried chicken, but her contribution would add a little variety to the meal. In the bedroom, a plastic crate against the back wall was stuffed with dried foods. He lifted it, ready to carry it to the kitchen, when he spotted the laptop on her mattress. Stifling a twinge of guilt—there was a missing girl in danger, after all—he hit the space bar, hoping she hadn't properly shut it down earlier.

The screen lit and filled with images of scantily clad young girls. And by young, he noted that most didn't even appear to be sixteen years old.

"For the discerning customer," he read.

James closed the computer, lips curled in disgust. What possible connection did it have to Lavender Mountain? This was no simple kidnapping.

Charlotte's soft voice drifted down the hallway as he made his way back. "I'm doing everything I can, Tanya. I promise I won't stop until I find her." A slight pause, and then, "We'll get her back. I know it's killing you, but remember to let me call you. Not the other way around. Okay?"

As if she had eyes in the back of her head, Charlotte spun around, cell phone at her ear, as James entered the room. "Gotta go, hon. Later."

"Sounds like this case is personal," he observed, taking a seat across from her. "Who's Tanya?"

Charlotte laid the phone down and sighed. "Why do I have the feeling you're going to pry every last detail from me?"

"Because I am," he said with a grin, spreading peanut butter on a cracker. But his amusement faded at the memory of the computer photos. "Is Tanya the mother of the missing Jenny?"

"Yes. And my best friend." Charlotte pushed away her plate. "You see why I can't quit, don't you? I mean, wouldn't you do the same for your best friend?"

He flashed back to that night in Bagram when he'd awakened in the barracks and realized the cot beside him was empty. He'd waited, figuring Steve might be in the bathroom, but the minutes had ticked by, and he knew something was wrong. Against orders, he'd sneaked out of the barracks and searched the compound until he'd found Steve—huddled behind the garbage dump, holding a gun next to his head.

It still haunted James. Another minute and his friend would have committed suicide. He'd carefully taken Steve's gun away and escorted him to the infirmary. To hell with alerting the sergeant first and following protocol for a missing soldier. He'd known in his gut that Steve was in danger. "You're not the only one with a black mark on your record," he admitted. "I understand that sometimes—"

A shot rang out.

James froze, his breathing labored. Had he imagined the sound? No, Charlotte's hands gripped the edges of the table—she'd heard it, too. This was real and in the here-and-now.

"They've found us," she whispered.

Chapter 4

Charlotte reached for her sidearm and felt nothing but bare denim at her hip. Damn. She kept forgetting James had confiscated her gun. Its absence made her feel vulnerable and powerless. First order of business in the morning was to get it back.

But that didn't help her now.

As if they'd done this together a dozen times before, she and James rose from the table and flattened their bodies against the side wall by the window.

"See anything?" she asked.

"Nothing but shadows."

"Still think it's nothing but a shot-happy hunter out there?"

"Getting a little too dark for a regular hunter," he admitted.

"As opposed to what—an irregular hunter?" she

quipped. "Maybe now you'll believe me when I tell you it's Jenny's kidnappers."

James kept his gaze out the window. "Shooter's motives don't matter at the moment."

"Right. Sorry. So what's the plan?"

"We wait."

"That's it? We wait?"

"And watch."

To hell with that. "We could get on your four-wheeler and see who's out there."

"And what if that shot was meant to draw you out? You'd be a sitting duck. Stop acting like this is your first rodeo."

He was right. Damn it. This was her least favorite part of the job—stakeouts and waiting for someone else to make their next move.

"There could be more than one, you know. Maybe they're going to surround the cabin." Hugging the wall, Charlotte made her way over to the den window on the opposite side of the cabin. "I'll keep a lookout here."

Dusk settled on the woods that were wrapped in a gray mist. The outline of her rental truck at the tree line was barely visible. The vehicle was useless to her now that she suspected it had been spotted. If there was time, she'd exchange it for another one tomorrow. Her eyes and ears tingled with focus as she tried to find shifting patterns in the shadows, or the whisper of an out-of-the-ordinary snap of twigs.

"We hear another shot, call for backup," James commented.

The minutes stretched on in a tense silence, and she shifted all her weight onto her left foot.

"Knee bothering you?" he asked, his gaze still concentrated on the gathering darkness.

How did he know with his back to her? Probably a good cop to be so observant of the slightest shift in details. "Hurts a little," she admitted.

James stepped away from the window. "Let's go. If there's a stalker out there, I believe they'd have made a move by now. No sense standing around all night. We'll come back at first light and take a look around."

"Sounds like a plan." Frankly, she was relieved. Her leg hurt like hell, and there was no way she'd be able to sleep in this cabin again without worrying she'd awaken staring down the barrel of a gun.

"You stay inside while I start the truck."

"No way. We go together."

He opened his mouth to speak, but he must have read her determination. "Okay. Anything you need to bring with you?"

She'd almost forgotten. "Yeah, let me grab my stuff. I'll be quick."

Charlotte scurried to the bedroom and then stuffed her laptop in the large duffel bag already filled with clothes and toiletries, prepacked necessities in case she'd needed to leave in a hurry. She rushed back down the hall, and a chill draft from the open door blew over her body. A truck engine started outside, and headlights pierced the darkness. How dare he? But the anger was soon replaced by a seed of fear. Was he leaving her alone in this compromised location? An image of a dark alley flashed across her mind—her old partners, Roy and Danny, fading into the shadows as they ran from the drug dealer flashing his small but lethal-looking pistol. She'd run, too, but not as fast. Not near fast enough to outrun a bullet. A quick peek behind her shoulder and she saw the dealer had aimed his gun at her.

She'd turned and faced him then. Better to see the flash of gunfire and take it head-on than be hit in the back while running away.

The drug dealer unexpectedly laughed and dropped his weapon. "Some friends you got there. You ain't no coward, I give you that." His arm had lowered to his side. His features had hardened. "Get out of here," he'd growled. "And don't ever forget this is my turf."

She didn't forget. Not the dealer, nor the partners who'd left her an easy target.

Faster than she'd ever believe possible with a bum leg, Charlotte flew out of the cabin and onto the porch, duffel bag clunking across the wooden floorboards.

The truck engine rumbled in Park. James wasn't leaving without her. She climbed in the king cab, throwing the bag into the back seat, where it landed next to the gallon jug of sassafras tea he must have grabbed from the fridge.

"You tricked me," she commented. But her words held no bite.

James shifted the truck into Drive. "I don't know about the big city, but around here, we try and protect women."

"I'm a cop, not a woman."

His brow quirked.

"Well, you know what I mean."

"I'm well aware you're a woman," he said drily.

The air was charged with something other than danger this time—the space between them sparked. Charlotte cleared her dry throat. "And a cop," she insisted. "Don't forget that part."

The truck jostled along the dirt driveway. "Uh-huh, right," he muttered.

"Wait. I'm not thinking clearly." She dug into her jeans pocket for her keys. "I can drive my own truck and then exchange it for a new one in the morning. Take me back."

James pulled onto the county road. "We'll worry about your truck in the morning when we come back. For now, I think it's best we leave it."

"Okay, then. I can't argue against your logic there." Charlotte stuffed the key in her pocket.

Heat blasted from the vents, and she held her hands up against the warm air.

"Cold?" James asked.

She shrugged. "My hands are always cold."

"No gloves?"

"Somewhere in my bag. I'll dig them out later."

James opened the console and pulled out a pair of black leather gloves. "Here."

"Thanks, but that's not nec—"

"Go on. No sense suffering." He laid them in her lap.

Charlotte slipped on the overlarge gloves. They were lined with fleece and felt comfy and toasty against her skin.

The truck sped through the night, and they were in town in ten minutes. Charlotte rubbed the passenger window, scrubbing away the condensation to peer at the street. "What motel do you recommend?"

"Neither of them. There's only two."

He turned the wheel sharply, and the lights of the

Dixie Diner blazed in front of her. "Why are we stopping here?" she asked.

"I'm starving. I'll pick us up a couple plates to go."

She frowned. He could have got his own meal after he dropped her off, but the rumble in her stomach couldn't argue with the need for food. Real food. Eating nothing but crackers and apples and granola bars for two days had gotten old. Charlotte followed him in, and her knees went weak at the smell of fried chicken. James ordered a meat-and-three plate for each of them, and her mouth salivated. She couldn't wait to check into her room, eat and then enjoy a long bath with no fear of intruders.

Back in the truck, James turned sideways in the seat and didn't start the motor. "This Jenny you're looking for—was she caught up in some kind of pornography ring?"

"You could say that."

"How about being a little more specific?"

It might have been framed as a question, but she knew it was a demand. Hell, if he knew this much, he might as well know the rest.

"A human trafficking ring. She's one of many girls who have been caught in its trap."

James nodded, but he didn't say a word as he started the truck and backed out of the parking space. He retraced his route and kept driving until downtown was visible only in the rearview mirror. They were far from anyone, on a lonely backroad where anything could happen.

A small frisson of fear chased down her spine. *Stop, just stop*, she chided herself. If he were one of the bad guys, he would hardly have stopped for fried chicken before doing her in. Or loaned her his gloves. Still, her hand sought the passenger door handle. "Where are we going?"

"My place."

"Now, wait a minute," she protested. "If you think—"

James held up a hand. "I have a spare bedroom. It's just a precaution."

She studied him—the hard planes of his face and his aura of calm command. Okay, she *would* feel safer staying with him. But he could have at least asked before assuming she'd follow along.

"I can't read you," she admitted. "Half the time you act like there are other explanations for the shootings, and the other half, you're extremely cautious."

"Blame my army training. I imagine all possible scenarios and then prepare for the worst."

Curiosity sparked to learn more about James. "What was it like in Afghanistan?"

His fingers drummed the dashboard as he considered his answer. "Lot of extremes. Hot during the day, cold at night. Periods of boredom followed by bursts of danger."

"I understand the boredom–danger thing. Lots of that with undercover work." Charlotte wondered if the experience had left him scarred. "What did you do in the army?"

"IED patrol."

She gave a low whistle. The man had put his life on the line with every mission. Lucky for him, he'd returned home in one piece. "Must have been tough. Do the memories ever bother you, now that you're home?" Charlotte bit her lip. This was none of her business.

"Never mind. I have no right to ask. I thank you for your service."

He was silent for so long, she didn't think he was going to respond, and she stretched her right leg, trying to find a position that didn't hurt.

"It only bothers me sometimes at night," James said quietly. "Insomnia's a bitch."

James shook out two of Miss Glory's herbal pills on the kitchen table along with a glass of sassafras tea. "Drink up."

"I'm fine. My leg's not—"

"Stop it. I've seen you wince whenever you stand up or sit down. The way you favor your right leg. Are you always this stubborn?"

Charlotte picked up one of the pills and held it in her palm, frowning. "I don't like feeling out of control. Like I could fall asleep and not wake up when there's a possibility of an intruder lurking."

"Remember that insomnia I mentioned? I'll be up all night." He felt his mouth twitch. "Let my problem at least benefit you."

She bit her lip, obviously debating the wisdom of taking the pills. "What the hell." In one swift motion, she popped them in her mouth and washed them down with tea. "I don't have much faith they'll be that strong, anyway."

"Hope they work. Others swear by her herbs and roots." He knew how to make her see it his way. "Besides, get a good night's rest, and you can work longer and harder tomorrow."

"Every day Jenny spends with that ring is torture for Tanya and Jenny. I never forget that. Not for a minute."

"I don't doubt your dedication. One night's sleep will help you think clearer, and means you can bring her and the others home sooner. I saw the photos on your laptop. The ones of those girls for sale." Disgust roiled in his stomach. Hungry as he'd been, he started regretting the fried chicken and gravy.

"When did you look at my laptop? How did you—"

"When we were back at the cabin."

"Seems like I'm not the only one with a suspicious nature."

"Comes with the territory in our line of work. Never know when it might save our ass."

She shook her head, a bemused smile lighting her green-blue eyes. "Next you'll have me thanking you for doubting me."

"Good. Now let me use my influence to get you to shower and then let me take a look at your injuries."

A tinge of red crept up her neck and face. "I can take care of myself."

"A little late for modesty. The first time we met, you weren't wearing pants."

Charlotte groaned and lifted her hands to her face. "I forgot about that."

He hadn't. Sure, at the time, he'd been a little distracted by the gun she'd aimed at him, but yeah, he'd noticed the bare, shapely legs. James rose from the table. "Go on. I'll see to cleaning up."

Charlotte rose, and again a slight wince crossed her face.

"I've got aspirin," he noted. "You don't have to strictly rely on Miss Glory's home remedies."

"Might as well give them time to work. I'll see how I feel after a bath."

Head held high, Charlotte left the kitchen, and then paused by the den's fireplace mantel. "What's this?" she asked, picking up a wooden carving of a deer and examining it closely.

"Something I whittled," he admitted, feeling self-conscious. "It's a hobby, kind of relaxing."

"This is beautiful," she murmured. "How long did it take you to make this?"

"Hard to say. I whittled on it here and there in the evenings."

"It would take me a lifetime," she said with a laugh, placing the wooden deer back on the mantel. "Besides having zero artistic talent, I'm never accused of being a patient person."

Charlotte headed to the hallway. Despite the stiff set of her back and shoulders, it was obvious that the injury bothered her.

Whether she was willing or not, if the cuts showed infection, he was taking her to a real doctor.

James stacked the paper plates and napkins, pausing at the sound of running water. Right now, Charlotte was stripping. In his house. Just down the hall. He pictured her curvy body stepping into the steamy tub and groaned. It had been way too long since he'd been with a woman.

All his nights were long, but this one might be the longest yet. Resolutely, he put up the leftover mashed potatoes and green beans. He'd get through it. He'd been through much worse.

James settled on the couch and fired up his laptop. Five minutes later, he'd confirmed that Charlotte worked for the Atlanta PD. By the time she emerged, he'd flipped on the television and attempted to watch a basketball game, but his mind was focused elsewhere.

Charlotte cleared her throat and entered the room. "This is silly, but if you must, you can see that the cuts are fine. And my knee's only a little swollen."

Her skin was damp and pink, and she tugged at the bottom of the oversize T-shirt that barely covered her underwear. James stifled his amusement. How could such a hard-ass cop be so shy?

"Come here," he said hoarsely.

She advanced to within a couple of feet and turned to the side. Slashes of jagged crimson marred the otherwise smooth, pink flesh of her leg.

James swallowed hard. "Doesn't appear to be infected. Have a seat. I'll apply some of Miss Glory's balm and put a bandage on it."

"I can do it myself."

He didn't bother arguing, just picked up the antiseptic from the coffee table and applied some to a pad of cotton. "I'll be gentle."

"You'd better be."

She sat down beside him and angled her body on her left hip, leaning her elbow on the sofa's arm. Although she hissed as he applied the antiseptic to her head wound and cuts, she didn't say a word in protest. He opened the jar of balm from Miss Glory and dabbed it on with his index finger, barely grazing the torn flesh. Quickly he put on the gauze bandage. "All done." Damn if his voice wasn't several octaves deeper.

Charlotte nodded and sat up straight. "Thank you," she said simply. "I feel better already. I can't believe it, but those herbal pills really work." She gave a lopsided, loopy grin. "I'm getting drowsy."

He wished he could say the same. Instead, every cell in his body pulsed with energy, acutely aware of the beautiful woman who stared at him with such gratitude.

"Not too early to go to bed," he suggested.

Bed. More images played in his head of Charlotte sleeping across the hall in his guest bedroom.

She scooted sideways and lay down. "I could fall asleep right here," she murmured, wiggling her toes. Even her pink-painted toenails were adorable. As if of their own volition, his hands wrapped around her arches and he massaged her feet.

"Um, that's so nice." Her voice was husky and deep, and her eyelids fluttered.

"You must be wiped out."

"That and the pills." Her eyes widened, and she struggled to a half-seated position. Her thin T-shirt twisted, revealing a pair of lacy panties.

James reached for the afghan and covered her bare legs. A man could only take so much temptation, but he hadn't sunk so low as to take advantage of a half-drugged stranger. Hard to believe he'd known her only a day. Charlotte Helms had stormed into his life like some badass angel of justice, shaking up his quiet, orderly world.

"Do you have a girlfriend or—" her face tightened "—a wife?"

"Nope." He'd had a fiancée this time last year, but Ashley had brushed him off with a Dear John letter while he was in Afghanistan. Not that he could blame her frustration with his absence, but it rankled. Last he'd heard, she was already engaged to another man.

"What about you?" He'd assumed she wasn't married, but what did he really know about her?

She snorted. "Hell, no."

Irrational relief flowed over him.

"My profession doesn't exactly lend itself to maintaining close personal relationships," she continued. "Haven't even seen my own parents in months."

"That must be hard."

"Yeah, it's tough." Charlotte sighed and ran a hand through her long hair. "It never used to bother me, but lately…"

"Lately what?" he prompted.

"After seeing the hell Tanya's going through with her missing daughter—it kind of makes you stop and think. You shouldn't take family for granted."

"I get it. My dad and one of my sisters died last year. Made me appreciate Lilah—she's my younger sister." Lately he'd even been talking more to his estranged mother. Something he never thought he'd do after she'd run off with another man when he was in high school and had left them all high and dry.

"Lilah Tedder," she murmured, gently probing the knot by her right temple.

"She's Lilah Sampson now. Married the sheriff."

Charlotte snapped her fingers. "Thought it sounded familiar. There was a serial killer up here and—"

"Yeah, she was lucky to escape. My dad and Darla weren't so fortunate."

James shut down. He never talked about the incident. What good did it do to rehash old sorrow?

"Must have been tough," she whispered. "And then to find out the real killer was—"

"I'd rather not discuss it," he said, removing her feet from his lap and standing up.

"Of course, I understand. It's just that—"

Annoyed, James strode to the window and pushed aside an inch of curtain. A strong whipping wind battered barren treetops.

"Sorry. I'm not normally one to pry. Let's blame it on Miss Glory's herbs."

"I'm sure you read all about the case in the Atlanta papers. Heard it made the national news for a whole fifteen minutes." Even he heard the bitterness in his own voice. "Old news," he added dismissively.

Charlotte pushed aside the afghan and struggled to her feet. "How about we make some coffee? I'm good to pull my weight for a night shift. You've had a long day, too."

"Not necessary. We weren't followed. Besides, I never sleep much. No sense in you staying up, too."

"I never sleep well, either," she admitted.

He fixed his gaze on her. She'd probably witnessed a lot of the dark side of life and had her own demons, as well.

"Go on to bed. I've got this."

She yawned and cocked her head to the side. "Wake me up in about four hours?"

"Sure." He wouldn't, but he feared she'd never agree to sleep otherwise.

"Okay, then. Good night."

Charlotte started to turn, and then hesitated. Instead of leaving him, she slowly walked toward him, an uncertain gleam in her teal eyes.

She wasn't...surely, no. But she kept walking until

she stood close enough that he could smell the soap from her recent bath.

"Thank you," she breathed, standing on her tiptoes.

Her lips pressed under his jaw, along the side of his neck. Before he could react, it was over. Bemused, he watched as she left the room. It was as though her kiss had sealed his fate. He would do everything in his power to help her find the traffickers. Whether it was for Jenny and the other trapped children, or whether it was for this maddening woman—or some combination of both—James couldn't say. Indeed, such soul-searching was pointless. He'd thrown in his lot with the charismatic Charlotte.

It was going to be a long, long night.

Chapter 5

James surveyed her efforts with a critical eye. "You didn't quite get it all," he pronounced, tucking an errant lock of hair into the knitted hat. His nearness and touch made her breath hitch, although he appeared unfazed by the contact. "Don't need your flaming hair blowing in the wind like a red flag."

"Does it really matter? They're bound to hear your four-wheeler before they see anything."

"With any luck, the roar of the wind will drown out most of the noise."

Despite last night's intimacy, this morning, James was all business. Charlotte inwardly cringed, thinking of the unsolicited kiss she'd planted on him. Totally uncharacteristic of her. She recalled Miss Glory's whispered words at the shop yesterday. *"Open your heart."*

Yeah, she'd understood the older woman. Probably fancied herself the local matchmaker.

James swung a long leg over the ATV and pointed to the back seat. "Hop on," he commanded.

Charlotte climbed onto it, grateful that her injuries had improved leaps and bounds overnight. Only a slight soreness remained. Once she brought Jenny home—and she would—she'd pay Miss Glory another visit and present her with a big tip.

With a lurch, James gassed the ATV, and she wrapped her arms around his waist to keep from falling. Lordy, he felt good—strong, and warm, and reliable. She resisted an impulse to bury her head against his broad back. What was it about him that drew her so? No sense falling for someone who appeared to temporarily be her partner. Emphasis on *temporarily*. She'd been burned before mixing business with pleasure. Danny had proven to be a rat bastard. Once this case was over, she'd return to Atlanta, and James Tedder would continue on with his relatively peaceful life here on Lavender Mountain. With no complications from her.

The wind was brutal in the early morning chill. Luckily James possessed more than one pair of gloves, and she'd donned the loaner ones. How cold must he be? His body shielded her from the worst of the wind.

The four-wheeler jostled and righted itself as they drove off his cabin's property and entered the main trail leading to Falling Creek.

Finding the exact spot where she'd been shot at and searching for the left-behind shell casings wasn't likely, but they had to try. She hoped the guards were still there at the house she'd spotted, although unarmed this time. If nothing else, this morning's excursion would prove she'd told the truth about the shooting, and that there was nothing accidental about it.

Charlotte kept her eyes glued to the passing trees and brush until she spotted the clearing where she'd run off the trail. Another thirty yards or so, and they'd be in the general area. She leaned to the side. "Slow down," she called out to James. "We're close."

Close enough to also see the line of mansions on the Falling Rock bluff.

He let up on the gas and swerved off the beaten path, parking the ATV in a copse of pines, right under a handmade sign stapled to a tree. "Private Property. Trespassers will be shot on sight."

"These people are crazy," she commented, pointing to the sign.

"Yeah, you trespassed. That tends to get people shot."

She hopped off and pulled the binoculars from her backpack.

The two guards were there at the same house, but apparently hadn't heard their approach as they conversed with one another.

"See anything?" James asked.

Charlotte pointed to the mansion in question and handed him the binoculars.

"They could be gardeners," he commented. "One's holding a rake and the other a hoe."

"Bet you could watch them an hour and you wouldn't see either of them using those tools. They're props."

"We'll keep an eye out. Where should we start looking for the casing?"

She sighed. "Here's as good a spot as any."

They separated and began combing the grounds. Charlotte hugged her arms to her waist, eyes focused on finding the small object amid the dead leaves and brown twigs. You'd think it would stand out, but they were hampered by being unable to pinpoint the exact location of the shooting. Too bad she hadn't thought to leave some sort of mark behind. That way, they could estimate how far away the shooter was when he fired his weapon.

"Found one," James called.

"Really? Damn, you must have eagle eyes." She scurried over.

James held it up to the sun, squinting at it a moment before dropping the casing into a small plastic baggie.

"What now?" she asked through chattering teeth. "Keep watching the guards?" She lifted her binoculars. They were still talking, gesturing broadly with their hands, the garden implements dangling uselessly by their sides. The men started pushing and shoving. "We're in luck today. They're too busy fighting each other to notice us."

"Then let's push it. We'll ride down the trail—it turns and runs perpendicular to the houses."

"What if they see us?"

He shrugged. "They'll just think we're out on a joyride."

"In this weather?" she asked skeptically.

"I want to gauge their reaction for myself."

Some small part of him still had reservations about her story. "You're the one sitting in front. If they shoot—"

"Exactly." James stuffed the baggie in his coat pocket and climbed on the ATV.

Charlotte lifted the binoculars one last time. The guards were throwing actual punches. Good to know the idiot thugs were so easily distracted. She tilted the binoculars upward, scanning the windows.

A face appeared. A young girl with long blond hair, nose almost pressed to the windowpane. The look of misery and longing in her blue eyes punched Charlotte in the gut. "I see a possible victim," she whispered, the sound of her voice lost in the wind.

"What's that?" James asked, immediately by her side. "Let me see."

She passed him the binoculars and hurriedly dug into her backpack for the camera. "Top left window."

James peered through the lens. "I don't see anything."

"Give it here." Charlotte dropped the camera, grabbed the field glasses, and pinpointed the target.

Nothing. The blinds were drawn closed. She hadn't imagined it—Jenny had been there seconds ago. "Damn it! Jenny was just there. I promise you."

"Too bad. If she'd stayed thirty seconds longer, you could have snapped a photo. Would have been solid proof to justify a search warrant of the house."

"I know," she said with a groan. "Who knows when or if she'll appear again?"

He laid a warm, heavy hand on her shoulder and gave it a quick squeeze. "At least we know where to focus our efforts now if that particular household doesn't claim children."

Our efforts. The world went bleary through a thick haze of tears, and Charlotte angrily blinked them back. She cleared her throat. "Does this mean you believe me? You'll help bring those bastards down?"

James stared ahead. "I saw the pictures of those missing children." A muscle worked in his jaw. "If they're being held there—" he nodded at the house "—then I'll stop at nothing to get them out."

Something tight in her shoulders relaxed slightly— a tension she hadn't been aware she was carrying. "That's where they are. I know for sure now, even if I can't prove it to anyone else."

Again she felt for the missing gun at her side. Maybe it was a good thing that James had confiscated it. She wanted nothing more than to force her way inside and search the premises. But even armed, it would take more than one person to get the captives out alive. *Soon*, she silently promised Jenny.

"Let's take 'er for a spin," James said, hopping on the ATV.

Privately she was unconvinced of the wisdom of that particular move, but partnerships were a give-and-take. She'd voiced her concern, and he'd overridden it. Fair enough. He'd been accommodating in other matters.

Charlotte resumed her position on the back seat, and they blazed down the trail. At last they were close enough to the guards that the men must have heard the oncoming vehicle. They pulled apart, warily eyeing their approach. Both drew their right hands to their hips as if reaching for sidearms.

Surely they weren't so brazen as to shoot two people in broad daylight.

But perhaps he'd been a fool to count on that. He couldn't let anything happen to Charlotte. Coming out here had been his idea. James threw up his right hand in a friendly wave, as if he were merely passing through without a care in the world.

They didn't return the wave or the smile, but they didn't fire, either.

James turned to the left and followed the path that led away from the territory the men guarded. Might be best not to return the same way, just to be safe. Another half mile ahead, he could cut across Old Man Broward's field and return to the cabin in a more round-about fashion.

Charlotte tugged violently on his right arm. "Stop!"

Had they been followed? James veered the ATV sideways, slamming on the brakes. His eyes cut to the path behind them. "What is it?"

Before the ATV completely sputtered to a stop, Charlotte hopped off and rushed to the side of the road, pointing. "Is that blood?"

Dark crimson dotted and swiped across dried leaves.

"The drag pattern indicates something was shot and dragged here," he mused.

"Or *someone*," Charlotte said, rubbing her arms. "Oh, God, I hope it's not Jenny. Not that I want any-one dead, of course. It's just, I couldn't ear for Tanya to lose her only child. Her marriage went south last year, and Jenny is her world."

"Every girl is somebody's daughter. Somebody's world, too. But I know what you mean."

He dug another plastic bag from his coat pocket and bent down to collect a sample. "An eventful morning," he said grimly.

"Wait. Let me take a photo of this before you start collecting."

He waited, studying the blood. No way to tell if it

was animal or human without running tests. There was a lot of it. If it was from a human, chances were they were dead. The body—or possibly a deer carcass—had been dragged a couple of feet before being hauled off.

A few snaps and clicks later, James quickly gathered up enough blood for lab testing and then drove the meandering route back to the cabin.

During the truck ride to the sheriff's department, Charlotte was unusually quiet and withdrawn. James took her hand. "We're going to free Jenny and the others," he promised, parking the truck.

She squeezed his hand, and he withdrew it. James stepped out of the vehicle, and she fell into place beside him as they entered the sheriff's office. Why did he always feel the need to touch Charlotte? Totally inappropriate and nothing he'd ever felt the urge to do on the few patrols he'd run with Jolene, the only female officer in the department. Must be because this case was personal for Charlotte and she was passionate about freeing the prisoners. She cared deeply about this assignment.

Hell, so did he. Hard to believe in America, and right here in his county, young girls were brutalized and sold to men like sides of beef. Made it damn hard to sleep at night, imagining their suffering.

The clatter and whir of printers and scanners abruptly stopped. Necks craned, and fingers stilled over keyboards. For a good five seconds, he and Charlotte were scrutinized by Elmore County's finest.

Sammy arose from his desk and walked over to greet them. "Wondered where you were this morning," he remarked. He extended a hand to Charlotte. "Sam Armstrong."

"Detective Helms." She gave a polite nod but volunteered nothing further about herself. Sammy turned back to James. "You're late this morning. Boss wants to see you. Pronto."

That sounded fairly ominous. As the newest officer, he had no authority deciding what cases to take, much less setting his own schedule.

"Shall I go with you?" Charlotte asked, squaring her shoulders.

"Later. Let me talk to him first." He'd sent Harlan a couple of brief texts stating only that he was investigating a trafficking ring with an Atlanta cop. No doubt Harlan was less than pleased at being left out.

"How about some coffee?" Sammy asked, steering Charlotte toward the back of the lobby.

"Sure. Just point me in the right direction."

Once she walked a few feet away, Sammy leaned in, amusement flickering in his eyes. "Want me to handcuff her to the desk this time? She appears to be a flight risk."

"You can try, but I have a suspicion you'd end up the one chained to my desk. Not Charlotte."

Sammy laughed. "I like her spirit."

"Guess I better go face the music with Harlan."

"He's in a rotten mood this morning," Sammy cheerily informed him.

James stifled a groan and strode the hallway to Harlan's office. The sheriff sat at his desk, a newspaper sprawled out in front of him.

"Sir?" James asked, always formal in the workplace. He didn't want Harlan or anyone else to think he courted favor because the sheriff was his brother-in-law.

Harlan scowled, impatiently waving for him to take a seat. "Cut the *sir* crap. You aren't in the army anymore."

A fact James never intended to use to his advantage. "Yes, s—"

"Call me Harlan like everybody else around here." He leaned back in his chair, steepling his fingers. "What the hell is this about a human trafficking ring, and who's working undercover in my county?"

"Yesterday I found a woman camped out in Dad's old cabin. Turns out she's an undercover cop with Atlanta's special crimes unit. Her name's Detective Helms." He tried not to grimace as Harlan punched her name into his computer.

"Might as well tell you," James said. "Char— Detective Helms—is currently on suspension with them for insubordination."

Harlan stopped typing and cast him a surprised scowl. "Why?"

"She was ordered to drop her search and was reassigned another case. She refused."

"Why?" Harlan barked again. It seemed to be his favorite word.

"Because one of the victims is the daughter of her best friend."

"An officer can't allow personal emotions to interfere with duty," Harlan objected. "If she was ordered to cease, then that's the end of the matter."

James quirked a brow. "Like you did when J.D. ordered you to mind your own business last year when Lilah was in danger?"

What an ass the former sheriff had been. He'd never cared for the guy and wasn't a bit surprised when he returned home and learned J.D. was in jail. Especially since he'd protected the identity of James's father and sister's killer. Mentally James shook off the memory of his own tragedy.

Harlan shifted in his seat. "If I had stopped my investigation, your sister might have been the next victim."

"I'm not complaining, merely pointing out that sometimes it's impossible to give up."

It was easy to read Harlan's discomfort as his boss realized the hypocrisy of the situation. James went in for the kill.

"What harm can it be to work with her for a time? Worst-case scenario, it's been a waste of one officer's time. Best case, we find the traffickers, and you get all the glory for the capture."

"You really think that's all I care about? What people will think of me?"

He'd overstepped his bounds. Of course Harlan cared how all this would reflect on him as sheriff. It was an elected position, after all. But he was also a decent man intent on keeping crime out of the county.

"I was out of line," James admitted. "But I know you. If young girls are being held against their will and sold into the sex slave market, you'll do your best to stop it."

"Damn right," Harlan grumbled.

"So you'll let me continue working the case with Detective Helms?"

Harlan regarded him silently for several heartbeats. "With reservations. I'm going to speak with her supervisor and get more information on this suspension. In the meantime, tell me what, if anything, you've discovered that validates her claim of a ring operating out of Lavender Mountain."

Quickly he filled Harlan in on the attempted shooting, being tailed by an unmarked sedan, the shot in the dark last night and Charlotte's claim of seeing a young girl's face at the window this morning. "And then there's this," he added, pulling out the baggie of bloody leaves. "Found them close to the Falling Rock subdivision."

Harlan leaned over his desk and picked up the evidence, holding it up to the light. "Could be from a deer."

"Or it could be human."

Harlan nodded. "I'll send it to the lab straightaway and pull strings. They should know in a day or two if it's animal or human, but the DNA tests to determine whose blood it is could take weeks. And even then, we can only match DNA if the person has a DNA sample on file."

Then he drummed his fingers against the wooden desk. "So far, you haven't proven anything sinister is going on at Falling Rock, but I don't want to take chances, either. I'll get the lowdown on this Helms woman, but in the meantime, check out her story." Harlan narrowed his eyes. "Heard she's a real looker. You aren't getting sucked in by a pretty face, are you?"

"'Course not." James swallowed back his irritation. "She's sacrificing everything to rescue her friend's daughter and whoever else is held captive."

Harlan let out a sigh. "So she claims. How long does she plan on staying?"

"As long as it takes."

"And where's she staying?"

Heat blossomed on his neck and face. "I've offered her my place." That sounded bad. Really bad. But he hated the idea of Charlotte staying in town and being exposed to danger.

Thankfully Harlan let that pass. "Suspension or not, Atlanta should have informed me of suspicious activity in this area. We've got enough problems without being in the dark on any leads they have. It's an insult to this office. An insult to me."

"Don't take it personally. It's the nature of undercover work. And Elmore County's reputation is ruined after all the crap J.D. pulled as sheriff."

Harlan didn't appear the least mollified. "They're still going to hear my complaint. Are you still sure this Helms woman is on the up-and-up?"

James immediately leaped to her defense. "Yes. A bit reckless, but brave and determined."

"Reckless?" asked a high-pitched voice.

Charlotte stood in the doorway, arms folded and chin lifted. "Nothing's ever been accomplished without taking action based on calculated risks."

Harlan stood and assessed her with narrow eyes. "I don't want my officer placed at risk with any wild plans you might harbor for accomplishing your mission. Got it? Any evidence you find, you run it by me, and I'll decide what action to take."

"Got it." Her lips tightened to a thin line, and James was willing to bet she told Harlan only what he wanted to hear. Obedience didn't appear to be her strong suit.

"Excellent," Harlan said crisply. "As long as we have that understanding, Officer Tedder can work with you a few days to see if you two can turn up evidence. We'll issue you a uniform and a cover story that you're our new employee on probation and learning the ropes. Not being undercover will allow you to freely explore the area. That sound fair?"

"Perfectly."

Harlan buzzed the intercom on his desk and his secretary, Zelda, appeared immediately. "Escort Detective Helms to inventory and see she's issued a suitable uniform," he told her. "If there's not one in her size, check around with a few of the neighboring sheriffs and see if they have a spare."

"I'm on it."

Zelda motioned for Charlotte to follow, and James was alone again with his boss.

"I appreciate this," James began. "I realize I'm still fairly new, and if it turns out—"

"We're already understaffed, and all my other officers have a huge workload as it is." Harlan relaxed and sat back down. "Besides, I wouldn't have hired you if I didn't think you were up for the job, and any assignment, brother-in-law or not."

James had his doubts about that. Lilah had fussed over him ever since he'd returned from Afghanistan, convinced he needed to get out of the house more. No one seemed to understand that after all he'd seen overseas, living alone and keeping to himself was his idea of paradise. He wanted nothing more than peace and quiet, but he suspected that ship had sailed.

The phone rang, and Harlan glanced at the screen. "Got to take this. Keep me informed. And James… keep your guard up, okay?"

With that, Harlan lifted the phone's handset, and James returned to his desk, mulling over the conversation. His feelings were mixed. It *was* an interesting case and one he'd campaigned to stay on. One that beat the hell out of roaming the back roads on patrol. But Charlotte unsettled him. He couldn't stop thinking about her haunted eyes when she mentioned Jenny. The need to leap to her defense had been surprising—and not in a good way.

Was he being fooled by a pretty face, as Harlan suggested?

He'd take his brother-in-law's warning to heart. Proceed slow and easy. And for God's sake, he'd resist the impulse to touch her. Detective Charlotte Helms was temporarily his new partner—and nothing more.

Chapter 6

"May I have my gun back now—partner?" Charlotte self-consciously tugged at the front of her too-tight uniform blouse. First opportunity, she'd buy some dark brown tank tops to wear underneath the shirt. Pink skin on her chest and stomach peeked out in the gap between the buttons. She was a quarter-pound cheeseburger away from completely popping out.

James's eyes slid down her uniform, and she barely resisted the urge to squirm. The pants were as tight as the top, hugging her hips and ass in a way that made her feel exposed.

"Right. Your gun." He unlocked a desk drawer. "Zelda's made arrangements for better-fitting uniforms to be overnighted."

Was it her imagination, or had his voice deepened and slowed? Suddenly it wasn't just her uniform that felt tight. The very room felt compressed and the air thick with tension.

Sexual tension.

Might as well call it what it was. Charlotte swallowed hard, eyes focused on his large hands as they palmed her weapon—metal caressed by muscle. Mesmerizing. What would it be like to have his hands stroke her naked flesh?

"Here," James said, his hand reaching for hers.

Lifting her arm was like a magnetic pull through molasses—slow and steady and inevitable. Her fingers wrapped around the gun's barrel, and she fastened it to her belt clip. She didn't dare face James. Didn't dare trust her eyes not to betray the sudden passion.

"Thank you," she murmured. Damn if her voice wasn't as gruff as his.

Buck up. He's officially your partner now. Passion meant distraction. And they each needed all their wits to break the trafficking ring. Not to mention, they also needed focus to keep their hides intact in the face of flying bullets. No wonder romantic relationships were taboo in law enforcement—they could get you killed. And once you broke up with a coworker? The worst. Danny had taught her that.

"For you."

Her eyes snapped to the doorway as Sam entered the room waving a thick manila envelope, which he tossed in James's inbox. His forehead crinkled. "Something going on in here?"

"No, thanks for—" James began.

"Nope," she denied.

He glanced between them, realization dawning in his eyes. "Right. Whatever you say."

Charlotte rummaged through her backpack for her case files, ignoring Sam as he swept out of the room. The situation was awkward enough without the man's teasing. She cleared her throat and spread her files across his desk. "Let's get down to it, shall we? Here's a photo of Jenny."

The blown-up color print portrayed a smiling girl, her mother's arm slung across her shoulder. The girl's eyes and skin had that glow that came only with youth. Tanya's grin was carefree and proud—in contrast to the past two weeks, when her eyes had been practically swollen shut from crying and her face puffy with misery. As thankful as Tanya would be when her daughter returned home—and Charlotte vowed to make it so—she suspected that Tanya's carefree look was gone forever.

"Jenny Ashbury," she said softly. "I also have photos of other missing girls ages twelve to sixteen, although most are twelve to fourteen years old. We tried a sting operation using me as bait, but I only drew men wanting to hire me as a prostitute. I'm too old to be considered a prime target for trafficking."

"Too old?" James shook his head in disgust and looked over the mug shots.

"Anyone look familiar?" she asked.

"No."

"Well, that was a long shot, but it could be helpful if you familiarized yourself with their faces and names. Never know when they might slip up and one of the girls escapes."

"Will do. I'm printing out the owner names and information for all the houses at Falling Rock. In the meantime, fill me in on everything you have."

Charlotte settled into a seat. "We've known for some time that a woman is locating and luring vulnerable young girls—runaways, foster children, the homeless, you get the picture. We don't know her name, but our nickname for her is Piper, short for Pied Piper."

"Where are you getting your info?"

"Mostly from Karen Hicks, a thirteen-year-old runaway who managed to escape. Piper befriended her after discovering her roaming around on Peachtree Street. Bought her a meal and offered to put her up for a night at a motel."

James frowned. "Your Piper's a class act. But I don't see the connection. Lavender Mountain's a long way from downtown Atlanta."

Charlotte couldn't mask her distaste. "According to Karen, two armed men forced her and three other girls into a van, bound and blindfolded them, then drove them around for a couple of hours. They were offloaded at a huge, luxurious house…and then they spent the next week being instructed in the finer points of sexual relations."

"Lovely," James muttered.

"Oh, it gets better. Karen found out that there was to be a party that weekend where Piper's clients could come and sample the goods. If they liked what they found, the girls were to be sold at a price—either as exclusive property to their new owner, or to a man who would pimp them out to others."

Charlotte shook her head. Poor Karen. At first glimpse, her prison must have seemed like a fairy-tale castle. But it hadn't taken long for the illusion to shatter—there would be no happily-ever-after on the horizon.

"How did she manage to escape?"

"Luckily for Karen, one of the rapists who visited there was not only excited but also stupid. He forgot to lock them up from the outside of the bedroom door before he asked her to tie him up and gag him. Karen happily complied, managed to slip out the back door, and then hitched rides back to Atlanta."

James tapped an index finger to his lips, a thoughtful expression in his eyes. "And Karen claims this happened at Falling Rock?"

"When she escaped, she noticed the entrance sign on the subdivision gate. Unfortunately, she never got the house address. She and the others were kept in the basement, and once she got free, she didn't stop running to look back."

"What about a description of the captors?"

"Middle-aged white couple of medium build. Man had gray hair and woman had brown hair. Both blue-eyed. In other words, generic."

"We can show Karen photos of the different property owners and have her identify which couple held—"

"Karen's long gone. I can only assume she's left the Atlanta area. No family or friends have heard from her in weeks." Charlotte feared the worst for her former informant.

James pulled the plat map of Falling Rock from the printer and circled one property in red. "Pretty sure this is the house we observed with the gardeners out back and where you saw the girl at the window. It belongs to Richard and Madeline Stowers, who have no children. We're in luck."

Her heartbeat quickened. "Why? Do you know them?"

"Barely. Not like we run in the same social circles. But next week, they're hosting the annual fund-raiser for the sheriff's office." He gave a grim smile. "And we're always invited to attend. Every officer—including new trainees."

Charlotte slapped her hands on the desk and grinned. Finally, an opportunity to access the grounds. "Bam. We can take advantage of that and sneak around." But as suddenly as elation surged through her body, it deflated. "Still, a whole week…they'll have moved the girls out by then. Sure, it's brazen enough that they're holding y'all a fund-raiser, but to keep the girls locked up for hours with a dozen lawmen in the same house? I don't see it happening."

"Oh, the fund-raiser won't be at their house. They hold it at the Falling Rock Community Clubhouse." He pointed to the map. "The clubhouse is only three doors down from the Stowerses' cabin, though. They plan on trying to sell the girls practically right under our noses."

"Perfect cover," she pointed out. "Invite all the law enforcement officers to the ball—which leaves no one patrolling the streets." Charlotte stood, restless and hungry with the need for action. "I want to see their home and the clubhouse from the front. I couldn't do a safe drive-by in my rental, but what if we took a patrol car for a spin? We'd be providing a routine public service, right?"

"I'm all in." He pushed back his chair and grabbed his jacket. "Don't forget your camera. With any luck, you'll catch a glimpse of Jenny."

James kept his gaze fixed on the winding mountain road. Something had happened back there in the office—unspoken, unexpected and unwanted. Sure, there had been a few flashes of heat before, but now their chemistry crackled and burned with tension. Charlotte's presence filled the vehicle, filled his mind and filled his senses.

"Fancy, shmancy," she commented as the Falling Rock entrance came into view. By the gatehouse was a large stone wall with a six-foot waterfall feature.

"Only the best for these folks." Despite all his years away and his overseas stints, James's nerves were still set on edge whenever he crossed into the exclusive community. Growing up as the son of a local moonshiner hadn't been easy. Even by Lavender Mountain standards, his family had been poor and looked down upon. In many ways, the situation was even worse since the Tedder name had been linked to a string of murders last year. The disparity between the rich and poor couldn't be more evident.

Charlotte's voice wrenched him out of his thoughts. "Do they keep this gate manned 24/7?"

"Yep. The guards are paid out of homeowner association fees. Must pay them fairly well, too—there's seldom any turnover. Then again," he admitted, "steady jobs are hard to come by around here."

"Could be the Stowerses pay them a little something extra to turn a blind eye to their comings and goings," she mused.

James pulled up to the gate and rolled down his window. Les Phelps leaned out the gatehouse window with a clipboard. "Afternoon, Officer Tedder. Cold day today."

"Hey, Les. Meet our new officer, Bailey Hanson.

I'm showing her around the area. Letting her get a feel for the lay of the land."

His gaunt face lit on Charlotte with interest. "Howdy, ma'am. Pleasure to meet ya."

Charlotte leaned forward and gave a friendly wave. "You write down every vehicle that comes and goes here?"

"Yes, ma'am. Make, model, time of arrival and time of departure. Always take a quick glance at strangers' driver's licenses, too. All day, every day."

"Bet nothing gets by you," she said with a coy smile.

"No, ma'am. It surely don't." He blushed and continued staring at Charlotte. "I take my job seriously."

"I don't doubt it for a minute." Her voice practically purred.

Irritation spiked James's blood pressure. Charlotte never spoke to *him* that way. "Thanks, Les," he muttered, then rolled up the window and hit the gas pedal.

Charlotte eased back into her seat. "How well do you know that guy?"

"I've seen him around. He was a couple grades behind me in school."

"Trustworthy or no?"

"Never been in trouble with the law, as far as I know. Seemed an okay kid."

"Not exactly a ringing endorsement."

He shrugged. "How can you ever really know what goes on in other people's lives? We all wear a mask to some degree. For all I know, Les might be a serial killer."

And he wasn't being flippant. Even family members sometimes weren't what they seemed—as he well knew.

Charlotte snorted. "And here I thought *I* was jaded. You're just as bad."

The road climbed until they rounded a bend and faced the first behemoth of stone and wood and glass. Charlotte gave an appreciative whistle. "Sweet little mansions you've got here. I bet most of the owners don't even live here full-time."

"Most don't," he agreed. "We hardly ever see them during the cold months unless it's for the fund-raiser or a holiday." James slowed the car. "And here we are. Third house on the left belongs to the Stowerses."

"Nice digs," she commented, studying the house. "Would it be possible to get an architect's drawing of the floorplan? Could come in handy later."

"I'll check. Shouldn't be a problem since the architect lives in Falling Rock. He'll want to help keep his community safe and clean."

"I take it there's only one entrance to Falling Rock?"

"It's the only paved road, yes."

"Good point. I noticed the jeep and four-wheeler trails along the back of the properties on this side of the street. We'll need a lookout posted front and back to secure the neighborhood."

"Harlan would agree to the needed manpower if we could show some proof that the girls are trapped there."

"Proof?" Charlotte slapped the dashboard and huffed, "She's there. It's so frustrating trying to prove it."

"You're a cop. You know how this works."

"I know," she muttered, staring at the dashboard. "I'm just... I call Tanya every night and have to give her bad news."

"But tonight you'll have good news. You saw Jenny. As long as she's alive, there's hope."

She sighed and rubbed her temples. "You're right. I can't imagine what it's like for Tanya, though."

He didn't want to do it, damn it, but he couldn't resist. Couldn't bear to see the misery in her eyes. James reached across the console and took her hand. Her fingers encircled his and held on. They didn't speak as they left Falling Rock and traveled back down Blood Mountain.

Peace settled over James. It was inappropriate, ill-advised and one step closer to heartbreak. Charlotte was his partner—a temporary one, at that. Once this case was over, she'd return to her life in Atlanta and forget all about him, just as Ashley had forgotten him while he was in Afghanistan.

And yet he held on to her hand.

A black car slowly exited Falling Rock and fell into place behind their vehicle. Although darkness had not yet fallen, it was impossible to make out the driver through the tinted windows. Reluctantly James removed his hand from Charlotte's and placed it on the steering wheel.

She instantly sensed trouble. "What is it?"

"Black sedan behind us. Just keeping an eye out since you were followed by one in town."

She straightened in her seat and turned her neck. "Holy," she grunted. "I'm glad I have a gun this time. And you beside me."

The five-mile stretch between them and town was practically deserted. A growing unease prickled his scalp as the sedan picked up speed and drew closer. Close enough that if he came to a sudden stop, the vehicle would ram into theirs. Two men were in that car, but he couldn't make out their individual features. James hit the accelerator.

The sedan did the same. An arm emerged from its passenger-side window, and a gun took aim.

"Get down!" he shouted, and shoved Charlotte's head below the glass. "They've got a—"

The ping of gunfire erupted, followed immediately by the grate of metal against metal as a bullet connected with fender.

His mind cleared and narrowed to a crystallized focus. He had to get them to safety. His brain worked at warp speed, calculating his options. It was another four miles to town, and he was willing to bet that the snipers wouldn't shoot with eyewitnesses around. And he knew every hairpin twist on this road— advantage, him. So…his best bet was to drive fast and weave the cruiser so that the snipers would have a more difficult shot.

Charlotte turned on the walkie-talkie. "Come in. This is Officer Hanson. We're at mile marker three on County Road 143. Officers needs help. Shots fired. All available backup needed *immediately.*"

James rounded a curve and jerked the steering wheel to the left. Another bullet fired, missing them completely. Quickly he maneuvered back into the right lane. Paved road and faded lines of white paint rose to greet him at a dizzying speed.

Ping. Glass shards exploded from the back window. He slowed for an instant, ensuring Charlotte was unharmed.

"That's it, damn it!" Charlotte loaded her gun, unrolled the passenger window, and halfway leaned out.

"What are you—"

The roar of her shot exploded, and James tugged at her jacket. "Get down!"

"No way." She took aim and fired again. "Missed. At least they're slowing."

"How the hell am I supposed to drive? One sharp turn and your ass will fall out that window."

"Don't worry about me. You focus on the road."

James gritted his teeth. If they managed to survive the next five minutes, Charlotte was in for a tongue lashing of a magnitude she'd never experienced. He was the lead, and as such, he had the right to—

A red pickup truck swerved around the corner, and James jerked the car back into his own lane. Only inches of space separated their vehicles. There was barely time to register the man's shocked face, and then he heard him lay on his horn. No doubt Harlan would be getting a civilian complaint about his reckless driving. So be it.

Another mile and a half passed. A few sprinklings of barns and cabins dotted the wintry landscape. They were getting closer to safety.

Charlotte fired again. "Got 'em! Bullet went through their windshield, but I'm not sure if it hit one of them."

And her tone indicated she hoped that the bullet found its human mark. A surge of admiration, mixed with adrenaline, rushed through him. He'd take Charlotte Helms as a partner any day, every day.

His bubble of appreciation burst as their cruiser suddenly pitched to the left. The sniper had shot out his left rear tire. James fought to keep the cruiser from veering over the side of the mountain. The flimsy guardrails would never hold back over three tons of speeding metal. Soon the heat from the tire rim grinding on pavement might lock up his brakes.

And that would be it. They'd come to a dead halt and be a sitting target. Orange and red sparks tunneled upward from the rear of the cruiser.

From a distance, the whirring of sirens approached. Would it be too late?

The sedan surged forward, trying to pass him on the left. Its right front fender crashed into them, and the cruiser spun out of control.

Round and round they flew in a circus ride of terror. He caught glimpses of Charlotte's face, which was set, grim and determined, even if her voice shook. "I'm ready to face them," she declared, one hand on the dashboard to keep from flying about, the other gripping her weapon.

The cruiser slowed its spin, and James withdrew his gun. This was it.

Another burst of gunfire erupted from beside him. "I hit their front tire," Charlotte said. "Take *that*, you bastards!"

The sedan took a sudden dive to the right, flipping over the guardrail like dandelion seeds in the wind. James slammed on the brakes, abandoned his vehicle and rushed to the rail, Charlotte one step ahead of him.

On and on it rolled. "Radio for an ambulance," he said.

"I'm going down." Charlotte hopped over the mangled guardrail and slowly walked down the steep incline, holstering her weapon.

"What the hell," he muttered. Backup was on the way. It was more important that he stay close to Charlotte. Bastards were like cats—they always seemed to have nine lives. No way would he risk letting one of them shoot at her. And she still favored her right leg after yesterday's flesh wound.

"Careful," he warned. "They might still be alive and dangerous."

"As if this is my first day as a cop," she muttered as she continued the slow descent. Rocks and roots marred the surface, and bits of gravel tumbled beneath his feet.

Oomph. Charlotte went down, feet flying out from under her, and tumbled a good ten feet on her side. James stumbled and slid to a halt beside her. "You okay?"

"Hell, no." Her breathing was jagged and raspy, her forehead scratched and bleeding. "My side hurts."

No blood that he could observe. Gently he ran a hand down her left rib cage. "Here?"

Charlotte moaned and batted his hand away.

"Probably cracked ribs," he said. "And maybe even internal injury."

"Who cares? Just go. Don't let those guys get away."

"You sure?"

She waved a hand. "Go!"

The siren wails grew louder—the cavalry would arrive soon enough.

"I'll send the backup your way," she urged.

He nodded and scrambled down the incline. Two men dressed in black pants and navy T-shirts crawled out of the sedan. One ran for the tree line, cradling his arm, and the other tried to run, but clutched his right leg and limped along at a slower clip.

James picked up his pace, half sliding and half jogging downward. What rotten luck that a tree hadn't broken the sedan's fall. Instead, it had rolled to a stop twenty yards from the edge of the woods. Gray smoke from its engine spiraled upward. Damn, the sedan could go up in flames at any moment.

The smell of leaking fuel brought him to a standstill. A whoosh of dizziness descended and he was again sucked into that quicksand of a flashback. A merciless sun beat down on the top of his head and his skin gritted and stung from an Afghan sandstorm. The enemy jeep approached and he was powerless to escape. Brain, body and lungs tightened into paralysis. He couldn't move or think past the boa-constricting fear that wrapped around his chest and squeezed and squeezed and squeezed.

"Look out!" Charlotte called, the words barely audible in the heavy gusts. But her voice cut through the time and distance his mind had created. The constriction in his chest loosened and he ran to the side of the smoking sedan, keeping plenty of distance between the smoking vehicle and himself. A curl of fire arose, licking the engine.

He ran as fast as he could, yet when the sedan exploded, the heat from the conflagration scorched his body like a blast furnace. How long had he been standing there, body present but his mind a thousand miles away? Probably enough time for the men to escape. They were nowhere in sight. He couldn't let them disappear and perhaps ruin their best chance of cracking the ring.

He ran into the woods, the brightness of the day dropping away. James withdrew his gun, stepped behind a tree, and surveyed the area. The men could be standing behind one of the wider oaks or curled down behind dense shrubbery and foliage. "Drop your weapons and give yourselves up!" he shouted.

The wind whistled and tree limbs rattled, but no other sounds emerged. How far had they managed to run?

At the distant shouts from behind him, James turned to find several officers making a slow descent down the mountain. Once more backup arrived, they could all spread out and search the area, but the sinking despair in his stomach said it would be fruitless. He knew only too well that it was easy for a man to hide out in these parts. The land was wild and tangled, populated with caves and plenty of nooks and crannies for desperate—or lucky—fugitives.

Damn it to hell. When were they going to catch a break in this case?

Chapter 7

A helicopter roared overhead in the almost black sky, making conversation difficult. Harlan gestured for James and Charlotte to follow him to his cruiser. Inside, James took the back seat with Charlotte while Harlan started the engine and cranked up the heater. He took off his gloves and warmed his hands over the vent.

"Sure you don't want to go to the hospital and have your injuries looked at?" he asked, spinning around and addressing Charlotte.

"For the last time, *no*. All I've got is a scratch on the forehead and some bruised ribs."

Despite his misery of self-disgust over the PTSD issues, James's lips quirked upward. The woman obviously had a thing against doctors.

"No point in you both hanging around all night," Harlan said. "I'm keeping an officer on patrol at Falling Rock in case the men return there on foot. And I'm sending the rest of the search party home, helicopter included. I'll deploy men again at first light. For now, we've done all we can do."

James ran a hand through his close-cropped hair. "How about we question Les one more time—"

"Forget it. He's told us all he knows. Thanks to him, we have the sedan's tag number, at least."

"For all the good that did," Charlotte grumbled.

Another dead end in the case. The sedan was rented from an Atlanta company, but the driver had provided a fake ID. Shame lanced through him yet again. That damn PTSD. So far, Charlotte hadn't brought up today's failure, but he couldn't let it go.

"More bad news," Harlan continued. "Sammy got ahold of the Stowerses. He and his wife are still in Atlanta, and he claims no knowledge of who the men could be. I tend to believe him. Listen, y'all go ahead and crash for the evening. You've had enough excitement for one day. And you're bound to be bruised and sore come morning."

James was fine and wound-up enough to work all night, to make up for his lapse. But despite her bravado, Charlotte's eyes sported half moons of dark shadows, and she kept rubbing her temples as if trying to ward off a headache.

"I agree." Charlotte's mouth opened to object, and James sped up to stop her argument. "The best course is for us to get a good night's sleep and start fresh in the morning." He ached to reach an arm around Charlotte, but if Harlan saw the attraction between them, he'd more than likely assign another officer to work with her.

James wasn't about to let that happen.

Harlan nodded approval and pulled out onto the road. "I'll give you a lift home. Come to the station as soon as you're able in the morning, and we'll work out a plan of attack."

They left behind the strobing blue lights of a dozen cop cars and entered the thick blackness of unlit country roads. In the crystal coldness, the stars and moon were lit like a jeweled candelabra. At the edge of town, Harlan pulled into James's driveway. A familiar red car was parked outside, and the lights inside were on.

"Lilah's here," Harlan explained. "Soon as she heard you were okay after the accident, she insisted on cooking y'all a hearty dinner. You know how she is."

And Lilah was no doubt dying to meet his new, live-in partner. He and Harlan exchanged an amused glance. She was curious as a cat, and nothing deterred her from exploring the unknown. A trait that had almost cost Lilah her life.

"Here's something for you to think about, Sheriff," Charlotte suddenly said. "Those men who chased us were tipped off that we were exploring Falling Rock. Soon as we announced at the office that we were going to patrol the area, the men were lying in wait. It's time you considered whether one of your own officers alerted them."

Harlan's spine straightened, and his jaw clenched. Oh, hell, he took those kinds of remarks personally and was about to flip. After the corruption of the previous sheriff, he was hypersensitive to criticism. "Could have been the gatekeeper or just plain bad luck," James said quickly, hoping to diffuse the bomb before it went off.

Charlotte shot him a thanks-for-backing-me-up

smirk. "Sticking your head in the sand never helps the situation."

"Don't be so quick to judge," Harlan said, snapping his fingers. "I run a clean operation and personally vetted every officer when I became sheriff."

"Still doesn't mean one of your staff isn't on the take," Charlotte said.

Harlan jerked the car to an abrupt halt.

James opened the back door, eager to forestall the argument. "Thanks for the lift. We'll see you in the morning."

Charlotte shot Harlan another sharp glance but climbed out without further comment.

Before James could follow her, Harlan muttered, "Like to speak to you a moment. In private."

Great. Just what he needed after this long, hellacious day. "Be there in a minute," he called to Charlotte. She continued walking to the porch without bothering to turn around and acknowledge him.

"No wonder she's been suspended for insubordination," Harlan remarked drily.

He leaped to her defense. "Look, she's got trust issues, okay? Probably had a few rats and sour deals go down after all those years working undercover. Their lives depend on suspecting the worst of everyone."

"I don't give a damn about her attitude. It's her… state of mind that concerns me. I spoke with her boss today in Atlanta. He insinuated Detective Helms has emotional issues. Her behavior has been erratic of late—refusing to be reassigned new duties, anger with a couple of other cops she claimed abandoned her during a drug bust, and taking an interest in one particular victim way too personally."

"Her best friend's daughter is one of the kidnapped children. You can't blame her for refusing to give up and taking it to heart. Didn't you take it personally when Lilah was in danger?"

Harlan blew out a deep breath. "Yeah, that's true. You don't have to keep bringing that up."

"And you broke every rule J.D. laid down during his past few weeks as sheriff. You even managed to get yourself fired. Imagine if another agency looked at your record during that time to evaluate your trustworthiness as a potential employee."

"Point taken."

James stuck his hands in his jacket and stared ahead. "There's something you should know. I messed up today. I was in pursuit of those men, but when I got near their vehicle and smelled gasoline...well, I froze."

"The PTSD got to you?"

"Yeah. I warned you about it before I took the job. If you want my badge, it's yours."

Harlan stared straight ahead, as well. "Still seeing that counselor?"

"Twice a month."

He nodded. "If it gets worse, or you want out, let me know. Until then, I have no complaints about your job performance. The men probably would have escaped no matter what."

"We'll never know. But I wanted to set the record straight. I'm the screwup around here, not Charlotte."

Harlan gave him a considering appraisal. "Don't think I haven't noticed the way you've been looking at her. Just remember that she's only here temporarily."

He knew that, but Harlan's warning still twisted his gut.

"She might as well be from across the country," Harlan continued. "The differences between here and Atlanta couldn't be greater."

"I *know*," he said wearily. "I'm not stupid enough to think she'd ever want to stay in Lavender Mountain." Unless one was born and raised in Appalachia, it wasn't an area one often wanted to move *to*— usually, people want to move *out*. He understood this. And Charlotte wasn't seeing the mountains at their greenest and proudest time of year, either.

"This is ridiculous," he muttered, more to himself than Harlan. "I barely know her."

"That's the spirit," Harlan said as James headed to the porch. "Tell my wife not to stay too long, ya hear?"

As if Lilah would listen to either one of them. She pretty much did as she pleased.

He waved a hand in dismissal and entered the house. The scent of chicken and dumplings almost made him weak in the knees. He hadn't even realized he was hungry.

Charlotte was already seated at the kitchen table and blowing on a spoon to cool the dumplings. "I'm starving," she admitted. "Your sister is an angel."

"You might be the first to ever call her that," he said with a snort. "Where's Ellie?" Lilah was almost never without his niece on her hip.

"With the babysitter," said Lilah. "She's under the weather, so I didn't want to take her out."

"What's wrong?" he asked quickly. He hated that little Ellie wasn't her usual bright, babbling self. He'd never figured himself for the liking-kids type, but since the day she was born, Ellie had enchanted him.

"A bit of a cold and sore throat. She'll be fine."

Assured Ellie was going to be okay, he fixed a bowl of dumplings and sat across from Charlotte. Under the kitchen light, her red hair shone with a heat that his fingers itched to stroke. The bright warmth of the kitchen and intimacy of the home-cooked meal loosened the tension of the day.

He could get used to this.

And that scared him more than any high-speed chase.

"We need to do something about this. James told me your red hair really stood out. It's beautiful, but not practical for undercover work, huh?" Lilah reached across the table and twirled a strand of Charlotte's hair. "Picked up some temporary hair dye for you in town, the brown tank tops you requested and a few little extra somethings."

If by "a few little somethings" she meant underwear, Charlotte would be eternally grateful. She hadn't packed enough clothes, and there'd been no time to do laundry, which landed her in a desperate situation. Going commando wasn't her style.

James stood and peeked in the store bags on the counter, then pulled out a box. "Are you going blond or brunette?"

Charlotte eyed it warily. "Appears I'm going brunette." A wig would have been simpler and less fuss, but this wouldn't be her first dye job to go under the radar.

James continued rustling about in the bag.

"There's nothing in there for you," Lilah said. "Stop—"

He pulled out a six-pack of women's panties and a

box of tampons. He dropped both items back into the bag as if it'd scalded his fingers and handed the purchases to Charlotte. "For you," he said drily.

"There's a peach pie for dessert," Lilah commented. "Why don't you get some and go watch television or something?"

"You don't have to tell me twice to get out of the way," he mumbled.

Charlotte suppressed a giggle before a wave of nostalgia washed over her. How long had it been since she'd enjoyed sparring with her two brothers? She did a quick mental calculation. It'd been two Christmases ago.

Way too long.

"Shall we get started?" Lilah asked, opening the hair color box and eyeing the directions.

"No need. I've done this before."

Disappointed blue eyes nailed her. "But I want to help. I've been shut in with a sick baby for two days and could use some serious girl time."

Dang. James's sister was as easy to like as he was. But Harlan's scowling face came to mind. "Your husband probably wants you to head on home."

"Harlan? Nah." She flicked her wrist. "His supper's in the oven, and he can fend for himself for one evening."

Was it wrong that she took a little pleasure in Harlan's forced solitude? She rose and headed to the bathroom. "Let's do this."

Ten minutes later, Charlotte cracked the bathroom window to air out the peroxide fumes. She wrinkled her nose at the mirrored reflection. The dye looked like shellacked tar coating her locks. This couldn't be good.

"Maybe we should rinse this out in twenty minutes instead of thirty," she said, dubiously eyeing the mess.

Lilah bit her lip. "The saleslady helped me pick out the color. Made it sound real easy, too."

"It'll be fine," Charlotte reassured her, adjusting the towel around her neck. "It's just hair. It can always be fixed."

"If you say so."

Her tone did not inspire confidence.

Charlotte emptied out the shopping bag, glad to see all the essentials—panties, tampons, shampoo, conditioner, body wash. "Thanks so much."

"You need anything else, let me know. Do you already have a dress for the fund-raiser party?"

"I've got one in my Atlanta apartment I can fetch later. You going?"

"As the sheriff's wife, it's expected. Besides the cash infusion for Harlan's office, those property owners wield lots of political power. Much as my husband hates politics, it'd be foolish not to hobnob with them."

No wonder everyone was so cautious about descending on Falling Rock. "Wouldn't want to tick them off in any way," she slowly agreed.

Lilah nodded. "Not unless absolutely necessary. But Harlan will do whatever it takes to solve this case. Even if it means angering the wrong people."

"He's told you about the trafficking ring?"

"Of course. The whole thought of something so evil happening close by makes me sick." Lilah shrugged and took a deep breath. "I didn't come to talk shop. Y'all have enough of that on the job. Honestly, I'm looking forward to the fund-raising ball. Wouldn't miss it for the world. I've never gone before. Last year, I had the baby the night before the ball."

"They hire musicians?"

"Only the best. Or so I've heard." Her eyes grew dreamy. "I've always wanted to go inside one of the mansions on Blood Mountain. When I was a little girl, I thought the whole neighborhood was a fairyland of castles."

"Surprised you've never had the opportunity to go in one over the years."

The dreamy expression vanished. "Me? Not hardly."

"Why?"

Lilah let out a long sigh. "You're not from around here, so you wouldn't know. But you've seen the tiny cabin where I grew up. For a whole lot of reasons, the Tedder name isn't one to land you a ticket to a fancy ball."

"Sounds like class bias is everywhere."

"It wasn't just the poverty," Lilah explained. "James hasn't told you our illustrious family history? I thought you two were close."

"He hasn't said much." Charlotte hesitated to bring up the past, but Lilah had broached it first. "I do read the papers, though. The serial killer incident made the Atlanta news."

Lilah's blue eyes darkened, but in spite of the painful memory, she seemed to quickly shrug it off. "Growing up in our household wasn't easy. My dad was a moonshiner with a monster temper, and my parents argued constantly until Mom moved out."

"I'm sorry. James hasn't mentioned any of that to me. Look, I don't want you to get the wrong idea about us. We're business partners. And I'm grateful to him for helping me with this case, of course."

Lilah raised a brow. "That's all there is to it?"

She flushed, thinking of his kisses. "What has he told you about me?"

"Nothing. But anyone can see the sparks between you two. And it's more than that. I've seen the way he looks at you."

She couldn't stop the warm glow that lit her belly or the smile that lifted her lips. "Really?"

"Positive. I've worried about James since he returned from Afghanistan. He's been withdrawn and alone for too long."

The warm glow faded. "You know I work undercover. Our living together is temporary. I won't be staying long."

"Atlanta's not so far you can't visit on weekends," Lilah said. "You have to come back to Lavender Mountain in the spring, when the whole forest comes alive. Or the fall, when the leaves are changing color. Right now, we're not at our best."

Lilah sounded as if she worked at the local tourist office. "I'm sure it's beautiful. But working undercover isn't like being a regular cop. I can't always come and go as I please. It's not a job. It's a lifestyle."

"Sounds extremely demanding and not much fun."

Fun? No. The fun had worn off years ago. Charlotte couldn't remember the last time she found it even remotely pleasurable. But she did important work. Work that few others wanted to take on.

Ding. The portable kitchen timer startled them both.

That time had gone by quickly. After rinsing the dye, Charlotte realized she'd have to eat her earlier words about it being "just hair" that could always "be fixed."

Lilah let out a startled wail.

Charlotte's formerly auburn locks were now a mess

of tangled black straw. All she needed was a hawk of a nose and a wart on her chin for a perfect Halloween witch disguise.

Too bad it was November.

A knock rapped the bathroom door. "Everything okay in there?" James asked.

Quickly she wrapped her ruined hair up in a turban. The guy was probably impatient for a shower. "One minute," she called out.

"Sorry," Lilah breathed.

"No big deal. During work hours, I always wear it in a ponytail anyway."

Lilah washed and dried her hands and opened the door. "Guess I'll be heading home now. Ellie might wake up feeling miserable and want me." Her face lit up. "Have I showed you her picture?" Without waiting for an answer, Lilah lifted her purse from the table and pulled out a cell phone.

James groaned. "Here we go."

"Just one quick look," his sister promised, holding out the phone to Charlotte.

Ellie's toothless grin and folds of baby fat were typical, but the crystal blue eyes were not. They were the startling blue shared by James and Lilah. She'd recognize that shade anywhere.

The towel slipped from her hair and dropped to the floor.

James stared at her, eyes wide and jaw slack. "What happened to your hair?" he asked, voice booming.

Lilah poked her brother in the side and scowled.

"I mean… I'm sure it'll look better when it dries," he amended.

"Sure." Like hell it would. She sat down at the table

and felt the tangled tumbleweed of hair. The damage might be beyond repair. Maybe she should cut it supershort. Absently she said goodbye to Lilah, and the door opened and closed.

James sat down beside her. "So…you got some conditioner? Darla—my other sister—once had a dye job disaster. She went around the house slathered in hair conditioner for a week to repair the damage."

Charlotte sucked in her breath at the mention of Darla. That sister's name had been all over the news last year. She couldn't imagine how much it would hurt if something tragic happened with her brothers—no matter how big of a pain in the ass they could be. "Yeah, Lilah bought a bottle. It's in the bathroom."

He rose from the table and returned with it in hand. "Let's see what we can do."

Before she could protest, he poured half the bottle in her hair and gently ran his fingers over the knots.

"You don't have to—"

"Shhh…relax," he whispered.

His fingers pressed into her scalp and neck, massaging and caressing. She closed her eyes and gave herself up to the pleasure of the moment. Not even cold glops of conditioner running down her face and nape deterred from the comfort of his touch.

A vision of Ellie's blue eyes flashed through her mind, and a primitive urge to procreate clenched her gut. Hell, she hadn't known she had a biological clock. That wasn't anywhere on her radar.

Until now.

That realization almost made her want to run from the hills.

Chapter 8

"The bloodwork came in," James announced at his office the next morning, slamming the phone down. "That was no deer killed in the woods. The blood was human."

Charlotte's face paled, and panic lit her eyes. "It wasn't… It can't be Jenny's. Maybe someone's just been injured—"

He hastened to reassure her. "We won't have the DNA results for weeks. And it's not necessarily from any of the captive girls. Anyone could have had an accident on a four-wheeler."

"We checked the hospitals and clinics. No serious accidents were reported near the vicinity. It *has* to be one of those girls."

Privately he agreed, but kept his mouth shut. "We'll

find out soon enough. Harlan wants us and Sammy in his office right now to work out a plan."

As they scurried down the hall, their coworker joined them midway. "What the hell?" Sammy asked, pointing to Charlotte's hair.

"Red hair is a little too conspicuous," she answered stiffly. "I took corrective measures."

James stifled a grin at her tight French braid. But Charlotte could dye her hair green and purple, and it wouldn't detract from her beauty one iota.

Zelda was seated by Harlan's desk, taking notes. "Subpoena the gatekeeper's records," Harlan ordered.

She adjusted the glasses on the bridge of her nose. "How far back ya want me to go?"

"At least a year."

Zelda nodded and left the room.

"Let's hit the ground running today," Harlan announced, slapping his hands on the desk. "I won't have my officers blindsided again like y'all were yesterday." He slid a pair of car keys across the table. "Here's your new vehicle. A temporary loaner from Floyd County until the destroyed cruiser is replaced. James and Detective Helms will canvass the Falling Rock neighborhood today, show photos of the Ashbury girl, and see if anyone's spotted her, or if their reaction is suspicious. Sammy, I want you to—"

Charlotte abruptly stood. "No. This isn't a good idea."

James shook his head. She never ceased to surprise him. "I thought you'd want to take action. You've been champing at the bit ever since you got here."

"If we do this, the traffickers will know something's up, and they'll find a way to transport the girls out."

"We can have an officer watch the gate to search any suspicious vehicles that leave," he suggested.

"What about the dirt path out back? If we give them any wiggle room, we can kiss the whole operation goodbye. I've been tracking them for over a damn year, and I won't have the girls' lives jeopardized."

He stood as well, standing toe to toe with her. So much for last night's détente. "Nobody wants that. But we can't just sit on our asses and do nothing."

Charlotte turned to Harlan. "Can't you do something to speed up those DNA results? All we need is one concrete piece of evidence for a judge."

"So, what's your great plan?" James interrupted, stung at her quick dismissal of him. "Keep sitting out in the woods every day and hoping Jenny or one of the others happens to look out the window again?"

Her face flushed, staining her cheeks crimson.

"Simmer down, you two," Harlan said.

They breathed hard, staring at one another. Sammy gave a low, amused whistle.

"I said sit *down*," Harlan thundered. "Last I checked, I'm the one running this show, and I'll decide what strategy to take."

James felt like a chastened schoolboy as he settled back in his chair.

"Now, here's what we're going to do. Sammy will guard the back of the Stowerses' property to make sure no one leaves via four-wheelers or a jeep on those back roads. He'll let us know at once if there's any suspicious activity."

"There are lives at stake here," Charlotte cautioned. "I know we all want to rush in and rescue them." Her fists clenched and unclenched by her sides. "But they're in a volatile situation. We can't make it worse for them by arousing premature suspicion. I say we keep an eye out from afar until the fund-raiser. Monitor the gate to make sure no one enters or exits Falling Rock to ensure that the captives stay where they are. Then, at the fund-raiser, we all spread out and find what we can inside the Stowerses' house."

"Search without a warrant? Highly illegal," James pointed out. "And how are we supposed to get in there?"

"You said they always had lots of out-of-town guests staying over for the event. There's bound to be lots of foot traffic between their place and the clubhouse. We'll try and blend in with the crowd."

"And we don't have to exactly call it a search," Harlan said slowly. "I'd phrase it more like *keeping our eyes open*. If you know what I mean."

"You can call it what you want. I won't leave until I've gone through every room in that house," Charlotte retorted.

"Ditto," James agreed. "Although I still don't see the harm in questioning the neighborhood today about who might have been driving that black sedan and if anyone's seen Jenny Ashbury. Only good can come when a community is alerted. Plus, it'll make future trafficking that much harder to slip by unnoticed if residents are on the lookout for unusual activity." James turned to Sammy. "What do you think?"

"I say let's head out there now." Sammy gave Charlotte an apologetic smile. "Sorry, Detective. Looks like you're in the minority."

She ran a hand over the black wisps of hair that had escaped her braid. "At least let me be the one to question the Stowerses. That is, if they even answer the door."

"Not alone, you aren't," James said quickly. Did she think she could brush aside their partnership so easily? Hurt, mixed equally with anger, coursed through his body.

"I can handle it," she said curtly. "I've been doing this kind of work for years. Much longer than you have."

Ouch. Bitten in the ass by his own logic.

"You'll go together," Harlan ordered. "It shouldn't be me. The Stowerses would view a personal visit by the sheriff as more threatening and suspicious. They might be more open with James."

"Doubt that," James muttered. "If you're hoping they'll invite me in for coffee and cookies, then you've forgotten what the Tedder name means around here."

Harlan shrugged. "Times are changing." His eyes and face softened. "A lot of that is thanks to Lilah. She has a real way with people."

Sammy stood. "Shall we get started?"

They all rose, and Harlan passed out copies of Jenny's photo. "Zelda got copies ready for us this morning. I'll form a blockade by the gatehouse and personally check every vehicle that passes by. Everyone all set?"

They nodded and left his office. It was a tense walk to their new department-issued vehicle. James opened the door and Charlotte edged up to him.

"Why don't I drive today?"

"I'm more familiar with the area. An advantage if another vehicle tails us again."

She didn't look happy about his answer, but walked over to the passenger side and got in. He faced Charlotte before starting the car. "Why all the hostility in there? Thought we were a team."

"That doesn't mean I quietly accept ideas that I think are wrong."

"I can't believe you're opposed to this questioning. You've been raring for action."

"I've already expressed my reservations. No need to rehash the issue. Let me do the talking when we get to the Stowerses'."

"No way," he said, starting the engine and backing out of the parking space. "The cover story is that you're a new trainee. It'll look suspicious if you take the lead."

"Oh, alright," she conceded in a huff. "I can admit when I'm wrong. You take the lead."

"Thank you."

They didn't speak again until the Falling Rock gate-house came into view. Charlotte placed a hand on his arm. "Sorry you felt attacked in there," she said quietly. "I just… I can't screw this up."

He took her hand and gave it a quick squeeze. "I know what this case means to you and to Jenny's mother. I'd never do anything to jeopardize the girl's safety."

Charlotte nodded. "And James, there's no one I'd rather do this with than you."

She might have been opposed to the plan, but Charlotte's heart skipped with excitement as they walked up the stone pathway to the Stowerses' house. Most of the neighbors hadn't been home today, but the few that were claimed no knowledge of a black sedan and said they didn't recognize Jenny's photo. But that was what they'd expected, anyway.

This was it. The real reason for questioning Falling Rock residents. She was walking on the very ground where Jenny was being held against her will.

James quirked a brow. "I'm lead. Right?"

"Right," she said grudgingly, stuffing her hands in the brown uniform jacket. Besides the fact that it would look suspicious for a trainee to do most of the talking, her personal involvement might make her too aggressive in questioning and blow up the case.

The front door was a massive wooden showpiece, hand-carved with a mountain range design. James rang the doorbell, which seemed to echo in the cavernous interior.

A petite older lady answered the door, wearing a gray dress with a spotless white apron. Her once-auburn hair was streaked with gray and pulled back into a tight bun. She even wore a frilly lace maid's cap like Charlotte had seen only in the movies.

Fear snapped in the woman's dark eyes. "May I help you?" she asked with a strong accent that Charlotte couldn't quite place. Irish, perhaps, given the red hair and fair skin.

"May we speak to the lady of the house?" James asked.

"One moment. I'll go see."

The ornate door closed, and Charlotte shared a look with James. The sound of it clicking shut echoed in the pit of her stomach like doom. She might have been opposed to the visit originally, but getting this close— only to be denied entrance—was excruciating.

Yet she said nothing and stared straight ahead. You never knew when cameras or audio tapes might be rolling. If she were in the traffickers' position, she'd certainly take those precautions.

A staccato percussion sounded on the hard floor, and the door creaked open. "Hello, officers," said Madeline Stowers. "To what do I owe the pleasure?"

Long silver hair was loosely gathered at her nape in a stylish coif that was much too elegant to have been accidental. Self-consciously, Charlotte touched her hand to her own dyed hack job.

Maddie's face was beautiful and possessed the underlying bone structure of a model's, although a faint tightness suggested plastic surgery accounted in part for the firm, barely wrinkled skin. Her brown eyes were wide and her eyebrows thin and arched. A tasteful shade of rose-red glistened on her lips. She wore a black shirt with a deep V that belted at the waist and a black pencil skirt that highlighted her slim physique.

"Mrs. Stowers?" James asked.

"Call me Maddie." She glanced at their nametags. "Officers Tedder and Hanson?" Her slight frown did nothing to mar the smooth plane of her forehead.

Botox, Charlotte guessed.

"Yes, ma'am," James answered. "May we come in?"

It took willpower not to sneak a surprised glance his way. A bold move. He hadn't requested to enter anyone else's home.

A heartbeat of hesitation, and then, "Of course, do come in." Maddie stepped aside and waved them along with a graceful sweep of an arm.

Charlotte entered and picked up a familiar, powdery-sweet scent of black violets mixed with citrus. Maddie used the same brand of designer perfume that her late grandmother once favored. They passed through the foyer and entered the den. She felt her jaw drop, but she couldn't contain her split-second reaction to the opulence. This was a whole new criminal class from what she was normally accustomed to dealing with. Usually the ones she sought undercover lived in squalor in a crack house or some back alley.

The entire back wall was covered in plate-glass windows that afforded a stunning view of trees and mountains. Everywhere she looked, from the paneled, beamed ceilings and walls to the fireplace, the house consisted of custom wood, glass or stone. The only exception was the rustic touch of a twisting iron staircase that led upstairs.

The mountain outdoor element also continued indoors, so much so that even a water element was featured by a huge, man-made rock waterfall that poured into a custom inlaid pool edged with stone and set by the crackling fireplace. The faint scent of burning oak gave the place a ski resort vibe. Two rolled towels were set by the pool, an invitation to indulge in luxury.

"Please, come have a seat," Maddie said, leading them to a leather sectional sofa that could easily accommodate a dozen people. "I take it you're here to discuss some aspect of the fund-raiser? I'm surprised the sheriff didn't contact me directly, though."

"No, ma'am. That's not why we're here," James said.

Charlotte sank onto the sofa next to him while Maddie seated herself opposite, crossing her long legs and smoothing the front of her skirt.

"Sounds ominous," she said with a tinkling laugh. "It's usually so peaceful here. That's why Richard and I bought this place, to escape the noise and the crowds of Atlanta. Don't even get me started on the city traffic. The older we get, the more time we seem to spend here at Falling Rock. Excuse my manners. Would you care for some coffee?"

"Yes—" Charlotte began.

"No." James shrugged. "Okay, coffee would be great. Thanks."

Maddie turned her head and motioned to the maid. "Colleen, serve us coffee and a few slices of that lemon pound cake the chef baked this morning." She faced them again. "It's loaded with sugar, but delicious. Do try a piece."

Hard to believe the perfect woman in front of them ever ate anything but carrots and tofu. She must have an iron will to keep that figure with a pastry chef in the house, Charlotte mused.

James pulled a five-by-seven photograph of Jenny from his coat pocket. "Do you know this person?"

Maddie took the photo and examined it for several seconds. "No. Sorry. Is she in some sort of trouble?"

"She's been missing for two weeks," James said.

Damn, Charlotte had to give it to him. He might have been working in law enforcement for only a few months, but he had the poker face of an officer experienced at interrogating people.

"That poor girl," Maddie cooed, returning the photo. "I take it she's from Lavender Mountain?"

"No, metro Atlanta," Charlotte piped in.

"Is that so?" One perfectly tweezed brow arched, again with no accompanying wrinkles.

It was freaky, Charlotte decided. Unnatural.

"Why on earth are you looking for her way out here, then?" Maddie asked, directing her attention at James. "Does she have family in the area?"

"We're following a tip," he commented, giving nothing away.

"Hard to believe she's landed in such a remote area. I'd imagine strangers in our community would be easily noticeable, at least during this time of year, with the tourist season over."

"So you'd think," James agreed. "But so far, no one's claimed to have seen her."

"Then I'm afraid your tip must have been a bad one. Perhaps an attempt to steer you in the wrong direction?"

James nodded. "That's very astute of you."

Oh, yes, the man was definitely good at his job. Charlotte stood and casually stretched her shoulders. "That's an amazing view you have here," she said, stepping over to the windows against the back wall. Down below, she observed four muscled men dressed in jeans and sporting navy T-shirts. They'd obviously stepped up their security game. She squinted but failed to spot Sammy. Wherever he was staked out, he'd done a fine job of camouflaging his presence.

"It is lovely, isn't it? Ah, Colleen, that was quick. Thank you."

The maid set down a tray on the coffee table and then quickly left the room as Maddie leaned over to pour.

"I'd like to wash up first," Charlotte said. "If you don't mind."

"Down the hall and fifth door on your left," Maddie replied with apparent unconcern.

A quick glance at James's face showed a caution warning in his eyes. He might be a good officer, but this wasn't her first search. Well, technically, this was *not* a search. It was a mere observation of the property that could be legally obtained through a casual stroll.

She slowly walked down the hallway, grateful for the open doors. She passed three bedrooms, each huge with large windows and carpet that appeared to be inches thick, the kind that would feel like walking on pillows. The furniture was heavy wood, and the dressers were empty of any sign that someone actually slept there.

She looked up in the corners of the hallways and bedrooms, curious to see if there were any cameras. Nothing obvious, though they could be cleverly hidden and out of sight. But if she were caught spying on their camera, she could claim she'd mistakenly taken a wrong turn.

Charlotte stepped into one of the bedrooms. The carpeting was as plush as she'd imagined. She halted in the middle of the room, furrowing her brow as if she'd mistakenly entered. If nothing else, a decent undercover cop knew how to put on an act.

But her side excursion didn't help. The closet doors were shut, and even on the opposite side of the dresser bureau, there was no stray clothing or any strewn item to suggest a person used the room. No, the girls were more likely locked in a basement as Karen had claimed—although these bedrooms on the main floor might be used by potential clients to "try out the wares."

The mere thought stiffened her spine and strengthened her resolve to save Jenny. Charlotte left the room and located the bathroom. Gleaming white bounced from walls to ceiling with marble tiles, counters and flooring. As much as she admired the cozy opulence of the rest of the main floor, the white-on-white décor smacked too much of a sterile hospital to suit her tastes.

A camera in here would be inappropriate in all kind of ways, but anyone who kidnapped teenage girls for trafficking was not above installing a discreet bathroom camera. Charlotte leisurely washed her hands and let her eyes rove. Again, everything was meticulously clean and devoid of human personality. She opened cabinet drawers stocked with unopened toothbrushes and toothpaste for guests. The far-left drawer held a pewter hairbrush, but the few hairs in it were long and silver—Maddie's. Charlotte strained her ears, opening her senses to even the faintest whisper.

But only James's and Maddie's voices droned from the den. Disappointed, she returned to them. James fired a quick inquiring glance over his coffee cup, and she shook her head in an almost imperceptible move.

"Will you be in attendance at the fund-raiser?" Maddie asked. "We always invite the officers and their families, even young children. That is, if they're old enough to be awake in the later hours of the evening. It's a real family affair."

"Wouldn't miss it," he declared.

"Me neither," Charlotte said, sitting down by James. "Rookies are invited, too, I take it."

Maddie's smile never wavered, but a cold snap flashed for a second in her dark eyes. "Of course, dear."

So the platinum witch was one of those who viewed other females as competition. That, or Maddie had somehow guessed her true identity. Game on. Charlotte picked up her coffee cup and settled into the cushions, as if intending to make herself at home for a very long time.

"I hear there will be live music." Charlotte sipped the black coffee. "I can't speak for any of the other officers, but I plan on dancing until the music stops and the maids have to shoo me away at dawn."

"Lovely," Maddie said drily, shifting her attention back to James. "I heard about the commotion yesterday near Falling Rock. So shocking. Hope the officers involved are all okay?"

"We're both fine."

"Oh? It was you and—" Maddie leaned forward and scrutinized Charlotte's badge. "Officer Bailey Hanson."

Her name on the badge was a fake. A precautionary measure.

Charlotte lifted her chin. "We're still kicking. Obviously. Not so sure about the other guys, though. Any of your men show up hurt today, by chance?"

Maddie blinked. "As far as I know, they're just fine. You suspect one of them was involved in the incident?"

She made a mental note to ask Sammy if any of the workers outside looked as if they'd suffered injuries.

"It could be anyone," James said. "We've been talking to everyone in the neighborhood who's home."

Charlotte helped herself to a slice of the pound cake and bit into the buttery goodness. "Yum. This is delicious. Will you be catering the fund-raiser?"

"Of course. The menu's set. We'll have hors d'oeuvres and shrimp canapés and tea cakes. Plenty of champagne, as well."

Charlotte turned to James. "That should keep us all busy."

"What do you mean?" Maddie asked.

"All the catering and staff coming in and out of here

will be monitored. We've set up camp at the gatehouse to record every vehicle and person that enters and exits Falling Rock. Can't be too careful. Kidnappers are on the loose." Charlotte set her plate down with a clatter. Let Maddie stew over that bit of information.

James stood. "See you soon, Mrs. Stowers. Thanks for the coffee."

Maddie stood, as well, smoothing down the front of her skirt again, then following them to the door. "My pleasure. We'll look forward to the event. Richard and I always enjoy this occasion. It's the least we can do to give back to this community. Lavender Mountain is our little home away from home. I understand that the proceeds from our event provides as much as twenty-five percent of your annual budget."

Charlotte almost snorted. Way to plug her political influence.

"The sheriff, and all of us, are most grateful," James said.

"I believe in giving back."

Charlotte hated the self-righteous tone of Maddie's voice.

"In Atlanta, I do lots of volunteer work, as well," the woman continued. "My favorite is working at the teen suicide hotline. So many young lives in crisis."

Charlotte's nerve endings tingled, and her mouth went dry.

James nodded. "Thank you for your service."

Maddie closed the door softly behind them, and Charlotte followed James to the cruiser. Inside, he turned to her. "What gives? I saw you tense up there at the end."

"The crisis hotline. My source about the Stowerses?

Karen Hicks was suicidal and had called a hotline for help not long before she was kidnapped."

"Well," he said, starting the car, "it appears we've found our Pied Piper."

Chapter 9

"Why are we stopping here?" Charlotte asked.

James mentally shook himself and stared at his father's cabin. Yet again, it seemed like the old homestead drew him even when he had no conscious plan to visit. Not that he'd admit that to Charlotte. It smacked of a weak character.

"Thought we'd visit Sammy. Check to see if any of the Stowerses' men have shown signs of injury. See if there's anything unusual."

She shrugged. "Beats doing nothing."

Her voice sounded as discouraged as his thoughts. For the last several days, all their knocking on doors and combing through the gatekeeper's records had yielded nothing other than an immediate complaint from the Falling Rock management corporation and the ire of the residents.

"My four-wheeler's still parked in the shed. Shouldn't take too long to go have a look."

Dispiritedly, Charlotte tagged along beside him as he pulled out the ATV. The case weighed heavily on her. For several nights, he couldn't help overhearing bits and pieces of Charlotte's conversation with her friend, Tanya. She'd tried to convey optimism, but after hanging up the phone, her face would be tight and withdrawn.

He knew that helpless feeling. When his own family had been in crisis, he'd been stuck in Afghanistan and unable to protect his sisters. Sometimes at night, he had lain awake on his cot, and worry had buzzed his brain like a storm of hungry gnats.

If she was anything like him—and he suspected Charlotte was—then the best cure was to keep busy, keep digging and poking even when there seemed no point. Even the tiniest clue could often make or break a case.

Charlotte zipped her uniform jacket all the way up and donned gloves and earmuffs. "You're not worried about blowing Sammy's cover?"

"Not particularly." He started the engine, and it sparked to life on the second try. "They already know we're watching them," he explained, raising his voice above the running motor. "Hop on."

She climbed on the back seat, and the contact of her body against his made him grit his teeth. Never had he once imagined being turned on by a partner when he entered into the life of an easygoing, small-town deputy. His dream of a quiet life wasn't panning out, but as he ran over a rut and Charlotte's body bounced against his back, James knew he wouldn't want it any other way.

He accelerated the engine. Trees and shrubs raced past his vision, and the chill mountain air invigorated his body and spirits. The land here never failed him—it was vast and constant, and every hill and hollow was imprinted in his DNA. His old army buddies questioned his decision to return to Lavender Mountain, but James knew this was his home, his land. The place he belonged.

He almost drove right past Sammy, who'd parked his camouflaged ATV behind a dense clump of evergreens. Only the sun glinting off the binocular lenses gave away his location. No surprise there. Sammy and Harlan and he used to hunt together, and each knew how to blend into the woods. James drew up beside him.

"Trying to blow my cover?" Sammy asked, but his eyes held their usual good humor.

"Doesn't much matter. They know we're keeping watch."

"Anything new happening?"

"Not a damn thing," Charlotte said, swinging one leg over the side and stepping down to the ground. "I want to nail Maddie Stowers so bad. She has the moral compass of a sociopath."

"The steel magnolia type, eh?" Sammy asked.

"In an evil way, yes. My theory is that Maddie often finds vulnerable, at-risk girls while working at a teen suicide hotline and then lures them into the trafficking ring. Either that or she preys on the homeless… whoever she can find who's vulnerable. Seen any unusual activity?"

"Nope. Just these men half-assed picking up broken branches and debris. Must be paid by the hour," he joked.

"Nobody staring out the window?"

James's heart pinched. She was desperate to know Jenny was alive and well.

"Sorry, Detective. Nothing."

James took the binoculars from Sammy's hands and stared at the crew. None appeared scratched-up or marred as though they'd experienced a near-fatal car crash days ago. But the Stowerses certainly had enough resources to keep hiring as many men as needed to maintain security. If one or two went down, they could easily hire more staff as replacements. Human trafficking was a lucrative business.

He recalled the immense house with its indoor heated pool and every other amenity for two people who lived there only part-time. No doubt their Atlanta mansion was just as opulent. And all of it earned off the misery of abused children.

Charlotte tugged at his jacket sleeve. "What do you see? My turn."

He handed her the binoculars and climbed back on the ATV. "Guess we'll go for a spin down the road a bit," he told Sammy. "Check out the area."

Charlotte sighed and returned the field glasses.

Again he reveled in the weight of her body braced against his as they rode, the ATV shaking and pitching in the deeply rutted dirt path. But as they rounded the curve leading away from Falling Rock, Charlotte yelled, "Stop!" waving an arm and pointing behind her.

James slammed on the brakes, and the ATV spun in a semicircle, sending up bits of mud and leaves. "What is it?"

"Over there, near the edge of the clearing. There are two men with shovels and a garbage bag. Do you think—"

"That they're digging a shallow grave?" He thought of the spilled blood they'd found earlier in the week. "Yeah. Could be. Or could they might be 'sengers."

"What's that?"

"I'll explain later." James stepped on the gas and reversed direction. "Let's find out which it is."

The two men abruptly stopped digging and eyed them warily. The eldest, sporting a long gray beard, hugged a garbage bag to his chest as he high-tailed it to a four-wheeler. The other guy, who looked young enough to be his son, or even grandson, dropped both his shovel and bag and also made a beeline for their mud-splattered vehicle.

"Halt!" James yelled.

Their old motor engine turned over once, then twice, before it started. James pulled in beside them, and the old man reached for a shotgun mounted on the hood.

Damn it. The old coot had a couple of seconds' bead on him. No way he could stop his ATV and withdraw his sidearm before he was already looking down the barrel of the mountain man's shotgun.

"Drop it!" Charlotte commanded. She half fell off the back seat, and then landed on her feet like a cat, gun drawn and aimed.

A blur of brown came between him and the old dude.

"Hell, no." The old man abandoned the attempt to grab his weapon and hit the gas. The old contraption lurched forward.

This was a chase the men had no chance of winning. "Get back on," he ordered Charlotte.

"Hell with that." She fired a warning shot, the blast echoing through the hollow.

The younger man glanced back, eyes round as a full moon. The ATV jerked to the right. The driver had enough smarts to get off the main path and try to lose them in the woods.

Charlotte dropped her weapon. "I had a shot at their back tire, but he switched directions on me at the last minute."

James revved the engine. "Get on. We'll catch them."

Quickly she climbed on board, and he gave chase. Had it been summer, the men might have been able to conceal their whereabouts, using green foliage as camouflage. But in the November barrenness, they were dead meat.

A shot rang out.

Son of a bitch. Did they really expect to get away with shooting two officers of the law in broad daylight? And then escaping on an old ATV that probably had a maximum speed of only thirty miles per hour? What the hell did they think they were doing? If they were guilty of illegally harvesting wild ginseng, as he now suspected, the pickers had way overreacted.

The trail narrowed. Did the men have a plan, or had they fled on a knee-jerk impulse? Soon there would be nowhere left to drive. Worst-case scenario, they were part of a larger group that was nearby and could be recruited to assist their fight. Or maybe there was a drying shed nearby that the men hoped to hole up in.

Both possibilities became moot as the men's four-wheeler crashed into a huge oak.

James drew out his sidearm as he raced forward. This time he'd be ready.

Charlotte's heart nearly burst with anticipation. They'd get these men and force them to talk. With any luck, they'd provide a clue to help catch the traffickers.

Both men jumped off the ATV, the eldest clutching his shotgun. She and James did likewise with their pistols. But the yahoo mountain outlaws still weren't done fleeing, and the two ran in opposite directions.

So it was going to be one of *those* arrests. Lots of trouble and a real pain in the ass.

"You go after the younger," James shouted.

Of *course* he chose the armed man to chase, and it ticked her off. She was as capable as any male cop when it came to apprehending felons. No time to argue, though. Later she'd set him straight on that score.

Charlotte took off, legs pumping and heart pounding double-time with adrenaline. Fortunately, the past several days had been event-free, allowing her injuries to heal. Problem was, her target was just as hyped as she was.

From below, brambles sliced and shredded her pants legs while low-lying tree branches from above slapped her torso. On and on he ran. Whatever the guy had done, she'd make sure a fleeing arrest charge stick. That and whatever else she could slap on him.

The dude was fast and crafty, darting from tree to tree in a zigzag pattern. She briefly wondered if James had caught up with the old man.

"Stop!" she ordered.

He didn't look back or slow down. The jerk. He wasn't getting away. Not even if it meant her heart exploded from exertion. "You're just making—" Charlotte gulped oxygen into her burning lungs "—it harder on yourself." She drew a few more gasping breaths. "Give it up."

"Up yours," he shouted, flipping her the middle finger.

Nice guy. But she'd seen and heard worse. *Far* worse.

Abruptly the trail widened, and he stumbled into the open. He glanced back at her, eyes bewildered and panicked. Charlotte smiled and raised her gun. "Halt!" she called out. "Got a clear shot" —she panted, though her aim never wavered— "at you this time."

He hesitated, running a hand through his dark, shoulder-length hair, and then raised both arms high in defeat.

Charlotte approached, cautious. She didn't trust his sudden surrender for a second. Backup would be cool right about now, but she was used to working alone. She only hoped Sammy had heard the fired shots and had left his post to find James.

"On the ground," she ordered. "Facedown."

He dropped, and she was pleased to note the rise and fall of his chest. Apparently, the run had tired him out, as well—but he might yet have some fight left in him.

"Hands behind your back, and spread your legs wide."

He grudgingly complied. "Bitch," he muttered, then spit.

"Careful. You might hurt my tender feelings." She

stood over him and used her right leg to spread his legs out further. "Got any weapons?"

"If I did, I'd have used 'em on you by now."

Dude was charming. Defiant to the end. She tucked her gun into her side holster and withdrew a pair of handcuffs.

"That ain't necessary."

She bent to one knee and slapped a cuff on his left wrist. "I'll decide what's necessary."

Charlotte grabbed his right wrist, but he twisted and jerked away. He reached into his jacket pocket. Must have a weapon after all. She'd expected no less.

Quickly she rose as he pulled out a knife and flicked it open. Sunlight touched the silver blade, and it glinted with malicious promise. She had one second to prevent an attack that could leave her gutted. Another second, and she'd have to run and would turn from hunter to prey. *Not happening.* Charlotte lifted her right foot and then stomped with all her might on his right hand.

"Owww…son of a bitch!" His fingers loosened their hold on the knife, and he curled into a fetal position. "I think you broke it!"

She stuffed the knife in her pocket, then bent down again and cuffed his wrists together. "What you got here?" Inside his other jacket pocket was yet another knife. "Any more weapons? Tell me now, and I won't have to hurt you again."

"One more knife. Right pants pocket."

She retrieved the weapon and patted down his legs before ordering him to roll over. Swiftly her hands ran down his arms, chest and hips.

"You need to git me to a doc," he said with a piti-ful moan.

The adrenaline left her system with a rush, and she sank onto her haunches several yards from his curled-up body. She reached for her walkie-talkie and then let out a moan of her own. Either she'd left it in the truck or had lost it during the chase. Just terrific. "Looks like we're in for a hike."

"Can't," he protested.

"You've got a broken wrist, not a broken leg."

His face flushed scarlet, and his eyes were bright with tears. Whether from pain or anger, she didn't know and didn't much care.

"Heartless bitch. I'm suing your ass. Police brutality."

"That's me. Coldhearted," she cheerily agreed. "Some perp twice my size tries to gut me with a knife, and I dare defend myself. Wonder who the judge and jury will rule for at trial?"

He scrambled to a sitting position, turned his head to the side, and spat again. "There's more than one way to get justice 'round here."

Anger blazed behind her temples, and she stuffed her fists into her jacket. What she really wanted to do was pummel some sense into the guy, but that was a line she'd never cross. In and out she breathed, willing her temper to cool. Dude hit a nerve for sure. This wasn't the first time she'd heard such a threat, and she didn't take it idly. One day her past might catch up to her. She'd return to her one-bedroom apartment some night, and someone would be there, waiting for her in the darkness.

"You want to sit around all day and exchange pleasantries, or shall we return to our ATV? I'm sure Officer Tedder has your partner in custody by now."

"Betcha Grandpa got away." A smirk twisted his thin lips.

Charlotte jumped to her feet. Why was she lollygagging? James might need her assistance. "Rest is over. Time to hit the trail."

"You go. I'll wait here."

"The hell you will." Charlotte leaned over and yanked at his cuffs.

A high-pitched wail escaped his mouth.

"C'mon, big guy," she said as he struggled to his feet. "Play nice, and I won't tell your grandpa and your future cellmates that I made you cry like a girl."

He opened his mouth, no doubt to call her another choice name, but then clamped it shut. "I'm coming," he said, his face scrunched in sullenness.

Frankly, he could pout all he wanted as long as he followed orders. Charlotte made a sweeping gesture. "You go first."

She followed a couple of feet behind as they made their way back through the underbrush. Only the crunch of their shoes and an occasional bird call ruffled the wooded silence. Where was James? With every step, her worry increased.

The crashed ATV came into view, still overturned and lying on its side. And still no sign of James. The cuffed suspect turned and grinned. "What'd I tell ya? Grandpa's long gone."

"Yeah, gone to jail," she snapped. But her uneasiness grew, pinching at her lungs and heart.

One of the large black garbage bags the men carried had fallen two feet from the ATV. What was in them—drugs? Weapons? Body parts? Curious, she scooped it up and looked inside. The bag held...vegetables? She pulled out one of the plants and held it in her palms. It had a green stem about twelve inches long that was topped with five leaves. Long, stringy roots resembling white carrots were attached to the base of the stem.

"What's this? Albino carrots?" she asked.

He snorted. "It's 'seng."

She blinked. "Come again?"

"Ginseng. You ain't never heard of it?"

"It's an herb, right? But…what's the big deal? Why the hell did y'all run from us?"

A voice called from behind, "Because it's highly profitable and highly illegal."

Charlotte whipped her head around. James strode her way, grandpa cuffed beside him. Relief jellied her knees, and for one horrible moment, she thought she might faint. So this must be what Southern belles called a swoon back in the old days. She straightened her shoulders and frowned. Since when had James's well-being mattered as much or more than her own? She had a job to do here, one that required all her focus.

"Thought you'd got away," the younger guy muttered, clearly disappointed. "Did he rough you up any? I think this one broke my damn wrist."

James quirked a brow at her, amusement dancing in his eyes.

"He neglected to mention he sustained the injury while attempting to stab me," she said.

Her partner's amusement flashed to fury. His eyes were flaming blue orbs, and his whole body grew taut, filling the air with a crackling tension. He left grandpa behind, all his focus on the younger man.

Now the dude wasn't so cocky. He stepped backward and held up his cuffed hands. "I'm hurt," he whined.

James grabbed him up by the collar and pushed his body against a pine.

This was a side of James she'd never seen. "Wait." She tried to wedge herself between the two men. "Stop. I handled the situation. It's over."

James let go but kept glaring at the guy.

A little redirection was in order. She retrieved a pen and small notepad from her uniform shirt. "Okay. Junior claims to need a doctor, so let's get the ball rolling. Y'all have any identification on you?"

Grandpa shook his head. "Don't need it to drive my four-wheeler."

"Name, please." Her pen hovered over the notepad.

"Linton Harold Drexler the Fourth. And this here's my grandson." A grand name for grandpa.

"And yours?" she asked Junior.

"Ross Drexler, you—"

"Careful," James warned with a growl.

She scribbled down the information, then held up the plastic bag. "Ross told me they were digging up ginseng, and that appears to be what's in the bags they carried."

"Yep. If they hadn't resisted arrest, they'd be charged with poaching and trespassing, which usually only carries a small fine."

"You questioned them yet about seeing or hearing anything?"

"We ain't no snitches," Ross piped up.

"If you know something, you *will* tell me," Charlotte said through gritted teeth.

"Shut up, Ross," Grandpa said. "I done told ya digging for 'seng so close to them fancy-pancy houses were beggin' fer trouble, and I was right." He turned his back on Ross. "We heard some terrible screaming one day, and it ain't been sittin' right on my conscience, neither."

Charlotte swallowed hard. Sure, she was aware of the methods traffickers used to break down their captives, but she'd kept that knowledge tucked away in a don't-go-there zone. Now it was all she could think about. Jenny was one of the screamers. And jackasses like Linton and Ross heard them and did nothing to stop it.

"When?" James pressed.

"It's been since we found that patch last week. At first, I thought I was a-hearin' thangs, but several days passed, there weren't no mistakin' that a girl was screaming. Spooked me. We hightailed it outta there, and 'bout five minutes later, a shot was fired."

"But did you actually see anything?" Charlotte asked. "If we had a witness—"

Grandpa shook his head so hard that his beard whipped from side to side. "No, ma'am. We ain't seen nothin'."

"What about you?" James asked Ross.

"I ain't seen nothin'."

Charlotte sighed and gestured for James to follow. About six feet away from the men, she stopped by a copse of pines. "I'm surprised Sammy didn't hear the shots and drive over." She kept her voice low.

"He heard and radioed me. I told him to stay put, thinking these guys might have been hired to provide a distraction while the kidnappers transferred the captives out. If I'd known you were in danger..."

She waved a hand in dismissal. "I've handled worse. So how are we going to transport these two to the station?"

"Sammy's already taken care of it. A cruiser should be on the main path any minute."

Whew. She'd had enough exercise for the day without having a mile trek to James's cabin with two fugitives in tow. "Junior will be glad to hear it. He's been whimpering like a baby ever since I stomped that knife out of his hands."

Oops. Mistake to bring that up. James's jaw clenched again, and she sensed the anger seething from his entire body. "Old man give you any trouble?" she asked quickly. "I kept expecting to hear his shotgun fire."

"Nah, once he saw the writing on the wall, he gave it up quick. Sorry. I should have chased the younger one. Would have if I'd known he had a weapon."

"That shouldn't enter into your decision. We're partners—equals." She held up the bag. "How much is this stuff worth?"

"You can fetch anywhere from five hundred to a thousand bucks a pound for wild ginseng."

She whistled and glanced down at the strange-looking plants. "You're joking, right?"

"'Fraid not. They've been poached so much it's possible they'll become extinct in a few years."

What a damn shame.

"What's so magical about ginseng?" she asked.

"People claim it can cure anything from cancer to diabetes to weight loss."

James regarded the poachers, rubbing his chin. "Forget your occasional murderer preying on lone hikers walking the trail. Between the moonshiners, pot farmers and 'sengers, Appalachia can be a dangerous place. Atlanta's crime rate has got nothing on us."

"And now you've even got human trafficking."

"Not for long," he vowed. "Not on my mountain."

Chapter 10

James settled into a chair in Harlan's office. The hot seat, judging by Harlan's scowl. That, and the fact his boss had told him to come alone and leave "that woman" behind, clued him in that this wasn't going to be a pleasant conversation. James mentally reviewed the ginseng poacher arrests he'd made yesterday with Charlotte. Everything had proceeded smoothly. This had to be about the trafficking case. Harlan leaned back and ran a hand through his hair.

"What's up?" James asked.

"I've just spoken to the mayor. There's been a backlash from our questioning at Falling Rock. Numerous complaints and a formal petition for the mayor to 'do something about me.'"

"Rich folks' complaints. We've done nothing wrong

and the mayor knows it. Did Madeline Stowers and her husband lead the charge on the petition?"

"He didn't mention any names, but it wouldn't surprise me."

He'd be lousy at Harlan's job and the ensuing political pressure that came with holding a public position. Mostly he'd hate the necessary kowtowing to the rich and powerful that came with an elected office. But James had enough sense to realize his resentment of the upper echelon was partly a result of his own upbringing as a Tedder. People had always judged him by the black sheep in his family and it had left him with a huge chip—no, make that a *boulder*—to carry.

"Surely he understood the necessity for questioning everyone," James said.

"He did—but he's still not happy about the situation."

Anger flushed the back of James's neck. "Maybe the mayor should be more concerned about the safety of his officers and the welfare of the people in his city than he is with keeping up an all-is-well appearance about crime in the area."

"Was that little speech for my benefit, too?" Harlan asked brusquely. "Because if it was, I can assure you that I have my priorities straight."

He said nothing. Let Harlan make of it what he wanted. Bad enough to have this tension at work, but the fact that this man was his brother-in-law might make the next family get-together awfully awkward.

"I've been reviewing my conversation with Captain Burkhart, Charlotte's supervisor. Her claim that the traffickers operate here stems from an unreliable witness."

"But don't forget that she saw a young girl at the window."

"Exactly. *She* saw it—not you."

Heat lanced his gut. "You accusing her of being a liar?"

"Not deliberately. Hell, James, sometimes people are so determined to prove a theory that they actually invent things in their own mind as proof and believe it's real. Detective Helms has admitted to a personal involvement in the case and that's always dangerous. It can cloud your judgment."

Harlan was nothing if not stubborn. "What about the men who tried to run us off the road? You can't blame that on a figment of imagination."

"No. But it's possible the incident had nothing to do with covering up a human trafficking ring."

"What else could it be?"

"Let me put it to you this way," Harlan said slowly. "Ever since you found that woman in your cabin, trouble has followed. We know something is going on, but is it really what she claims it is? I'm concerned about Detective Helms's mental health."

James jumped to his feet. "Like hell you are. You're concerned about not making waves with the mayor and the Falling Rock residents."

"That's not fair," Harlan snapped.

A voice sounded from the doorway. "I can assure you, Sheriff, that I'm not unhinged. Although I'm not sure how one goes about proving their own sanity."

Charlotte leaned against the door, face washed of emotion. It was as though she'd donned a professional mask of indifference. But Harlan's words had to cut her deeply.

"You don't have to prove anything," James said hotly.

"Sorry you overheard it this way," Harlan apologized. He turned to James. "I'm afraid she does have to set my mind at ease. I can't risk your safety, or any of my other officers' safety, unless I'm convinced there's good cause."

"Can you give me until the night of the fund-raiser to prove my case?" Charlotte asked. "Just a few more days."

He nodded stiffly. "Sounds fair. In return, I ask that any inquiry you make into the alleged trafficking ring is done discreetly. This office can't afford to alienate the mayor and a significant portion of the people we're here to serve."

"Understood."

With that terse word, Charlotte turned on her heel and left.

Tension clouded the air between him and his boss. "May I be excused?" James asked.

Harlan waved a hand toward the door. "You two have until this Sunday to find enough proof of the trafficking to obtain a subpoena, or better yet, get this matter resolved."

"You've made that very clear." James strode to the doorway.

"Wait a minute. James…don't let your emotions blind you to the facts."

"Don't worry yourself on my account. And don't you let the bigwigs dictate what your office can and should investigate."

He retreated before Harlan could whip out another angry retort.

The ride home had been tense and quiet. "I don't want to talk about it" was all Charlotte would say about the matter.

He stirred the camp stew and took the cornbread from the oven.

"I'm glad you know how to cook," she commented, setting out the plates and silverware. "Because I sure don't."

"You can thank Lilah. She always cooks more than enough for her family and then sends me the frozen leftovers."

"She's too good for Harlan." Charlotte clasped a hand over her mouth. "Oops. Didn't mean to say that out loud."

"Harlan's okay. We used to be best friends in high school. The two of us and Sammy used to go hunting and camping almost every weekend during deer and duck season. We did our share of sipping moonshine together under the Appalachian moon."

"Sounds like a real manly bonding experience. Did it bother you when he married your sister?"

"Took a little getting used to." He set the stew on the table. "Did feel strange at first when I got back from my tour of duty."

"And he offered you a job working for him?"

He returned to the kitchen for the cornbread as Charlotte ladled the stew into their bowls. "Yeah. Not sure how much of that was Lilah's doing, or whether or not he really needed me."

"You're a good cop. He's lucky to have you. Do you like the work?"

"Surprisingly, yes. Solving cases is like putting together the pieces of a puzzle."

A smile curled her lips. "I see you haven't had time to get jaded yet."

"The army already did that for me." His cell phone vibrated, signaling a text message. He picked it up from the table and swiped the screen.

Back off.

What the hell? The phone number didn't ring a bell. He'd run a check on it tomorrow, but odds were that it was generated from a burner phone.

"Problem?" she asked.

"Nothing to worry about." He turned off the phone and laid it down. What good would it do to tell her of the vague threat? And he certainly didn't plan on mentioning it to Harlan, either. He'd only point out that Charlotte might have sent it, or that the threat could be about anything and not necessarily the trafficking case.

"I have to admit this is nice." Charlotte bit into a piece of buttered cornbread and then took a sip of sassafras tea. Her knee injury was almost completely healed. Luckily she enjoyed the tea's strong, tangy flavor and dutifully drank a glass or two a day.

"What's nice?"

"Being able to relax in the evening and have dinner with a friend. Usually I grab fast food, when I remember to eat, and scarf it down in front of the TV."

Friend? To hell with that. He wanted to sleep with her the night through and wake up with her every morning in his bed. Images of her spread on his couch in T-shirt and panties the night he'd tended her wound interrupted his train of thought. What had she just said? Something about food. He cleared his throat.

"I can relate. If not for Lilah, I'd never get a home-cooked meal."

"Ribs still hurt?" He'd insisted on X-rays and was relieved to discover none of her ribs were broken.

"Not too bad. The bruising looks worse than it feels."

He reached for the butter at the same moment as Charlotte. Their fingers touched. Heat traveled up his arm like an electrical charge—hard, fast and almost painful. He'd tried to be hands-off, but these nights alone with her had taken their toll. Everything she did and said drew him deeper into her spell.

She jerked her hand away from his as if the contact had burned. Charlotte felt the fire, too. He read it in the spots of color staining her cheeks, in the sharp inhalation of her breath. James reached for her hand and held fast. Her gaze moved slowly up from their clasped hands until her teal eyes, darkened to the color of the forest, bore into his own.

"Charlotte," he breathed. His heart skittered as if he'd run a race for his very life. He pushed back his chair. Wordlessly she rose from the table and came to him, never breaking their handhold.

It was as if every ounce of her considerable willpower had flown the coop. She dropped into his lap, pressing her hands into the top of his shoulders.

And then he kissed her.

His tongue danced inside her mouth and she was drowning in a flood of desire. She needed him—all of him. His fingers raked through her hair and then pressed into her scalp, drawing their mouths even closer. His desire pressed against her left hip. James stood and his hands cupped her ass, pressing her more intimately into his erection.

"Wait. Stop." She withdrew from his kiss and took a deep breath. "This is too fast…"

He let go immediately, leaving her dazed and disoriented, as if she'd lost her mooring. Charlotte grasped the edge of the table behind her for balance.

James ran a hand through his hair. "If you're not ready, okay. I thought…"

"It's not that I don't want you," she quickly assured him. "It's just… I don't want you to think it changes anything. No matter what happens at the fund-raiser, by this time next week I'm back in Atlanta."

A momentary flash of some emotion—pain? Sadness?—swept across his normally stoic features. "I get that. But it's not like Atlanta's on the other side of the country. We could visit."

"No. You don't understand." How could she make him see? "Being undercover is nothing like a regular job with regular hours. If you visited my place at the wrong time, you could jeopardize my cover."

"So? I'll call first or we could meet elsewhere."

Charlotte stepped away from his intense scrutiny and paced the kitchen. "There's more. Sometimes an assignment requires me to be away for weeks at a time. That's why undercover officers hardly ever have intimate relationships. Or if they do, it rarely lasts."

"We could try," he insisted.

Damn, James was stubborn. She threw up her hands, exasperated. "Don't you get it? I'd be terrible for you, for any man. Harlan's right—trouble follows me. I never know when some ex-con with revenge on his mind might find me."

He held up a hand, warding off her objections. "I'm willing to tolerate a little inconvenience. And as far as danger, I can handle it, so stop borrowing trouble. We can take this one day at a time."

"Are you sure?" She anxiously searched his face. He deserved more than what she had to offer. He deserved a Lavender Mountain woman who could spend her evenings with him, share these cozy meals and be there to listen as he unwound at night and talked about his day.

She was not that woman.

"You're an all-or-nothing kind of man, James. With strong views about right and wrong. I don't want to hurt you."

"Let me worry about my own feelings." He crooked a finger and gave a lopsided grin. "I'm a big boy and can take of myself. Trust me?"

Like no one else. He'd never abandon her when danger went down, unlike Danny. And James cared about her.

She slowly walked toward him, drawn to his strength and to her body's urgent need to feel him inside her. To know him intimately. His hands rested on either side of her hips and he kissed her forehead, his lips tender and warm.

The tenderness completely undid her. Some small knot of reserve deep inside melted. Charlotte buried her head against his chest and shuddered.

"You alright?" he asked gruffly.

His voice rumbled against her cheek, the vibration setting off a corresponding rumble in her heart and a seismic shift in her soul. This wouldn't do. *"One day at a time,"* he'd said. For tonight, she'd find pleasure in his arms and not analyze her feelings. The trick was to focus on the physical, to imagine this as a temporary fling.

Charlotte raised her chin and found his mouth, eagerly succumbing to the passion. She pressed her body against his so hard that the table slid against the wall. He groaned, and the knowledge of his need fueled her own even more.

His hands were everywhere at once, down her back, against her ass, then roaming up the sides of her ribs toward her breasts. All while his lips trailed kisses down her neck and to the hollow of her throat. Impatiently she tugged at his belt. Without missing a beat, James undid the buckle and she pushed down his uniform pants.

He groaned again—or wait—was that her? Or both of them? Didn't matter. She cupped his most intimate parts and felt the velvet steel of his erection. "I need you. Now."

"Not yet."

He suckled her nipples and inserted a finger into her core. When had he removed her pants? Her fevered brain hadn't noticed anything but the unbearable throbbing at the apex of her thighs, the need to be joined. "Now. Please," she whimpered against his mouth.

"Hell, yeah," he growled. "You're so hot and ready for me."

He took her hand, evidently intending to lead her to the bedroom. But that would take way—way—*way* too long. She couldn't, wouldn't, wait. Charlotte shook her head. "Here. Now."

"If you're sure you really—"

She smothered his mouth with kisses and wrapped her arms around his neck.

As if she weighed nothing, James hoisted her legs around his hips and flipped their positions so that she was seated on top of the table. He entered her quickly and she met his thrusts with an increasing urgency.

Harder, harder, harder...faster, faster, faster. Her body tensed and then exploded with pleasure and release. The muscles on James's back tightened and spasmed beneath her hands as he reached his own orgasm.

His head sank onto her shoulders and the sound of their labored breathing joined together. Her fingers gently traced lazy circles down his sides.

"I think I need to sleep," she said with amusement. "About ten hours or so."

He laughed and swept her into his arms. "I don't know about sleeping, but I'm all for going to bed early and often. No more sleeping in the guest bedroom for you." He waggled his brows.

Charlotte returned his grin, feeling more relaxed and carefree than she had since Tanya had called two weeks ago saying that Jenny was missing. "Lucky for you—" she began.

An angry buzz vibrated the tabletop.

"Not again." He stared at it, frowning.

"Better answer. It could be work."

"It is." He let her down and she hastily pulled her clothes together.

"Officer Tedder," he said. A moment's pause. "Okay, we're on our way."

Hope fluttered in her chest. "Any news on the traffickers?"

"Nope. Domestic disturbance."

"No one else is available?" Resentment quickly spoiled her afterglow, followed by the familiar weight of guilt. It was her own fault the sheriff's office was stretched thin.

"The surveillance at Falling Rock leaves us short-handed. This shouldn't take long; the disturbance is just a small piece down the road."

Amusement tugged his lips as he surveyed the spilled camp stew that ran off the table and puddled on the floor. "This will be a mess to clean up later."

Charlotte put her hands on her hips and arched a brow. "Are you complaining?"

"No, ma'am. I wouldn't change what happened between us, even if it means staying up all night scrubbing floors."

His lopsided grin made her breath catch. Who was she kidding by thinking that sex with James could be a mere physical fling? That her life and heart could continue on same as before?

Tonight had changed everything.

Chapter 11

Blue strobe lights flashed across the night landscape, illuminating a disheveled clapboard house that had enough junk lying around the yard and porch to stock a small store. James hopped out of the car and headed for the door. "Stay behind me," he ordered.

Charlotte shot him the dagger look. "Like hell I will. And next time it's my turn to drive."

So much for postcoital afterglow. It was back to business as usual.

Screams reverberated off the house walls.

"You cheatin' sack of—"

"—crazy heifer. Put that poker down or I'll—"

"—who is she? I'll kill you first and then I'll kill her."

James shook his head. "I believe we can ascertain the root of the argument here. Which was no doubt enhanced by shots of moonshine." Idly he wondered if it might be some old batch of 'shine his father and uncle had produced. The irony of that never escaped his notice.

"You been called to this house before?"

"No, but these domestic disputes are amazingly similar."

Charlotte kicked an old tricycle out of her path. "Voluminous consumption of alcohol and a short fuse by one or both partners?"

"Followed by a cooling off period and teary reconciliation until the next round of drinks. You got it. Remember, these types of calls can turn out to be the most dangerous."

"Even undercover cops know that," she said, voice brusque.

James pulled open the screen and wrapped on the door. "Sheriff's office. Open up."

"See what you done did, woman?" a man shouted from inside.

"What I did? What *I* did? You stupid, lying—"

James turned the knob and discovered it was unlocked. He entered and took in the scene at once.

A heavyset woman in a floral print dress brandished a poker in her right hand. The man wore only a pair of boxers. Blood ran down his nose and he swayed slightly, off balance. But James's focus quickly passed the couple arguing and traveled to the couch where two young girls—probably ages four and five—huddled together beneath a Hello Kitty blanket.

"Ma'am, put down the poker," he said firmly. "Let's discuss this calmly."

"Ain't nothin' to discuss. I told him to git out and he won't leave."

"This is my house," the man bellowed. "You go."

James caught a movement from the corner of his eye—Charlotte reaching for her firearm. He flicked his wrist downward, motioning her to put it away. She raised a brow, hand hovering over the sidearm, but nodded and dropped her hand to her side.

"I'm ordering you to drop that weapon," James said, stepping between the two.

The woman lowered her gaze and stared at the poker blankly, as if she'd forgotten she held it. Her face was flushed and her eyes wild with rage.

Charlotte also stepped between the couple, facing the man and spreading her arms out wide. Together, the two of them provided a visual and physical barrier between the couple.

"There we go," James said, his voice softer. He stepped closer and took the poker from her shaking hands. "That's better. Could you do me a favor, please?"

"What the hell do you want? I ain't done talking to him yet." She tried to walk around him and James blocked her path.

"Ma'am, see your kids over there on the couch?" he asked. "Maybe it'd be a good idea to take them to their bedroom. You don't want them to witness this. You're a good mom and know this isn't good—"

"It's his fault," she muttered. "Pulls my chain every time."

"Officer Hanson, could you go with her and the kids? Sir, I need to you take a seat over there." He pointed to the recliner across from the sofa.

The man did as told, and Charlotte walked to the children, giving them an encouraging smile. "Everything's going to be alright. Your mom's going to tuck you in bed. Good deal?"

The youngest girl clutched her doll tighter and regarded Charlotte with solemn eyes that belied her age. The older one asked her mom, "You want us to go?"

The mother pursed her lips into a tight line and faced Charlotte. "I want him gone, ya hear?"

"We'll discuss that later," Charlotte said. She bent her knees and came eye-level with the youngest girl. "Such a pretty doll. What's her name?"

"Emily."

"Nice. What's your name?"

"Sarah Slackum. I'm four years old and live at 19 Pence Street." Sarah smiled at her mom. "I 'membered, Mama."

The woman teared up. "Ya done good, honey. Said everything like I told ya to do if'n ya was lost or the police asked ya questions."

James kept his focus on the man as the women left the room. "What happened here? Did she hit you in the face with that poker?"

"Damn sure did." He grasped the arms of the recliner and held tight.

The man had the nervous energy of an angry, caged tiger. He still needed to be talked down a few notches.

"How did this get started?"

"I come home late and she started accusing me of being with another woman. I've had it up to here." He karate chopped the air by his neck.

"Been drinking?" James nodded at the mason jar of applejack moonshine on the coffee table.

"A wee bit," he admitted. "But so did Edna."

"You need to go to the hospital?"

"Nah. This ain't nothin'."

"You want to press charges?"

The man snorted. "I'd hear no end of that at the factory. Everyone would make fun of me getting whupped by a woman."

"This a regular occurrence with you and your wife?"

"This ain't the first time," he admitted. "Ought to be in yer records somewhere about us."

"It's not good for the children. Ever considered getting counseling?"

"I ain't no alcoholic."

"That may or may not be. But I'm suggesting that you and your wife take anger management classes."

"But she hit *me*. Edna's the one that needs them there classes."

"Think about it for your children's sake. I'm reporting this domestic disturbance to a social worker. She'll talk to you and your wife about the classes and check out the children's safety. Be expecting a visit."

"What's he still doin' here?" Edna cried out, striding toward them.

Charlotte blocked her path and ordered her to sit on the couch. Surprisingly, Edna complied, putting her head in her hands. Her whole body shook with sobs.

"You'll be glad to know your husband isn't pressing assault charges," James said.

Edna dropped her hands and snapped her face up. "But it was his—"

James held up a hand. "You can't assault people. Ever. For now, let's just try to get through this evening without this situation escalating. Think of your children."

Silence at last descended in the room.

"For tonight, I think it's a good idea if you two are separated. Have either of you got somewhere you can go for a night?"

"I ain't a-leavin' my children," Edna said. "Make Boone go."

Boone rose. "Didn't plan on stayin' here's no way. I'm staying with Grady." He grabbed a jacket and weaved his way outside of the house.

James followed him onto the porch. "How do you plan to get there? You can't drive anywhere in your condition."

Boone held up a cell phone. "I'm callin' my brother to come git me."

"We could give you a lift."

"Nah, Grady be here in less than five minutes. I'll wait here on the porch for him."

They watched as Boone climbed into his brother's pickup.

"Great job in there," she said, leaning her head back in the car seat. "Nice touch about contacting the social worker."

James nodded and started the cruiser. "I'll make sure either life gets more peaceful in that house, or the children are removed if they're in danger."

She cast a sideways glance, studying his strong profile. He'd be a great father one day—calm but firm, and loving. Tonight's call had been tense, but they'd worked together as a team, and every time she saw James in action, her respect for the man grew.

"I see how your department is a real asset to the community," she observed thoughtfully. Normally she measured success by the number of arrests made and the amount of contraband recovered. But there was another side of law enforcement, too. One where officers worked with more normal citizens and aided the vulnerable who needed them to intervene on their behalf.

"We try. The job has turned out to be a lot more enjoyable and interesting than I imagined it would be."

"What made you take it to begin with?"

"I was drifting after getting out of the army. Had become a bit of a recluse, actually. Then the opportunity came along and I took the job, thinking it would be easy, steady work."

"Must have been difficult reacclimating to civilian life after leaving the army."

"A little," he admitted. "I wanted peace and quiet when I returned home."

"Pretty rough over there?"

"I've seen and heard things that no man can easily forget. Ended up with a mild case of PTSD." He shot her an uneasy glance. "As my partner, I probably should have mentioned that to you sooner."

"I trust you, and evidently Harlan does, as well."

"Overall, I'm grateful for my experience in the army. It's defined who I am."

And he was a damn fine man—if a little bossy.

He might claim the job was coincidental, but there was more to it than that. "I don't believe you went into law enforcement only because it was convenient. You went in because you believe in justice, especially considering what's happened to your family."

He slanted her a thoughtful look. "Maybe. Glad to

know I have your trust. I have a feeling you don't trust others easily."

"I don't." She drew a deep breath. What had Miss Glory said about opening her heart? James had opened his a crack, she could do the same. "My partner before you, Danny, ran out on me during a botched drug bust. Left me alone with a pretty scary suspect who had pulled a gun on us."

"What a son of a bitch."

"It gets worse. We…had a thing going for several weeks before this happened." There. She'd spit it out. What a fool she'd been.

"A double betrayal," he said, mouth grim. "That explains a lot."

The police radio crackled. "Fire reported at 101 County Road 14. Fire truck en route. Nearest officer please respond."

Charlotte rolled her eyes. "Is there a full moon tonight?"

"What the…" James picked up the mike. "Officers en route."

"Can't someone else take this call?" she asked. "We've done enough—"

"That's my cabin." He flipped on the blue lights and siren, hit the accelerator and spun the cruiser onto the road.

Charlotte held on to the door pull. "Your cabin," she repeated slowly. Coincidence? No. That old place had been standing for decades. This was a message.

She licked her suddenly dry lips. Guilt weighted her shoulders. She'd brought this on James.

They raced through the darkness in silence. Did he blame her for his old homestead going up in flames?

Her phone vibrated in her pocket and she pulled it out.

This is just the start.

Damn. The anonymous text left no room for doubt. The fire had been intentionally set. Charlotte slipped the cell phone back into her jacket pocket without comment. She'd tell James about it later. He had enough on his mind at the moment.

In record time, James pulled the cruiser onto the cabin property. At least a dozen other vehicles were parked helter-skelter in the yard and spectators had already gathered, watching as firefighters sprayed giant hoses on the inferno. Orange flames toasted the black sky and the fire's roar muffled the murmur of human voices.

There was no saving the family cabin. There wasn't even the possibility of saving any items inside, though she doubted anything of sentimental value had been left behind. Anger blazed inside her, as hot as the wall of heat emanating from the burning building. The perpetrators were probably long gone—if this was a professional job orchestrated by Maddie. If so, the bitch was probably standing at the window of her plush mansion, watching as fire glow lit the woods below.

But if the arson was a mere crime of opportunity by a pervert…her gaze drifted to the tree line. He could be hiding behind one of those trees, getting off watching the sight of his work. She glanced at James, but his focus was all on the cabin. His hands were on his hips, his face stoic. She longed to touch him, offer words of sympathy, but that would hardly do in public. Besides, she'd be of more use to him by finding the perp.

Charlotte slipped into the crowd and then hurried around to the back of the cabin. Only one lone firefighter fought the flames from the opposite direction. She jogged toward the woods, right hand resting on the holster of her gun.

A crash boomed from behind and she whirled around. The left cabin sidewall collapsed to the ground and the roof sank on top of it, shooting sparks like the Fourth of July. The smell of burnt pine stung her eyes and enveloped her nose and lungs. She swiped at her eyes and continued into the woods.

Leaves, twigs and pine needles crunched underfoot, loud as firecrackers in the sudden stillness. Only a few feet past the tree line and the noise of the fire and firefighters was already muffled.

Screech.

Her stomach cartwheeled and she raised her gun, spinning in a circle to discover where and what had sounded. Blood pounded in her temples.

And again, the cacophony arose. *Whoo whoo.*

"Just…just a barred owl," she whispered. Creepy thing was loud as a foghorn. "Nothing to fear."

But it took several seconds before her heart ceased its rapid pounding and her breathing returned to normal. Charlotte lowered her gun and searched the inky blackness for signs of anyone hiding.

Nothing was out of the ordinary. Barren tree limbs reached skyward and the tops of shrubs were laced with crisscrossed shadows from moonbeams. The wind whispered above and around her.

So why was she so sure that she wasn't alone?

Awareness prickled her scalp and snaked down her spine. Someone watched. She listened and strained to pinpoint a location.

"Charlotte? Charlotte? Are you out there?"

James. She exhaled in a whoosh and cautiously stepped forward.

Twigs snapped like a mini explosion from her left side. Footfalls vibrated the ground and at last she could make out the tall figure of a man running deeper into the woods.

"Halt," she called out.

The man kept running, just as she'd expected.

"Charlotte? Everything okay?"

"I'm fine," she reassured him. "Be right out."

She stepped out of the forest and quirked a brow at his stern face. "I was checking to see if our arsonist was watching all the excitement."

"Without backup? What were you thinking?"

His dad's cabin was in flames, so she bit off an angry retort. He had enough on his plate without her reminders that he wasn't her protector on the job. "You were busy," she said mildly. "Any leads about what started the fire?"

"They won't say yet but we both know what happened here. Especially since…" He clamped his mouth shut.

"Especially since what?"

"I wasn't going to mention it but I had a text last night saying to back off."

She shook her head in disgust. "Why didn't you tell me?"

"Didn't seem important. I mean, c'mon, it changes

nothing. Neither of us will ever back down from pursuing this."

She marched past him, eager to leave the dark shadow of the woods and whoever had been out there hiding. "You still should have told me. If you were working with Sammy, I bet you would have, right?"

"Maybe," he agreed, falling into step beside her. "And don't think I'm finished. Promise me you won't run off on your own again without at least telling me what you're doing. That's professional courtesy at the very least."

"I can admit when I'm wrong. Sorry. I won't do it again."

"Excellent. I take it you didn't see anyone?"

Charlotte hesitated, but she could hardly withhold information after she'd just chastised him for doing the same. "There was someone out there, but he took off running and I never saw his face."

"You could have been..." He broke off his chain of thought. "Never mind. You're here and safe."

"I had a text, too, on the way over. It said, 'This is just the start.'"

"The Stowerses are getting desperate and they know we're the ones investigating."

"I wonder how much else they know."

They trudged back to the fire, wrapped in their own thoughts.

The fire wasn't quite as bright and the flames were lower. It wouldn't take much longer before the firefighters had it completely extinguished.

"Sorry about your dad's cabin."

James shrugged. "Maybe it's all for the best. The

place was a hard sell for buyers and neither Lilah nor I had any desire to move in."

"Speaking of Lilah, I see she and Harlan are here."

"And she's brought Ellie. At least you'll get to meet my niece."

The little family headed toward them. Lilah appeared solemn, but the toddler at her hip was clearly entranced by the fire, and stared at it with saucer-wide eyes.

"Hey, Ellie," James said, holding out his arms.

Charlotte ran a hand down Ellie's blond curls. "Such a pretty girl."

Ellie graced her with a cherubic smile before turning her attention back to James. "See the fire, Uncle Jim Bob," she squealed.

Charlotte snickered.

He winced. "Uncle James," he corrected her mildly, taking Ellie into his arms. "You okay, Lilah?"

She nodded, but her lips trembled slightly. "Yeah. A little sad, though. Me, you and Darla had some good times there."

They watched in silence as the hoses continued to beat down the flames. Most of the spectators drifted away, driving off in their vehicles. Harlan put an arm around Lilah's shoulder. "No point hanging around," he said quietly. "The cold air can't be good for Ellie's cold."

"You're probably right," she agreed.

They all walked together to Harlan's car and James strapped Ellie into her car seat.

"Sorry about the cabin," she said to Lilah.

Lilah wasn't her usual vivacious self, but she mustered a tight smile. "It represented our past. And it held as many painful memories as good ones. As for me, I'll keep my focus on the present."

Harlan glanced significantly at James. "Like I said—trouble," he muttered.

Resentment sliced through Charlotte, but she said nothing in protest. How could she? Harlan was right. She'd brought nothing but trouble to James.

Soon, she reminded herself, this would all be over. She'd leave Lavender Mountain and leave James. In time, he'd forget her and move on with his life—as would she. The thought should have been comforting, but it filled her with sadness.

Harlan dug into his jacket pocket. "I'd been on the way over to your house to deliver this." He held out a certified letter. "Captain Burkhart called me and said to make sure to find you. You've been formally summoned to a hearing tomorrow to discuss dismissal for job abandonment. Your suspension was over yesterday and you were supposed to have reported back to work today."

Damn. She hadn't paid any attention to the date. Atlanta seemed a lifetime ago. "Tomorrow," she repeated dully.

"We'll go together," James said, shooting Harlan a defiant look.

She stuffed the envelope into her pocket. "This isn't your problem."

"You're not going alone. End of argument."

Like hell it was.

Chapter 12

"The choice is yours. Report for work here tomorrow morning or be dismissed."

"I need more time," Charlotte pleaded. "Just a few more days and—"

"You're fired," Captain Burkhart said, smugness evident in his pronouncement.

She clamped her jaw shut and arranged her features to show no emotion. She wouldn't give him the satisfaction of knowing how those words hurt.

The man had never liked her. Whether it was because he was a sexist cop or because he'd taken offense for some other unknown reason, Charlotte couldn't say. But in the two years he'd been her supervisor, he'd made her job hell.

When she'd reported Danny and Roy's abandonment at the alley, he hadn't believed her. Instead he bought into her partners' lies that she'd been at fault for the life-threatening danger with the drug dealer. According to their false version of the story, she'd carelessly blown their cover and then fled the scene. Valiant men that they were, her partners claimed they stayed behind and pursued the drug dealer—at great risk to their lives.

Charlotte shook off the old memories and fought for composure. The two other detectives at the hearing stared at her with a modicum of sympathy.

She rose and lifted her chin. "I used my suspension to pursue this case. My only fault is checking back in a day late. The punishment's a little stiff for the offense. All I'm asking is permission to use my annual leave for the next few days."

Burkhart slapped his hands on the desk. "Enough. We've been through this. You're insubordinate and I don't believe you ever intend to return to duty."

"Not until I have my arrests," she agreed.

"And now you'll never get one." He also rose from behind his desk. "You no longer have any authority as a police officer. Turn in your badge on the way out."

She bit the inside of her mouth, not wanting to lash out and set him straight. She might no longer be employed by the Atlanta PD, but Harlan could still deputize her to work in his jurisdiction until she'd arrested the Stowerses. Right now, she couldn't think about her future career. All that mattered was rescuing Jenny. After that, she'd have to come to grips with the mess.

"Richard and Maddie Stowers will be arrested by the end of the week. You can count on it," she promised.

Burkhart's face reddened. "Not by you. Let it go, Helms."

Hell, no. Easy for him to say. He didn't have a personal connection to the case. Nor did he have to interview trafficking victims and hear the pain in their voices and the horror in their eyes. She couldn't save everyone, but she could and would save Jenny.

She snatched up her purse and marched to the exit, slamming the door behind her. James was sprawled on a bench in the hallway. For the first time, she was secretly glad he'd insisted on accompanying her on the trip to Atlanta.

He quirked a brow. "Bad news, I take it?"

"I want out of here." The institutional-green walls and gray linoleum flooring, combined with the faint scent of industrial cleaner mixed with sweat and tobacco, were a sudden anathema.

"Couldn't agree with you more."

He matched her step for step as they left the building and climbed into her car. She turned on the engine and they headed into the late afternoon traffic.

"I'd hate to drive this every day," he observed from the passenger side.

She cast him a wry smile. "We're not even in rush hour traffic. Sure you don't want to drive like usual?"

"Nope. It's all yours."

Well, at least she'd won that battle today. Wordlessly she weaved along the crowded interstate, stewing over the long day spent at the hearing.

James interrupted her thoughts. "You can always appeal their decision, you know."

"And go through another kangaroo court?" She laughed dispiritedly. "Six years of stellar service— all down the drain on my first transgression."

"Sounds pretty stiff. You should fight it, or at least file a complaint about the severity of the judgment."

"Maybe." But she couldn't muster enthusiasm for the task. When had she stopped loving her job? It had happened so gradually. "I used to enjoy working undercover," she said. "It was exciting and it felt like I was making a difference. Stupid, huh? For everyone I arrested, it seemed like three more criminals replaced them by the next week."

"Would have been even worse on the streets if you didn't catch the ones you did."

"I suppose. But I get sick of the whole underground culture, too. And not getting to see my family as often as I want."

"Now you're free."

"Now I'm broke." A sudden worry assaulted her. "You really think Harlan will temporarily deputize me until the end of the week?"

He winked. "He's my brother-in-law, so I have some influence. Lilah could make life hell for him if he didn't help us out on this. Besides, you're a great cop and he knows it."

The words were a balm to her injured pride. Much as she'd grown to hate her job, she'd never been fired before, and the idea rankled. Maybe James was right. She should file a complaint and get her employment record cleaned up from this hit. Plus, it would have the added benefit of irking Captain Burkhart— always a plus.

It took forty minutes to drive the ten miles to her apartment, but at last she pulled into the parking lot and they headed up the stairs. While she was nearby, it'd be crazy not to pick up more street clothes, a fancy gown for the fund-raiser event and a few other little odds and ends.

They climbed the concrete stairwell and she dug the keys from her purse. A strong hand rested on her forearm. "What—?"

James frowned and cocked his head at the slightly ajar door. "You leave it unlocked?" he asked in a low voice.

She felt the blood drain from her face. "Maybe the landlord had to get in." Not likely.

James drew his gun and stepped in front of her. "I'll check it out."

"Not alone you won't."

He shot her an irate look. "Just stay back."

She unholstered her own sidearm and tried to squeeze her body in front of his. "Me first. It's my apartment and I know the layout better than you," she argued.

James muscled her behind him and slowly opened the door.

Books and sofa cushions littered the den floor. Every item on her bookshelf had been dumped and furniture was pulled away from the walls. James took a step in and she followed, her eyes sweeping from the kitchen to the dining room and balcony. The same mayhem from ransacking was everywhere, but no one was in sight.

That left the bedroom and two bathrooms to check. She carefully picked her way through the junk on the floor, sliding past James. He wasn't happy about that, but could hardly argue the point.

The hall bathroom was empty, all the contents of her medicine cabinet toppled into the sink. Which left the bedroom—the only room where lights weren't blazing. An unnatural stillness lifted the hairs at the back of her neck. If someone was in there, they knew she'd returned. She flattened herself against one side of the door, and James joined her on the other. She was about to enter, when he beat her to the punch.

He kicked the door and it slammed against the far wall. Charlotte flipped on the light switch.

Two men dressed head to toe in black, their faces hidden under dark ski masks, erupted from the closet. The two barreled toward them, so quickly she barely had time to catch her breath—much less shoot. One of the men chopped her arm holding the gun, and her weapon hit the floor by her feet. Strong arms grabbed her just above both elbows and then violently threw her to the side. She was airborne for two seconds before rolling clear across the bed. Her forehead smacked the bedpost and pain radiated through her head. Warm liquid trickled into her eyes and she swiped at them, seeking James in the melee.

Her attacker had fled, but James was wrestling on the floor with the other man. She had to help him. She located her gun and tucked it back into her holster.

"Go get the other guy," James grunted.

"No way."

"I got this," he insisted.

The need to help James warred with her need to catch the other intruder. They'd violated her sacred space. Every nightmare come true. If she didn't catch the fleeing felon, she would always worry that he would return one night. And the next time she might not be lucky enough to have a partner by her side.

"Be right back," she promised, racing to the stairwell.

The steps were slick with rain and she lost her footing, tumbling down the first flight. Ignoring the burning shinbone scrapes, Charlotte ran on and scanned the back of the property.

A silhouette in black crouched behind a garbage can. At first sight of her, the intruder took off running again, knocking over the dumpster can, spewing trash everywhere. But she was close enough—in shooting range—if her aim was accurate. Charlotte touched the gun she'd slipped back into her holster. *You aren't officially a cop anymore. You shoot the guy and you've got a mess on your hands.*

The moment's hesitation cost her a chance. He reached the street, blending with traffic and pedestrians.

She bent over, hands on knees, and took deep breaths that burned her chest. *Get it together. James might need you.* Charlotte straightened and ran back upstairs, ignoring the jabbing stitch in her side.

Pausing to reason with Charlotte had cost him the advantage in the fight. The masked man fought with the desperation of a cornered animal. Trying to wrestle him back down was like trying to bathe an angry wildcat.

"Who the hell are you?" James panted as they rolled on the floor.

No answer.

The scent of sweat and cheap aftershave filled his nostrils and lungs. He fought against the downward spiral that might tunnel into another flashback. *Keep it together.*

Pain seared his left thigh as the man landed a vicious kick.

Had he momentarily blanked out and weakened his hold? James groaned and grabbed one of the attacker's feet, trying to prevent another kick. Where was Charlotte? Fear pinched his gut. What if this guy's accomplice stopped running and went on the attack? To hell with this wrestling match. Charlotte's safety was his priority.

But he could accomplish one important victory—get a good look at who was behind the attack. If he was lucky, he'd find this criminal later. James released his grip and reached for the knit ski mask, ripping it off his face.

Startled gray eyes met his. James soaked in every detail possible—cropped brown hair, ruddy complexion, a hawk nose, thin lips. His gaze dropped lower and hit the jackpot—on the right side of his neck was a dagger tattoo. The mark looked to be a crude prison job with its lack of detail and grayish-black coloring.

The guy rushed the doorway and James gave chase. Halfway down the stairs, he spotted Charlotte coming toward them—alone and seemingly intact, but blood trickled down her face. Relief chased down his neck and spine. The man she'd been chasing was nowhere in sight, but she was now in the direct path of the gray eyes.

"Look out," he shouted.

Too late. The intruder never slowed, but he raised one muscled arm and knocked her out of his way. In horror, James saw her petite body absorb the pounding of concrete until she lay motionless at the bottom of the stairwell.

"Charlotte!" He rushed to her prone body and pushed the hair from her face. In the space of mere minutes, hell had unleashed its fury. She was pale, the whiteness contrasting with the crimson ribbons of blood on her face.

She groaned. "You okay? Did they get away?"

"Yes, on both counts. How bad are you hurt? I don't want to lift you if anything's broken."

She struggled up onto one elbow and drew several shuddering breaths. "I think I'm okay. Give me a minute."

"That's one nasty cut above your left eye." He pulled a handkerchief from his jacket and gently dabbed at the open wound.

She flinched and reached for his arm. "Stop. I'm going to try to stand."

He supported her weight on one side of his body and she sagged against him. "This is officially the worst day of my life," she joked. "Lose my job and then get the crap beat out of me. Now I get to return to my destroyed apartment and pick up the mess."

"Leave it. I'll lock up while you wait in the car. Where's the nearest hospital? You need stitches."

"I won't argue with you this time. We can stop at a doc-in-the-box on our way back to Lavender Mountain."

James quickly locked up her apartment. Slowly, they returned to the cruiser, his arm bracing her around the waist. "Think you might have sustained internal injuries?" he asked anxiously. Each time pain flickered in her green eyes, he sank lower into guilt. At last they reached the car and he carefully tucked her inside before entering it on the opposite side.

James keyed the engine and turned up the heat. Charlotte leaned back in the seat and flipped the mirror down. "Holy crap, I'm a mess. I promise I don't feel as bad as I look."

She faced him. "So what's wrong?"

"What's wrong? Everything. You're hurt and it's my fault."

"Don't say that." She pointed to the cut on her forehead. "That was caused by an unknown assailant. Not you."

"Yeah, an assailant who escaped me."

"We were surprised by an attack and neither one of us is to blame. I noticed you were limping. What happened?"

"Bastard landed a lucky kick." He gripped the steering wheel and stared out into the rainy darkness.

A warm, soft touch on his right hand startled him, and he glanced down. Charlotte's small hand caressed his tense fingers, which were white at the knuckles.

"I'm okay," she whispered, her breath clouding the air. "Those men did enough of a number on us without us piling on and beating ourselves up."

"Back there. I might have lost it for a couple of seconds in the fight," he admitted. "I'm not sure."

"Doesn't matter. My mind was a tilt-a-whirl a good thirty seconds after I crashed into the bedpost. As they say, shit happens. All we can do is our best."

But what if his best wasn't good enough? Some small part deep inside still felt broken from the war. It was getting better—much better—in large part because the insomnia had finally been laid to rest. The past nights he'd spent with Charlotte in his arms, he'd drifted into deep slumber. James loosened his grip from the steering wheel and held her hand, staring at their enjoined fingers. Every word, every touch from Charlotte was a balm to his spirit—that is, when they weren't arguing. A smile curled his lips. Fussing with Charlotte was still more fun and invigorating than normal conversation with anyone else.

The rain came down harder, a metallic din that thundered above and around them. Water washed across the car windows in sheets. It seemed as though they were separated from the rest of the world in a warm, safe cocoon.

Her hand traveled up his arm, and even through the jacket, the contact set his heart pounding as loud as the rain outside. She brushed her mouth across the edge of his bottom lip. "There's no need to hurry back. Let's wait out the storm together."

He kissed the top of her scalp. "If you're sure the stitches can wait."

"Kiss me and I'll forget all about the cut."

"I aim to please." His mouth met hers. What he'd intended as a tender gesture escalated at once into a roaring desire and he pulled away. "Not the time or place," he said with a frustrated laugh.

"Tonight, then."

The promise and passion in her eyes wiped away all pain and all misgivings. Somehow, someway, they belonged together.

Chapter 13

The last three days before the Stowerses' fund-raiser event sped by way too fast. She and James spent most of their days outlining their plan of action for rescuing Jenny, and their nights...well, she'd never been happier. It was going to hurt like hell to return to her dreary apartment in Atlanta once this case was over. There was nothing there for her—no job, no lover and no friends. Her undercover work had consumed all her energy for far too long.

Charlotte checked the cruiser's pull-down mirror and smoothed back the few stray locks that escaped the bun on the back of her head. Her dyed ebony locks had faded a bit from repeated washings, and the gallon of conditioner she'd used had helped the damage, but it was still a disaster. The stitches above her left eye were removed yesterday, but no amount of makeup could cover the nasty bruise.

James laid a hand on the top of her bare shoulders. "You look beautiful," he assured her.

She smoothed a hand across the long green evening gown, thankful that its length would cover all her shinbone scrapes. Sure, she was being vain and embarrassed that James guessed her trivial concern. Crisply she closed the mirror and raised the sunshield flap to its original position. "Doesn't matter what I look like—all that matters is finding Jenny. And you look pretty spiffy yourself, by the way."

Did he ever. He filled out the tuxedo like nobody's business. The suit emphasized his lean, muscular build and lent an elegance to his high cheekbones and strong jaw. Her admiration must have been clear because his eyes darkened and his gaze shifted to her lips.

"Don't you dare kiss me," she warned.

Teasing mischief danced in his eyes. "Afraid you'll need to have me right here and right now if I do?"

"No, I just don't want you to ruin my lipstick."

"Liar."

She knew what he was trying to do—lighten the tension before they entered the Stowerses' mansion.

"Good thing our plan doesn't include having to actually dance. That bruise on your thigh looks rough."

Music spilled from the main level of the Falling Rock Community Clubhouse and every window was lit. It appeared so elegant and enchanting—if one weren't aware of the dark underside that funded such privileged wealth. If she had her way tonight, the Stowerses would spend the rest of their years in a dark, damp cell with no music. And even that wouldn't atone for all the lives they'd ruined. *I'll have Jenny home to you by dawn*, she silently promised Tanya.

James lifted her hand and kissed the inside of her palm. "We'll find Jenny and the others," he promised. "We've got our plans in place."

"Right." She inhaled deeply.

"One more thing."

She gazed once more at the glittering clubhouse, a hand reaching for the door, impatient to get started.

James placed a finger under her chin and gently turned her face to his. "I love you."

"Wh-what?" No, oh no. This wasn't supposed to happen. She'd let him get too close.

"You heard me. Does that really surprise you? I thought after last night…"

She swallowed hard. Last night had been magical. There'd been a certain tenderness along with the passion, emotions that she didn't want to examine at the moment.

"Don't love me," she whispered. The hurt in his eyes matched the hurt in her heart. "I bring trouble to everyone. Can't you see that?"

"I've told you before that I don't care. We can face anything together." He sighed and ran a hand through his hair. "Never mind. I shouldn't have brought it up now."

"You'll always be special to me…the best friend I ever had."

Friend? The word crushed his spirit. He wanted it to be so much more than that.

"James…" Tears threatened to ruin her carefully made-up face, and she couldn't control the tremble in her lips.

"Sorry. Really. You don't have to say anything." He cleared his throat. "Is your mike secured?"

Relieved to get the conversation back to the job at hand, she checked to make sure it was safely tucked into the front of the low-cut gown. "Yes. Ready when you are."

He nodded and opened the car door. "Showtime."

The wind chilled her bare skin and she hastily threw the gown's matching wrap over her shoulders.

They walked side by side to the front door, min-gling with several other couples also on their way to the party. Everyone else looked excited and happy to be going to the annual fund-raising event, while a hard knot of misery twisted her stomach. She'd hurt James and she'd never meant to do so. He deserved a woman who would fill his life with good things—not her.

The door opened and they entered into the bright warmth. A live band played classical music that under-scored the chattering of the houseful of guests.

Her eyes quickly swept the room of beautiful peo-ple dressed in formal attire. Serving staff milled about with glasses of champagne and shrimp canapés. She'd thought the Stowerses' house beautiful, but it was noth-ing compared to the present festive glory of the club-house.

"Thank you for joining us." Maddie appeared in the foyer dressed in a red low-cut gown that managed to be bold yet flattering. She ignored Charlotte and extended a hand to James. "Officer Tedder, if I remember cor-rectly? Richard and I appreciate all you do in keeping peace and order in our community."

Yeah, I bet she appreciates us. Phony witch.

"I believe y'all are the last of the officers to arrive,"

Maddie said, still avoiding Charlotte. "Harlan said everyone's made it here except for one officer left manning the fort and another who's home sick."

That would be Sammy, who was guarding the back of the place, and Charlotte wouldn't be surprised if the Stowerses were aware of that fact.

"I don't believe you've met my husband before?" Maddie swept her hand toward the man at her side, who gulped a healthy swig of bourbon from a crystal glass.

Richard Stowers glanced Charlotte's way and discreetly looked her body over. But not so discreetly that it escaped her attention. A cheesy smile lit his puffy, albeit handsome, face, and he extended a hand. "And you must be Officer Tedder's wife?"

"Partner. Officer Hanson." She masked her displeasure at his handshake, which he held two seconds longer than customary.

His eyes narrowed in on her forehead. "Nasty cut you have there. What happened?"

As if he didn't know. As if the two of them hadn't sent those men to search her apartment for clues on how much she knew about their trafficking ring. Unless…unless Maddie were the brains behind everything while he merely enjoyed the fruits of her ill-gotten gains. Richard certainly didn't look or act the part of a criminal mastermind. His ruddy complexion, and the web of broken veins around his nose, suggested he either imbibed quite frequently or was an alcoholic.

His remark finally drew Maddie's attention her way. Brown eyes flashed at her, barely able to disguise anger.

Charlotte offered a cool smile to Richard. "I took a tumble down a flight of concrete stairs."

"Ouch. Guess it could have been worse, though," he said jovially.

Maddie's sharp chin jutted out even further than normal. "Colleen," she said peremptorily, summoning her housekeeper, who apparently served double duty at social functions. "Please take their jackets." Maddie faced them both with a chilly smile. "Enjoy your evening. Let's move along, Richard."

Charlotte removed her wrap, uncomfortably aware of Richard ogling the low-cut V of her gown before obediently tagging along behind his wife.

"Your purse, ma'am?" Colleen held out her hand.

She firmly pulled the sequin purse closer to her side. "I prefer to keep it with me, thank you."

Richard sidled up close to Charlotte and she drew back an inch. Annoyance stiffened her spine. The last thing she needed was to have this man clinging to her side while she searched his house.

James took her arm and guided her away. "Excuse us. We'd like to catch up to our friends by the buffet."

"Certainly." Richard took her other hand and pressed it into his coarse palm. "See you in a bit. Perhaps a dance later?"

Not if she spotted him first. Next time she saw Richard, she vowed it would be to handcuff the creep.

"Of course," she lied, accompanying James into the den, where a long buffet table was spread out the length of the entire room. Once they were out of earshot she quickly whispered, "Thanks for helping me escape."

James nodded. "I see my sister and Harlan. We'll talk a bit and then…"

Then, they implemented their plan. She nodded in silent agreement. With any luck, Richard would be too drunk to seek her out by the time they began the house search.

"Champagne, ma'am?" She accepted a slender flute from the waiter. He was tall and stocky and clearly uncomfortable in his ill-fitted uniform. No doubt he was also employed as a guard, same as the Stowerses' supposed gardeners. She exchanged a knowing glance with James.

"Be careful," he muttered.

The man just couldn't help himself when it came to unnecessary warnings. "Don't worry about me. I can take care of myself. Focus on your own—"

"Look at you all spiffed up in a tux!" Lilah rushed over and hugged James. "I haven't seen you in one of these since your high school prom." Her gaze swept to Charlotte and she clasped her hands in admiration. "Stunning."

"As are you," Charlotte said. Lilah's long blond hair was loose and she wore a lavender tea-length dress. But even more striking was her happy confidence. You'd think she'd grown up attending swanky parties every weekend. But as for Harlan...she stifled a grin. He tugged at his collar and looked as if he wanted to be anywhere but here.

Lilah's gaze fell to Charlotte's feet and she let out an exasperated *tsk*. "Too bad I couldn't talk you into high heels, or at least wedge pumps."

As if she'd attempt smuggling out Jenny and the other girls while tottering in high heels. She caught Harlan's warning glance—Lilah was in the dark about tonight's mission. Just as well. Let her have her fairy-castle, enchanting illusion for the evening. The less people that knew, the better their chance for success.

The band came to an abrupt halt.

"May I have your attention, please?"

Maddie and Richard posed in front of the band, and her cultured voice swept over the crowd. Conversations halted.

"As everyone is aware, we've gathered here tonight to honor our sheriff, Harlan Sampson, and all of the men and women employed by the Elmore County Sheriff's Department."

Richard raised his glass in the air. "Hear, hear!" he called out a tad too loudly.

Maddie slanted him a look.

"Bet she gives him hell later," James murmured by her ear.

"Not if they're locked in separate cells."

He clinked his champagne glass against hers and smirked. "Hear, hear."

Maddie continued. "It's because of their hard work and dedication that the Lavender Mountain community is such a peaceful haven."

A smattering of applause broke out.

"And now I'd like to ask Sheriff Sampson to come forward and say a few words."

"Damn," Harlan muttered.

"Speech," Lilah said with a grin, giving him a playful shove forward.

Now was the time to slip away. "I'm going to the ladies' room. Be back in a bit," Charlotte lied.

"Wait until after Harlan's speech and I'll go with you," Lilah offered.

"Sorry. It can't wait."

She cast a last look at James. His face was stoic, but she knew he hated her operating alone. Yet they'd both agreed beforehand that it would be less conspicuous if they searched apart from one another. She gave him a reassuring smile and strolled toward the side exit of the clubhouse, all while casually sipping the flute of champagne.

At the rear of the main ballroom she stopped at the buffet table and picked up a canapé, using the opportunity to check if she were being watched. Luckily all eyes appeared focused on Harlan's clipped speech. She dabbed at her mouth with a paper napkin and then whisked out of the room and into a back hallway with an exit door.

One last furtive glance behind, and Charlotte slipped outdoors. Cool wind whipped through the thin material of her evening gown and she shivered, thinking longingly of her jacket. But soon enough, she'd be back inside. On the sidewalk, she passed a couple decked out in their finery, obviously out of town guests on the way to the party. The woman's voice was a tad too loud and the man practically carried her as she stumbled about in her high heels.

Charlotte waved at them cheerily. "Forgot my lipstick," she said. "See you in a bit at the party. The band's fantastic."

"Oh, damn." The woman placed a hand over her mouth. "I believe I forgot mine, too. I'm going back, Thomas."

Thomas rolled his eyes. "You look fine. Let's go."

Charlotte beamed at him, practically bestowing a conspiratorial wink. "You go on. Me and—" She glanced at the woman.

"Alyssa," she supplied. "Alyssa Renfroe."

"Alyssa and I will go in together and meet you in a few minutes."

"You sure?" he asked doubtfully.

"No problem."

He transferred the weight of Alyssa to Charlotte's arm, and she fought to keep her balance while propping up Alyssa. Their progression to the Stowerses' house was slow and arduous, but Charlotte was grateful for Alyssa. What a struck of luck. Now she didn't have to sneak into the house. Alyssa had unwittingly provided an alibi.

Once at the Stowerses' entrance, Charlotte didn't bother knocking and opened the door like she had every right to be there.

A tall, husky man entered the foyer and gave them the once-over.

"We forgot our… What did we forget?" Alyssa asked with a giggle.

"Lipstick." Charlotte smiled at the man and kept walking. "I'm staying in the east wing. Are you?" she asked Alyssa.

Her smooth forehead puckered. "I—I'm not sure."

"Don't worry. We'll find your room."

It took several minutes to make it down the hallway, but at last Alyssa came to a halt. "This is it," she declared. "I recognize my perfume bottles on the dresser."

"Great. My room's further down. I'll be back in a few minutes," Charlotte lied, relieved to be rid of her drunken burden.

She'd been down this particular hallway on her previous visit with James and didn't expect Jenny or the others to be kept so close to the party. But for the sake of thoroughness, they'd leave no room unexamined.

Every bedroom off the hallway was presently empty, but appeared to be used as a guest bedroom for the weekend. Each contained luggage, clothes hung in the closets and a few toiletries were set on the nightstands. Charlotte peeked out of the last room she'd entered to make sure the coast was clear before stepping back into the hallway.

"So sorry you are feelin' poorly, ma'am," Colleen said in her distinctive Irish accent as Charlotte started to enter the den.

Charlotte ducked back inside the nearest bedroom and flattened herself against the wall.

"Let me help you find your room," Colleen continued. "This way, please, ma'am."

She let out a deep breath and listened to the women make their way down the hall. Time to slip away.

Charlotte scurried out of the room, still clutching the small sequined purse that was just large enough to hold her cell phone and a small gun. The hallway made an L-turn and she ventured on, but it was more of the same—empty rooms.

Until she entered the last room on the right.

Someone was in there. A mattress squeaked and a man and woman groaned. Uh-oh. Hastily she backed out and softly shut the door. Had they heard her?

She waited a few heartbeats, prepared to make a lame excuse if they came after her, but the mattress squeaks never slowed.

Whew, bullet dodged. Charlotte retrieved her cell phone and texted James.

East wing complete. Negative. No need to break in.
Go inside and say your name is Thomas Renfroe and
you are checking on your wife, Alyssa, who returned
for some lipstick.

A rough hand grasped her elbow. "What the hell
are you doing here?"

The band resumed playing and James waited several
minutes before strolling through the crowd, biding his
time until he had an opportunity to leave unnoticed. A
teenage girl clutched the arms of an older gentleman
and her gray eyes were wide and...not exactly scared,
but apprehensive. Was the man her father or one of the
Stowerses' clients? He needed to check the west wing
of the Stowerses' house and then find Charlotte—the
quicker the better. But he couldn't ignore the girl, either. He turned and scanned the crowd for Harlan.

His brother-in-law was surrounded by people con-
gratulating him on his speech, but as if he had an extra
sense for danger, Harlan raised his head and made eye
contact. James cocked his head at the old-man-young-
girl couple and Harlan nodded in understanding. He'd
check it out.

"Look at her," a lady said close by. "Never thought
I'd see a Tedder at an event like this."

Another voice murmured assent. "Heard Sampson's
hired her brother now."

"Harlan's in bed with the dregs of our community,"
another chimed in. "Disgraceful."

Heat fevered his brain. They could say what they
wanted about him, but not his sister. She was off limits.

James squared his shoulders and eyed the small

clique. "Lilah Tedder is one of the kindest, smartest women you'll ever meet. Harlan's lucky to have her for a wife." He focused his gaze on the sole male among the group. "And if you've got a problem with me, let's discuss it now."

"No problem," the man said quickly. "Ladies, let's head to the buffet table for refreshments."

They made a quick beeline to move away and James took a deep breath. He shouldn't have confronted them. The last thing he needed was to make a scene. Their plan depended on acting as unobtrusive as possible. He meandered out of the room, relieved nobody paid him any mind. At the back door of the clubhouse, he exited onto the deck. No one was around. Quickly he walked through the backyard. If someone asked what he was doing, he'd claim he needed fresh air.

His cell phone vibrated and he read the text message. Great. Charlotte was safe. Soon as he finished searching the west wing, they were to meet by the kitchen.

Sure enough, he easily got past the man monitoring the front door. The moment he was alone, James began his search, going into every room—a couple of bedrooms and baths, a fully equipped gymnasium including a sauna and a movie theater room.

The hallway was eerily quiet. The Stowerses had excellent acoustics in their place. Perhaps they'd built the mansion that way to contain the screams of desperate children. His pace picked up. No way he'd leave this place without every room searched. If Jenny was here, they'd find her.

His spirits sank with each empty room. But the most likely place the girls were hidden would be either on the upper level of rooms or in the basement. They'd expected this going in. James entered the den and searched for Charlotte. No luck. She might already be hanging around the kitchen area. He hurried to the door—but still no Charlotte. Stealthily he opened the door several inches, but the room was dark and quiet.

No Charlotte.

Unease tingled at the back of his neck. Where was she? He pulled out his phone and checked the time the text was sent—five minutes ago. She should be here.

He pushed away from the kitchen and reached for his phone. A familiar smell of roses startled him. "Charlotte?" He whirled around.

"The one and only." Her voice was light but her expression subtly strained.

"Where were you?" he whispered fiercely. "What happened?"

"One of the male serving staff grabbed me and asked what I was doing in that area. I tried to play it off as if I were lost and looking for the bathroom, but he wasn't buying it."

He stood between her and the doors, half expecting security to arrive and escort them out of the house. Or worse. "How did you get away?"

"I acted all embarrassed and haltingly admitted that I'd gone there in search of my married lover. Claimed we'd made a rendezvous, but I couldn't remember which room we were supposed to sneak into. Then I put on my best snooty air and said that Maddie and Richard were close personal friends and if he didn't leave me alone I'd have to report him."

"Quick thinking. Guess you learned it on the job."

"Sink or swim, as they say." She shivered and

rubbed her arms. "I'm okay. Let's get on with it. We don't want to draw attention to ourselves in case guards are lurking about."

"Agreed." He kept his voice low as they walked by the pantry. "Kitchen appears normal but we can take another quick peek before heading upstairs."

"I want to see as much as possible before we search the attic and basement. Make sure no child is left behind when the raid begins."

People liked to tease him about his military rigidity, but Charlotte was just as thorough in her job process.

What a shame this gorgeous house was owned by such a despicable couple. How many years had the Stowerses managed to conceal their illegal activity and live this lifestyle?

A deep voice suddenly boomed from around the corner. "Did you see that drunk chick—Alice or something—stumbling around the house?"

"Her boobs were practically hanging out of her dress," another man replied, chuckling.

Quickly James took Charlotte's hand and they ducked into a side room as the men made their way past.

"That was close," she breathed at his side as they slowly eased their way back into the hallway and proceeded to the staircase. Sneaking upstairs would be even trickier than the basement. Anyone passing through the foyer would see them. Timing was everything.

A quick look back and then they bounded up the stairs together. Again, he was struck by the unnatural quiet as they left the den and walked the hallway. As mapped out earlier, he searched the rooms on the right while Charlotte worked the left. They made quick work of it. He glanced in the last empty room on his side and joined Charlotte for her last search.

A heavy padlock hanging on the outside door set him on edge. Even if it wasn't locked now—why was it ever necessary to lock someone inside?

Half a dozen cheap cots lined a stark room that was unlike the opulence of the rest of the living quarters. The beds were meticulously tidy, even though they were made up with only threadbare sheets and blankets. He entered and shut the door behind him while Charlotte flipped on the light.

A scratched armoire was the only other piece of furniture besides the cots, and Charlotte flicked it open. A few lone wire hangers dangled from the top dowel, but it was otherwise empty.

"Could be the maid's quarters," he said quietly.

"This isn't the Victorian era where indentured servants were forced to live in substandard hidey-holes."

She walked to the lone, narrow window and pulled back the tattered curtain. "And then there's this," she whispered.

He ran a finger down the pane's tinted liner. "Bingo."

Charlotte's eyes grew misty. "They're gone. Sold. I'm too late."

"There's still the basement." But his own spirits grew low.

The scrape of a shoe sounded far down the hall. With unspoken accord, they rushed to the door and positioned themselves on either side, backs flat against the wall. Charlotte flipped off the light switch.

A crescent moon struggled to shine through the tinted and curtained window.

Creak. Another step closer.

James hardly dared to breath, concentrating on the patterns of sound.

Creak, creak. Just one person. He carefully extracted the gun from his vest and closed his finger on the trigger, the metal cool and lethal in his hands. A rustle of movement beside him, and Charlotte extracted a gun from her beaded purse. Her face was pale but composed in the faint light.

A flashlight beam crisscrossed on the floor outside their door. He was closer now. With any luck, the man was only on a routine security check.

The footsteps reached the end of the hallway and stopped.

Silence as thick as the stale, dark air weighted down on him. He noted the rise and fall of Charlotte's chest, although she made no sound. What was the man doing on the other side of the door? James gave her a slight nod. *Be ready for anything*, he silently willed her with his mind.

The world exploded in a firestorm of splintered wood as the man kicked down the door and entered. The scent of sweat and cheap aftershave stabbed through the chaos of his mind. *The intruder at Charlotte's apartment.*

A metallic clatter ripped through the darkness, like the sound of automatic gunfire in Afghanistan. James shook off the memory. *Not now. Stay in the moment.* His eyes focused and he realized that Charlotte had knocked the gun out of the man's hand. That noise had only been the sound of it harmlessly hitting the floor.

The man raised a fist to her, ready to strike.

James lowered the boom. Raising his arms high, he

thrust downward with his gun and knocked the guy on the back of the head. He never saw it coming and crumpled to the ground with a heavy thud.

"Go get some pillowcases and blankets," he told Charlotte, kneeling beside the injured guard. Handcuffs were in his pocket, but the first order of business was to gag the intruder. One loud yell and their gig was up. James rolled him flat on his back. Had he killed the guy?

He moaned. James hastily grabbed the sheet from Charlotte, rolled it into a cylinder and gagged him. "Get another sheet and tie his feet while I cuff his hands."

They worked quickly, and all the while he strained to listen for more footsteps. So far, so good.

"Here." Charlotte pressed the intruder's flashlight into his hands. "We might need it."

Curious, James flicked it on and shone it on the man's face, glancing at the dagger tattoo on his neck. Gray eyes glared back, defiant to the end.

"Got you now," James said with grim satisfaction.

Charlotte tugged at his tux sleeve. "Let's go find Jenny."

Chapter 14

Charlotte gathered up the hem of her long gown and checked the hallway before entering.

Behind her, James spoke softly into his mike, filling Harlan in on their progress. "Bound suspect upstairs, heading to basement. Any news?"

Charlotte held her breath. What if they'd been spotted entering upstairs? Harlan might call off the whole mission if Maddie was breathing down his neck.

James winced. "Ten-four."

"Well?" she asked.

"Sammy hasn't seen any activity out back and the gate officer reported no young females have exited Falling Rock. We're on."

"So what's the bad news? I saw that look on your face."

"The usual. He says abandon the mission and don't

attempt a rescue if there's more than one guard down there. And call backup if needed."

Charlotte bit her lip, hoping for James's sake there wasn't more than one guard so that he wouldn't have to break Harlan's orders. Secretly she and James had agreed to take on two guards if necessary.

And in her heart of hearts, Charlotte made her own secret vow. She wouldn't jeopardize James's life if there were three or more guards—but she'd return alone and attempt a solo rescue operation, despite all the odds against success.

At the end of the hallway, James suddenly pulled her in for an embrace and gave her a quick, fierce kiss. "Be safe," he ordered.

Love and worry blazed from his blue-hot eyes. It took her breath away. But before she could even process her thoughts, James stepped around her and surveyed the area. "We're clear."

Together they hurried down the stairs. In the foyer, she pressed his hand. "Good luck."

This is where they parted ways again.

She hurried past the kitchen and started by the main entrance.

According to the architectural drawing, there was another entrance to the basement behind the main level utility room, third door past the kitchen. She swept inside and locked the utility room door behind her. To the right of the washer and dryer was yet another door. Quickly Charlotte hurried over and gave the knob a turn.

Locked. Of course it was.

She opened her purse and extracted the tiny pick and tension wrench that both fit in the palm of one hand.

She and James had practiced for this eventuality, and he'd been taken aback at her skill. This wasn't her first time to pick a lock.

Assured no one was about to witness the break-in, Charlotte set to work inserting the wrench into the bottom of the keyhole and the pick at the top of the lock. She scrubbed the pick back and forth. A little twist here and there and—*ping*—the metallic click fell into place. She turned the knob and cracked the door open.

"—getting hungry," she heard a deep voice say. "We should go upstairs and filch some of their alcohol."

"Hell, no. Maddie would have a fit. Ain't worth it."

Damn, there were two guards at least. She listened harder, praying a third voice didn't chime in.

"Stop acting like a wuss. She won't know. Don't need two of us to guard one door. Them bitches are locked up tight. They ain't goin' nowhere."

A smile curled her lips. She wasn't too late. Jenny and the other girls were so very, very close. She and James had a shot at making this work. Charlotte dropped the wrench and pick in her purse and texted James on her cell phone.

I'm in. Only two guards. Girls locked in storage room inside basement.

Setting her purse behind the dryer, she lifted out her gun. It took all her self-control not to rush in with her gun blazing and demand their release. But she and James had a plan. For now—she waited.

James returned his cell phone to his pocket with a sigh of relief. That had taken a little longer than anticipated. On his end, the basement entrance door hadn't been locked so he'd already deduced that if the girls were downstairs, they were locked in one of the two storage rooms. If he were the Stowerses, he'd have taken those extra precautions.

Taking a deep breath, he threw open the door and stomped down the narrow stairs. "Halloo," he called out, slurring his voice. "Where's da bathroom?" he asked, belching loudly. "I need to—"

"Hey, you can't be down here," a man quickly answered.

"Whaddaya mean by that?"

A burly guy appeared at the bottom of the steps. "No guests allowed down here."

"That's b-b-bullshit." James staggered and clutched the handrail, as if he were too drunk to keep his balance.

"Sir, you have to go. Now."

With satisfaction, he watched the guard start up the stairs. "But, but I—I'm Richard's pal." James fell on his rear end and stumbled down two steps. He let go of the rail and waved his hands in the air. "Whoa. Them stairs are st-steep."

The guard scowled, climbed up to him, and grabbed his arm. "You have to—"

With all his strength, James pulled the guard down with both arms. The man gaped in surprise and James landed a swift punch to his gut before the guard regained his senses and realized what was happening.

The man doubled over in pain but had the presence of mind to keep his arms locked around James. Together, they tumbled down the stairs. James's mike and cell phone clattered to the ground.

"Hey, what's going on?" he heard another male voice shout.

Excruciating pain suddenly radiated from his right shoulder. The son of a bitch had bitten him. James kneed the man in the groin and the pain eased as the man stopped biting and let out a strangled yelp.

"What the hell?" the other guard shouted. James saw him reach for a gun that was belted at his waist. Where was Charlotte? Right about now would be a good time for her to make an appearance.

From his position on the floor at the bottom of the stairwell, he spied her flat green shoes and a swatch of green fabric advancing toward them. His avenging angel in emerald. He strained his neck upward and watched as she pushed her gun into the second guard's back.

"Drop your weapon," she demanded in a hard voice.

"Who? What? Ah, damn it." The guard bent his knees and placed his weapon on the ground. Charlotte kicked at the gun and it spun several feet across the concrete floor, out of grabbing reach.

James rolled his prisoner onto his stomach and jerked one of his hands behind his back. "Sheriff's office. Don't resist arrest. You'll only make matters worse for yourself."

"Okay, okay," he groaned. "Don't hurt me."

He made short work of slapping on the cuffs. "Say one word and you're dead," he warned before leaping to his feet. "You, too," he told the other guard.

Charlotte spoke, nudging her pistol into the suspect's back. "Get on the ground spread-eagle, hands out in front."

He complied without a word of complaint, and James quickly cuffed him.

"We need more gags," Charlotte whispered.

"We'll make do." He tore off his tie and gagged one of the prostrate men on the floor.

Charlotte glanced down, running her hands down her hips over the sleek gown and frowned. "I don't have anything… Wait." She raised her hands and tugged at the velvet ribbon holding the bun at the top of her hair. Her hair cascaded down and she held the ribbon in front of her, eyeing it critically. "Not as strong as I'd like, but it will do."

"Give it to me," he said.

"Get the storage key from him first."

James grabbed the man's chin. "Where's the key?"

"You won't get away with this," he grunted. "Guards are everywhere patrolling the grounds. Let me go and I'll cooperate."

Charlotte knelt beside him. "We don't need your co-operation, Ricky—that is your name, isn't it? You're the one who shot at me."

James patted down the man's pockets. "Nothing here."

Charlotte turned to the other prisoner. "I'll pat him down."

James pulled the ribbon tight between his fists, holding it in front of the guard's face. "Last chance to talk."

"Okay, okay," Ricky said, breathing hard. "But remember I cooperated later if I get arrested."

James said nothing, advancing the gag toward his mouth. There'd be no deals for scumbags like Ricky. He wanted everyone involved in the trafficking business to get the stiffest sentence possible.

"It's in my right shoe."

James exchanged a bemused glance with Charlotte, and then untied the man's sneaker and shoved it off his foot.

A small brass key dropped on the concrete.

Charlotte snatched it up with a trembling hand and they stared at one another, disheveled and breathing hard. "We did it," she whispered. Her green eyes shone with tears.

Bittersweetness gnawed at his heart. He loved Charlotte's strength and courage, but even more he loved her vulnerability and fierce loyalty. She might not love him, but he'd stood beside her when no one else would believe or help in her quest to rescue Jenny. That would count for something in Charlotte's book, and he'd take what he could get.

He took her hand and helped her to her feet. "Only one thing left to do."

She nodded and ran a hand through her hair. "Right. I just…should be prepared for whatever we find behind that locked door. It'll be an ugly sight."

"Maybe it won't be too bad," he said gently. "After all, they want these girls to look pretty for their clients."

Anger crackled in her eyes and she lifted her chin. "That's not happening again. Let's go finish our job."

Chapter 15

Charlotte held her breath as she turned the key in the lock.

"Wait." James's hand held her back. "Could be a trap or another guard waiting. I'll go first."

She shook off his hand. "We'll go in together." Before he could argue further, she thrust the door open.

The room was almost pitch black, with only a faint trickle of light from a high, small window. The stale, moldy scent of damp air assaulted her nose. Her eyes adjusted to the darkness and she saw the faint, pale outline of three young girls huddled together in a back corner. Groping along the concrete wall, she located the light switch and flipped it on.

The large, square block room was devoid of anything except the girls and a half-dozen cots with thin mattresses. James drew his gun and circled the middle of the basement for any hidden surprises.

"Don't shoot us," one of the girls screamed. "We've been good."

"Don't scream. Nobody's going to hurt you. I promise." Charlotte approached them slowly as James put away his weapon. She blinked at the unexpected sight.

The girls were gussied up to look like living Barbie dolls. They wore bright-colored, low-cut evening gowns, their hair was elaborately curled and styled, and their young faces were painted with red lipstick and heavy rouge. Their eyes were thickly lined in black kohl. In a gray room that held all the charm of a steel garbage can, they popped like discarded roses.

It took Charlotte several moments to realize the blonde in the middle was Jenny. She looked nothing like the last time she'd seen her with Tanya. Then she'd been fresh-faced, wearing blue jeans and a T-shirt, and sporting a wide, easy grin.

"Jenny. It's me—Charlotte. Your mom's been so worried about you."

Jenny hunched her thin shoulders and shrank back until she was pinned against the wall. "Don't tell her where you found me," she whispered.

"But, but…" Charlotte floundered, unsure how to proceed. This was hardly the grand welcome she'd expected.

A petite Asian girl with bobbed black hair eyed them warily. "Who sent you?"

James flashed his badge. "Sheriff's office. We're here to help you."

A whimper escaped the lips of the third girl, another blonde who appeared to only be about twelve years old.

Charlotte scrutinized the girl's features. She'd seen her photo listed in their book of missing children. "Lisa Burns?" she guessed.

Lisa's eyes grew even more terrified, but she left the other two girls and approached James and Charlotte on wobbly legs. "I'll do whatever you say."

"Hey, are y'all really cops?" the Asian girl asked. "Did you just come for Jenny?"

"We're here for *all* of you," Charlotte assured her.

The mistrust melted on her face and she ran to Charlotte, wrapping boney arms around her waist. "I want out. My name is Amy Chang."

"We'll get you out." Charlotte ran a hand over her smooth hair and eyed Jenny, who'd sunk onto a cot and curled into a ball. Leg cuffs bound her slim ankles.

"Promise?" Amy pulled away and swiped at her eyes. Mascara and liner ran down her face.

Lisa gasped and put a hand on her red lips. "You're all messed up now, Amy. They're gonna hurt you if we don't get outta here. We're supposed to be all pretty."

"Nobody's going to be hurt," James said. "You're safe with us."

"Safe?" Amy thrust out her right hand, wrist down. Deep scars crisscrossed the veins. "I almost killed myself six months ago. A few weeks ago, I got messed up one night, thinking crazy thoughts, and got scared I'd do it again. I called a teen suicide hotline. That's how I met Piper. She was so nice. Asked to meet me. Said she'd take care of me and keep me safe. I thought she was my friend." Amy's lower lip trembled.

Charlotte's heart squeezed until it ached.

"Stop it!" Lisa cried. "We're going to get in trouble.

They'll come shoot us like they did Mandy when she tried to run away."

"Mandy?" Charlotte and James exchanged a look. The human blood on the leaves... That poor kid. She hadn't been as lucky as Karen.

"We should go," James said, casting a swift glance at the stairs.

Charlotte eyed the teary Lisa and recalcitrant Jenny. "Might be easier to call Harlan and have him come down here with backup."

"You still got your phone? Mine's probably busted."

"It's upstairs in my purse. I'll use my mike to contact Harlan."

"Good. Because mine fell in the tumble down the stairs."

Charlotte removed the small black disc tucked into her gown. "Officer Hanson to Sheriff Sampson."

Nothing. Not even a whisper of static. Charlotte blew into the mouthpiece. "Testing, testing."

"Damn it," James muttered. "I'll go search for my dropped phone under the stairs. There's an off-chance it's not smashed to smithereens."

Charlotte put a hand on Amy's and Lisa's shoulders, guiding them to the cot where Jenny lay. "Let's go talk to Jenny a minute."

They offered no resistance, as docile as lambs, and stood close by while she sat on the cot beside Jenny. Tentatively, Charlotte touched one of Jenny's delicate cuffed ankles. Besides being bound, she wore ridiculous sequined high heels. "Why the leg cuffs?" she asked. The others weren't cuffed.

"She tried to run away the first night," Amy volunteered. "She didn't even make it out of the house before they caught her."

Charlotte could only imagine the severe punishment for that defiance. No wonder she was so scared to try to escape again. "Jenny. Are you afraid to leave? You know me. I promise I won't let anyone hurt you."

Jenny's face was buried in a blanket and she vehemently shook her head. "No. I won't go."

"Why not?"

"Because." Sobs shook her body.

"Because why?"

Jenny suddenly sat up and faced her. "I've done... bad things with bad men."

"It's not your fault, sweetie."

"Yes, it is. I-I'm a bad girl. I ran away from home and then...they got me."

Charlotte wrapped her arms around Jenny and laid her cheek on the top of Jenny's head. "Shh. It's okay."

"But my mom... I don't want her to know."

"Tanya just wants you home. She misses you terribly and has been out of her mind with worry."

Jenny turned her head to the wall, refusing to listen. It was going to take lots of time and therapy to get this child over the brainwashing and abuse. And she'd been troubled to begin with. Tanya had finally admitted to her that Jenny had threatened suicide several times after her father had left home. But Charlotte didn't have time or therapist skills. Every second they spent in the basement meant the odds of rescue dramatically decreased.

Lisa suddenly screamed and cowered to the ground. Amy's mouth opened in horror. Charlotte's stomach cartwheeled as she jumped up from the cot and whirled around.

Footsteps creaked on the wooden stairs. Through the open step slats flashed a pair of shiny men's shoes and gray flannel pants. James heard it, too and ran to the stairs.

Richard Stowers stepped down and faced them, a gun drawn.

Charlotte blinked. This Richard was deadly sober. The affable albeit lecherous drunk from earlier at the party had transformed into a maleficent, hard column of a man whose eyes shone with a vicious intent. Or—more likely—this was no transformation, but an unmasking of his true self. The show of drunkenness might have been just that—an act to throw people off. It had certainly fooled her.

"Had a feeling I'd find you two down here," Richard said coolly. "Maddie might have underestimated y'all, but I didn't."

The utter calm of his voice was all the more terrifying for its unruffled focus. This was a man who could not be reasoned with or distracted.

James stepped in front of her and raised his gun. Charlotte maneuvered to his side. If they went down, they went down together.

"Drop it," Richard ordered.

"Hell, no. We appear to be at a standoff."

Amy let out a banshee wail that echoed in the chamber like an explosion. Richard turned his head a fraction to determine the cause of the noise.

This was Charlotte's chance.

She dived toward Richard's knees. He stumbled

backward half a step. Time slowed and her whole body attuned to every nuance of detail—

The stiff fabric of Richard's pants.

Amy's wails.

James shouting her name.

The thundering of her own heart in her ears.

A whoosh of air as Richard raised his arm.

His furious dark eyes intent on killing.

The cylindrical chamber of metal pointed at her head.

She'd always known it would come to this one day. But she didn't shut her eyes and she didn't regret her decision. Her mantra was always to see a job through to the end. No matter what.

Another swoosh of air and Richard was falling. Charlotte swiftly rolled toward the back wall. Richard's gun fired. An explosion of smoke and noise assaulted her senses—but no bullet ripped into her flesh. She was unharmed.

James jumped on top of Richard and landed a solid punch to the man's gut. The gun fell out of Richard's hand and she picked it up, scrambling to her feet. "Stop fighting, Richard. Or I'll shoot."

The men stilled and eyed her, Richard gaping in surprise, and James with a grin.

"No need for that," James said. "Stowers is going to play nice now." He grabbed an arm and twisted it behind Richard. "Roll onto your stomach and put your hands behind your back."

"Damn you both," Richard ground out harshly. "It's not over yet. Do you hear me? This is *my* house. And those bitches back there are mine, too."

Charlotte's anger rose to match his. "They aren't bitches and they don't belong to anybody."

James slapped the cuffs on Stowers's wrists.

Richard bent his knees and managed a sitting position. "They've already been bought and paid for. This isn't over yet. You'll never make it out of here with those whores."

"Shut your mouth," James warned, grabbing a fistful of the man's starched shirt. "Unless you want me to gag you like I did your guards."

Richard glowered but kept his mouth shut as James frisked him for weapons. He pulled out a cell phone from Richard's pocket and tossed it to Charlotte.

"Give me that back," Richard cried out. "You've no right to search my house like you did. When my lawyer's through with you— Hey!"

James pulled off the tie from around Stowerses' neck. "You had your chance."

Charlotte smiled grimly as James gagged the guy. Actually, the threat of his lawyers was a problem, but she'd cross that bridge later and she damn sure wasn't going to let the bastard know she was worried.

"I expect nothing but commendations from law enforcement for breaking this case," she boasted.

James stood and raised a brow at her. "After all, we did hear the victims cry for help when we entered the house to escort a guest to their room. I'd say that gave us a right to investigate."

Nothing but muffled curses escaped from Stowers's gag.

"Go on and take the girls upstairs and let Harlan knows what's happening," James said.

"But I can't get Jenny to agree to leave, and her feet are cuffed anyway."

"Then you go ahead and take the other two while I deal with Jenny. If I have to carry her out of here screaming, then that's what I'll do."

"Okay. Lisa, Amy, let's get out of here." Charlotte walked over to Jenny's cot and ran a hand through her blond hair. "Officer Tedder's going to carry you out. You can trust him, okay?"

Jenny's entire body started to shake. "No! Just leave me alone."

Charlotte dropped her hand and stared at her, unsure what to do.

James sank to his knees by Jenny and cocked his head toward the stairs, signaling for Charlotte to leave.

Taking Lisa and Amy by the hand, Charlotte ushered them across the basement. At the foot of the stairs, she glanced back once more.

James nodded. "I won't leave without Jenny," he promised.

And she believed him. He'd take a bullet before he broke that vow. Something fierce and warm and wonderful pulsed through her body. A feeling she'd never expected to happen again. She loved James. Loved and trusted him with a deep faith she hadn't imagined possible. She wanted to tell him, but now wasn't the right time or place. These girls desperately needed to get away.

"I know you will," she called out. Charlotte let go of Amy's and Lisa's hands. "I'll go first. Stay close to me and follow my orders."

The girls nodded in understanding, their eyes huge with fear.

They rapidly climbed the stairs. Each moment, Charlotte expected Maddie or one of her guards to appear at the open door. But the utility room was blessedly empty and she waved her hand at Amy and Lisa to follow her.

Charlotte gave them an encouraging smile, then turned toward the doorway and caught sight of her purse where she'd stashed it earlier behind the dryer. Quickly Charlotte dug out her phone and punched in Harlan's number.

They were so close to rescuing Jenny and the girls. All that was left was to find Harlan and get backup in place before arresting Maddie and Richard. Their guests were in for a real surprise tonight. This year's fund-raising event would be remembered for years to come.

Now if she could just get Harlan to answer the phone.

Chapter 16

"It's time to go."

James strove for a firm yet gentle tone with the traumatized Jenny.

"You don't get it. They'll catch us and kill us."

How must it feel to be sixteen years old and think you're forever doomed to a life of sexual slavery? To not be able to see help when it was in front of your very eyes?

He took her hand. "We're going. Whatever it takes, I'm going to make sure you leave here and never come back. I don't want to force you, but if that's what I need to do, so be it."

"No." She shrank further from him. "You can't make me and if—"

Enough. He'd wasted a good five minutes trying to gain her cooperation and it wasn't working. James quickly uncuffed her leg irons, then put one arm under her knees and the other across her back, lifting her effortlessly. Jenny gasped and he placed a finger against her lips. "Not another word," he said sternly.

She blinked at him and slowly nodded. It hurt to use that tone with her, but her life was more important than hurt feelings. He crossed the room with the light burden in his arms, relieved tonight was almost over.

James started up the steps, but paused on the third rung. Sharp, staccato footsteps sounded above, from behind the door. Not the soft padding Charlotte made with her flats. The steps grew louder.

Jenny whimpered and turned her face into his chest, afraid of who it might be.

He wasn't so thrilled himself. His only options were to turn back and hide Jenny while he attacked their confronter—or push ahead at full speed and perhaps catch the guard off balance. Too late to retreat, he decided. Press on.

James plowed forward, but Jenny had a different reaction to the danger. She reached her hands out to either side, clinging to the walls in an attempt to slow him down. She twisted and squirmed in his arms, surprisingly feisty. The desperate always managed to draw strength when panicked.

A figure appeared at the top of the stairs—tall, dark and deadly.

"What's this?" Maddie asked with a hiss.

It looked like Maddie, same red outfit and elegant veneer, but her eyes were bereft of even a speck of human warmth. They crackled with aggrieved outrage. She didn't wait for an answer. "You're not going anywhere with my property."

She raised a pistol at them. "Turn around and go downstairs."

If Jenny wasn't in his arms, he'd take his chances—rush Maddie and knock her to the ground. But she was, and he'd do anything to keep her safe.

"Be reasonable, Mrs. Stowers. Your home's crawling with law enforcement and they'll be here at any moment."

Where the hell was Harlan? There'd been plenty of time for Charlotte to have alerted him. His skin flushed hot, then cold. Had something happened to Charlotte?

"Bullshit," she said flatly.

The profanity startled him. He'd thought her much too cultured and uptight to be coarse. "Nobody's coming to save either of you. Now move it."

He wouldn't turn his back on Maddie. Too dangerous. Instead, he slowly descended one step. The longer he delayed entrapment in the basement, the better.

Maddie slammed the door shut and waved her gun. "If I shoot, my aim's at the girl."

Jenny's nails dug through his shirt as she clung to him, her body tense and shaking.

"I'm going," he reassured Maddie. "This is between us. Leave Jenny out of it."

Another step down and still no hint of the cavalry coming to save them. He had to face this alone.

The scent of violets grew strong as Maddie closed in. The clamor of bells spun in his mind, a dizzying vortex of sound.

It was happening all over again. His skin burned as though he was back in Bagram, and his body felt lightweight and unbalanced. He stumbled on the last step and fell backward.

Get it together. Don't hurt Jenny.

He held tight onto her thin frame, absorbing the impact of the cement floor as they tumbled. "Stay behind me," he whispered to Jenny, grabbing her hand and pulling her behind him as he rose to his feet.

Maddie was closing in. He watched as she scanned the room and caught sight of the guards and her husband bound and gagged on the floor.

"Richard?" Her lips curled and her patrician nose flared. "You incompetent fool. What the fuck are you doing down here? You should have sent me to handle this situation."

She waved her gun at the guards, shaking her head in disgust. "I'll deal with the two of you later."

It was clear who was in control of the trafficking ring. And it wasn't Richard Stowers.

Maddie turned her back on the hapless men and focused her attention on the matter at hand. "It won't do you any good to hide behind the cop, Jenny. Did you really think you were going to get away? Come out and face me. Time I taught you a real lesson in obedience."

James slightly raised his arms to the side, shielding Jenny.

"Give it up, Maddie. Cooperate with me now and it will go better for you."

Her lips curled into a sneer. "That might have worked on these idiots—" she half-turned and waved her gun at Richard and the guards "—but your empty threats don't scare me one iota."

Jenny slipped beneath his right arm and shuffled forward.

"I'll be good," she said around the sobs that wracked

her slender body. She dropped to her knees. "Please don't kill us."

"You'll be the first to die. It's you they've been searching for all along. You've been way too much trouble."

She means to gun us both down.

Death permeated the room, settling its dreaded weight on his shoulders. The last seconds of his life played out before him. Had Charlotte made it to safety with the other two girls? He hoped that would be some consolation to her when she discovered their bodies.

"Kill me. Let her go," he said in a last-ditch effort to bargain for Jenny's life. "She's your—" he stumbled over the next word "—*property*. Wouldn't want to miss recouping on your investment, would you?"

He stepped in front of Jenny again as Maddie wavered, clearly weighing the options. Would her greed win over her caution in leaving a witness to his murder? Once Jenny was sold and her ownership transferred to another person, Maddie would no longer have any control over what Jenny might say in the future.

Footsteps pounded down the basement steps and he turned.

Charlotte's voice floated down. "James? Backup's on the way. Where have you—"

She stopped short at the sight of Maddie's gun.

James squeezed his eyes shut momentarily and groaned. Why had she come back downstairs alone? That wasn't the plan.

Maddie frowned. "Hands up. Come on down and join the crowd, Detective Charlotte Helms. Yes, that's right. I know who you are."

Charlotte's eyes widened as she approached, hands

held high. "How long have you known my real identity?"

Charlotte was playing his same game. Keep Maddie engaged, keep her talking, until help arrived.

If they were coming at all.

"Since day one," Maddie said crisply. "That bitch, Karen Hicks, tipped you off about our operation. I intend to make her pay for that, too."

"I don't know anyone by that name," Charlotte said. James admired her loyalty. She'd go to her death and not reveal an informant's name.

"Liar! I thought when Larry fired you, you'd go away. Should have known better."

"Larry?" Charlotte's brows drew together and then smoothed.

"That's right. Your very own Captain Burkhart. He's kept us protected for years."

Damn. Burkhart was in for one serious asskicking—that is, if he ever got out of this freaking basement.

"Son of a bitch," Charlotte breathed.

Heavy footfalls rained down from the room above. Had Harlan arrived with backup—or was it more of the Stowerses' guards?

Maddie's fingers tightened on the trigger and her eyes narrowed.

A chill chased the length of his spine and a roaring pounded in his brain. Holy hell, she was going to kill Charlotte. He recognized the murderous intent in her eyes, the subtle micromovement of her hands before shooting. He'd witnessed it too many times in combat. With every ounce of willpower he possessed, James tamped down the spiraling sensations that threatened to tunnel him back in time and place. Right here, right now, he had to save Charlotte.

He launched his body in front of Charlotte.

Please don't let me be too late.

James's body flashed in front of her, blocking Charlotte's view of Maddie's madness.

The crack of gunfire exploded.

Blood. A thin stream of crimson arched upward and then fell like droplets of red rain. James pitched forward, landing face-first on the concrete.

Charlotte swallowed the acrid, burnt scent of gunpowder. She registered the chaos of noise and movement coming from behind her back, and the screams of Jenny curled on the floor, hands over her ears.

Not James. Dear God, no.

She had to touch him, had to know he still breathed. Charlotte dropped to the floor and touched the back of his head, fingers curling over his short, sandy hair.

The whistle of a speeding bullet passed inches above her head. Unfazed by the danger, she moved her hand lower, down to the familiar, sensitive nape of his neck. Miss Glory had told her to open her heart, but right now her heart felt as if it were breaking. Her fingers probed and explored, finding the beat of his pulse.

He lived.

Hope renewed her mind and heart. They still had a chance to get out of this alive…and together. She homed in on the pandemonium surrounding them, crystallizing her focus.

"Drop it, Stowers."

It was Harlan. And he wasn't alone. A cavalcade of footsteps treaded the wooden floor, and from the corners of her eyes she noted dozens of black shoes and the hems of suit pants.

Maddie retreated a step. "You have no right to be here," she screeched. "This is *my* house. *My* property. *My* land."

Charlotte didn't have to look up and see Maddie's face to know that the woman was losing it. Her shrill voice trembled with panic and fury. Charlotte imagined that Maddie felt trapped as officers pressed in and surrounded her. A criminal mastermind like her might be unhinged at her lack of control in the situation. And that made her very, very dangerous.

Any moment, and Maddie could fire off a round of bullets, killing many of them before she was shot or taken down.

She had to stop her. Maddie's attention was on Harlan. Now was her chance. Charlotte lunged forward, latching onto Maddie's right ankle. Charlotte yanked at the woman's leg with all her strength.

Maddie shrieked and tried to kick her hand away, but Charlotte held on like a bulldog and pulled on Maddie's leg with both hands.

The elegantly thin Maddie crumpled to the floor, landing on her skinny ass.

Officers stormed from all sides, seizing Maddie's weapon and cuffing her.

"Do you know who I am?" Maddie screamed. "You can't do this. I'll sue you. I'll—"

Charlotte ignored her desperate ramblings and all the mayhem from above. She crawled to Jenny. The girl's stunned, wide-eyed stare was fixed on James's bleeding wound.

"It's my fault," she whispered. "All my fault. He

kept trying to get me to go with him, and I wouldn't. And now he's d—"

"Shh. He's not dead," Charlotte assured her, patting Jenny's hand. "But he needs an ambulance, quick."

She left Jenny and hurried over to James.

He moaned and the sound was heavenly to her ears, much as she hated that he was in pain. She flipped him over onto his back and assessed the damage. All the bleeding stemmed from his right shoulder. It probably hurt like hell, but his heart and vital organs should be fine.

"Here, take this," Harlan said, handing her his jacket. "Medics will be here in a moment. I had them on standby. They said to staunch the bleeding as much as possible until they arrive."

She took the jacket and pressed it against the wound.

James groaned again and his eyelids lifted. Blue eyes shimmered with an equal measure of humor and pain. "Are you trying to kill me?"

"Trying to save you." She cried and laughed through tears. "Don't you ever jump in front of a bullet again. You got that?"

He grimaced and raised up on one elbow. "I don't plan on it."

"Hey, buddy," Harlan said, bending down on his knees. "That was a damn fool thing to do. Don't try to get up. Medics will take you out on a stretcher."

James clenched his jaw and raised to a half-seated position. "I'm fine."

"Like hell you are." Charlotte barely suppressed a snort. James was pale and had lost blood. "Just stay put and—"

"Are Amy and Lisa okay?" he interrupted.

"They're upstairs with Sammy." Charlotte turned and motioned Jenny over. "So is Jenny, or she will be, once she sees you're going to be alright."

James mustered a smile for the young girl. "Told you I wouldn't leave you behind."

Jenny threw himself at him, throwing her arms around his neck. "I'm sorry. It's my fault you got hurt."

Charlotte winced. That hug had to hurt.

James patted her with his uninjured arm. "You're not to blame. Not at all. I'm fine."

Charlotte placed a hand on Jenny's shoulder and drew her away. "He's hurt. Give him a little breathing room," she said lightly.

EMTs clamored down the steps as fast as they could with their bulky stretcher, and Charlotte exhaled a sigh of relief. She hated seeing James in pain. He needed to be stitched up, medicated, and then put to bed.

Maddie's voice rose again over the crowd. "You can't do this to me. Wait until my attorneys hear this…"

Charlotte watched as officers grabbed Maddie by both arms and forced her to move forward.

"Richard, do something," Maddie ordered.

The two guards and Richard Stowers were on their feet and their gags removed. They were also being read their rights.

"Shut the hell up, Maddie. It's over," Richard snapped.

Jenny hugged her knees to her chin, making herself small, watching Maddie's imminent approach. They'd have to pass close by on their way out. Charlotte moved to shield Jenny from the sight, but Maddie spotted her.

"You little bitch," she screamed, venting her ire at

her former captive. "Everything was fine until you came along."

A change swept over Jenny's face. Her eyes flickered from fear to fury and she jumped to her feet, hands clenched into fists. "I hate you," she screamed, her voice even louder than Maddie's. "Hate you, hate you, HATE you."

Maddie blinked. The woman had probably never had a comeuppance before from one of her young, vulnerable victims.

Charlotte wanted to applaud. She'd much rather see her angry than scared. Jenny had spirit. With lots of counseling and her mother's love, she would have the strength to move on with her life.

And hopefully it would be a damn good life.

"Get the Stowerses out of here," Harlan ordered.

His officers hustled Maddie up the steps, her husband and their two guards close in tow. Maddie didn't say another word.

Charlotte put an arm around Jenny. "You'll never have to see that woman again," she promised. "We'll do all we can to see she stays in prison until she's a very old lady."

Jenny swiped at her eyes and nodded. "I want my mom now."

"Of course." Eagerness burst inside Charlotte like a dam. This was the moment she'd been waiting for ever since she came to Lavender Mountain.

Harlan handed her his cell phone. "Call your friend. She's waited a long time to hear this news."

Charlotte punched in the numbers with shaking hands. "Tanya? Hey, I called because...no, Jenny's not hurt. Just the opposite. Deep breath, hon. I have good news." Charlotte inhaled deeply herself, relieved the ordeal was almost over. She caught James's glance, and he smiled and gave a thumbs-up as an EMT bandaged his wound. For a moment, her lungs choked and she couldn't speak. "Tanya, there's someone here who wants to talk to you."

Wordlessly she handed the phone to Jenny.

"Mom? It's me." Tears, mixed with black mascara, streamed down her heavily made-up cheeks. "Can you come bring me home?"

There wasn't a freaking dry eye in the basement that was still swarming with law enforcement officers—supposedly hardened men and women used to horrendous crimes. Harlan's chest rose and fell and he cleared his throat.

James was suddenly beside her. Stubborn man. He shouldn't be standing at all. But she nestled into his solid warmth. Leaving her job and coming to Lavender Mountain was the best decision she'd ever made.

She'd found Jenny, and so much more.

Chapter 17

James shifted in his seat. The stitches on his right shoulder pinched uncomfortably under his shirt. Not that he'd admit that fact to anyone. Charlotte and Lilah had fussed over him for the last two days and he'd had enough.

"You okay?" Harlan asked, leaning back in his chair.

He groaned. "Don't you start with that, too. I came back to work to escape."

"Nothing but desk duty for you, at least for another couple of weeks." Harlan shoved over a mound of paperwork and gave him an evil grin. "This should be loads of fun for you."

"Yeah, right. Looks like you've let filing go for at least six months. What the hell does Zelda do around here?"

"Everything but filing. She hates it."

James rifled through the papers. Escaping the incessant nursing at home wasn't the only reason he'd returned to the office. But he dallied, reluctant to state his real reason. He changed the subject. "How are Amy and Lisa? Heard any word?"

"Lisa was returned to her home. Unfortunately, Amy tried to commit suicide again. But the good news is that she's been placed in an intensive psychiatric care facility. Hopefully they can put this behind them. How are Jenny and her mom doing?"

"Healing. Glad the nightmare's over, but struggling. It will take time. Charlotte plans on paying them a visit in a couple weeks."

Harlan scowled. "Never would have imagined a human trafficking ring had connections with Lavender Mountain. I'm trying my best to keep Elmore County crime-free, but by the time I clean up one mess, something new and unexpected pops up."

"No need to beat yourself up. The ring hadn't been here long."

Investigation had already revealed that the trafficking ring had been in Lavender Mountain for less than six months. The Stowerses were based in Atlanta, but they'd felt heat from the cops closing in, so they'd decided to cool things off a bit by temporarily switching their base to Falling Rock.

"After all, they'd been running this operation close to a decade in Atlanta," James continued. "There's always something new popping up, too. It's the nature of the job." And his brother-in-law was doing a damn good job. Credibility in the sheriff's office was finally returning after the disastrous tenure of the old sheriff. "What's the latest on the Stowerses' case?"

"Nothing new there. They're still awaiting trial in Atlanta. The real news is that Captain Larry Burkhart was arrested. Created quite the shake-up in their police department."

"Nothing worse than a dirty cop. After the way he treated Charlotte, I couldn't be happier to hear he's gone."

"I regret that I listened to his nonsense about Charlotte's mental stability."

"You should tell her, not me."

Harlan nodded and cleared his throat. "I intend to."

It was clear that Harlan wasn't looking forward to eating crow, but when he was wrong, he was man enough to own up to it.

"Speaking of Charlotte..." Harlan began. "What are her plans for the future? I'm assuming she'll be offered her old position, given that Burkhart was behind the firing."

"They called this morning. She told them she wasn't interested."

And hadn't he breathed a sigh of relief at that announcement? But Charlotte hadn't said she'd stay with him, either. It was an issue they hadn't discussed yet. But now that he'd recovered from his injury, there was nothing to tie Charlotte to this mountain—or to him.

Their living arrangements were in limbo and it made him uneasy.

Harlan tapped a pencil on his desk, a sure sign he was about to speak on a topic that made him uncomfortable. "You know our office policy. Since you obviously have some kind of—intimate relationship—the two of you can't work together anymore as partners."

"I'm aware. That's another reason I came back to

work today." James opened the folder in his lap and took out its only contents—a single typed sheet of paper. "This is my official two-week notice, although if you need me to stay a little longer, I will. But I'm resigning."

He reached across Harlan's desk to hand him the notice, but Harlan didn't take it. James shrugged and let it fall onto the rest of his boss's paperwork.

"There's no need for this. You can both stay on, but work different shifts with different partners."

"The job isn't for me. I appreciate the opportunity, but I'd—"

"You've done damn good work," Harlan interrupted. "What don't you like about it?"

He knew his brother-in-law wasn't going to take the news well and he hated disappointing him. Harlan had given him a job when he'd returned from military duty, and he was floundering on what he wanted to do next.

"I'm pursuing an old dream. I want to go in business for myself as a carpenter."

"I always knew you were good with your hands... but are you sure about this?"

"Positive." He'd stayed up most of last night, resolving everything in his mind. Nothing like getting shot at point-blank range to make a man rethink his direction in life.

"I may be leaving, but you should keep Charlotte on. She's a fantastic cop."

"Agreed. Although I could find a place for both of you. If you change your mind, the door's always open."

James stood and they shook hands. "Guess I'll be getting a start on all this." He nodded at the stack of papers Harlan had unloaded on him.

"Count on me working you like hell for the next two weeks, buddy."

James grinned. "No problem. I'll see what I can do to get this stuff filed and organized—since you and Zelda obviously won't ever get around to it."

He turned to leave and had almost slipped out the door when Harlan spoke again.

"It's none of my business, but I hope you intend doing your part to get Charlotte to stay on here at Lavender Mountain. Seeing as how you've left me shorthanded. Least you could do."

James narrowed his eyes and gave a slow smile. "I believe you may be as nosy as Lilah."

And with that nonanswer, he made his exit.

"You shouldn't be driving," Charlotte scolded. "You worked late and then insisted on helping me clean up after dinner. Don't you need some rest?"

"Stop fretting over me. I'm fine." James backed the car out of the driveway and eased onto the dark road.

"Where are we going?"

"Nowhere in particular," he lied. "I was cooped up in the house for two days and then spent all day at the office. Thought it'd be nice to get out for a spell."

They settled into a comfortable silence as they traveled up the steep mountain road. A deep peace filled him since he'd turned in his notice. His career path was clear. At least that part of his life was in order.

Charlotte played with a lock of her hair. "I've been thinking—"

"Always dangerous," he teased.

She gave him a hard stare. "I'm going back to Atlanta this weekend."

His chest squeezed tight. "Why?"

"My apartment is a wreck. Remember? I need to clean it up and take care of my bills. You know, all the daily routine stuff that's gone undone."

His chest relaxed a fraction. "A temporary visit, then?"

"For now. The police commissioner asked if I'd meet with him."

His hands tightened on the steering wheel as he rounded a bend. "They really want you back."

"Maybe. Or maybe he wants reassurance that I won't go to the press about the way Burkhart ordered me to quit the case and then fired me when I refused."

The Atlanta news media was having a field day with the news that a high-ranking member of the police department had helped cover up a human trafficking ring.

"When are you leaving? Friday?"

"Bright and early."

Seemed like he was already losing her. Could she really be happy working and living in such a remote area? He didn't want Charlotte to settle. He wanted her to live out all her dreams. And if that meant living in Atlanta, he wouldn't stop her.

The confidence he'd felt earlier vanished. She hadn't told him yet that she loved him. He'd been so sure he'd seen it in her eyes down in the Stowerses' basement after he'd been shot. Had read a desperate concern in her eyes as she'd hovered over him once he'd been shot.

But he might be wrong.

Another silence descended—though this time not as peaceful. James continued up the mountain, then turned onto the familiar dirt driveway. Headlight beams illuminated the charred remnants of his old family cabin.

Charlotte glanced his way, brows raised. "You really want to see this place again? The last time we were here was so sad."

"Not all my memories here are bad ones."

"Right," Charlotte touched his arm. "You grew up in that cabin. I'm sure you had lots of great times."

He pulled around to the back of the yard. Yep, the old metal glider swing remained. He stopped the car and stuffed the keys in his pocket. "But my favorite memory of all is that this is where I first met you."

A delighted grin broke across her face. "Aww... that's so sweet."

"Come on." He got out and headed for the trunk.

"For a minute," she agreed, climbing out. "It's cold out here."

James opened the trunk and pulled out a thick quilt. "I've got you covered."

"Looks like you had this planned from the get-go."

"True," he confessed. He put an arm around her and led her to the glider.

"Did your mom make this quilt?"

"Grandmother. Mom wasn't into all the domestic stuff."

Charlotte sat down and he tucked the quilt around her legs before sitting beside her.

She giggled. "How could I forget the first time we met? That look on your face when you ordered me to stop running—so ferocious."

"Of course it was. You pointed a gun at me."

"Because I thought you were one of them and had come to finish me off."

A grin split his face. "Freezing cold and you had on nothing but an oversize camouflage shirt and black panties. All long, sexy legs, wild red hair and an attitude."

She jostled his side with her elbow. "Is that why you followed me everywhere and wouldn't leave me alone? You lusted after my body?"

"You were a mystery. One I had to solve."

"It's what makes you a good officer."

"About that… I turned in my two-week notice today."

Surprised widened her teal-green eyes. "Why?"

"It's not for me. I've been longing to go back to my old job. To work with my hands again."

"Doing what?"

"Carpentry."

He studied her face closely. Carpentry wasn't exactly a sexy kind of job, and it might take some time before he became established in the community. For some women, that could be a real turnoff.

"A carpenter," she murmured thoughtfully. "You're full of surprises. I should have guessed with the whittling piece at your house. If that's what makes you happy, then you should absolutely go for it."

His gaze drifted to what remained of the burnt pine structure. "My first job will be to tear down what's left of Dad's cabin and rebuild it into a new home."

"I love that idea, James." She paused a few heartbeats. "And I love you."

The tension in his shoulders relaxed. Charlotte loved him. They could figure the rest out later—together. He stroked her hair and ran his fingers over the delicate features of her face.

"Forever?" he asked quietly, hardly daring to breathe.

Her teal eyes sparkled and shimmered. "Yes. And I promise I'll never run away from you again."

Epilogue

Charlotte's breath caught at the stunning vista. A woman couldn't ask for a more perfect wedding day. Dogwoods blossomed on top of Lavender Mountain and the lush greenness of the forest contrasted with the turquoise sky. To think by summer's end she'd be living here, waking up each morning next to James and admiring this gorgeous view from their new home.

Her gaze sought his through the throng of well-wishers. He was deep in conversation with Sammy and Harlan. The threesome looked so arresting in their tuxes that her breath caught. Of course, James was the most handsome by far. How lucky was she?

As if attuned to her every nuance, James lifted his eyes and scanned the crowd until they settled on her. A slow, sexy grin lit his face.

Lilah was suddenly by her side. "Pretty impressive, huh?" she asked.

"He is," Charlotte murmured, gaze still locked on her groom.

Lilah laughed and slapped her arm. "I'm talking about the cabin, silly. Not my brother."

Charlotte wrenched her gaze from James and stared at his handiwork. The burnt remains of his dad's old place had been torn down, and a new home for the two of them was coming along at a quick pace. James had hired a crew and worked sunup until sundown, returning home every night sweaty and dirty, with a huge smile lighting his face. And he slept soundly at night, the insomnia a thing of the past.

"It doesn't have the grandeur of a Falling Rock mansion, but it'll do, right?"

Again she had to snap her thoughts back to the conversation at hand. "It's perfect."

Lilah hugged her. "I'm so glad you're marrying my brother. I haven't seen him this happy since before his first overseas tour of duty. You're good for him."

"And he's good for me. I was lonely and totally burned out working undercover." She hadn't even known how miserable she was until she met James and came to Lavender Mountain.

"I only wish Dad and Darla were here to see your wedding. And the new house."

"Me, too." She and James had talked about it just last night. His father would have been proud of James's accomplishments. "This work has been good for James. It's as if he's laying to rest the ghosts from his past with every board he cuts."

"What's this about ghosts of the past?" James was

beside her, and Lilah waved goodbye, strolling over to Harlan and Sammy.

"Nothing. From here on out, it's nothing but new beginnings," she promised.

"No second thoughts about marrying a carpenter?" His voice was light and teasing, but his eyes hinted at worry.

"Not when you've built us this gorgeous house complete with custom cabinets and bookshelves." She winked. "Who am I to complain? You should be the worried one. I work crazy hours with Sammy and I've made plenty of enemies over the years."

"You're safe with me. Forever." James lifted her left hand, and her engagement ring sparkled in the late afternoon sun.

"I know," she whispered.

He lifted a strand of her red hair and smiled. "Glad it's back to its fiery color. It suits you." Then he kissed her. It started out as a quick press of the lips, but he deepened the kiss and she was lost in the moment.

Cheers and whistles from the wedding guests brought her back to reality. Before she could pull away, James whisked her into his arms and spun her around.

In a dizzying whirl, she saw them all there—her mom and dad and brothers, Harlan and all her coworkers, even Tanya and Jenny had come for the celebration. Finally, she was at home. At peace. In a place where she could plant roots and spend the rest of her life. Lavender Mountain was the haven she hadn't even known she was seeking.

Miss Glory had told her to open her heart, and at last she finally had.

* * * * *

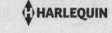
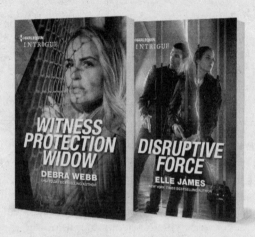

SPECIAL EXCERPT FROM

ⓗ HARLEQUIN
INTRIGUE

*When a young woman is discovered buried alive,
Colorado ME Dr. Chloe Pascale knows that the
relentless serial killer she barely escaped has found her.
To stop him, she must trust police chief
Weston Ford with her darkest secrets. But getting
too close is putting their guarded hearts at risk—and
leading into an inescapable trap...*

Read on for a sneak preview of
Grave Danger,
*part of the Defenders of Battle Mountain series
from Nichole Severn.*

Three months ago...
When I'm done, you're going to beg me for the pain.

Chloe Pascale struggled to open her eyes. She blinked against
the brightness of the sky. Trees. Snow. Cold. Her head pounded in
rhythm to her racing heartbeat. Shuffling reached her ears as her
last memories lightninged across her mind like a half-remembered
dream. She'd gone out for a run on the trail near her house. Then...
Fear clawed at her insides, her hands curling into fists. He'd come
out of the woods. He'd... She licked her lips, her mouth dry. He'd
drugged her, but with what and how many milliliters, she wasn't
sure. The haze of unconsciousness slipped from her mind, and a
new terrifying reality forced her from ignorance. "Where am I?"

Dead leaves crunched off to her left. Her attacker's dark outline
shifted in her peripheral vision. Black ski mask. Lean build. Tall.
Well over six feet. Unfamiliar voice. Black jeans. His knees popped
as he crouched beside her, the long shovel in his left hand digging

HIEXP0122A

into the soil near her head. The tip of the tool was coated in mud. Reaching a gloved hand toward her, he stroked the left side of her jawline, ear to chin, and a shiver chased down her spine against her wishes. "Don't worry, Dr. Miles. It'll all be over soon."

His voice… It sounded…off. Disguised?

"How do you know my name? What do you want?" She blinked to clear her head. The injection site at the base of her neck itched, then burned, and she brought her hands up to assess the damage. Ropes encircled her wrists, and she lifted her head from the ground. Her ankles had been bound, too. She pulled against the strands, but she couldn't break through. Then, almost as though demanding her attention, she caught sight of the refrigerator. Old. Light blue. Something out of the '50s with curves and heavy steel doors.

"I know everything about you, Chloe. Can I call you Chloe?" he asked. "I know where you live. I know where you work. I know your running route and how many hours you spend at the clinic. You really should change up your routine. Who knows who could be out there watching you? As for what I want, well, I'm going to let you figure that part out once you're inside."

Pressure built in her chest. She dug her heels into the ground, but the soil only gave way. No. No, no, no, no. This wasn't happening. Not to her. Darkness closed in around the edges of her vision, her breath coming in short bursts. Pulling at the ropes again, she locked her jaw against the scream working up her throat. She wasn't going in that refrigerator like the other victim she'd heard about on the news. Dr. Roberta Ellis. Buried alive, killed by asphyxiation. Tears burned in her eyes as he straightened and turned his back to her to finish the work he'd started with the shovel.

Don't miss
Grave Danger *by Nichole Severn,*
available February 2022 wherever
Harlequin books and ebooks are sold.

Harlequin.com

Love Harlequin romance?

DISCOVER.

Be the first to find out about promotions,
news and exclusive content!

Facebook.com/HarlequinBooks

Twitter.com/HarlequinBooks

Instagram.com/HarlequinBooks

Pinterest.com/HarlequinBooks

YouTube.com/HarlequinBooks

ReaderService.com

EXPLORE.

Sign up for the Harlequin e-newsletter and
download a free book from any series at
TryHarlequin.com

CONNECT.

Join our Harlequin community to
share your thoughts and connect
with other romance readers!
Facebook.com/groups/HarlequinConnection

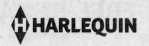
HARLEQUIN

Heartfelt or thrilling, passionate or uplifting—Harlequin is more than just happily-ever-after.

With twelve different series to choose from and new books available every month, you are sure to find stories that will move you, uplift you, inspire and delight you.

SIGN UP FOR THE HARLEQUIN NEWSLETTER

Be the first to hear about great new reads and exciting offers!

Harlequin.com/newsletters